The Smoke Series

JUNIPER
SMOKE

Amazon Bestselling Author
SADIA ASH

JUNIPER
SMOKE

Read On

PRAISE FOR
JUNIPER SMOKE

"The Smoke books are the must-read nerdy romance series."

"Sadia Ashraf is a master storyteller. She combines heart-stopping romance, drama, and dark revenge with such expert finesse. I was addicted from page one. I defy anyone to be able to put down this book until it's finished."

"Juniper Smoke cuts a sweet story of love and nostalgia with the razor edge of modern dating."

"I cannot wait for Finding Juniper. Sadia…you are such an amazing writer. I read Juniper Smoke and I can tell you it was one of my top reads of 2016—magic!"

"Sadia's foray into the romance genre paid off, not only do we get a stunning novel, but a feature film to go with it."

"Juniper Smoke is an odyssey, a fantastic, sexy, funny, smart and heart-stopping journey that I never wanted to end. There is just so much to love about this book that I want to yell from the rooftops for everyone to read it!"

"Intense, romantic story that gives you a book hangover for a very long time. The chemistry between Kyle and Juniper is swoon worthy. Beautifully written debut book by Sadia Ash—a perfect romance book to remember for a long time. A definite five-star read!"

"What you seek is seeking you."

RUMI

KYLE

October 30, 4:28 p.m. 34 seconds
(Historical Museum, Ann Arbor)

K yle Castillo Paxton did not wear a watch but he knew exactly what time it was, precisely where on earth's longitude and latitude coordinates (42.280826 by 83.743038) he stood and how far he was from his home (2418.4 miles). But it wasn't a home, he thought, as he pulled up the museum's north entrance. It was a structure of concrete and glass—as empty and cold as him.

Kyle parked his car and in a picosecond calculated it was 2 hours 31 minutes and 24 seconds before the event was to start. He took 187 measured steps from the parking lot to the museum's emergency door. Hands in his tuxedo pocket, he read the security sign. If he opened the door, the alarm would go off. He smiled.

The museum was still using an obsolete wireless system that relied on radio frequency signals and sensors to trigger the alarm. It took Kyle only 36 seconds to disable the alarm with his phone. It was easy. He jammed the communication between the museum and its security by sending radio noise to stop the signal from travelling between the sensors and control panel.

He thrust the door open and scanned the hall. Even though he tried to turn his calculator mind off, he estimated its total area was 57,280 square feet. He walked to a sign map of the museum galleries—Greco-Roman, Egyptian, American, European Painting—everything was basic and non-specific. This irritated him, for Kyle liked efficiency and precision.

Entering the Egyptian Hall, he shook his head. Everything in the museum was stuck in a time warp. Exactly the way he remembered. Ancient artifacts. Real and replicated. Expensive and cheap. Dusty. Old. Outdated.

The museum needed a big overhaul.

By the tomb exhibits, he stopped dead in his tracks. There was a scaffolding in the middle of the hall. Using visual spatial cognition, he calculated the scaffolding was 62 feet away from him, 55 feet high and 14 feet wide. And the heels lying on the floor were 4 inches long. It was all so out of place. He tilted his head, like an AI cyborg confused by new data.

Then he heard a muffled but unmistakable scream. Tick tock went his heartbeats.

He ran.

CHAPTER 1

I, Juniper Mills, always run away from the people I love. It is the story and sequel of my life. A wise guy once told me that I knew exactly what I wanted, but I kept running in the other direction. I found out the hard way…running doesn't make your troubles go away. You run into new ones. And one day you look in the mirror and realize…it's all inside.

The whispers. The troubles. The battles.

And you can't run away from yourself.

The day I met this wise guy, the day it all began, was the day of the gala.

I was a Junior Curator at the Historical Museum of Ann Arbor, Michigan and it was a special day. In few hours our annual gala was to start. I was on my final inspection round when I saw the scaffolding—smack dab in the middle of the Egyptian Antiquities Hall. I stopped short.

Why is the scaffolding still here? It should have been moved last night.

"Dave? Are you up there?" Dave was the museum's restoration artist.

Silence.

"Dave, you do know what today is?"

Silence.

No one came to the Egypt hall when the museum was closed, but soon the place would be crawling with guests, board members and the press. The gala was our little engine-that-could, the museum's annual funding source, and it was my job to make sure things ran smoothly. Time was not on my side today, so I called his phone. It went to straight to voicemail.

"Dave, this is Juniper. Call me back ASAP."

I looked up. Maybe, he was still there painting with ear-splitting headphones. The scaffolding was a scary mass of steel poles, wood platforms and ropes tied to bracings. There was water damage on the Egyptian ceiling mural and Dave should have finished restoring it a week ago. As usual, he had procrastinated and I had allowed it.

If my boss, the museum's director, Roger Ipswich, saw the scaffolding in the middle of the Egyptian Hall—today of all the days—his lush white mustache would twitch, his neck veins pop, and he would yell at me in front of the gala guests.

That is why Mr. Ipswich was on a strict, need-to-know basis.

"Dave, you there?" In the domed hall, my voice echoed like an air raid siren. I hoped he was not high today. Last year at our Christmas party, I had found him passed out in the Greek Gallery by a mural restoration. "Please tell me you're not high on pixie dust. Not today."

Please. Please, don't be baked today.

Oh no. What if he's hurt?

Or dead.

My panic button went off. Craning my neck back, I took a deep breath. The scaffolding spelled danger (with a side order of possible death) but I had no choice. Ignoring my klutziness, my touch of vertigo, and my lack of yoga-elastic limbs, I decided to climb up myself.

I checked the wheel casters to make sure they were locked in position. Clutching the metal poles, I began to climb the rickety slats. Half-hoping he would peer over the edge, I said, "Dave, if you're stoned, you're fired. Just because I'm an epic boss doesn't mean I won't fire you."

That would not scare him. He knew me too well.

Midway up, I looked down and swallowed.

The ceiling was fifty feet high and I was already too far up for my sanity. On top of it all, my absurdly long heels grated against each rung, the thin straps cutting into my ankles. In my defense, I don't usually wear torture contraptions disguised as fashion. Dragging my shoes against the step, I flung them off. I winced at the clatter of leather and metal on the marble floor. If the only pair of designer shoes I owned (and had gotten from Bargain Barn at a steep discount) was damaged, I would lose it. I enjoyed an image of my hands on Dave's scrawny neck.

When I got to the top, I groaned. He was not there.

The platform was a jumble of brushes in rank oil jars and paint tubes on dirty rags, under which I was sure hid a nest of spiders. Heaving myself gingerly onto the platform, I squinted at the ceiling. Tape and plastic laced a life-sized Nefertiti and I saw the sheen of wet paint on the herons and palms around her. I shook my head. There was no time for Dave to finish today. The only option was to take off the plastic and tape and hope no one noticed from below.

The museum had opened in 1946 and needed constant upkeep. Our conservation artists hung on ladders and crouched on scaffoldings to repaint fading murals and restore water damaged frescos. They also removed the artwork school kids left behind—gum in sculpture nostrils and lollipops in the intimate crevices of priceless artifacts. When expert artists were out of the budget, Dave was the sale option. Since I hired him, his mistakes were my fault.

I gave Nefertiti an apologetic smile. "We'll finish you. Promise." Using my nails, I eased the painter's tape off the wall, trying not to damage the original artwork. I rolled up the plastic sheet in a tarp, careful not to get paint on my dress.

There. Done. That was the easy part. Now I had to get down. Fast. Not brave enough to stand on the ratty platform, I inched backwards on my knees. I stared down. My belly clenched. The marble floor seemed so, so, so far away. It was like bungee jumping down a Grand Canyon peak.

I can't. A big sack of nopes.

I crawled away from the edge, the rough plywood scraping my palms and knees. Sitting down on my haunches, I winced in pain. I counted five red scratches on my knees and thighs from nails sticking in the wood. *Oh, joy.*

I fingered the hem of my dress and wished I were not already dressed for the gala. My black knee-length dress once had soft, satin waves and now it was bunched up like a broken umbrella..

Loud music jarred my senses. My phone's ringtone, "Where is My Mind" by the Pixies, echoed in the hall. It was a jolt of energy.

Let's go, Juniper. You can do this.

I flipped over and stepped on the second rung. The scaffolding lurched. So did my heart. A reflex scream escaped my lips. I looked down. Big mistake. Below me, the world spun. The hall was a topsy-turvy haze of glass exhibits, mummies in sarcophagi and vats of pottery.

Climbing up the wobbly made-for-himself-scaffolding by Genius Dave was bonkers but predictable, as I routinely do dumb stuff. I could slip. I could die. And I did not want to die at twenty-six. Ironically, I thought I might die from gala fatigue and now I was actually going to be killed by this gala.

I groaned. "If I don't die, I will be fired. Both lead me six feet under."

Hearing a muffled laugh, I froze.

"Who's there?"

Silence.

There was no one but me in the hall. I was losing my mind. Does one hallucinate in a life-and-death situation? I slumped against the ladder, my nose flattened on a steel rung. My legs were paralyzed. But my lips were not.

"Dave? Dave. If I survive this, I'll kill you. Curse of Sekhmet on you. 'There will be judgment and an end shall be made for him. I shall seize his neck like a bird. You shall meet death by a disease that shall cast the fear into you.' Do you remember that? You painted it above the tomb of Sekhmet."

Without warning, a deep male voice rang out from below me. "Curse or no curse, I was told there were some impressive exhibits up here. But I had no idea how impressive."

Petrified beyond words, I looked down. I caught my breath. Right below me stood a stranger, looking up at me. A handsome stranger. Scratch that, a ridiculously handsome stranger. My heart skipped a beat. I was now doubly dizzy. How had he crept up without a sound?

"You scared me," I yelled.

"I think you beat me to that," he said.

"Who are you?"

It was too early for the gala guests. If he were wearing an embalming strip kilt, I would think he was the risen spirit of Wepwawet, the Wolf-God of War—for he had the grim, brawny and wolfish looks to qualify for the role. But he was wearing a tuxedo, like all the waiters, so I assumed he must be one of the caterers.

"At this moment, your liberator. Looks like you need help."

Twisting my head his way, I saw dark hair, flawless features—golden ratio compatible, I might add—and even from high up, I made out broad shoulders stretching the fabric of his black jacket and the long lean muscles of his restless limbs. If he flexed his upper arms right now, he'd Hulk-out and rip his shoulder seams.

My heart fluttered. *I'm up high and now I have a view. Sweet angels.*

"Look, I don't need your help. I was just resting for a second."

He crossed his arms. "Really? My hearing's pretty good. And I recall you cursed this poor Dave in the life-and-death situation you're in. Now, shall I come up and carry you down? Or will you jump and I catch you?"

I inched my legs closer and caught the flash of his super white teeth. Wolfish, indeed. "Will you please leave? And stop looking up."

"Give me a reason to stop looking up."

Great. A Comedy Central reject.

"Are you one of the waiters?"

"Hmm. Telekinesis. I think I've found my soul mate."

Is he trying to flirt?

My heart beat like a Neil Peart drum solo. An unfamiliar sensation quivered through my body. I blushed. *Wait. I am not shy and I don't blush. What is going on?*

Without a doubt, he was one of the most handsome and magnetic men I had ever met. Then again, I don't meet a lot of men, so that may not be saying much.

I twisted to give him another look. He looked too polished to be a caterer. He must be a failed actor-turned-waiter. There were a lot of those floating around Ann Arbor now that Michigan offered tax incentives for Hollywood films.

Clearing my throat, I spoke in my brisk work voice, "Sir, you're not allowed here. This area is for museum staff only. Please go back to the catering section. Follow the exit signs."

His smile got wider, but he did not move.

I tried to take one more step down. My leg swung in the air and the scaffolding creaked. I yelped like a tiny Pomeranian and my bare foot quickly found the ladder again. Hands super-glued to the poles, I gulped. I had not really thought through this "getting down" thing.

My spectator walked leisurely to a large pillar, leaned against it and crossed his legs. "Damn good show. Wish I had popcorn."

"Dude, really. If you value your pathetic job, leave now."

"My job is pathetic, so I don't really value it."

"Troglodyte. You'll regret this."

"Hmm. Nerd cursing. Me and the absent Dave both tremble in fear," he said with his hands spread out in the air.

"The absent Dave and I both tremble in fear," I corrected.

"Wow. Hangs on for dear life. Still corrects grammar."

"Look, caterers are not allowed here. Who's your manager?"

"Someone who can't control me."

"What's your name?"

"Kyle Castillo."

"Mr. K.C., you are dead."

He chuckled. "Sweetheart, the odds of your death are higher right now."

Damn him. All right, audience or not, I could do this. Grasping the poles so tight my palms hurt, I put one tentative foot down the ladder.

"Careful now," he advised.

Thanks, Captain Obvious.

Breathing like an exhaust fan, I came down two more steps. The scaffolding shook again. A wave of terror hit me. It was enough to make me shut my eyes and cry out, "Help."

"Stay. Don't move."

Kyle's footsteps pounded on the marble floor and he prodded the base of the scaffolding. In a flash, he began to climb up. Opening one eye, I tilted my head to check him out. He moved with the speed of a cartoon Tarzan and the core strength of an Olympic rock climber. Caught up by the superb view, I forgot the gravitas of my situation and my pessimistic spirit left me for one happy second.

When he was a few rungs below me, Kyle stilled. Then he moved up rung by rung, until his large body enclosed mine. Muscular arms snaked around my waist and he said, "I've got you."

"Thank you. Thank you."

Still holding the poles, I sagged against him. I don't think I had ever felt safer in my life. Soon all I felt was his body pressing against mine. Solid. Snug. Tight. I felt the breadth of his chest, the strength of his biceps and the power of his legs straddling mine—*wowza*, some rock-hard quadriceps muscle there.

"Listen. I'm gonna get you down. Safely. So let go." Kyle's breath was a warm breeze on my neck.

I was silent. Our proximity replaced fear with an alien feeling. My senses pulsed with the slow burn of desire. It had been ages since a man had held me—yup, that's how sad, single and pathetic I was. Hanging from a ladder, dangling forty feet in the air, in terror of death and thinking about pleasure. *Sheesh.*

"Did you hear me? Let go."

"Okay," I lied.

He shifted me closer, my back warmed by his body and the rest of me aching for his touch. I inhaled his male scent. It was alluring, unmistakably expensive and yummy with a hint of cedar, bergamot, lime, mandarin, and agarwood. And was that a minty aftershave? Or his mouthwash? My curator nose has mad olfactory skills.

I might never come down this ladder.

What if I become a ladder-hugger and spend the rest of my life up here with this insanely attractive man spooning me?

Sounds like a plan.

"Lady, I need you to let go of the ladder."

"I can't." I tried to declaw my hands but I was scared stiff, my fingers red, knuckles white.

"Yes, you can. Relax. I have you secure in my arms."

I know that. Stop reminding me.

This was the most action I had gotten this year. My heart pounded and I colored. *Damn it.* In a few seconds I had gone from a rational antiquities scholar to a silly ingénue, my feminist life goals dissolved in a heap of salt.

Focus, Juniper.

"What if our combined weight tips us over?"

"It's safe. The scaffolding creaks but it's not dangerous. I checked the stability before coming up. Okay?"

I did not move.

He said, "Just let go. You'll be fine." When I still did not budge, he tried humor. "Are you perhaps a closet claustrophobic?"

I smiled. "I think I have scaffolding vertigo."

"Did your ear crystals get loose?"

"Huh?"

"Dizziness can be caused by loose crystals in your ear canals."

I laughed. "Really? I have ear crystals?"

"Yes. Calcium carbonate crystals stuck in in the utricle gel of the ear canal. If loose they can cause benign paroxysmal positional vertigo. Or BPPV. You should get it checked out."

"Okay. You a doc or something?"

"No. I go rock climbing a lot and have seen my share of BPPV."

Rock climbing? An image of a shirtless Kyle scaling down a sandstone behemoth in Utah popped up in my head. Dang, I should be able to climb down a scaffolding. I moved one finger off the metal post, and then another. One of my hands was now free.

We did it.

My phone rang again and I slammed my hand back.

He tensed. "What the hell is that?"

"Sorry. It's just my stupid ringtone." I choked back laughter at the absurdity of it all.

Ooh, stop
With your feet on the air
And your head on the ground
Try this trick and spin it, yeah
Your head'll collapse
If there's nothing in it
And then you'll ask yourself
Where is my mind?
Where is my mind?

It stopped and he said, "Wow. It's cosmic—that song. How do you manage to set your ringtone to your shenanigans?"

"Just rescue me; don't mock me."

12

"Can I mock you? Then you don't have to thank me."

"I'm allergic to mocking. Try irony. I have a shot for that."

He laughed, and it was a pleasant, deep-throated sound. He held me so close, it vibrated in my body. *Wow.* If I could record and harness Kyle's remarkable laugh all the world's babies would stop crying and maybe the adults would be moved to work for peace. I felt happiness I had never known before. Then I got sad, for very soon I would never see this hot and mysterious stranger again.

Closing my eyes, I let go of my other hand. "Okay. I'm ready."

"Together now. One step at a time. Follow my lead."

With one arm taut around my waist, Kyle began to descend, one foot at a time. In a few short seconds, we were down. As soon as he got to the last step, he eased me away from his powerful grip. Torn from his warmth, my body went cold.

"You okay?"

"Yes. Thanks so much." I stumbled on the floor trying to find my balance, my legs the strings of a broken guitar.

"Whoa." Instantly his hands seized my midriff and I was steadied. "You do not look all right. Can I take you somewhere? Call someone?"

"I'm fine."

Our eyes met and he took a sharp breath. As his gaze knifed mine, I could not move. He assessed every inch of my face and his bold eyes dipped to the rest of my body. I returned the favor and skimmed him head to toe. I could not help it. He was tall. At least six feet. Five inches taller than me. Ripped. Wide shouldered. Striking. *Did I mention hawt?*

I caught my breath. In my estimate, his level of allocated looks was rather unfair. The level of Roman-statues-smelted to make him. Statue was right. There was something stiff and static about him. Robotic. Inflexible.

13

Machine-like. As if, he was a superior android AI and the human part of him did not get fully downloaded.

He was so golden tanned, I expected dark eyes and was shocked to find his were intense, ocean blue. His tan was not Oopmpa Loompa orange and induced but bronze and natural, from being outdoors in the open wild or surfing too long on sunlit days. Or maybe it was just the luck of genealogy. My eyes dipped to the dark and well-groomed stubble that lined his laser-cut jawline. Not too scruffy. Not too neat. Thick black hair sculpted by pomade shone to the edge of his shirt collar. Not too long. Not too short.

I longed to twist my fingers in his hair and make it unruly. His lips were firm—very male but lush. Deep inside me grew an ache that could only be defeated if he kissed me long and hard, right here against the scaffolding.

As if he read my thoughts, Kyle leaned closer, his lips parting a few inches over my mouth.

I wanted to kiss this guy. So bad.

But I can't. Not with my baggage.

A master at deflecting unwanted advances, I jerked back. He blinked and smiled, his eyes meeting mine. Had I not been so oddly attracted to him, I might have slapped him for his primitive ways. Instead, I tore my gaze away. But I did not shift from the hands encircling my waist. I trembled under Kyle's intrusive stare as he gave me another once over.

Compared to this demi-god, I felt basic and austere. My brown hair, hazel eyes and nonathletic, puny figure with narrow stooped shoulders seemed unworthy of his appraisal. Sharp as electron probes, his eyes figured out my secret—that I hunched my shoulders to hide my ample breasts, which were a bit big for my waist. I was lucky I did not need silicon, but as Michigan's youngest Antiquities Curator, I didn't want to advertise my breast-to-waist ratio to the world, so I always wore loose-fitting clothes.

My phone rang again and I reluctantly pulled away from the promised land of his arms. I picked up my phone. "Rats on a stick, I have to go."

"Where? Your Cirque de Soleil audition?"

"Wow. Aren't you a crack shot wit?" Stumbling to my heels like a newborn lamb, I hopped on one foot to get my shoes on.

Entertained by my clumsy antics, my schadenfreude savior said, "Baby steps. Baby steps."

"Hey, thanks for saving me. That was very kind. You should get back to the kitchen. I won't tell your supervisor you strayed."

"You won't? Lucky me."

I picked up my phone. *Shoot.* In a few minutes, dozens of text messages had piled up. From Mr. Ipswich, my boss. From the two interns I was training. From the MC. From the event planner. From the auctioneer. From guests looking for directions and last minute tickets. Mentally groaning, I scanned my texts. "FML."

"Why?" He came behind me and leaned over my shoulder.

"Dude. Thanks for saving my life, but we have work to do." When he did not budge, I said, "God, please leave."

"Not God. Only human." His tone was chilly but he still stood close behind me.

"Why the heck are you still here? Run off, or I'll report you." My voice was harsher than I intended.

I spun to face him and gulped at the glints of fury in his eyes. Strange. For a guy who worked in the services industry—he was not used to being commanded. Or following orders. He probably assumed I was rude to my inferiors. This was not true. I was just crazy busy today. And I wasn't always nice to strange men. Or men, in general.

Black and sharp eyebrows rose up a bronzed forehead and I was pinned by a haughty stare. Perched on his aquiline nose were chic thick-rimmed glasses over aloof eyes. I had not noticed his glasses before, so he must have just put them on. The hot nerd look suited him.

He dug his hands in his pockets. "You look like a girl who microwaves butterflies for a living."

Okay. I deserve that.

"Moths, actually." I brushed past him and walked toward the exit. "I have to go. Please follow me. I'll take you back."

He walked up to me. "Tell me your name, busy girl."

"Juniper."

Falling into step with me, he whistled. "Juniper. What were your parents thinking, naming you after a tree?"

I gave him a side-eye. "Most people think it's pretty."

"Not me. A coniferous mountain tree from the cypress family. What's your last name? Evergreen?"

"Ha. No, it's Pine." It was, in fact, Mills.

"So Miss Pine, what do you do at the museum?" He smiled and my body thawed like I'd been dunked in a hot Jacuzzi on a winter's night.

"A bit of this and that." I waved my arms around the hall. There was no way I was giving him my name and title. I knew too many creeps.

His smile deepened but he did not probe further. We walked past glass cases, suhets, sarcophagi, and my heart swelled with pride at the exhibits my colleagues and I had spent years acquiring from all over the planet. He too was riveted. When we entered a long glass tunnel with a recreation of Queen Nefertiti's tomb, Kyle's eyes widened. "This is new."

"You've been here before?"

"As a kid." He looked around with interest and lingered, slowing us.

This maddened me and I quickened my pace. Kyle ignored me and dawdled at every glass display. Slower—I swear.

At the end of the tunnel, he pointed to a sculpture of Sekhmet. "Ah. The curse you used. Can you tell me about this dame?"

My curator mode was activated to on. "Yes. This is the tomb of Sekhmet, the celestial daughter of Netjer of the Sun, from the reign of Amenhotep III. She was a kickass dynamo. Her very name Sekhmet, means girl power. That is why she has a head of a lioness on the body of a lovely woman. The patron of Priests and Healers, she was a terrifying goddess whose very curse could kill."

He grinned. "Poor Dave. So I guess you are a tour guide at the museum."

Wrong, Sherlock.

My phone rang. It was Stacy, one of my interns. "Stace? Get four of the crew to the Egyptian hall. There's a scaffolding there. Top Priority. Capisce? Yes. Yes. The band is set. Sound check done. Get Travis to set up the Nile jewel collection in the VIP lounge. Two security guys need to be there. At all times. Is the step-and-repeat ready? Good. Meet you at registration." I hung up.

Kyle smiled. "You run a tight ship, Miss Pine. No shirkers permitted, eh?"

Certain it was not a compliment, I gave him a sharp look. "It's all teamwork."

"So are you an event planner here?"

Wrong again.

My phone rang again. An unknown number. "Hell-oo," I said, ready to hang up if it was another guest asking for directions. My breath lodged in my lungs and I stopped short. "Oh. Mr. Clive Anderson. Is it really you?"

Clive was an A-list British actor who had played the role of Professor Shadow in a trilogy of blockbusters shot in Michigan. I had been trying for months to get him to our event and had called his agent in Los Angeles only a million times. We were sold out and five hundred of Michigan's most affluent would be here soon; and if Clive Anderson was coming, we could raise double the money for the museum tonight.

"Yes. I'll be there tonight," said a charming melt-your-garters British accent I knew well from his movies.

Though I shook in excitement, I kept my voice level. "Cool. Red carpet at seven. Gala at eight." As we talked, I began to hop. In the midst of a happy dance, I mouthed, *Yay. Yay. He's coming.* I jumped in my four-inch pencil heels and froze. In my excitement, I had forgotten about Kyle.

Navy eyes bright with laughter, he was watching me. He stood in front of an Anubis sculpture—the menacing, chilling, alert-eyed jackal god of death rites—so very fitting. My bronchial tract constricted, like I had asthma out of the blue. I don't know what it was about this stranger that I found so fascinating and scary, all at once.

"Is there a green room away from the mob?" asked Clive.

"Yes, Mr. Anderson. And security guards. And a limo."

"Forget the limo. I'll be there at seven." Clive yawned as if bored already.

"Thank you. I'll meet you by the north gate."

"Okay." *Click.* He hung up.

"You're not going to believe who it was," I cried out.

"Your high school crush?" Hands in his pockets, Kyle walked up to me with a devil-may-care expression.

"Excuse me? No. Clive Anderson. Only the world's top action hero."

"You invited your screen crush to the event?" He leaned closer to me. "Hmm. Whatta girl. Clumsy, smart and kinky."

I stiffened and the words came out before I could stop them. "What's your problem? You're probably a failed actor, just jealous of Clive."

Kyle took off his glasses and put them in his pocket. Jet black brows knotted over a steely gaze fixed on me. It was so intense, my belly clenched with longing. My heartbeat was as loud as marbles falling down a metal staircase. Did every girl he meet get the same level of scrutiny? He looked more disappointed than injured—as if I had fallen lower in his estimation.

Who cares what he thinks?

I was sure Kyle was as arrogant as he was handsome. In my limited experience, men this good looking were natural-born devious jerks. He was probably married with a girlfriend *and* a side chick. And women doubtless made a single file to him, happy to be spiced, tossed and ground up in the meat factory that is today's dating scene. I was usually not so pejorative, but Kyle pushed all my cheesed-off buttons, without saying a word. He didn't have to. It was not him, it was me.

See, I was raised to hate men.

My mother didn't raise me to believe in fairytales. Only unfairy tales.

The dark Grimm kind, where princesses' hands could be chopped off and mermaids danced till they bled. Stories where stepmothers planned infanticide and little boys were buried in gardens and their blood and flesh turned into roots and sprouted juniper trees.

My bedtime stories were never about Prince Charming, but about Norman Bates and serial killers who crushed little girls by tormenting them and locking them in basements.

I was a terrified little girl.

Safe—yes. Normal—nope.

When I grew older, I realized my terrors and insecurities were far from normal. They were the upshot of the bunch of lies my mom told me. But by now it was too late. The damage was permanent.

At the advanced age of twenty-six, I had never been in a relationship with a man.

I don't know who had fried my mom's brains, but if I ever met that bastard, I'd sucker punch him.

The phone rang again, and I took the call, tired now. It was Anne, our publicist. She wanted to know if Clive Anderson confirmed. She had only called me a zillion times today.

"Yes. He is coming," I said. "But is it too late to get the press?" I had asked Anne to not call national media until Clive said yes.

She shrieked and I pulled the phone away from my ears. "No. I already told them all. There will be dozens. Even global press," she said, in a giggly tone.

"I told you to wait. It'd be a national humiliation if he didn't come."

"Don't worry. It's all set. Even the Guardian's Chicago affiliate is coming." Our little museum was never more than a blip in local papers and thanks to Clive, the stakes just got higher.

When I hung up, Kyle and I walked in silence to the catering kitchen hall. I pushed the heavy swivel door open and he held it still for me. The smell of gourmet food mingled with fresh fruit and the heady scent of champagne rosé being set up for five hundred people. Above us, the harsh florescent lights hurt my eyes, after the soft gold lights of the exhibit halls.

"Kyle. Kitchen's there. Thanks a million for helping me. Bye now." I gave him one final, long look and I could not help but feel a pang of sadness at saying goodbye to this man—who was so high on the intriguing-men-I've-met scale.

"Goodbye, Juniper." His voice was crisp as a paper's edge. Without a backwards glance, he stalked off.

As I ran in the opposite direction, heels clunking on the concrete floor, I forced myself to shift from sad mode to busy mode. Like White Rabbit, I had a squillion things to do. *Oh my furry whiskers. I'm late I'm late I'm late.*

KYLE

K yle Paxton stared after the nervy girl. She left. But some part of her lingered in the air still. Somewhere in his ribcage he felt a knocking. Like a drumstick beating a hollow tube. It echoed. What just happened? He was still numb, but in a different way than he had been in a long time. A different way than he had been for seven years. Precisely 7 years 2 months 4 days 16 hours and 42 minutes. Since Chloe.

Who is that girl?

She said, 'rats on a stick'. Who says that?

At first glance, she wasn't much to look at. By his jerk standards, she was average. Her hair fell short of being golden brown and her eyes fell short of being green. Her figure fell short of being sexy and her height fell short of being statuesque. But then, he looked again. There was something unusual and alluring about her. It wasn't her looks. It was something primal inside her that screamed at him and forced him to take a second look. That

21

forced him to think about her.

That made her linger—even when she was gone.

He liked the way she stopped to think. As if thinking meant putting a pause button on. As if she could actually chew on her thoughts. When she paused to think, her body froze and her eyelids moved as fast as a camera shutter.

What the heck?

Why am I thinking about her?

Why am I thinking about her like that?

But he couldn't stop. He needed to know who she was.

Juniper.

What kind of irresponsible parents name their child that? He wasn't buying her last name was Pine. His hand slipped in his tuxedo pocket and he pulled out his phone.

He called Evan. "I need info. About the museum. About someone. I have a first name only. Juniper."

CHAPTER 2

It was game time. Half an hour before the gala was to start, I stood in the Greek Gallery to take a breather. Usually, the hall housed our Hellenic sculptures, but today it was set up with fifty draped tables around a stage. Our hit-you-in-the-head theme was Ancient Egyptian Nights and restraint was not our style. The stage was decorated with Egyptian artifacts, where musicians dressed in linen tunics and leather belts played ancient melodies with flutes, cymbals, harps and barrel drums. Potted palm trees lined the pillars and hieroglyphics pennants fluttered high above us and Nile-blue strobe lights made the room magical.

Bracing myself, I plunged through the crowd to get to the entrance hall. Filled with guests dressed to the nines, it was a crush. Our gala was always a dullish fundraiser, well-attended but predictable. With word out that Clive Anderson was coming, it had become the event of the season. Star power is the most powerful force in the universe.

Clive had arrived a while ago and I had situated him in the green room. And now I was going to take him to the red carpet where the press was waiting for him. My wireless radio earplug buzzed.

It was Stacy. "Heading to green room now. You coming?"

"On my way," I said.

I caught up with Stacy in the Americana Hall and our heels clicked in the welcome silence. "Where's Trevor?" I asked.

"He's in there." She pointed to her earplug, her blond bob jutting by her chin.

"I can hear you, Juniper," Trevor said in my ear.

I smiled. The museum's best interns and my personal unpaid laborers, Trevor and Stacy were archeology students at the University of Michigan and always glued at the hips.

At the green room door, Stacy bent to adjust her hem. A lovely curvy girl who dressed for dramatic effect, Stacy wore a scarlet dress, an Empress Hatshepsut gold-and-turquoise cuff bracelet and Louboutin shoes. I stared at her with affection. At times, I felt Stacy was me from six years ago, when I was a student and interned at the museum. Yeah, I was her without the trust fund. Without the beauty. Without the curves. Without the confidence. So…maybe not.

We flashed our museum badges and the security guards let us in. As the door opened, Stacy clutched my wrist in excitement. Clive Anderson was sprawled on a couch, legs on the sofa arm, chatting on his cell. Seeing us, he looked up and smiled. His tuxedo jacket lay on the cocktail table by an uneaten cheese platter and a half-empty wine bottle.

My heart sank. I hoped he wasn't drunk.

After we exchanged hellos, he reached for his jacket and jumped up. "Right then. Time to face the paparazzi?"

"I promise it won't be for more than fifteen minutes," I said.

"Let the schmoozing begin." He smiled at the way Stacy and I gawked at him. Insanely pumped and butch for the Professor Shadow, Clive was a bulky six-foot four inches of swoon worthy male. Built like a lumbering Spanish bull, he had shoulders the size of doors, a narrow torso, long muscular legs, and all manner of big deltoids and biceps visible under his crisp white shirt.

"This is Stacy." I propelled her forward.

As his eyes flicked over her, her legs buckled. I did not blame her. Clive had celestial brown eyes, bronze arched eyebrows, comic-book hero features and sun-kissed surfer dude hair. There was also the mandatory celebrity charisma, a magnetic field pulling poor ion filings like us in.

"She'll take care of you and stay in your visual arc at all times." As we walked out, I nodded at the security. "These guys will shadow you."

"Yes, boss." Clive gave me a salute.

"Did you read the talking points I gave you?"

"Nope."

I sighed. "Today we're raising money for the Egyptian exhibits. In your speech, please say we're a nonprofit and donations are tax-deductible."

"Yes, ma'am. You know, you remind me of my agent."

Chewing my lips, I gave him a thoughtful glance. "Is that a good thing?"

"Bad thing. But you'd do well in L.A., Ringmaster Chick." Clive grinned and the megawatt movie star smile made me pause.

I made a whip gesture in the air. "I can tame any wild beast."

He laughed and then got distracted by a phone call.

Stacy winced and whispered in my ear, "Bad humor is why sometimes I don't want to live on this planet anymore."

"Millennial humor is everything that is wrong with our civilization," I whispered back. "Human existence reduced to a meme."

Stacy gave me a pert smile. "Um. GIF newsflash, you're one of us. You're only four years older than me."

"Yes, but I have a socially maladaptive old soul. So I don't count."

"Anyone who uses words like maladaptive shouldn't count," she whispered, rolling her eyes. "And did you see how much shade I threw at you?"

"Shade? I don't get it."

By now we were in the reception hall, where the crowd had doubled. Flanking Clive, Stacy and I pushed through a mass of people to get to the red carpet. The area was roped off to the reporters, photographers and fans armed with cell phones. There was a rush to us as people recognized Clive. Gasps and excited screams rose up and the cameras swiveled his way. The flashes glinted nonstop and the noise volume rose. Clive waved and smiled. A flurry of phones, paper, photos, and sharpies were thrust at him from all directions. The security guards moved closer to him.

A dozen girls shrieked, "I love you, Clive Anderson."

A few screamed, "Marry me, Clive."

As a behind-the-stage person, I felt suffocated and turned to leave, but Clive grabbed my arm tight. "Stay with me. I wewee scawed of beeg baad paparazzi by my weettle self."

"Not a chance, Professor Shadow. I have five hundred people to take care of. Stacy, stay with him." Frantic, I looked around for her but she had been swallowed by the crowd.

"No, you stay with me." Clive's arms wound around my waist.

I tensed until I saw that he just felt at ease with me. The sight of Clive with his arm around me while he signed autographs drove the press crazy and a few voices clamored up in the madness.

"Clive, who is that?"

"Is that your new girl?"

"Hey, tell us her name."

"What happened to Willow?"

Caught like a deer in headlights, I covered my face and mumbled, "Clive, gotta go."

"Fine. But tell your sheep to get lost. I'll only work with you. I need a ringmaster or I become a bad boy." He gave me a wide grin, revealing perfect square pearls.

His charming British accent sent shivers up my spine and I admired the spiky gold stubble on his comic-book jaw. To my shock, he leaned and kissed my cheek. Before he could kiss my other cheek, I spun to leave the red carpet.

My eyes widened in shock.

I felt a kick in the teeth.

Standing in front of me was Kyle! My catering-waiter savior. And he was noting my exchange with Clive with tightened eyes. He posed in front of the step-and-repeat, in front of the velvet ropes, in front of the press. Why on earth was he posing like a celebrity?

Without thinking, I ran to Kyle and yanked his arm. "Hey, what are you doing here?"

"Please wait." Freeing his arm from my clutches, he turned away.

To my stupefaction, I realized the cameramen seem to know him.

"Kyle, look this way," they said.

"Kyle, please turn to your left."

Stressed out and confused, I tried to leave, but Clive blocked my way. Trapped between the two men who seemed to have no intention of letting me pass, I just stood there…awkward and blinded by the flashes.

Well, this is actually happening.

On seeing Kyle, Clive yelled, "Hey there, Mate. I'm here."

"I see that. Thanks for coming," Kyle said, quietly.

"You called, 'course I came," said Clive, putting an arm around me and jerking me close.

This elicited a glacial scowl from Kyle.

Who is this Kyle Castillo guy?

I knew everybody on the guest list. I had personally invited all of them. Clearly, he wasn't one of the waitstaff. Why had I been so clueless? I mean, Kyle radiated an aura of power, wealth and control, as confident and in command of the world around him as a Cro-Magnon. Why did I not see it before? My ears sizzled in shame as I recalled the way I treated him. In general, I did not treat anyone badly, but he had annoyed me in an insane moment in time.

What if he complained? Would I get fired?

My heart dived to my belly button.

I have to get out of here.

But I was still trapped between the two hunky men like useless mayonnaise in a perfect Cuban sandwich. On one side of me was the roped-off press and on the other side the step-and-repeat. Arms on my face, I pulled away from Clive and made a final push to leave. I was blocked by an excited guest who tore through security to get to Clive.

It was Mathilda, an important board member's daughter. I waved at the security to let her through.

Let loose, she launched herself at Clive like a deranged fangirl. "Oh my God. Oh my God. Sweet mother of God! Clive Anderson. I've seen all your movies. You have no idea." Her hands flew from cupping her face to groping Clive's biceps. "I feel like I know you. Do you know who I am?"

He shook his head.

She giggled. "Silly. I'm Mathilda Marston and my daddy made the museum."

Clive braced himself for assault and Kyle's frown deepened.

My earpiece buzzed. It was Trevor. "Juniper. The MC needs you on stage. Now."

Ignoring Kyle's searching gaze, I tore my arm away from Clive, pushed past Mathilda, the press, the screaming fangirls, and finally made it to the main hall. On stage, I met Dan Lopez, the MC of the evening, who was getting wired with a lavalier mic. Dan was the Detroit NBC Local 4 anchor and as the homeboy-turned-star, he always hosted our events.

After we went over the event timeline, I asked, "Did you get Clive's bio?"

"I did. So Professor Shadow made it?" he asked.

"Yep. When you fundraise, call him on stage. Let's raise a million dollars today."

"Okay, dreamer. Good luck tonight." Smiling, he leaned and kissed my cheek.

I hugged him and jumped off the stage steps. At that moment, who should I see but Kyle, strolling past the stage, eyes raking me, his face sardonic and derisive. I swore he mouthed: *Déjà vu.*

Oh joy. In just ten minutes, he sees two men kissing me.

Flushing, I looked away. Why I broke out in unprompted blushes at his appearance was a mystery. I ran backstage. Breathing hard, I leaned on the curtained-off brick wall. It was the best place to get away from those navy eyes. Eyes that glowed like cigarette ends in the dark.

For a while I forgot about Kyle and ran around putting out small fires and puppet-mastering twenty people on my wireless set. Five minutes before the event was to start, my friend Lila came backstage looking for me. The sight of her cheered me up.

Lila Malouf and I had been best friends since the first day of preschool when she had shared her apple juice box with me, pressing it in my palm with her sticky little fingers. We had been inseparable since that juicy day and even went to the University of Michigan together, where I got my Masters in Art History while she was a medical student.

Lila gripped me in a tight hug. "Junie. Junie. Break a leg. The event looks amazing, as always."

"Thanks for coming, sweetie." She wore a black dress with an Egyptian collar that I fingered. "Nice, babe. Very accurate."

Of Lebanese descent, Lila was a stunner with a curvy hourglass figure, black hair rippling to her waist, big kohl-lined eyes and golden skin I envied. She glowed like Cyalume—even in the dark.

She grabbed my chin and screeched, "Junie, you did not wear makeup, as always."

"No time, chica."

"There is always time for beauty. Come now."

"No, I can't. The event starts in five."

Despite my protests, she dragged me to the bathroom and forced some kohl and fire red lipstick on me. The color was shocking on me since I rarely used even lip gloss.

"Pretty. Pretty," she said, admiring her handiwork.

I whistled at the expertly applied makeup. "Why are you a doctor? You should own Lila's Salon."

"Before Lebanese babies are born, they are told, 'Don't come out unless you become a doctor.'"

"Ha-ha. What about your brother, the realtor slash artist?"

"A total disgrace to the family."

Laughing, I turned to go. "Now I hafta run."

She grabbed me by my ponytail and lugged me back. "Don't tie up your hair."

I stayed put. "Ow. Does your fiancé know you're such a dominatrix?"

"He'd better." Brushing out my hair in long waves down my back, she mused, "You're lucky you have beautiful bones, Junie. Even granny buns look good on you. And I'd kill for your straight nose."

Startled, I stared at the mirror. I had never looked at my bones, and now I arched my neck, examined my cheekbones and lifted my reflection nose. "Standard issue. Don't know what yer yapping about."

"Um, hello? Cheekbones of a goat, a giraffe's neck and those cat eyes."

"So I'm Mufasa's zombie bride now? Thanks." I had brown hair with caramel highlights, which grew straight and thick like a plant that did not need water. My eyes were wide and hazel—the changeable kind—ranging from greenish gray indoors to lime under the sun and brown when I wore black, like tonight.

When my hair was done, Lila said, "Off with you now."

Kissing her cheek, I ran back. By now, the hall was dark and all five hundred guests were seated. Dan was waiting for a signal from me to start the event. Just as I got to the stage stairs, I heard somebody shouting my name. My heart dropped.

Of course, Walrus needs me now.

Cursing under my breath, I made it to the VIP table where my boss sat with our big donors.

"Ah, there she is." Mr. Ipswich stood up. A portly man in his early sixties with puffy eyes, round cheeks and a white mustache sweeping his jowls, he deserved the nickname Walrus. He smiled.

I blinked. Mr. Ipswich never smiled.

"This is Juniper Mills. She is a Junior Curator here, but a senior in fundraising."

A tall man sitting next to him stood up and smirked at me.

Someone catch me. I am going to faint.

"This is Mr. Kyle Paxton," said Mr. Ipswich.

My eyes widened. My ears picked up Paxton like an ear tick—not as in the name Nolan Paxton? Paxton was the name inscribed all over our museum. Why had he said his name was Kyle Castillo?

Oh God. Oh my God. He's a Paxton. Kill me now.

With wicked glints in his eyes, Kyle held out a hand to me, as though we shared a dirty secret. "Miss Mills, such a pleasure to meet you."

"Likewise." Lips parted in shock, I stared at Kyle. My heart raced out of control as I took his hand.

God damn. Am I in trouble?

He held my hand longer and harder than necessary and I could've sworn his fingers caressed my palms inappropriately. A frisson went up my spine and down to my knees. Enjoying my discomfort, he inspected my newly applied red lipstick with hooded eyes and a half-smile. So intimate was our contact, everyone else melted and we were the only two people in the hall. In the world. For a few long beats, we just stared at each other.

I tore my hand away and the spell broke.

Mr. Ipswich gripped my shoulders and thrust me closer to Kyle. "Juniper, Kyle is Davis Paxton's son. I wanted you kids to meet. You will be working together a lot on funding."

Our museum was once called the Paxton Museum of Ann Arbor, as the long deceased John Nolan Paxton had founded it. And his son, Davis Paxton, was the current museum Board president. Davis was Ann Arbor's richest businessman and the most notable patron of the museum.

Kyle is his son? Why have I never met him before?

"Recently we got some sad news. Davis is sick and can no longer serve on the board," Mr. Ipswich said.

"Sorry to hear about your father," I said to Kyle.

He shrugged.

"I asked for another Paxton to replace him and Kyle agreed to step into his father's shoes. It was kind of him to fly down for our event. Juniper, Kyle is a tech genius and serves on the board of the Modern Museum of San Francisco. In fact, he found a glitch in our security system today on entering the museum. We simply, really, truly don't deserve him," Mr. Ipswich said, with more than usual fawning adulation.

"Oh, I think you deserve me." Kyle was looking straight at me.

I cringed under the heat of his gaze.

"And Kyle, Juniper is the heart-and-soul of our museum. She has spearheaded exhibits from all the museums in the world. To date, she has raised four million in fundraisers and grants. Truly the lifeblood of our little art island in the wild."

Say what?

My ears burned. I could not believe it. Mr. Ipswich never praised me, let alone recognized my work. He hated all my ideas and I had to fight him for all my exhibits. He generally acted like a dungeon master, and now, he could not stop singing my praises like a medieval trumpeter.

Too many champagne glasses, I think.

"You are indeed impressive," Kyle said. Slowly.

"All thanks to our village chief here." I squirmed. Why did his compliments sound like insults? I recalled his first words to me, earlier. *I was told there were some impressive exhibits up here. But I had no idea how impressive.*

33

Kyle's eyebrows elevated as if he knew how much I loathed Mr. Ipswich and how much ass-kissing was going on here. "You seem to have a talent for climbing scaffold—um, ladders of success."

A warmth crept up my face. *Your talent is mocking me.*

Just then, my earplug crackled. "Juniper. Where are you?"

"I have to start the event. Nice meeting you." I turned to leave.

"Wait, there's more, dear." Mr. Ipswich put an arm around my waist and planted a wet kiss on my cheek.

Ew. I just about fainted. Why did Walrus kiss me? He smelled of minerals and roses. Definitely too much champagne. I wiped my cheek, noting Kyle's entertained eyes. He seemed to say: Three men kissing you? Where's my kiss?

Bite me.

"Kyle agreed to do the keynote speech today. He will talk about his plans to add a modern wing to our museum. Isn't that great news?"

Wait, what? We're getting a modern wing?

I gave Mr. Ipswich a cold look, my palm itching to yank his big bushy mustache. Typical Walrus. Keeping key info in his hoarding head. When was he going to tell us?

"Yes. Great news." The squeak in my voice gave a great amount of pleasure to Mr. Kyle Nolan Castillo Paxton.

Sadist.

At that moment, a man inserted himself in our group. An impeccable, graying-at-the-temples-kinda-handsome man in his forties took Mr. Ipswich's hand. "Hello, apologies we're late. We had another event in Detroit."

Walrus and his mustache twitched with delight. "As luck would have it, we have two Paxtons in the house tonight. Juniper, this is Congressman

Royce Paxton, Kyle's older brother."

"My *step*brother." Kyle's jaw tightened and he gave his brother a glacial look.

Rude much? What's his beef?

"What's semantics with family?" Royce's warm brown eyes crinkled and he slapped Kyle's shoulders. "And it is half-brother."

Royce took my hand and said the expected polite things. He shot an arm into the darkness and pulled a woman into our circle. "This is my better half. My fiancée, Denise Mather, soon to be Denise Paxton. Denise, you've met Mr. Ipswich. Meet Juniper Mills."

"What a pleasure to meet you. What a lovely, unique name. Juniper," Denise said, taking my hand.

Sheathed in a sleek black gown, Denise was a dazzling Amazonian in her thirties with black hair, violet eyes and a sharp little nose. Her blood-red lips curved into a smile and for some reason I was reminded of fatal Sirens who lured sailors off ships to dash them on rocky cliffs. But she was so genuine and polite, I revised my first impression of her.

Kyle flinched and when Denise tried to shake his hand, he thrust his hands in his pockets. I did not have time to dwell on this knife's edge tension between the Paxtons, as my earpiece blared.

"Juniper. Stage. Now." Dan was on stage looking around for me, his eyes wild.

Mr. Ipswich, Royce and Denise sat down but Kyle did not.

I froze in front of him. The lights dimmed but a spotlight near the stage arced on just the two of us. Drenched in its glare, I lit up like a night parade float. I squinted. Kyle's eyes flicked from the halo around my hair down to the sparkle on my heels in such an invasive way that I think my blood curdled. In a hot way.

And when his dark blue gaze met mine, I was spellbound.

All of a sudden, a woman shot out of her seat and wrapped her bony arms around Kyle. She was as tall as he was and towered above me.

Tearing his eyes away from me, Kyle said, "Miss Mills, this is Isabelle Kyoda, Izzy for short. Izzy, meet Juniper, the heart-and-soul of this place."

"Hi." I stretched out a hand and she did not take it.

Giving me an indifferent nod, Izzy whispered in his ear. A cross between Iman and Halle Berry, she was one of the most beautiful women I had ever seen. Together, Kyle and Izzy looked like they had been torn out of the covers of GQ and Vogue. I swallowed. The magnetic pull between us was a cuckoo delusion of my mind.

Just my luck. He is taken.

Izzy looked familiar. Sultry and sensual, tall and leggy, she was taper thin and wore a white dress—a slinky, sequined, transparent creation— something Cleopatra would have worn if she shopped in Milan. I suddenly realized why she looked so familiar—Izzy was, in fact, a supermodel. Despite my limited knowledge of pop culture, photos of her in magazines, ads of her selling cars and burgers, wafted through my mind.

Naturally, Kyle Paxton only dated supermodels. *Typical Paxton.*

"Sit down, Pax." Izzy thrust a possessive hand inside Kyle's jacket and gave me a frosty look that screamed, *MINE.* The female equivalent of a child licking a dozen donuts.

My heart sank and I didn't know why I cared. Without another word, I stalked off. I snapped my fingers at Dan and he started the program. Backstage, I found Stacy running around like a headless chicken, cornflower blue eyes panicked as she spoke into her headset.

"Stace, listen. Davis Paxton's son will give the keynote."

"Who? I don't have his bio."

"Kyle Paxton. Google. Print. Give to Dan. Run."

Trevor came up behind us. "Ladies?"

I sighed in relief. "Trev. Find a Mr. Kyle Paxton. On Walrus's table. Ask him if he has a slideshow and get it to AV. Pronto."

KYLE

October 30, 8:10 p.m. 07 seconds

(Paxton Museum, Ann Arbor)

The event started 3 minutes ago. It started 7 minutes late, thought Kyle. Juniper Mills. That girl. It was her fault it started late. She had stood 16 inches away, staring up at him.

So close, yet so far.

He looked up. Juniper was gone and the mind-numbing MC, who had kissed her, was speaking on stage. Sitting next to him, Izzy was bored already. With a dramatic sigh, she flipped through her Instagram feed. She had 14,345 likes on the mirror selfie of her white dress, taken 47 minutes ago. Kyle saw there were 16 hashtags on the photo. #Egyptianstyle #walklikeanEgyptian #whitedress #boldfallchoice #smokyeyes #loveplumlips #celeblife #rebellife #fiercegirl #Orchidmakeup #...#...# on and on.

It made his head hurt.

She aimed her phone to take a selfie of the two of them and Kyle shook his head, eyes stern. She rolled her eyes and shifted her chair a few inches away from him. Izzy had informed him, post-coitus—exactly 5 hours and 16 minutes ago—that she was not ready to leave for the gala with him. She needed to groom and primp at a salon and would meet him post red-carpet, fashionably late. Kyle Paxton was a man of time and unpunctuality upset him more than anything on earth.

Kyle felt a gaze stabbing him in the semi-dark. The hair at the back of his neck rose. Denise. *Motherfucking Denise.*

She watched him with a soft smile on her blood-red lips. He scowled and slumped back in his seat so he was in her blind spot. He pinched the bridge of his nose and massaged his aching temples. What made his head hurt more was the idea of Denise and Royce being here. Sitting at the same table as him.

After what had happened…how dare they?

On stage, the MC was still droning. Kyle's eyes were not on him. His gaze followed the backstage curtains, drifting up. From the belly of the velvet curtains, the girl emerged, led by the hand like a child by a taller, heavier girl. His eyes narrowed and he leaned on the table for a better view.

Aha. She appears.

Holding a tablet, she was giving furious instructions to the girl with her. When the girl left, Juniper walked to the side of the stage. Leaning against the wall, she pushed into the deepest, darkest recesses of the curtain, as though she wanted to melt into the darkness. To become one with it. Face glowing in pride, she looked around the hall like she owned it. Making sure no one could see her, she waved her hands around in a clumsy ninja move.

He smiled.

CHAPTER 3

Everything in the event went without a hitch. During the speeches, there was dead silence. Aside from a handful of teenagers glued to their phone screens, no one's interest faltered. Proudly, I surveyed the room, nodding and swinging my imaginary nunchucks.

I'm an event ninja.

As a Junior Curator, I spent my year in scholarly research, cataloguing our acquisitions and writing about Iron Age artifacts. Every fall, I got to plan the October gala. On Monday, I would go back to my humdrum, quiet desk job and miss the noise and the madness.

When Dan announced the dinner break, the hall filled with conversation, laughter and the clink of silverware. My stomach growled, for I had not eaten all day. I walked to Lila's table, where she had saved a seat for me. To support my cause, she had bought an entire table and filled it with our friends. On seeing me, they gave me thumbs up for the event. I bowed, smiled and slid down next to Lila.

"The food is delish, babe," she said.

The swankiest restaurant in town, The Chrome Fig had donated the food. Dinner consisted of a salad of figs, pears and endives; an appetizer of shrimp and sea scallop brochette; a main course of Bird and Turf plate with purple potatoes, quail and veal medallions; and for dessert, we would be served brie mousse gateaux with figs. I took a few blissful bites and glanced at my phone. *Damn it.*

I had missed several texts from Clive, our actor extraordinaire.

Hey, J-girl. You there, babe?
Gal, I need you.
Junnnippperr pretty tree.
Come to me.

I jumped up and walked to Clive's table. Behind his table, a line of fans had formed and was being kept at bay by the security. His face lit up when he saw me. "Juniper, pretty tree."

"Did you need something?" I crouched down, knees on the carpet.

He put his mouth to my ear. "Hey, make sure they show my movie trailer. It's an indie I'm starring in, producing and directing. It's deep. About a homeless veteran in skid row who becomes an actor. But later on, he realizes he is an actor playing a homeless veteran. Or is he? Very deep. Oscar buzz likely. My agent sent you the video, right?"

"All news to me." I had no time for this and longed to pinch his self-obsessed thespian cheeks.

"Come with me now." Clive said he had a USB drive in his car and grabbed my hand. Seeing him get up, a few fans and photographers came running his way. We made a run for it. For awhile we sprinted through the museum until the security foiled the paparazzi and we were alone.

"How do you know Mr. Paxton?" I asked, when I caught my breath.

"Kyle? He and I go way back. I met him when I did an advert for his company."

"He has a company?"

"Yeah, BirdsEye. He's a rock star in the tech sector." He stopped abruptly at the exit doors. "Oye, it says emergency exit only."

"You're an emergency." I disabled the alarm and thrust the heavy glass and brass doors open. A massive gust of cold wind blew in. Recalling the exchange between Kyle and Clive on the red carpet, I asked, "So Kyle asked you to come today?"

"Yeah. I was knackered and in my pajamas but he called and I'd go anywhere for him."

Shocked, I stopped in my tracks. "Wait. Your agent didn't tell you about the gala?"

"No, sweet stuff. I get oodles of requests a day. Sid filters and filters. But I'll come anytime now for this geeky history stuff."

Kyle got him. And I had done a victory dance in front of him, after he had saved me from the scaffolding. *Kill me now.*

By the time we got to Clive's car, my heels were killing me. I took them off and walked barefoot on the asphalt behind him. Pointing to a flashy blue car parked in the front row, Clive said, "Thar she blows. My baby. My Lamborghini Veneno Roadster. You like my new baby?"

"Nope. To me it just looks like a small blue car."

He made a strangled sound and hit his chest hard. "You wound me deeply, museum-babe. This is one of the world's priciest cars."

I lifted one shoulder and smiled. "Unless it's an ancient artifact, it doesn't impress me much."

He laughed. "You are a barmy but scrummy girl."

As he rummaged inside his car, I walked to the pavement around the museum. The sky was lit up with milky clouds passing over the moon. It would have been a lovely, romantic night if it weren't for the wind chill factor. I shivered and wrapped my ice-cold arms around my waist.

I stilled. I heard muted voices and saw cigarette smoke wafting over my head. A man and a woman stood nearby, separated from me by a tall hedge. Craning my head, I peeked through a gap in the hedge. It was Kyle and Izzy. My heartbeat accelerated and I considered leaving. But I was developing an unhealthy crush on Kyle, so I stayed put.

Kyle flipped through his phone and leaning against him, Izzy smoked. "So boring. So bored. Mind melting bored. Stop taking me to dead events. In the Bay, it's okay. But in the Midwest, ugh, I'd rather slit my wrists."

"Events are part of the deal." He did not look up from his phone.

What deal? I leaned closer to hear them better, my heart pounding in guilt.

"So winter is almost over," she whispered.

He looked blankly at her. "It's just begun."

"I'm winter. I'm almost over."

"Izzy," he said, his voice a warning.

A shiver went up my spine that had nothing to do with the wind shaking the hedges and nipping my bare feet.

"Do you have summer all set up?"

He went back to his phone. "You're not allowed to ask me that."

"Tenth of December. I'll be gone."

"And then you'll be released. You got what you needed, as per the contract."

"And then on January tenth, comes summer. Oh, summer."

Even in the dark, I saw Kyle tense. He put his phone away and said, "What is up, Izzy? I have never seen you emotional."

"Maybe you misjudge me." Her voice was sad and she put her bony arms around his neck. She kissed his neck and moved up to his lips.

My heart pounded in guilt at my shameless spying, but I could not look away. I was mesmerized. They were such a hypnotic couple. And it was such a strange conversation. Contract? Release? Winter? What the hell? *Rich people. So messed up.*

"Dammit, Izzy. There is smoke in your breath." He turned away from her kisses with a low growl.

She inhaled deeply and blew a smoke cloud on his face. "I wish I could tell the world what you really are."

"If you do, I will have no option but to tie you in legal knots."

Rich people. So damned litigious.

I was right about Kyle. He was an arrogant, heartless player. The type of man who broke girls—even the unbreakable kind, like Izzy. I felt a tug of sadness on my heart. Strange. *Why am I sad?*

"Bastard," she hissed.

"It's the way you like 'em."

Wow. That's cold.

"Fuck you."

"Oh, you have."

"Fuck you, Kyle Paxton." She threw down her cigarette butt and crushed it with her heel.

"Tell me you're not on a nose candy diet in New York."

"Oh, I have addictive behavior? Funny coming from you." Izzy laughed coldly, groped in her clutch and put another cigarette in her lips with shaky hands.

"Let's go back in." Kyle jerked the cigarette out of her mouth and threw it away.

Just then, Clive came towards me, dangling the USB. "Found it."

Not waiting to see if they discovered me, I ran to him. Fast.

Whew. That. Was. Insane.

When we got back, the photographers raced after Clive. Holding my shoes to my face, I hid behind Clive, but he put a sociable hand around my waist, enjoying the spectacle. When he was seated, Clive looked like he wanted to run away again. I knew why.

Mathilda. The spoiled socialite and daughter of one of our board members, the always breathless, on-the-verge-of-hyperventilating, curvaceous, over-bejeweled and overdressed Mathilda Marston was the darling of the Detroit press and had come today only for Clive.

She leaned on his shoulders, her red curls spilling down his jacket and her newly augmented imitation bosom in his face. "Ooh, Clive darling, I missed you."

"Right then." Flinching, Clive moved his face away from her cleavage.

"Take a picture of us." Mathilda dropped her cell in my palm as if she would get a venereal disease if she touched me.

Used to being treated like the help by her, I complied.

She squeezed Clive's biceps. "I worked so terribly hard on this gala. Look around, Clive. This was all me and I'm just dog-gone drained. Tell him. Tell him. Tell him."

"Um, yeah. This. Today. All you. Smile please." Incredulous, I clicked a few photos. Work and Mathilda? That was a misnomer.

"Selfie time." Grabbing her phone back, she started to take duck-face selfies with him while yammering on about visiting him in England.

Clive tossed me a martyr's look and mouthed: *Save me.*

I shrugged and mouthed: *She's all yours.*

Grinning, I turned and felt ice cubes slide down my back. Leaning against Izzy's chair at the next table, Kyle's eyes followed me with cold scrutiny. Recalling the conversation I had overheard between him and Izzy, I blushed—yet again. He had *inamorata* issues and he was glaring and staring at me?

I went back to Lila's table and sighed. My plate was gone. I grabbed a few bites of her dessert and she dug an elbow in my waist. "Hey, get your own."

"Story of my life. Food, food everywhere, nor any drop to eat."

"Okay, you can have it if you shut up," she said, pushing the plate at me.

"Such a hater."

We grinned at each other.

On stage, Congressman Royce Paxton was speaking. His speech was banal politician-speak. Though he did not mention his personal politics, as we were a nonprofit, every word out of his mouth was a self-serving vanity card for his bid to stand up for Michigan Senator in the next election.

I listened with half an ear, but when Mr. Ipswich walked on stage to introduce Kyle, his name was like caffeine shots to my system. Walrus read Kyle's biography and inflated it with his own apple-polishing tributes. Kyle's company BirdsEye had totally failed at first—but was now a huge success due to his "American entrepreneur's risk-taking, indomitable spirit."

Or his father's money, I thought. When I heard Kyle had started his company seven years ago at the age of twenty-four, my interest peaked. *Great, an overachiever. To what end? So he can dangle famous models like keychains?*

I flinched. Since I had met Kyle, I had become very jealous and judgmental.

"So Ann Arborians, without further ado, I present Mr. Kyle Castillo Paxton, who like his grandfather is a philanthropist and inventor of unique cameras." Walrus gave Kyle an awkward hug and stumbled down the stairs.

As Kyle spoke, I admitted he was a riveting speaker, spare in his words but power packed with meaning, every sentence underscored by a new slide on the jumbo screens. He made a few apt but cheesy jokes. One in particular was so unlike him, I actually liked it. "Why couldn't the art handlers move the painting? They didn't have Monet for Degas to make the Van Gogh." That led to a fundraising pitch. "If you donate well, I'll cut my speech in half."

Lila leaned over to me and whispered, "Hubba hubba. Forget Clive. This guy's hotter than Professor Shadow."

"Lila, hush. He is the new board president, for God's sake. Kind of my new boss."

"Explain then…why is he smitten by you?"

"What? Stop it."

"Check it out. Giving the whole speech to you, like a lovesick puppy."

"He's not a puppy. I know his kind. Looks like a boy scout, smells like a douchelord."

She was startled and punched my upper arm. "Wow. Harsh, even for man-hater you."

I shot her a rueful smile. "Look, I don't hate men. I just haven't found any I like for myself. And as for Mr. Paxton, I hate guys who have a pretty girl on one arm and eyes on others. Why look at me when he has a supermodel girlfriend? I hate this taken-but-still-looking attitude." Plus, I was pretty sure he had tried to kiss me after he brought me down from the scaffolding, though I wasn't going to tell Lila that.

"Wait, what? Supermodel who?"

"You know the one on TV who sells Luster cars and Palm Burgers."

"You mean Izzy something? OMG, I follow her on Instagram. Is she here?"

I nodded.

She pulled up Izzy's Instagram account and thrust it under my nose. Izzy looked flawless in all the photos, each shot a calculated feat of selfie perfection, with quote gems like: "Imperfection is beautiful and you're not perfect," and "In the end, we only regret the chances we didn't take." As Lila flipped through hundreds of pictures of Izzy—frowning in front of cloud tipped skyscrapers, doing yoga on sunset beaches, dancing in clubs, getting makeup done for New York Fashion week, walking the runways in Paris, and attending movie premieres—I stared at my chipped nails and shabby shoes.

I suck.

My work life was hectic and my family life difficult, leaving me no time for shallow upkeep, but now I longed to turn back the clock and spend months polishing myself. Tweezing. Waxing. Creaming. Bleaching. Contouring. Curling. Ironing. Whatever the heck normal peach pie girls do. I wish I had better makeup or had worn a prettier jewel than my scarab beetle necklace today. I shook my head. Jewelry or makeup could not give me Izzy's bone structure.

Or Kyle Paxton.

Okay, there it was. I was outed in my mind.

I want Kyle Paxton.

And getting him was as easy as collecting the Pacific Ocean in a teacup. I was screwed.

"I don't see any pictures of Kyle here. You sure they're together?" Lila asked.

"Yeah, she pretty much licked him in front of me."

"Well then, they're not serious."

"He doesn't look like the type who gets serious."

"But he's got lay-me eyeballs on you." Lila tucked a strand of hair away from my face. "Check him checking you."

I looked at the stage. Even across the dark hall, I saw Kyle was delivering the speech to me as if we were the only two people in the room. Our eyes met. I gulped, my throat dry.

He held a clicker to advance the slides and a vintage camera appeared. "My grandfather built this museum to be an urban oasis in Ann Arbor. He believed he owed his mad success to this city. Grandpa got famous for inventing the Paxton Rangefinder, a low-cost 35 mm camera. He developed it in 1930 and perfected it in 1932. America fell in love with the size and ease of his portable camera. His catch phrase, 'Smile, America', took a life of its own. And boy, did America smile."

Behind him, breathtaking pictures raced in quick succession.

"These are photos the camera took in the forties and fifties. The Paxton Rangefinder was in the hands of Los Angeles paparazzi shooting Katherine Hepburn and Spenser Tracy. It was in the hands of fashion shutterbugs at Dior and Chanel shows in New York. It was in the hands of war photojournalists imbedded with soldiers in WWII. They brought back horrible but victorious war stories. My grandfather wanted to tell those stories and started an annual photo exhibit in his house. Three years later, he had built—this."

A vintage photo of the museum appeared.

"The Paxton History Museum."

His eyes drilled holes in my head, as he advanced the slide.

So help me God, he is without a doubt addressing me.

I swallowed. The lump in my throat did not go away. We had met four hours ago and already Kyle Paxton filled all the empty spaces of my mind. I crossed my legs, feeling jumpy and jittery, for I had never been attracted to someone who was a virtual stranger. In fact, I couldn't recall the last time I'd been attracted to a man not on my Netflix queue.

That is how tragically single I was.

"My grandfather was not a superhero like Professor Shadow." Kyle nodded at Clive and we all laughed. "He was just a boy with a dream. Ann Arbor granted my grandfather all his dreams. His factory. His company. His darling wife. He was born in a humble farmhouse, just a mile down the road. And when he died, he wanted to be buried in the museum. He wanted a mausoleum to bury him in this very room. Right there." Kyle pointed to the center of the room and paused at the laughter. "He loved it so much. Thank God, grandma was so feisty, she said, 'Over my dead body.'"

More laughter.

"They are buried side by side at Forest Hill Cemetery, together even in death."

Two photos of Kyle's grandparents lit up the screen. One when they were young and fresh and one when they were old and bent. In both, they faced each other, unmistakably in love. There was a respectful pause.

I teared up at the image of the married lovers gone and buried.

"Across the world, museums are losing money and this little museum is no exception. Long buried men, like my grandfather, built this country, built its hospitals, its universities and its museums. They are gone. It is our time now. I speak to the young ones in the room."

Breaking his gaze from me, Kyle's eyes swept the room. He nodded at Mathilda and saluted Trevor, who stood by the stage.

"Yes, that's right, Millennials and Generation Z, I'm talking to you. Baby boomers passed the baton. Gen X will do so soon. It is our turn to back what our ancestors started. And hey, Generation Z, if you lift your heads from Snapchat for a second, listen. Use your virtual power to kick-start us."

At the mention of Snapchat, some dazed teens looked up from their screens, blinked and went right back.

"If we don't support public arts, the ones after us will suffer an existential crisis. And since we'll be their elders that will suck for us. Don't let the baton drop. Open your checkbooks. Or Square apps. If you fund the museum's annual budget, my family promises to build a Modern wing here."

The screen flickered and there was a collective gasp. It was a digital image of our museum remodeled with a giant diamond glass monstrosity jutting out in front.

"Oh sweet baby Jesus. No. No. No." I leaned forward, lips parted and hands balled into fists.

I got a questioning look from Lila.

This man was a wrecking ball. This would be a failure of epic proportions. This is not the MET or the Louvre. This is not San Francisco, New York or Paris. This is time-honored, charming, university-town Ann Arbor—my turf. Though Ann Arbor has its art lovers—its art critics, appraisers and a fair share of artists—most of our museum's visitors barely appreciate Degas, let alone Damien Hirst. Moreover, the University of Michigan's museum had a large contemporary collection, adequate for our town.

Sullen, I sat back in my chair. The lights came on and my eyes met Kyle's. A spark sizzled in the space between us. I glared at him and he raised a brow and walked off the stage.

To his credit, we ended up raising a lot of money. Later on, Clive got up on stage and helped Dan with the fundraising and live auction. In the end, we didn't need a celebrity after all. Kyle had riled the crowd so much with his keynote speech, the checks and pledges poured in like sugar from a broken jar.

We raised eight hundred thousand dollars. Not a million.

But better than any fundraiser we ever had. Everyone was all smiles and it was universally declared to be the best event anyone had ever attended.

When it was all over and the guests finally left, the museum staff stayed to help wrap things up. I was charged with putting away the Nile Collection in the VIP lounge and I recruited Trevor to help me. Wearing gloves, we set the jewels back into their velvet lined glass cases as a museum guard waited outside to transport them back. Even as we yawned nonstop, Trevor and I summoned care and love in handling the priceless artifacts.

From the corner of my eye, I saw Mr. Ipswich and Kyle enter the room. I tensed. Did this man never leave? Was he now a permanent fixture of my workplace?

I turned. "Mr. Ipswich?"

"Ah, there she is. Juniper, stop what you're doing. Kyle wants to talk with you."

"Trevor, come and help me in the Greek Hall." Mr. Ipswich glared at Trevor and they walked away, leaving me alone with Kyle.

"Yes, sir?"

Flushing, I looked down at the floor as Kyle approached, my eyes on his sleek polished leather shoes. Italian, for sure. When he said nothing, I wondered if I was in hot water for my earlier behavior.

I looked up, my panic evident. "I'm sorry for earlier, sorry if...I mean, I hope. I am trying to apologize, I guess."

He stood near me, hands in his pockets. For a moment, he had a wicked look on his face, as if he were tempted to rip into me for sport, and then I saw a flicker of kindness in his eyes. It surprised both of us.

"I can tell it's hard for you. So don't even."

Relieved he was too classy to mention my gaffes, I exhaled.

He began his habitual visual sweep of my person and I had been eye-banged so many times by him today, I felt immune. Also, I was too tired to care. My hair was in a messy topknot, my kohl was smeared, my lipstick a pale shadow, my dress crinkled, and my heels lay on the floor...as I was mortifyingly barefoot.

And damn Kyle, he was looking as fine, sleek, and pomaded as this afternoon when we had met during Scaffold-Gate. Not a hair follicle out of place, not a wrinkle on his Armani tuxedo, not a crease in the crisp, white shirt under it. I hated him. Such neatness was surely a sign of a sick mind.

Speaking of sick minds. "Why did you say your name was Kyle Castillo?"

"Why did you say yours was Pine?"

We smiled at each other.

"Castillo is my maternal grandfather's name. It's what I use, but my official last name is Paxton."

"I see. By the way, thank you for helping us raise such a big amount. It'll make a huge difference for exhibit funding. And your speech was perfect. Direct and heartfelt."

"I'll let my publicity director know you approve of her words."

"Oh. I see."

"I don't have time to write pretty speeches and I feel no family affiliation, Miss Mills. But it's cute you think so."

I was confused. Conflicted. Was anything about this man real? This made me wonder why he was here. "Did you want me?"

"Maybe." He gave me an inscrutable smile, his eyes on my feet. Seeing I was barefoot, his smile widened. Seeing me cringe, he picked up a gold and lapis lazuli bracelet and held it to the bridge of his nose. "Lovely."

"No touching. Only looking. Museum rules." With a gloved hand, I eased it from his fingers and put the bracelet back in its glass case.

"I like rules." When I did not respond, he cocked his head to study me and asked, "Does it belong to us?"

"On loan from the British Museum. One of the twenty-first Dynasty items found at Tanis. It belonged to Nimlot A's wife. We think."

"Fun stuff. And what about that bug on your dress?"

Mystified, I looked down at my necklace, the bronze scarab beetle with faux turquoise stones nestled in my cleavage. "Oh this. It's a cheap imitation from the museum shop. Scarab beetles were held by the Egyptians as a symbol of rebirth, creation and luck."

"And did it...bring you luck?"

"I don't believe in luck. Only knocking down circumstances," I said, my eyes flying back to his shoes.

He paused as if reflecting on my words and said in a low voice, "You should look up more, Juniper. It's a shame to waste those beautiful eyes on the floor."

Shocked and pleased by his compliment, I looked at him and, under the force of his gaze, looked at the floor again. I paled at the intimacy of whatever this was—flirtation? Meaningless small talk? Casual appreciation? Or something shady...like gauging the available crop of bachelorettes on the big boss's new turf? I looked at the door, wondering if Izzy was lurking out there.

"Expecting someone?" he asked, following my gaze.

Tired and confused, I swiveled and carefully detached a silver amulet from a display. "Is there something you needed, sir?"

"I wanted to talk about the museum expansion."

"Sure thing."

"Mr. Ipswich tells me you are working on a few future exhibits. Everything will change now that I am in charge."

My head shot up and I faced him. A cad and a power-drunk boss? *I can't stay silent.*

"Wait, what? No. Are my new exhibits in jeopardy? Are you cutting them? You know, I fought Mr. Ipswich hard for approval, wrote the proposals and got the funding. A modern wing and now this."

His eyebrows rose up and the corners of his lips twitched. "Relax, Miss Mills. No one is cutting anything. It is just routine evaluation. And I will go over the changes with you."

Gulping, I nodded. "On Monday?"

"No. I fly back to San Francisco, so—"

"It is two a.m. Mr. Paxton, and some of us have lives outside the museum. I can't tonight. Too tired." My tone was snippy and I yawned involuntarily.

His navy eyes held mine with arctic coolness. "I know what time it is. You jump to conclusions too fast. Let me finish. I fly to San Francisco in an hour. I'll be back in two weeks. I expect you to show me all your exhibit proposals. Accounts, grants, everything. Now, good night. Or good morning." He strode to the door and said, without turning, "Oh, and Juniper, good job tonight."

KYLE

I t was windy and cold as Izzy and Kyle marched up the metal stairs of the jet. As always, the captain stood at the foot of the jet, smiling as he welcomed Kyle. Nodding at him, Kyle pulled his coat tighter and was surprised Izzy slipped hers off on the stairs. It was too cold to make a fashion statement.

Handing her coat to the stewardess, Izzy took the chilled champagne glass and sank in the leather seat. She posed for him, her long legs stretched till they touched his feet and her arms raised around her titled neck in a sexy way.

Kyle was not looking. He was miles away. Barefoot Girl. Scarab Beetle girl.

Why did I tell her she has beautiful eyes?

I don't believe in luck. Only knocking down circumstances.

Why did she say that?

Did you want me?

And why did she say that?

He. Wanted. Her.

Slippery slope.

Kyle frowned and leaned forward. "We have to talk, Izzy."

Her sultry eyes became angry slits. "About what?"

CHAPTER 4

"Pancakes," said the voice. "Juniper, I want pancakes."

"Here you go." I was on a driftwood raft sailing down a river, lined by pine and maple trees. The tide was swift and the water was strange, like thinly melted copper. I dipped a finger in the water and put it to my lips. Maple syrup. The river was made of syrup dripping from the maple trees with giant steel faucets.

"Pancakes now, Juniper," the voice said.

I turned to the voice, but there was no one, just gold lily pads all around me. No, not lily pads. Pancakes. Thousands of pancakes whizzed past the raft like darts. A harsh wind shook the trees, the red leaves fell, the sky got dark, and the pancakes sank in the maple river. A huge rock hit our raft and rushed it along faster.

With a sinking heart, I saw we would drop down the waterfall edge. Cypress would drown. I had to save him; he did not know how to swim. I screamed his name.

The raft rushed down fast and I saw a blur of blue sky, brown trunks and red leaves, like the folds of a Gerhard Richter painting. I looked up and saw the ceiling of Queen Nefertiti's murals, dripping in gold syrup. I was on a scaffolding going down a waterfall. My belly took a dive and my hair flew up in flags. We plunged a thousand feet to the sharp rocks below.

It was an endless fall. I fell. And fell.

"Juniper," he said.

I was on a ladder and his arms held me tight. A man. Someone nameless. Then I saw the name on the museum plaques. Kyle Paxton.

"I've got you, Juniper. I'll never let you fall."

I wanted him to hold me. I was warm. Safe. Alive.

I had to save Cypress, but Kyle shook his head and took me away in his arms. He kissed me hard and when I responded, he pushed me away. I saw black. I was trapped in a pitch black well. My world moved in fast frames until Cypress found me and pulled me up from the well with a long stretchy hand.

"Juniper, wake up."

Groaning, I lifted my head and saw a fuzzy face. A face I love. Cypress.

"Wake up. Make me pancakes."

"Gu gu...wazza." I looked around. I was in my room and my twin brother leaned over me, his shaggy hair tickling my nose. Sniffing, I pushed him away.

"Junie. You're awake."

"Sorta. What...time is it?" My voice was hoarse, like I just had a tonsillectomy.

"It is eleven twenty-two and thirty seconds, Eastern Standard time."

Rats. I had barely slept after last night's gala and my eyes ached. My head pounded like someone had used my face to mop up a mediaeval castle. Was

I dreaming of Kyle Paxton? Like a juvenile teenager. Son of a snap, I had it bad for him. Bad. In one day.

I smiled at Cypress. "Morning, Sunshine."

Lugging my weary body out of bed, I went to the bathroom. Cypress followed me and settled on the edge of the bathtub. Leaning over the sink, I reached for my toothbrush.

"Junie. Junie. I missed you last night."

"I hadda work, Cip. My big gala, remember? I feel bad I couldn't take you. You would not have liked it. There was too much light and noise."

"Too much noise? Like a concert? Did you know a 400,000-watt rock concert can reach ear-splitting decibel levels? Was it loud like fireworks? Or like the earth-shattering explosion of a volcano? The loudest volcano was one hundred eighty decibels of rock, ash, fire and pumice. Did you know?" He frowned and covered his ears for a second, his golden brown hair shaking like a cocker spaniel's.

"I did not. Not that loud. But there were too many people. Hundreds. All talking at once." I turned, brush in hand, the froth over my chin, the toothpaste suds muffling my voice.

"Heart attack. Glad I was home."

"Yes, safe at home with mom. But you like Lila, right? She was there."

"Yes. Lila is hashtag prettysmart prettysmart."

"Aw. You crushing on Lila?"

"No. No. No. Cypress is always a gentleman to Lila."

I mentally groaned. When it came to expressing feelings and human emotions, language acquisition—that had taken my special needs twin so long to acquire—flew out the window.

"Yes, I know you are. You're the most awesome soul on the planet."

Quickly rinsing, I went to hug him. His head nestled in my belly and I crushed him closer, kissing the top of his head. Pain rose in my throat, like the tender swelling of glands I could not control.

"I love you, Cypress."

"Me too. I love myself." He smiled at his joke and jumped off the edge of the bathtub dislodging us both. "Junie. Art pancakes. Animal shapes. No, do spaceships."

I groaned. My migraine was worse and my mop-face was now cleaning the inside of a volcano. "Buddy, lemme take headache pills. Then pancakes. Regular. No art."

We went to the kitchen and busied ourselves. Only one person could be comfortable here and Cypress and I constantly bumped into each other. Our apartment was a snug space and the kitchen was no exception. Mom was nowhere to be seen.

"Where is she?"

Cypress pointed to her shut bedroom door and shrugged.

Biting my lips, I heated the griddle as he dug in a drawer and handed me two migraine pills and a glass of water. Whisking the pancake batter, I watched Cypress make coffee. He was beautiful to look at—my handsome and scruffy twin. Even though he took a lot of showers, Cypress reminded me of a shaggy dog who had just shaken his mud off. Gangly and long-limbed, he had hazel eyes like mine with the same girly eyelashes. We both had brown sunlit hair; mine was straight, while his waved around his face and neck like brown seaweed with crinkled bronze edges.

My beautiful brother. A beautiful soul. A soul no one could see or stand. Except me. My eyes filled with tears and I quickly wiped them off. I never wanted him to know how much his kind smile and the crystal purity in his eyes—so different from other men of twenty-six—hurt me and reminded me of the pointless savagery of his condition. When I was young, I used to ask Mother, *'Why him, why not me?'*

Born two minutes after me, Cypress had PPD, Pervasive Development Disorder, which is on the Autism spectrum. As a kid, he had some good days and some bad days. Now it was all calm days. He had the cerebral IQ of a college student, but the EQ of a ten-year-old. Brainy and academic, Cypress was high-functioning on the spectrum—but when it came to social stuff, he was lost.

Except for me, he had no one.

And Mom was as useful as a frying pan made of toilet paper.

It was all my fault. Before birth, Cypress and I shared a fused placenta. According to the doctors, I had siphoned his oxygen in mom's womb and ruptured his amniotic sac. Though we were both preemies, I was born a pound heavier. To this day, I could not forgive myself for my pre-natal greed that ruined his chance of a normal life. Aside from PPD, Cypress had hypoplastic lung syndrome, GI Reflux disease, agoraphobia, panic disorders, auditory processing disorder and a load of other disabilities.

Because when life gives you lemons, it gives you a basketful.

"Aha. Found it." He turned from his cabinet hunting, jubilant. He held a squeeze bottle and before I could protest, he filled it with pancake batter, twisted the top and handed it to me.

"No art, Cip." I shot him a nippy smile, my arms akimbo.

"Art please, Junie."

"Fine. You win, kiddo. Who can resist those puppy dog eyes?"

"Elk."

"Nope. Too hard. Lion. Easy."

Cypress watched as I twirled a line of batter on the griddle. I drew a lion's face and filled it with layers of batter. The outline cooked first and when I flipped the pancake, it was a lion. I was no artist, but I had been making shape pancakes since we were twelve. Cypress's sappy smiles would not stop as the veritable zoo stack grew.

I realized that every time I blinked, I saw Kyle leaning against the Egyptian Hall pillars, eyes fixed on me as I swung from the scaffolding.

Why is that man stuck in my mind?

I just needed to clear my head. Pouring myself a cup of coffee, I swigged it down. But I still saw Kyle everywhere.

What is happening? I'm truly screwed.

I sat down next to Cypress and was baffled to see he had set four plates, each with a different pancake. I touched the rim of one plate. "Why four, buddy? We are three. Mommy, you and me."

"No. All mine. I want to admire Junie's art while I eat."

Smiling, I sat down next to him and put an arm around his shoulder, holding back tears of empathy. After we ate, he got to clean up the kitchen. Poles apart as we were, Cypress and I made a good team. I cooked, did the groceries and paid the bills, while he cleaned—and his pathological fear of dirt kept the apartment, our cars and garage spotless, organized and germ free.

Our third floor apartment in the Windy Hill Complex of central Ann Arbor had three small bedrooms, a tiny living room and a bare bones dining room. The minimalism helped Cypress from getting mentally cluttered. His room was spare—ascetic almost. My room was stark too, except for three overflowing bookshelves and stacked piles of books under my bed.

Mom's room was a different story. Bursting at the seams with thousands of Vogue magazines, vintage dresses, classic rock records, and fine china we'd never use, it suited the semi-hoarder in her. Cypress and I hated going there. It was like walking into her mind cave, an Hieronymus Bosch triptych on hell.

"I am going to clean my room," Cypress said, after he finished with the kitchen.

"Your room is already clean."

He shook his head, his hair waving like a flag in the wind. "No. No. Do you know a person can get MRSA, meticillin-resistant Staphylococcus aureus and Clostridium difficile just from a dirty room?"

"I did not." I added hypochondria to my checklist of Cypress's issues.

He held up a small, cell phone-like device. "See, I just bought an antimicrobial apparatus. It helps me see where the wicked algae, mold, mildew, fungi, and bacteria are hiding." He made a fierce face. "And then—zap. Die, bitches."

I laughed. "Wow. Amazing."

"I'll also do your room." Cypress snapped on surgical gloves, slipped on a facemask and picked up a bottle of all-purpose cleaner—like a boss.

He left and I went to the living room, which consisted of a beaten up tan couch, a faux Persian carpet and a metal TV trolley. It looked as sad and stale as I felt. I drew apart the cheap plastic blinds and pressed my nose on the glass, staring at the city of trees dotted with intermittent homes. The flat gray sky was a contrast to the flame and russet trees edged on the low hills. The fall leaves clustered on the trees like the garnets, ambers and rubies of an antique Mayan necklace I retained in the museum.

From up here, the trees were a blur, but I could classify each one of them. Right outside our apartments were bur and black oaks, while birches and flowering dogwood grew around Silver Tree Lake, and sycamore, hickory and elm trees lined the hills. On the peaks, emerald firs, pines and junipers of the cypress family stayed evergreen.

Since I was a little girl, I'd been obsessed with the classification of trees.

I thought if I could identify every North American tree, I could figure out who my father was. Cypress and I never knew our father. We had been named after evergreen trees and Mom never told us why. When we were younger we would press her—beg her—to tell us who our father was, but she would get upset, so we had given up on the Mystery of Why the Mills Twins Were Named after Trees.

Eyes shut, I pressed my cheeks against the cool glass. I stood at this spot often. It was where I came when I was worried about Cypress, upset at Mother, or angry at my missing father; and now all I could think about was a pair of ocean blues on me. Damn Kyle Paxton with his cigarette end eyes burning me, even as I stood by a frosted window.

Kyle. The Kyle of the famous Paxtons. What was he doing in my mind? After the gala, I'd been bone-tired but too alert to sleep. Staring at the ceiling, images of Kyle had kept me awake till dawn. The high of raising money was gone. I felt empty inside—like I was missing a few organs. I wondered if Kyle had also felt the air stirring between us. He had certainly stared and stared enough to peel away my skin.

My #lifegoals were suddenly clear: Get Kyle Paxton.

Um, Juniper, news update: He has a supermodel girlfriend.

But then, why did I feel this way? Experts say it only takes four minutes to fall in love. Is that what had happened to me?

Noooo. Don't go there.

Last night had been a rush. Over-taxed and driven, I had been an energizer bunny on wheels, my emotions on an unnatural high. When I met Kyle again in two weeks, we would both be professional and I would see this was a moment of insanity. I needed to stop thinking about him. ASAP. Pronto. Our polar opposite worlds collided once a year when the Paxtons came to our gala. I could not even imagine stepping into Kyle's stratosphere.

Never.

The Paxtons were the Pharaohs of Ann Arbor. Kyle's grandfather, John, had been the local boy genius turned celebrity. His son, Davis, was also legendary—but not in a good way. Kyle's father lived the American Capitalist dream on crack. With limitless funds, Davis was known for his many MTV cribs, baths in dollar bills, wild vacations and parties in paparazzi rags, and a dramatic bunch of wives, mistresses and divorces.

Through the museum grapevine, I heard he had ten kids from six wives sprinkled all over the world. I wondered which of his wives Kyle's mother was.

My feelings about Kyle were conflicted. To his credit, his speech revealed him to be a man of vision, a humanitarian and a genius inventor. But then, infidelity and frat boy habits ran with genius in the Paxton bloodline and Kyle was no exception.

He probably had a nice wife or mistress tucked away in San Francisco, pining for him. I was sure he saw women as pieces of hot tail, sorted into groups by heat index. And with his cool-boy charm, superhero body, mad success, and pots of his daddy's money, Kyle Paxton no doubt left a trail of broken hearts under his heels wherever he went.

Exactly the type of man I needed to stay away from.

He could tear someone like me apart.

As if he is even interested, Junie.

He is neck-deep in supermodels.

I swore under my breath. Every time I thought about the way I had fit into him on the scaffolding, I felt like someone gave me a warm hug. I wanted those muscular arms around my waist and those hard-and-soft lips on mine. Every day. All night long. Lucky Izzy. But judging from the conversation I had overheard, maybe she wasn't so lucky. What had she meant by her being gone by December tenth? And winter being over. All Tetris puzzle things to me.

"How was your event?" asked a low voice behind me.

I turned in surprise. My mother was sitting on the chintz couch staring at me like a pet cat. As always, she had crept up on me and I wondered how long she had been sitting there.

"Good. Same as usual." Not giving any more info, I gave her a distant smile.

She clicked on the TV remote, flicked through her recorded DVR list and put on Hoarders. "Juniper, can you get me some coffee and pancakes?"

"Sure." I got up and obeyed.

After I set the food down on the cocktail table, I plunked down next to her. Mom was shaking her head at a hoarding woman who lived with a dozen cats in a house that looked like a nest of old newspapers.

"I don't know how people get to that level of crazy."

"Are you kidding me, Mom? Your room isn't Disneyland. It's Hoarderland. And your job is couch potato."

She tossed me a look that spelled aren't-you-a-bitch. She was right. I had to try to be nicer. I twisted my fingers in my lap. There were a thousand things that led to her sustained sadness—the reason she was a hoarder. I was angry because she did not fight her sadness. I was angry for what she had done to Cypress and me when we were kids.

Or what she had not done.

Her neglect was payback for us being born and ruining her life. When I was younger, I felt cursed with a mother who was too depressed to be both mommy and daddy, too clueless to take care of an autistic son, too flaky and ditzy to get medical insurance or to send us to college. We did everything ourselves. I used to call her deadbeat mom. I was mean and wrong. As I got older, I realized Mom had as little to do with her situation as I did.

"I'm sorry," I whispered.

"Whatever."

When I was younger and ruder, I never let her forget I had to sacrifice my youth for her sins. In high school, I got a job flipping burgers since we were on welfare at that time. At times, I could not stop my words cutting her to ribbons. We'd get into screaming matches about how much she had screwed up our lives and poor Cypress would be reduced to tears in trying to referee us. It was partly due to his condition that I stopped yelling at my mother and accepted my lot.

My lot.

I would be here taking care of her and Cypress till they stuck me in the grave.

You sound bitter, Juniper. Think of something else.

"I really am sorry, Cindy." It was easy to say sorry to Cypress. He and I had a custom called Cuddle Attack. But my mother wasn't the cuddly type and I don't recall if we ever got hugs or high fives as kids. I sat there picking a loose thread on my fuzzy pajamas, watching her from the shade of my lashes.

"Fine. Can you get me tea? The coffee is too strong." She looked at me with those beautiful limpid jade eyes—the only color on her that had not faded.

"Sure. Peppermint tea, okay?"

She nodded and I went to the kitchen. As I watched the steam rise from the kettle, I thought about the enigma wrapped up in a crossword puzzle and stuffed like a cannoli with secrets that was my only parent.

My mother, Cindy Mills, was once a famous pageant queen and she had been Miss Detroit in the early eighties. The proof of her glory days lay under her bed, in a shoebox full of dusty newspaper clippings of her waving in shimmery dresses on stages, and Polaroid photos of her partying with frizzy crimped Madonna hair, conical bras, and chunky bangles.

If you looked closely now, you could see the traces of her beauty and spirit left in her sultry green eyes, long eyelashes, and pouty lips. But mostly you would see her frown lines, sunken cheeks, drawn eyebrows, and over-bleached thinning hair.

Pouring the tea in a porcelain cup painted with roses, I tried to imagine my mother when she was young and lively. All I had seen—all my life—was a broken woman. She was stuck in a solitary existence, like the Sentinelese islanders who live on the most isolated island on Earth. After she got the Miss Detroit title, my mother fell in with a wild crowd and partied a few years away.

A semi-alcoholic to begin with, she went up the drug ladder till she became a heroin addict. She lost her public support and her Miss Detroit title was stripped. This led her church going, straight-laced parents to kick her out, and even her sugar daddies abandoned her. To support her addiction, she became a stripper at Al's Hot Spot in downtown Detroit. Whatever the hell happened to her in the years she worked there broke her. She left, but some part of her was still there.

I went to the living room and handed her the peppermint tea. "Here you go."

She took it with a watery smile. "Thanks, Juniper. Where is Cip?"

"Cleaning, of course." I sat on the sofa edge staring at her, still lost in the past.

Cypress and I were born a year after Mom left Al's Hot Spot. We did not know who our father was and I doubt she did either. Though we were an oops-pregnancy, she decided not to get rid of the twin embryos that had (as she never let us forget) ruined her perfect pageant figure.

After we were born, she moved to Ann Arbor to work as a grocery store clerk. She hated it and was always in a state of suspension-on-the-edge-of-a-nervous-breakdown, so when I got a raise at the museum two years ago, I insisted she quit.

Once I started supporting the family, Mom checked out of life. She dug a subway to purgatory. And it ran deep. Hundreds of nights passed, years even, and we would find her sitting on the couch, vacant eyes on the TV screen. Cypress and I tried to get her to go to therapy, make friends, volunteer, go to church—anything but just sit there—but Cindy Mills had an army of maggots eating her mind. There's no antimicrobial apparatus for that.

Recently, she had regressed. Now that the gala was over and I had time, I had to do something.

I shot up from the couch. "Mom, how are you doing?"

She shot me a wary look. "Fine."

"You sure? You've been so quiet lately. And the last time you went out was like three months ago when the fire alarm went off. I'm worried about you. Look, don't freak out...but do you...do you...want to go to therapy? You know, Cip and I, we'll go with you."

"Juniper, stop."

"It might help. It's not healthy to be stuck home all day, on this ratty couch—"

"Just leave me alone." She shut her eyes and her head dropped back on the couch headrest.

"Okay. My bad." I sighed in resignation and went to pick up my car keys; I had to get out of here. "You need anything, Mom? I'm gonna go out."

"Can you go to Pricers and get a lot of candy?"

"A lot? Why?"

"It's Halloween. Today."

"I forgot. Sure. I'll get it. I'm running low on candy canes. You wanna come?"

Please say yes. Please say yes.

"No, no. You go ahead. I'm tired. Just get me some Klondike bars." She took the afghan off the couch arm, spread it on her legs and gave me another weak smile.

I went to Cypress's room, where he was playing video games on his PC and asked him to come with me. When he said he would, I smiled.

He too, rarely went out.

This was a good sign.

KYLE

November 2, 7:02 a.m. 19 seconds
(Seacliff, San Francisco)

Kyle inhaled, tapped twice on the diving board and plunged down 12 feet into the cold waters of the 14-foot deep pool. In exactly 26 seconds, he swam to the slate edge of the pool and strode back to the diving board. After 6 dives, he began to swim laps.

1 down, 66 laps to go.

In the water, he was in control. The 56 feet by 24 feet pool was exactly 95,517 gallons of cubic blue liquid reliability. The water didn't change; it stayed the way he wanted. Kyle could control it.

Unlike people.

Mainly—one person. Kyle calculated he had not seen the barefoot girl for 2 days 4 hours 17 minutes and 36 seconds. But he saw her. Everywhere.

Even in the reliable, constant water, Juniper was there. A variable bug. Intruding in his life. Trying to get rid of the image of her silver-green eyes lit up by the floodlight was impossible. But he didn't know that word. Impossible.

It did not exist in his lexicon.

Kyle focused on swimming. He knew the trick was the difference between force and momentum: Time. Each stroke had to be matched to time in a formula: Force $\times$ time $=$ mass $\times$ velocity. Tightening his biceps, he pushed against the water, shooting headfirst.

He did half a lap when he saw something he had never seen in a pool. Floating in the water beside him were eyes. Eyeballs with silver green irises, bloody optic nerves exposed. Kyle froze. The water felt electric. He tore to the surface and gasped for air. He got to the edge of the pool and pulled himself up.

For the first time in four years, he did not finish his morning 5200 meters. In 1 hour 23 minutes he would be at work. There, Kyle could delete Juniper's eyes. Sylvia would distract him.

CHAPTER 5

When I got to the museum on Monday morning, it was still buzzing with the special event. Everyone was talking about Kyle Paxton and the press we received because of Clive Anderson. The final donations came to the magic million number, for when Mr. Paxton had heard we were two hundred thousand short of our goal, he had given us another fat check.

Instead of Clive Anderson, our hero was Kyle Paxton. The fabled man—just an indestructible shield and latex jumpsuit short of Captain America—was now declared the best board president in the universe.

In a staff-wide meeting, Walrus went on about Kyle and how we owed him our livelihoods; and how we, needy Ann Arborean serfs, should bow down in eternal gratitude to Lord Kyle Paxton of Silicon Valleyshire, who—with one blow of his Minecraft sword—was going to revive Ann Arbor's tourism economy with the new modern wing.

How?

I looked around the conference table feeling like the only live body in a room of zombies. Apparently, I was the only cynic.

We sat in the Aztec Conference Room, which had a shelf wall of Mayan artifacts and Aztec pottery. Flanking me were Stacy and Trevor, bent over their phones, hashtagging each other on Instagram. Mr. Ipswich was at the head of the table, eating a croissant and spilling crumbs like a toddler. Lydia Pick, our Chief Curator, sat next to him, holding up her creepy birdlike hands to stop the hail of crumbs coming her way.

Across from me sat Reza Meza, the Ancient Civilization Curator, who had been recruited from Egypt. In his early thirties, he was handsome in a bold but sweet sort of way. When he had started at the museum, I'd gotten a bad crush on him—for all of two weeks—until I met his wife and kids at a Christmas party. Damn him for not wearing a ring. Thankfully, my heart no longer raced when I saw him.

Next to Reza, our sleepy Painting Curator, Aggie Manners, had her eyes closed and head slumped forward.

"Wake up," said Ruben, prodding her forehead with his pen.

I smiled. I liked Ruben Holders, Head of Education, who was in charge of lectures and publications and always said yes to my mad ideas. He sat across from Kathy Cardiff, our maternal Accounts and Human Resources Department in one. She was chatting with our Publicity Manager, Ann— and hidden behind Ann, was damn Dave, our absentee artist, rocking in his seat. His red-veined eyes made me think he'd snarfed a pot brownie for breakfast. Still pissed about the scaffolding, I glared at him and he smiled and blew me an air kiss.

I had to learn how to be more tyrannical.

"Listen up, people." Walrus gave us a warning look. "No one is to miss the landmark meeting with Kyle Paxton. He's on the bloody Modern Museum of San Francisco's board, for God's sake. He would not give two hoots for our piddling, two-bit garbage pile had his grandfather not built it. And there will be many, many, many changes now."

"What kind of changes?" I asked, with a thousand questions in my mind.

He tossed a *j'accuse* look around the table, frog eyes resting on me. "If anybody, and I mean especially you, Juniper, challenges Kyle Paxton, they will have to suck it up, buttercup. Or they will be in deep kimchi, as you kids say these days. Is that understood?"

What'd I do? Stop looking at me. I looked around the room with my most innocent look. My phone clinked and I looked down. It was a text from Stacy to Trevor and me:

ROFL. "Kids these days?" Or kids from the 1910s.

Trevor replied with a cartoon GIF of an angry walrus. We choked back our laughter.

Walrus glared at us. "Stop your hashbrowning, kids. Look, Kyle is a godsend. And his donation—pennies from heaven, I tell you. Our museum is deeply obligated to him and I need to see the gratitude in your eyeballs when he is here."

I sat back and bit my lips. What was happening to my beloved museum?

The next two weeks passed in a flurry of preparation for King Kyle's Coming. The day he was to arrive turned out to be a crisp and sunny day. I went to work early, as I had a meeting with a Gulf State businessman. The meeting had been finagled by Adam Malouf, my bestie Lila's brother.

I met Adam at the entrance lobby and he introduced me to Sayed. A wildly successful realtor in Detroit, Adam was eager to make his cultural mark in Michigan and I was grateful that he'd gotten Sayed Leen, the billionaire, to attend the gala and donate. As we toured the museum, Adam and I tag-teamed to convince Sayed of the benefits of having a permanent Arab art collection.

After the tour, I led them to a big avant-garde installation in the lobby. Crafted with turquoise, spring green and glass mosaics, it was like a sea of cubes crawling up the white wall.

Fingers on the mosaic, I said, "Gentlemen, this donor wall was made by local art grads. They were guided by Olafur Eliasson, who made the famous *Take Your Time* series. He uses light, water and air to create installations of the future."

"Always in motion is the future," said a deep voice behind us.

I turned around and gulped.

Kyle Paxton was standing there, his eyes irreverent and bright. "Apologies for the Yoda quote," he said, taking my hand in a firm grip.

"Uh, hello...um."

The electric currents from his extra-long handshake destroyed my poise. My heart pulsed in my throat. Why was this man always early? It was nine thirty and we were expecting him at ten. Was his biz war tactic to unsettle everyone on premature arrival? Well, it worked. I was totally unsettled. Every nerve in my body reacted to his presence. I blushed. My blush deepened when I noted the three men were watching me turn red with interest.

I took a sharp breath. "Gentlemen, you are in luck. This is Mr. Kyle Paxton. Our new board president. His grandfather—"

"Opened museum. I remember speech." Sayed smiled.

"Hey, good to meet you."

Adam held out his hand and Kyle shot him an assessing glance. Of average height, Adam was well-built and striking with large brown eyes and curly black hair. Despite the aura of wealth and power he exuded, Adam had a twitchy boyish energy. He was stylish, if a bit metrosexual, in his suit with a waistcoat, a pink tie and a pocket square.

In contrast, Sayed, the real powerhouse, was unassuming. His clothes were unkempt, his shoes well-worn, and he used a napkin to wipe his sweaty bald head and florid face, constantly.

"I forgot there's no traffic in Ann Arbor. So I'm early," Kyle said.

"Would you like me to call Mr. Ipswich?" I asked.

"No. Please continue. I'll tag along."

Kill me. Now.

With a fake smile, I turned back to the wall. "Mr. Sayed, our donors get a mosaic tile with their name. The tiles range from five thousand to half a million dollars, getting bigger by the sum."

"Was this wall your idea, Miss Mills?" Kyle asked. His voice was so neutral, I could not figure out whether he hated it or loved it.

"Yes." I nodded and turned to Sayed. "Now if you fund the entire exhibit in my plans, it'll be called Leen Hall. Plus, you'd get a coveted seat on our museum board."

Sayed had a lot of questions for me. My voice shook as I addressed them. Kyle's focus on my every word made me so jumpy, I second-guessed every syllable.

When there was a pause, Kyle asked, "The current Middle East exhibit is a circulating one?"

My eyes met his penetrating stare. Why had I not noticed his eyes were pure Azurite stone—a deep blue copper mineral? *Focus, Juniper. Look away from his hypnotic stare.*

"Yes. On loan by LACMA. Adam is a friend of mine and knew Mr. Sayed, who wants to fight terrorism with education, culture and art. I'm all for that."

"A noble pursuit and even nobler endorsement," Kyle said with a half-smile.

Not sure if he was mocking me, I blabbed on, "Local schools support the idea for curriculum diversity. The media loves it too."

Sayed bent to whisper something in Arabic in Adam's ear.

"Congrats." Adam nodded and beamed at me. "It looks like Sayed wishes to make a big contribution to the museum. We'll look at your plans, Juniper. Wow, this is thick." He held up my fabulous folders, chock-full of museum brochures, and my hundred page proposal.

"Wonderful. Thank you." I tried to keep in check the pure sugar rush I felt at this news. We could fund another permanent collection. Mission bloody accomplished. *Thug life, yeah.*

"No thank YOU, Junie. Lila will be stoked. She twisted my arm to do this," Adam said.

"Oh, she is mean when tenacious."

"Deadly. Hey, meet us in Detroit next time. We'll do lunch."

"I'd like that." I was conscious of Kyle's alert gaze on us.

"Bye, hon." Smiling, Adam pulled me into a warm hug and kissed both my cheeks, Arab style.

I pecked him back. When I scuttled out of his arms, I noticed Kyle scrutinizing us with what I could have sworn were jealous eyes. This surprised me. Adam was married with kids and our familiarity was due to the fact he was Lila's brother and we had practically grown up together.

I led Adam and Sayed to the front doors and nodded at our security guard. "Matthews, please escort these gentlemen out."

They waved and left.

Heart beating out of control, I turned to the spectacle of Kyle leaning against a Doric column a few feet away. I was reminded of our first meeting, when I was hanging from a scaffolding in Kyle's arms. I wondered if there was a way to trip myself just so I'd end up in his arms again. *Real mature, Juniper.*

"Miss Mills, do you make a habit of kissing every donor?"

I stopped in my tracks. "Excuse me?"

His steely gaze dissected me. It was clearly hostile. I felt like I was being assessed by a digital scanner, not human eyes. The empty eyes of a robot.

"No wonder your donor wall is so full."

"Adam is a good friend." Annoyed by his offensive question, I walked to the end of the Greek Gallery. "This way, please. Mr. Ipswich is waiting for you."

"Are you dating him?" He fell into step with me.

How is it your business?

I decided to have fun with him. "Yes. I am madly in love with Adam. Sadly, he is married with kids. We plan to murder his wife and run away. This weekend. Or the next. Depends."

Kyle did not respond but I noticed he was part surprised, part amused.

I recalled my place at work and his position here. "No, I'm not. Dating him."

I longed to ask him if Izzy was his girlfriend but did not dare. Thinking about his cavalier attitude, I shot him a hot and bothered glance. I caught my breath. Kyle was distractingly handsome. He was robotic, yes. But machines can be beautiful too.

Genetics had been kind to him. A human brain has around eighty billion neurons capable of unlocking the entire data of the galaxy, and all my shallow neurons rushed to admire the man. I could think of nothing else. Moreover, he was impeccable. Sophisticated. And casually menacing.

Kyle wore a black shirt and coat over dark low-slung jeans, the uniform of Silicon Valley CEOs. In my boring navy pencil skirt and blazer over a white blouse, I could be a nerdy airline hostess. I frowned at my sensible taupe pumps, wishing I had worn my longer heels. I nervously yanked at the silver and turquoise chain that swung to my midriff.

As we exited the Greek Gallery, Kyle began to whistle. It was a soft, low whistle and it sent shivers down my spine. I was happy when he stopped. It was way too diverting.

"Did you have a good trip?" I blurted to break the silence. *Mother of Medusa*. What kind of question was that after his Adam debriefing.

"Yes." He reached for the glasses in his blazer pocket and put them on. The light bounced on the black frames, glinted off the glass and blinded me. "I'm curious, why does Lydia not lead the patron meetings? Is she not the chief curator?"

I went still. What did he mean by that? Did he think I was too young? Or a nincompoop? How could I explain Lydia, a genius Renaissance scholar, had a painfully shy nature? I just had the buy-one-get-one-free combo of PR skills and art know-how needed to recruit new patrons.

"I—I—at times recruit...donors. Lydia publishes a lot, so I deal with them."

What's wrong with me? In my line of work, I sweet-talked politicians, got government grants, coaxed donations from savvy CEO's, but Kyle Paxton's mere presence turned me to a jar of jellied lychees.

"Don't worry, Miss Mills. I find you more than adequate in your duties. Just trying to figure out the dynamics here. So how long have you worked here?"

"Six years."

He shot me a surprised look. "As long as that?"

"Yep. Two years as an intern. Two as assistant. Two as junior curator."

"Whoa. I pegged you to be in your early twenties."

Really, you pegged me in your mind?

"I'm twenty-six."

Paying no attention to what I was saying, Kyle's hot gaze examined me again. "How are you so well preserved, Miss Mills, and not decaying like the rest of us?"

Try a steady diet of no men, no alcohol, no fun. It works.

"Oh, you know, I roll in the mummy tombs and rub on natron salts from the Nile Delta."

He grinned. "I figured. So you must have a lot of dots and dashes to your name."

"Not really. Most of my coworkers have doctorates. I just got a grad degree."

"I didn't even finish my Bachelor's. Dropped out."

And here you are: a multi-millionaire CEO, while I make pennies.

At the gala, Kyle had talked about Millennials helping museums. To me, that was a joke. Most of us could not even afford to move out of our parents' basements, while one-percenters like Kyle did not know the world outside their gold-plated yachts where they gulped down pearl-stuffed oysters with platinum spoons. I was not surprised he was a college dropout. I bet he owed his success to a sizable trust fund, while I went to the School of Hard Knocks, got an Archaeology degree and then a Master's in Art History. And now with my freaking average American salary, I was able to move to a basic apartment, pay our basic rent and get basic groceries.

I'd be able to afford a trip to Ireland by the time I turned sixty.

He was waiting for me to speak so I said, "Well, after grad school, I dropped out of a Ph.D. program. Dropped out of an Accounting course in college. Dropped out of a talk on my research last month. Dropped out of Brazilian jujitsu when I was a kid. I dropped out of piano. Debate. Theater. All the sports I tried. I'm an expert dropper-outer. So there."

He gave me a lopsided grin. "It's not the same thing. I am a high school graduate."

"Clearly education doesn't matter to success. Genius does."

"No genius, just a dad with money."

I found his honestly refreshing. "I'm sure that's not all."

"It is. Once you get to know me, you'll find only shallow waters here. So why'd you drop out of the Ph.D. program?"

His question tensed me. The answer still hurt. *I couldn't feed my family on the skimpy grad stipend.* Kyle inspected my face and I've been told I cannot lie because my face reflects every naked thought. Damn my face.

Not getting a response, he asked, "So what are your plans at the museum?"

I wondered how honest I could be as he was my boss's boss. "I am an Iron Age and Celtic specialist. I'd like to publish my work."

He gave me a surprised look. "So you want to stop raising money and become a pencil pusher?"

"Maybe…one day. I'm kinda stuck doing fundraising for now."

"So you're good at something you don't like doing, huh?"

"I'm grateful for my position here…but I'd love to focus on my research. However, Mr. Ipswich—" I stopped short and looked away.

"Continue. I'm here to make things better, Juniper."

I loved the way he said my name, his voice rolling over the syllables like cream dribbling down peaches and thunder echoing over hills. *Focus, Juniper.*

"My dream is to go to Ireland, finish my work and publish it. Here, they see I'm good at raising funds, so it's never gonna happen. That's life. I guess reality and dreams don't mix."

"Reality's overrated. Steve Jobs once said only crazy dreamers change the world."

"I don't want to change the world, Mr. Paxton, I just want to survive it."

Oh God, why'd I tell him that?

His face was unreadable as he thought about what I said. "I'm not a fan of letting dreams slide. There are no excuses, only cop-outs. If you want something, run to it. There's no other way to get it."

"What I want is irrelevant."

Shut up. He's your new boss, not your high school guidance counselor.

As we crossed the Americana Hall, he turned to me. "I read on the museum website your turf is Celtic history. What made you pick that?"

My head shot up. He'd read my biography, yet here I was, being chargrilled like a poblano pepper. We were even then; for I had been cyber-stalking him all week long.

"Well, I believe the Iron Age Celts are really underrated."

"Don't care about them. I asked about *your* interest in them."

We halted by the native Michigan exhibit, right in front of a diorama of fierce Iroquois warriors in a canoe. I rested a hand on the sign to steady myself and stared up at him. Kyle stepped close to me and I did not step back.

Great Spirit, when he looks at me that way...I'm a goner.

"I don't—I am—"

"You are not used to talking about yourself, are you, Juniper?"

"My forte is the museum."

"So *you* are not your forte?"

Dammit, he was tireless. "Mr. Paxton—"

"Please call me Kyle."

"I can't, you are the president—"

He took another step until we were inches apart and lifted my chin, running his fingers along my jaw. My breath hitched and he smiled at my reaction "Right now, I am just a man enjoying the company of a bright and beautiful girl."

A spark lit up inside me at the intimate tone in his voice. Flushing, I looked down at the matte marble floor. *Bright and beautiful, huh?* Score. Compliments were like diamond dust to me, as I never received any. Then the trained man-hater inside me activated and swiped his hand off my jaw. *Man, is he fresh.*

"Mr. um, Kyle, I started off in love with Egyptian archeology. So was everyone else. When I wrote my Master's thesis on Celtic mythology, I saw the lack of research on them."

"Is that why you became a curator?"

"Not really."

"Then why?"

"Because I love the past."

"Elaborate."

Pushy much?

"I don't know. As a kid I wished I could time travel, you know. And my high school history teacher used to say that the atoms we're made of don't belong to us. They're on loan, and each one has been around the world thousands of times and we're all from somewhere else. That made me love his class and led me here."

"His belief in reincarnation led you to become a curator?"

"No. He meant the people who came before us and the things they left behind. The clues they left: jewels, clothes, weapons, sculptures, tombs. I think of the souls who used them. I can't imagine the billions of goners alive, loving, fighting, dying for nothing. All their stories lost to dust. Their stories drove me to the past. Makes you think. It all has to mean something, right?"

"Huh." A shadow passed across his face and a muscle twitched in his jaw. My mood soared—perhaps my words affected him. But he shot me a terse look and turned to the Iroquois diorama. Maybe he concluded I was a sappy dork.

Gah. Why does he make me so nervous?

"I didn't mean to ramble," I whispered.

Kyle smiled and rubbed the crisp dark stubble lining his jaw. "Trust me, you don't ramble."

Resisting an urge to kiss that spectacular jaw, I gave him an apologetic smile. "I've been told the way I talk, it's how really drunk people talk."

He laughed. "Then you'd be one smart drunk. Hey, after today's meeting, I fly out. But I return for the board meeting next week. Can you show me around the museum? I'd rather you than anyone else."

"I'd be happy to."

Next week. Wildly happy at the idea of seeing him again, I tossed him a look of pure sugar. As our eyes met, I swallowed. Static sparked in the air and formed a wall of solid friction between us. I could not ignore this longing in me every time we met. If I was to be in an asinine state of emotional arousal every time I saw him, how could we work together? *Also, does he feel what I feel?*

To my relief, he sensed my discomfort and switched gears. "Listen, I wanna pick your brain. We'll be hiring a contemporary art curator but name a few artists you like."

"Contemporary ain't my specialty," I said as we resumed walking.

An inky black eyebrow went up and I followed its movement. Like a caterpillar dance. His eyebrows were so thick and dark. And distracting. "You don't like modern art?"

"I didn't say that. I'm in the minority and stand with the few rejectivism critics of out-there postmodern installation. I do love Dada and Surrealism, mostly the work of Kurt Schwitters and Dali."

"No clue who Schwitters is. But Dali, eh? Still off by a century. You, Miss Mills, are an ancient soul."

"Okay. In contemporary art I like Takashi Murakami and Yayoi Kusama. Do you know of their work? It's colorful bedlam."

"I only know the basics, pet. No idea who they are."

Pet? Did he just call me pet? "I'll bet you like Damien Hirst and Koons."

"Damn, am I that see through?"

"Yes. I think you'd pick the two most expensive artists—popular, but not kitschy. Let me guess. Your house has a few Hirsts. Dots. Skulls. Butterflies. One of each." My teasing him took guts, but I was now less intimidated by the great and glorious Kyle Paxton, and I got the feeling he liked my candor.

The expression on his face was that of a man bested in chess by an opponent he liked. "You're such an art snob."

We arrived at the conference room and I almost collided into a tall stranger, holding the glass doors open. Kyle put an arm at the small of my back and propelled me into the room. My body tingled at his touch.

"Juniper—I mean Miss Mills, this is Evan Marquez, my Executive Assistant, who runs my office and life."

Evan held out a hand and I took it, smiling. I was surprised he did not smile back. He looked to be about my age and was as tall as Kyle, but leaner and slicker. He had black curls, dark eyes, golden skin, and a thin hipster mustache. I was hit by the preppy tailoring of his skinny navy slacks, salmon striped shirt, fitted smoking jacket, and a checkered bow-tie. From his flawless chic, I guessed Evan was not into girls. He was a breath of fresh air in our stagnant town where men wore plaid over lumberjack boots and baggy jeans. And damn it, was everyone from the Bay Area so sizzling hot? I saw the women in the room rubbernecking from him to Kyle, dazed at the double sighting of such male beauty.

Worried the others would see the sparks leaping off me like wild spores, I tugged my elbow from Kyle's firm fingers. As I walked away, his words echoed in my head. *I'd rather you than anyone else.*

What did he mean by that? I wondered with a wistful sigh.

Simmer down, village eejit. He wants a museum tour, not custody of your heart.

Yeah, but he also admires me. And says things like: It's a shame to waste those beautiful eyes on the floor. Never forget that.

Maybe it was force of habit and he flirted with every girl he met. I pinched my arm to remind myself that my obsession with a man who had zero interest in me—who had a supermodel girlfriend, to boot—was bizarre, even for me. My extreme lack of experience with men was showing. I sat down between Stacy and Trevor and looked around.

The museum board members sitting around the table were mostly old-school men, as Mr. Ipswich pushed back against what he called creeping diversity. Any change, any drop of cultural variety was seen by him as a radical assault on good ole American values; and his bigotry was chiefly why I loved defying him. What the heck was the use of a museum if we were only going to showcase local stuff? Might as well stick a mirror in every hall and drop kick the universe to the curb.

It was cool that we had new female recruits on the board, though I was not thrilled to see Mathilda Marston replace her daddy. In my opinion, the dead-eyed ginger Siren was a waste of flesh and bones. At the gala, she had licked Clive to mark him. and now I noted how her eyes shone and her plastic chest perked up when Kyle entered the room. She slid down until she was seated next to him and ogled him like he was a Vegas buffet.

Revolting. It was only cool when I did it.

Walrus got up and introduced Kyle, ending with, "Socrates was a wise Greek who walked around giving advice to people, so they poisoned him. Now I avoid giving advice, ha-ha. But today I advise you to give Mr. Paxton your full attention."

This poor analogy made Stacy, Trevor and I choke back our laughter.

Kyle got up and began to talk about the museum extension plans, while Evan clicked a tablet to advance the slideshow behind him. Designed by San Francisco's top architect, the mock-ups revealed the sterile beauty of our updated museum that would take a year to build.

I noted how we were all gripped by Kyle, especially Mathilda, who was staring at him with sultry Jessica Rabbit eyes. By now, Kyle's spell on me had reached epic proportions and strains from Screamin' Jay Hawkins's song, "I Put a Spell on You," ran riot in my head. *What sorcery is this?* I wondered if he had put a love spell on me when he had helped me down from the scaffolding. Hmm…we did have the *Egyptian Handbook of Ritual Power, Invocations and Spells* in a display case in the Egyptian Hall…

Noting my preoccupation, Stacy whispered, "No mere mortal can help it. He is habanero pepper hot. I'd tap that."

"Um. Behave."

"How can I—when *that* is in front of me? It's like Clark Kent time traveled and hadda love child with Sophia Loren."

"Zip it, Stacy."

Reaching inside me to find the empowered girl who had slipped on the marbles she lost, I tore off the Kyle-bandage. It was my job to be objective. Chin in hand, I leaned forward and listened. When Kyle outlined the seven million dollar budget for the museum expansion and Walrus interrupted him to say that four million was Kyle's personal gift, we all gasped in unison. My ears perked up when Kyle said the two million needed to be raised by us. Mentally groaning, I knew that task would fall to me. It made me anxious. Even if Kyle gave us four million dollars, and the Michigan government granted us a million more for tourism incentives, any negative PR could destroy us. Like electric eels in a kiddie pool, my fears would not let me rest.

I was so caught up in Kyle's words, it came as a shock when I realized he was staring at me during his talk. *O-kay, this is not my imagination. He is eye-banging me.*

Looking for my bone marrow through my skin, Kyle was saying, "With its fun centers, interactive exhibits, modern galleries, the fifty thousand square-foot space will attract younger tourists in droves. Working with Michigan Visitor Bureaus, your staff—"

Question everything, Juniper. My hand went up.

Kyle's lips twitched. "It's not kindergarten, Miss Mills. Feel free to speak without raising your hand."

All the heads in the room turned my way and I felt Walrus shooting arrows of cease-and-desist. Ignoring him, I locked eyes with Kyle. "We may get a brief hike in museum visitors but what if we get pushback? When we see unemployment, poverty, a housing market crash, good folks homeless, a killer water crisis, and a decline in the industries that made the Detroit economy great, how will the media react? They might say Michigan—where the state fund revenue is off by six hundred million, with a new deficit of four hundred million—is the wrong place for over-the-top indulgence."

In the pin-drop silence, Kyle asked, "Is that a question or a comment?"

Evan stared at me as if I was a fly in the ointment.

Mathilda was shaking her head at me, as if to ask: *How dare you, help?*

Trevor shook his head and Stacy mouthed: *Yay, badass bitch.*

From across the room, I saw Mr. Ipswich turn purple. "Juniper, as you are not the finance or public director, leave your bravado ankle biter concerns to them."

"Fine." Chin jutting out with attitude, I sat down.

"Please let her finish. I'm happy to address her passionate concerns," Kyle said coolly to Walrus.

Passionate concerns? I stood up again. "Look, as primary fundraiser, I face the donors and public. Daily. We have to justify every dollar spent. When public art budgets have been chopped across the States, how can we justify seven million dollars, not to mention the hundreds of thousands added to our annual fiscal budget? People don't have the bandwidth to handle this much change. So I only ask, what do we do if one bit of whiny media goes viral?" I flopped down in my chair between Stacy and Trevor. *End rant.*

"Yeah, stick it to the man," Trevor whispered in my ear.

"You Juniperized him, all right," Stacy hissed in my other ear.

"Oh, Kyle, please continue your brilliant talk and ignore her." Mathilda frowned, her hand snaking on Kyle's bicep.

Brushing off her hand like a pesky insect, Kyle smiled at me. "Change, Miss Mills, is hard. Trust me, I know. Especially for a small town like Ann Arbor, especially with our big hairy audacious goal to double the museum." This elicited scattered laughter. "Dividends in education and tourism take synergy and time to build. But our pooled resources will create lasting core competencies for this town." He gave me a patronizing look and put a hand on his chest. "I welcome pushback. And only when you ruffle feathers do you know you are doing something right."

Kyle deflected my queries with corporate buzzwords and empty jargon, not real answers to my questions.

My feathers aren't ruffled. I'm not afraid of change. I chewed on that. Well, maybe I was. After all, I came from a family where I only went out for survival basics like work and groceries to prevent us from being deader than a whale in the Gobi Desert.

Kyle went back to talking about the new wing and I realized what this project meant to him. He was a big fish in a little pond here. In San Francisco, he was a minor blip on their museum board radar. With this new addition, his name would be everywhere. And the tax deduction on the four million donation would help his business with exemptions credit.

Hubris, Paxton style.

I folded my arms, raised an eyebrow and gave him my best pout. If I looked up at any point during his talk, Kyle seemed intrigued by my badass defiance.

After his talk ended, he said, "By the way, Miss Mills, objections are always welcome. I look forward to further objections from you."

I lifted my head up. "Objections are the hazards of a research job. I apologize, but I'm the inquiring kind."

"No need to apologize for your kind," he said with a smirk. There was a visible ripple of interest at this and everyone stared blankly from him to me.

What does that mean? Cheeks red, my head dropped on my chest. I wanted to hit my fat head on the glass wall behind me.

Lunch was served and our staff presented new projects to the board. Focused on his phone, Kyle listened with half an ear, but when it was my turn, I had his laser-like attention. As riled up as I was, it was flattering.

After lunch, Evan informed us we would be traveling to the Bay Area in December for a week-long mandatory staff training. Stacy, Trevor, Lydia, Reza, Ruben, Aggie, and even Dave, were all to go, and my name was called out, as well. Us lucky stiffs were to attend seminars at the Modern Museum of San Francisco and team up with their staff for future exhibits. A beat of excitement went through the room.

I clenched my palms. If this was mandatory, I'd surely be fired. I could not *ever* leave Ann Arbor. Cypress and I were joined at the spine and I couldn't abandon him, not even for a day. Nor my comatose momma. Apart from an enforced visit to Egypt for my archeology degree four years ago, I'd never traveled outside the Midwest. My two-week trip had nearly shattered Cypress. He had regressed and stopped talking for weeks. That freaked me out so much, I decided never to leave him again.

Shooting up, I headed for the door. As I slipped out, I felt Kyle's sharp eyes on me. He noticed everything about me. The meeting had not concluded, but I ran down the hall.

KYLE

The walls were closing in. Kyle looked around the room. It suffocated him. She had left, the barefoot girl. She was a prize fighter, he thought. Someone who fought all her life. Lots of small battles. One big war. He wanted to know who and what she faced. Now she was gone and he could not run after her. Stuck. He was stuck in the room with the strangers.

No matter. He had plans for her. Big plans.

Kyle looked at Evan and tacitly communicated his need. His want. Evan nodded.

Kyle sent him a text: *Did they email the full report on her?*

Evan nodded again. Kyle could not wait to get out of this room and read it.

CHAPTER 6

Counting down the hours till I would see Kyle again, the week was a snail traveling in honey. I didn't know it then, but my life was about to get turbo charged. In a big, fast way.

I couldn't stop thinking about Kyle and being furious for thinking about him. His semi-flirting and his curious jealousy of Adam made me wonder if he had broken up with Izzy.

Instead of sleeping at night, I spent time scouring the Internet for info on him.

Curiously, I found no mention of Izzy and no trace of a personal life. In his interviews, he refused to answer personal stuff. Kyle Paxton was as clammed-up as I was secluded. I asked Trevor to email the gala photos and found hundreds of sexy Kyles to drool over. There was only one photo of us together. A cringe-worthy moment. Me sandwiched between Kyle and Clive, hands on my face. Great. Now it was preserved till the end of time on Getty Images.

Deeper internet searches led to a few old photos of Kyle with stunning girls (who looked like underwear models) at red carpet events. My heart sank when I found one of him leaving Chateau Marmont in Los Angeles, wearing a cap and dark glasses and holding hands with Mona Atkins. She was a talented, gorgeous, famous actress known for her long string of affairs with leading male actors. The photo was dated two years ago.

Holy smoke. Mona Atkins.

Man, was he out of my league.

I read a few articles about Kyle and his company, BirdsEye. He was truly a rock star in the geeky tech world and always headlining at big conferences like TEDx and SXSW. For his inventions, he had won many business awards, including the Millennials Change the World Award, the Techie of the Year Award, and even Forbes 30 under 30.

He is remarkable. I'll give him that.

Kyle was in my head like a centipede in a rotten apple. I saved his photos on my laptop and at night, when I tossed and turned in bed, I imagined myself in the photos with him. I needed the slap of a reality check.

Dumb dreams. Dumber Juniper.

Two days before Kyle's visit, I was in my office, trying to focus on work. It was impossible. Lately, I had not even been working on my book about fierce Celtic women. After two hours of zombie-gaping at my PC monitor, I poked an eye with a pencil end.

I pulled up my book manuscript and realized I had not heard from my mentor for over a month. Professor Ian Scott was once the curator of Iron

Age and Celtic Artifacts at London History Museum. Now long retired, he was a writer of six books on his subject. Our oddball friendship began when he gave a lecture to my grad class. He lived in London, but had agreed to be my thesis director. He also consented to be the editor of my book.

I emailed him to ask him why he was MIA.

I tapped my desk, willing my mind not to go to Kyle again. I rummaged through my candy drawer and took out the handmade candy cane from Granny's Cranny store. My body needed a sugar fix. I was going through candy cane withdrawal symptoms—anxiety, dry throat and low blood sugar.

A few minutes later, I got an email back.

From: Dr. Scott
Sent: November 22, 10:32
To: Juniper Mills
Subject Re: How are you faring?

Dear Miss Mills,

Thank you for your email inquiring about Dr. Scott. From now on, his email is being routed to me. I have some news to share. May I please call you?

Sincerely,
A well-wisher

Who is this? Crunching on my candy cane, I replied: *Absolutely, please do.* My phone rang straight away.

"Is this Miss Mills?" It was a polite male voice with a distinct Irish accent.

"Yes." I put down my candy cane.

"My name is Dean D. Dillon—"

My hackles rose. *Dean D. Dillon? D.D.D? Is this a prank?* "Who is this?"

"This is Dr. Dillon. I worked with Professor Scott." A polite pause.

My head jerked up. I knew who Dr. Dillon was. He was one of the few other people on this planet writing about Celtic artifacts. *My homie.* Now a curator at the London Museum, he was also a star in our little Iron Age world, frequently interviewed by BBC and PBS.

"Oh, sorry. Yes, Dr. Scott mentioned you."

"I know it's strange—me calling you, Miss Mills. But I was his student and followed his quirky career path. Um…I have some important information to relay about Scotty. Er…we called him that here."

I listened with bated breath to his charming accent. His sentences sounded like questions, as was the Irish way. I could tell living in England had ironed out some of his native Irish dialect.

"Sure. Is he okay?"

"No. Miss Mills…actually, he is no longer with us."

I gasped for air, putting the phone on my desk.

"Are y'alright? Miss Mills, you there?"

I picked up the phone. "I'm here. That's terrible news. What happened?"

"Age."

"Oh." We were both silent, until I thanked him for letting me know.

"He was brilliant. But he was eighty-four. Only death could retire him. A fortnight ago, he died while writing his latest book. Peacefully. Scotch in hand, head on desk, manuscript in lap."

"Oh."

"By the way, I'm going to finish his book."

"That's nice," I whispered, still in shock.

We talked for awhile, connected by the man's legacy and what it meant personally to both of us. Finally he said, "Not to sound dodgy, Miss Mills, but I know all about you. There are very few Americans who're aces in Celtic research and I have seen parts of your manuscript—"

A soft exclamation escaped my lips. "He showed you my book?"

"Scotty was an old scatter-brain and I handled a fantastic bit of his work. I read your Master's Thesis, as well. In fact, I'm ashamed to say he sent you *my* feedback, not his."

"It's...fine. It was good feedback."

"Now, about your book...I wouldn't mind working on it, yeah?"

"That's wonderful."

"Miss Mills, I'm coming to America to speak at Northwestern University next month. Any chance we could meet up?"

"I'd love that." On finding out he was coming in February, I asked him if he had an extra day to come and speak at our museum. I could do a little lecture in conjunction with his visit.

Dean thought about it, asked me a few questions and agreed. "I'll do it."

"Great."

"Brilliant. This will give us a chance to meet up."

"You know, I always wanted to bring Dr. Scott here, but he always said his bones were too tired to fly."

He laughed. "Ay, sounds like Scotty. He would say my bones are too tired, but never this blasted mind. Or, my bones are too tired for pretty girls, but not this heart."

Before I hung up, I said, "Thank you, Dr. Dillion. Sad as his death is, I'm glad Dr. Scott lived such a complete life."

I quickly emailed Ruben Holders, my coworker who handled all the museum talks. He thought it was a great idea and I began to plan a special event, headlining Dr. Dean Dillon.

That night was hard. I read all of Dr. Scott's emails to me over the years and cried silently in my pillow. I never had a father, and I was always comforted by his role in my life.

And now he was gone.

By Wednesday, the day Kyle came to the Museum, I was a mass of nerves. I stayed in my office because the staff was not invited to attend the board-only meeting. I did not see Kyle arrive, but I knew the meeting was in session.

I wondered if he still needed a museum tour as he had requested last week. When I didn't hear anything by noon, I came to the sad conclusion Kyle must hate me for publicly calling him out. I stayed in my office, crunching candy canes.

But with every cell in my body longing for him, and Kyle Paxton sitting only a thousand feet from my office, I couldn't resist making an effort to see him. After lunch break, I leisurely traipsed by the conference room where the board members were deep in conversation. A thrill ran through me when I saw Kyle's profile etched by the window. However, he seemed not to notice me. I went back, crushed.

Just as I made it to my office door, I heard the swift fall of footsteps behind me. I gulped and turned. Kyle stood a few feet behind me! "Hello, Miss Mills."

He followed me?

"Oh, hi."

"I have not seen you all day." His eyes were cold. The friendly man from last week was gone.

Mood swings, much?

"I am…was…not supposed to be in the meeting."

"Are you rescinding your offer of my museum tour?" His eyebrows rose in an inquisitive, haughty way.

"No. Anytime you want." My voice was weak.

"I have some work to do remotely. Meet me at the Egypt Hall in two hours." Turning to go, he said over one shoulder, "Juniper, do *not* make any dinner plans. You will be eating with me tonight."

Damn, am I in trouble?

I bristled at his curt tone. "Wait, what? I was not told—"

He came real close, leaned against the wall, and inspected me from head to toe. "I just told you."

"Is it just me?" Realization dawned on me and I blushed.

"And me." He shot me a wry smile.

"No, I can't. It's Thanksgiving tomorrow and I have to go home and prepare for it."

He almost choked at my words, equally floored, I think, by what I said and possibly because no woman had ever denied him. "Say what?"

I noticed other staff members giving us curious looks as they petered back into their offices after lunch. I took a step back. "Let's talk about that later. I will see you in two hours."

Poker faced, Kyle walked away without a word.

I stood in the bathroom and washed my face with cold water, trembling at the image of Kyle leaning against the wall and asking—no, ordering me to have dinner with him. Despite my zilch experience with men, there was no mistaking his look and intent. Whatever was going on between us, he felt it too. He wanted to take me out to dinner and then what? What was Kyle expecting? Me for dessert? Did he think I'd be an easy lay? A willing member of his *help* to serve him?

If so, he was in for a surprise.

My mother's hatred of men, pooled with the tales of horror from her stripper days, had weaned me off of men early in life. The fear of a single step leading to the alleys Mom had gotten lost in kept me away from horny high school boys and drunken frat boys. A hard-earned scholarship was my only ticket to college and if my GPA went down, I would have lost the scholarship. I also interned at the museum at that time, so dating was not an option and partying was impossible.

I couldn't be a slacker; I had too much to lose.

After college, I dated from time to time, but no dude made me want to go back for a second date. My last date was over a year ago and had been a disaster as big as the Halifax explosion. Lydia had set me up with an insurance agent, Mike Seale. He had kind eyes and was cute and timid. It was hard not to like Mike.

I liked him for a grand total of fifteen minutes. He had spent the entire dinner griping about his cheating ex. To my horror, I learned he was stalking her and—*get this*—she was eating in the very same restaurant with her new boyfriend.

Gosh, I had no idea how the dating game even worked anymore. What would I do if Kyle wanted to date me? My other issue was my twin Cypress. Badly bullied all through high school, he was now a total shut-in. He had no one but me. The apartment and I were his comfort zones and I liked living in this comfort zone. My twin came first in my life. My museum second. My two loves. There was nothing else inside me.

No experiences. No boyfriends. No lovers.

At times, I got scared by my reflection in museum glass cases. It was a dusty old relic staring back at me. I expected to die a frigid virgin scholar in a musty house with Cypress, an army of cats, a few Celtic torcs, and a reservoir of books. I even had an epitaph picked out.

Here lies the mythical American creature. Juniper Mills, the old Virgin.

Though I knew Kyle was dangerous, I wanted him. Like I had never wanted anyone before. Until I met him, I'd never felt like this. This attraction was a pulley of chains on hooks inside me that pulled me his way. It did not matter that he had a girlfriend or a whole host of them. I was my mother's daughter after all.

Should I accept his dinner invitation?

Life doesn't come to you, Juniper. Go to it.

With shaking hands, I applied mascara and a taupe lipstick, the only makeup I had on me. At least my lashes looked defiant, thick and jet-black. My eyes were green-gray today and looked haunted and worried. My hair was in a sensible bun and I let it fall into caramel-seared waves down to my waist. I took off my blazer, patted down my sleeveless cream shirt and black pencil skirt, and strung my purse crossways on one shoulder.

Walking through the vacant halls, I noted the staff was gone. With Thanksgiving tomorrow, most of them had flights to catch. In one hour, the museum would lock up and Kyle and I would be alone, except for Stan, the night guard.

I entered the Egypt Hall. A wave of unease fluttered in my belly. Kyle was already there, leaning against a pillar. He must have heard me approach, but his attention was fully occupied by his phone. When I got closer, he said without looking up, "Gimme a minute."

KYLE

November 25, 3:58 p.m. 17 seconds
(Egypt Hall, Ann Arbor)

K yle was looking down, but his mind was on Juniper. She was walking into his trap. His mind was a C-clamp tool. His life was a steel bear trap. He depressed the springs, the jaw fell open, and in she walked. *Snap.* Trapped. Like all the others.

But she was as different from the others as air from water.

No. She is not special.

He heard her walking to him. No symmetry in that walk. She plodded. She wavered from straight lines. It provoked him. So when she came to him and stood 2 feet and 10 inches away, he did not look up from his phone. He wanted to punish her.

But when he did look up, the muscles of his heart contracted. He could not breathe. No woman had ever made Kyle Paxton stop breathing. Ever. Until now.

CHAPTER 7

Taking Kyle in, I stood there in silent admiration. My knees went weak, like my tibia bones were slowly melting. Even off-the-cuff Kyle was too disturbing. He wore dark jeans, a white shirt and a black cashmere sweater rolled up at the sleeves. His tanned forearms were splayed with thick, long veins and beautiful, corded muscles. A coil of his hair fell on his bronze forehead, and I longed to brush it away. I locked my fingers to stop myself from mauling him.

I'm screwed. I was acting like a hormonal teenager.

"Sorry about that." Kyle slipped the phone in his slacks pocket and inhaled hard.

I shrugged. "No matter."

"When I travel, my business goes haywire. I had only sixty important emails." His hot gaze raked over me. He noted my loose hair and that I'd taken off my blazer.

Worried my blouse shell publicized the curve of my breasts, I turned. "Let's start the tour."

"After you."

"Anything in particular? Old Americana? Greco-Roman? Iron Age?"

"Everything."

I stiffened and looked at my phone. It was four o'clock. "Really? That'll take several hours."

"I have time."

"I don't. I told you, tomorrow is Thanksgiving. I have to get back home."

"So tell me about your family. You still live with your parents?" He wound impatient fingers in his hair, brushing it off his face.

"Yes." I was taken aback at his personal question. *Some of us are not as lucky, Trust-Fund Tap.* I pointed the way. "Let's start with the Egyptian tombs."

Except for Lila, no one knew about my bizarre family dynamic and I wanted to keep it that way. But he was tenacious. Noting I skimmed over his question, he shot me a curious look.

"Have you always lived in Ann Arbor?"

Ignoring him, I said in a perky tone, "Ah. Here we go. The tomb of Perneb. Ancient Egyptians believed that after death, the unseen *ka*—the life force of a person—lived on. And it needed a place between life and the afterlife, so they built these complex tombs as the borders of mortal time and eternity. Reza, our Ancient Civilization Curator, got these items from the Cairo Museum. He submitted a proposal to get more from the British Museum. I'm sure he could use your help in funding that, Kyle."

During the tour, Kyle walked around with a thoughtful air. He asked a lot of questions about our loaned acquisitions, took photos and jotted down notes on his phone. At one point, I told him he was the most hands-on board member I had met. He knew it was not a compliment and shot me a cagey smile.

In two hours, I led him through most of the important displays and when we got to the Iron Age section, I noted a clear change had come over him. He was less occupied by the museum than by me. With no sense of personal space, he stood inches away as I spoke and made relentless eye contact, leaving me breathless. Every chance he got, Kyle put a light arm around my waist and brushed his hand against mine—as if it was the most natural thing in the world. I tried to carry on, but I got goosebumps all over my limbs. My heart beat with the dull thud of an ancient African Djembe drum.

Professional Kyle had fled the building.

I took him to my favorite piece of the Iron Age exhibit: Celtic Warrior Man. Waving a silver sword, the beefy wax figure was encased in a huge glass case. "This guy was a warrior chief from 70 BC. His bones were found in a North Ireland burial mound. Sadly, he died at thirty-four, which was a lifetime then. The items he left behind are a marvel of the Iron Age. His silver sword, gold collar and bronze helmet are different metals but each has the same linear design. Look at the leaf link in the torc."

"Torc?"

"The split-end collar Celts wore." I pointed to the heavy gold band on the warrior's neck. "See the twisted knots? They're a form of sacred geometry, a harmony of all things between man, life and nature."

"Harmony? What you're describing is chaos theory. In my experience, nothing is connected."

"Chaos theory?"

"Yes. The idea of the science of surprise. That we should expect the unexpected. The nonlinear dynamics of time in which events can happen from random equations."

I motioned to the torc. "Thankfully, chaos theory didn't exist when these knots were made, or the design would be random scribbles."

"Let me tell you a little secret. There is no destined harmony. It's all a fluke, kiddo. All of it."

Kiddo? He was probably five years older than me. I searched his face to see if he was mocking me. "Last week you were telling me rah rah rah fight fight fight never give up and now life is a fluke?"

"We are flukes. No one has the right answers. We're all just running around trying to make sense of the chaos. *I* set rules to manage the chaos."

"And how's that working out for you?"

He grinned and spread his arms like a super-villain about to take over the planet. "Quite well. I don't like the unexpected. I want to know the plan. To know what happens before it does."

"So you can predict the future? Or do you have a Tardis?" I scoffed.

"No, but I can control my future."

What arrogance. "Why do you need to do that?"

"Unpredictability is a huge waste of time. I don't waste my resources on things I can't predict. Or people I can't control."

Weird turn to this conversation.

Lacing my fingers at my waist, I cleared my throat. "As I was saying... the Anglo-Saxon and Celts believed in an endless wheel of life that wove nature, love, and mortality into an interlinked human existence."

"I disagree, but then primitive man only left useless bones and pointless theories."

I opened my mouth to argue, but let it go. "Well, there is an old Celtic saying, *Ni lia duine na baruil.* There are as many people as opinions."

"Well, facts trump opinions. So did you learn Celtic?" Kyle sounded intrigued.

"Celtic is a slack term. The Celts hail from Ireland, Scotland, Wales,

Brittany and Galicia, and they have many languages. I learned snatches of scholarly Irish, Scottish, and Gaelic. I don't know the other ones, but I swear in all of them."

"Hit me." He smiled and folded his arms.

"*Ifreann fuilteacha*. Bloody hell in Irish-Gaelic."

"Hit me harder."

"Okay. *Brisfaidh me do magairli*. I will break your balls."

He made a comical face. "Ay caramba."

We both burst out laughing.

"*Diolch yn fawr*," I stated. "Guess what I said?"

"Fuck you in Irish?"

"Nope. Thank you in Welsh."

This time he laughed long and hard and I looked down, a bit shocked by his answer.

Peering at glass exhibits, Kyle stopped at a placard on a Celtic jewelry display. "I'm assuming this is your work. What does that say?"

"Yeah. These are lines from a poem. *Go ba chóir dom a fanacht i ndiaidh Naoise—*" I began in Irish.

"Go on."

"First, I have to tell you the myth behind these words. May I?"

"Yes."

I pointed to a small painting that Dave had done for the exhibit, of a beautiful girl in a dress as green as her eyes, with crimson hair and a sorrowful face.

"This is Deirdre of the Sorrows, from Ulster, Ireland. Her beauty was a curse, for only sorrow came from it. The King Conchobhar wanted to marry her, but she fell in love with Naoise, a handsome warrior and singer. Before Christianity, Celtic women were free, fierce and empowered. They rode in war, hunted alongside men, led clans, and often chose their own lovers. Deirdre flouted the king and fled to Scotland with her lover. They wandered for years, hunting and living off the land. But her beauty ensnared the Scottish king too."

"The Kim Kardashian of her era, huh?" Kyle said.

I laughed. "Not quite. She grew afraid and homesick. When they returned, the Irish king had Naoise killed. Then the king married her and taunted and tortured her so much, she died of grief. She's known as the Swan Maiden. Epic sad tale."

Kyle was smiling at me, like I was a child telling him a bedtime story. "Well, she did cheat on a king."

Okay, that's callous. You don't mess with my homie, Deirdre.

"These lines are from an old poem about her." I pointed to the placard. "That I should remain after Naoise. Let no one in the world suppose. After Ardan and Ainle. My time would not be long."

I was gratified by the sheer focus of his gaze on me, framed by those black rectangle glasses. He asked me to repeat the lines. I was startled to see him look lost. I did not take him to be a man touched by poetry.

"Interesting. Did you ever go to Ireland?"

"Never."

"We'll have to fix that. Set up a fund for curators to travel for work. Making mental note."

My heart raced at the idea of actually being able to see Cashel Rock, Megalithic Cemetery and Aran Islands. But then, there was my odd family situation. I could not leave Cypress alone with my lifeless mom.

Kyle searched my face, trying to figure out my thoughts. "Are you carrying on your research, Juniper?"

"Yes. I got published in a few museum journals. And now...now I'm writing a book about Celtic women." I couldn't believe I told him that. Except for Dr. Dillion, no one knew that I was writing a book—not even Lydia, my direct supervisor. "But no one knows, yet. Except you. I have ages to go. Right now, it's just a tangled mess of research."

"What's the book title?"

"It'll be my last few words. But the subtitle is History of the Ancient Celts, Chiefly the Chronicles of Fierce Females told through their Artifacts and Mythology."

"For sanity fuck's sake, that should not be the title."

"For anything's sake."

We stood there smiling at each other, and suddenly the main track lights went off and only the low recessed lights were on.

In shock, I glanced up. "Dang it. I forgot the lights go off at seven."

"To dinner. Onwards."

I sad-smiled like a kid refusing Disneyland tickets. "I cannot, thanks. I have to get back to my family."

"Who? Your husband?" Suddenly his arms went around my waist. His hand plucked at my left hand and his long fingers caressed my ring finger. "No ring. No husband. No fiancé."

I went rigid and my heart slammed into my throat. This intimacy made me anxious but I did not push him away or snatch my hand back. In fact, I loved his touch and a blaze of desire lit up inside me. This was unusual for me. Usually when a man touched me, I went into cold fish mode.

I got the courage to meet his gaze. "What if I have a ring in my office desk?"

"I say you don't. But you are married to the museum."

"What about a boyfriend? I might have one, you know."

Kyle's face dipped down, his warm breath stroking my cheeks. He gave such a robotic vibe, I expected his breath to be cold. He lifted my chin and

I held my breath. Two fingers traced my jaw and linked to the fluttering wings in my belly. "Judging from your racing pulse and reaction to my touch, I say no boyfriend. Except for maybe Celtic wax man here."

I was shaking in his arms. "Is everyone in San Francisco so very presumptuous?"

"Only me."

When I eased my face away, he let his arm drop, only to wrap it around my waist. He bent his head to kiss me. From years of reflex training, I pulled away from his embrace with a jerk. Sanity poured over my heated body like the Ice Bucket Challenge. It was pooled with the knowledge that there were security cameras everywhere.

"What about you? I met your girlfriend."

"Who? Oh, Izzy." He had the gall to look surprised. "She's not my girlfriend."

I recalled their conversation I'd snooped on and it seemed she thought she was. I gave him my best museum curator look. "Thanks for your dinner offer, Mr. Paxton, but I need to go home. Now." I turned on my heels and walked to the exit.

He followed me to the automatic glass doors and as they swung open, he said, "I don't think so."

"You coming?"

"Nope."

I swiveled around. Barely lit by the can lights, a wicked grin swept across Kyle's well-sculpted lips as he stared at the glass display of my beloved Celtic warrior. He walked backwards, eyes pinned on me. To my utter horror, he reached for an Irish cremation urn, which had no alarm since it was just an imitation space-filler. He picked up the urn and aimed it at the glass display.

"What are you doing?" Heels pounding on the marble floor, I ran to him as he took a few mock swings of the urn on the glass case.

"If you say no to dinner, Celtic warrior gets it."

"Kyle Paxton! What are you doing? Stop. Stop. I'm calling security."

"One security guard. Separated by thirty thousand feet. Dozens of halls. Low lights. With the fastest trajectory for maximum force, I say wax guy gets it precisely three minutes thirty-eight seconds before he gets here."

"Let go. He is priceless." Hopping up, I tried to grab the urn from his hands.

"So is having dinner with me." He grinned and raised the urn higher, the sweater stretching up his muscular forearms.

"You're insane. I'm gonna report you."

"Say yes: Pure joy. Say no: Bang smash. If you report me, I'll say it was an accident."

Hands clenched into fists, I took an uncertain step back. "You can't blackmail me. Plus, there are security cameras everywhere."

"There are only two cameras in this room. They are not NVR cameras, missy. Nor is there a live feed. It's recorded. It's the Ann Arbor History Museum, not the MET. The cameras are not optimized for dark or sound and the screen will pick up a grainy scuffle, which is why I stood here after calculating the blind spot of both cameras." He moved the urn closer to the glass again. "Tsk. Tsk. So sad. Say buh-bye to Celtic dude."

"Stop. Yes. I will go out to dinner."

"Yaaas." He lowered his arm and put the urn back.

I wagged a finger at him as we walked to the exit. "Why are you not in a happy farm? You are certifiable."

"As long as I'm winning in life, I don't care." He looked cool and collected, as if the entire juvenile spectacle had not taken place. Whipping out his phone, he started to text.

"Is that your secret sauce? Bully everyone to get your way?"

"Nope. I only bully those I like." He tucked his phone back.

He likes me? Completely dazzled by the Kyle Variety Show, I blushed. "I, uh, have to call my family."

He nodded with a half-lidded stare, as if it was adorable I still had to call my family for permission. "I have reservations at The Chrome Fig. We will take my car."

He already had reservations? Some nerve on this man. "I know where that is. I'll meet you there."

"No. Come with me." He snatched my phone and jabbed at the screen. "My number. Text me your address. My assistant, Evan, will take care of your car."

"Not necessary."

"Is."

We glared at each other. This was an impasse. I shook my head and took a few steps back. I did not want anyone coming to my apartment and alarming Cypress or meeting my mother. What's more, I was quite attached to my car. "No one drives Tomato but me."

"What?"

"My car. My vintage 1964 tomato red Ford Mustang."

"You drive a wreck?" he asked, trying to hide his smile.

"No, an antique. Fully restored. News flash, Kyle, I like old things."

"With any luck, you'll get attached to new things after tonight," he said, quietly.

By now, we stood in the intimate room that connected to the Italian sculpture display. It was one of my favorite spaces of the museum. Barely visible in the dark, the faux grotto was inset with small sculptures to mimic a Flemish garden, complete with fountains and a rockery wall.

Crossing my arms, I sagged against the wall. "I'll go out to dinner with you. That is all. After dinner, nothing else."

"Agreed," he said from across the room. In a flash, he strode over and his arms splayed my back. The force of velocity pushed me hard against the rough wall, while he drew me to him.

"What are you doing?"

"Keeping my promise. After dinner, nothing else. But I never said anything about before dinner." His face bent over mine, his breath grazing my lips.

"Stop."

He did. Then he raised an eyebrow. "Do you really want me to?"

I smiled and shook my head. "Nope."

At that, one of his hands grabbed both my wrists and forced them above my head on the jagged stone grotto wall. His other hand drew me closer to the hardened planes of his muscular body. I was confined by his legs. Though his thighs felt like steel beams, I noticed his touch was firm but not painful. I stopped breathing as his hand traveled from my back to my neck and caressed it as he made relentless eye contact. Every cell in my body went into a dazed alert. I wanted him to kiss me, and lord knows what else, right there. So bad.

"Why are you doing this, Kyle?"

"Because when you are near, I feel a physical tension, like molecules torn apart."

"Molecules, really?" In spite of our situation, I lifted an entertained eyebrow.

"Okay, that's bad." His smile was sheepish. "But I'm a scientist, not a Celtic poet."

"I could get in a lot of trouble."

"I don't kiss-and-tell. And there are no cameras in this room. I have to know…"

His lips parted and descended on mine, nudging my lips open. Terrified of the consequences of kissing the board president at work, I tore my mouth away. In his cobalt irises, I saw a rush of confusion and vulnerability and it surprised me. I never thought Kyle Paxton could be hesitant about anything.

"Know what?"

"This. What this is between us. I can't stop thinking about you. All I know is, ever since I met you, I've wanted to do this."

He bent down. My lips met his, hesitant at first, then eager. The kiss was more of an act of discovery on his part— as if he wanted to shake off this urge, this electric charge between us, as a mistake or a specious moment of insanity. But it was our undoing. His lips on mine confirmed our collective fears. This was no ordinary kiss. I never wanted him to stop.

Even with my lack of experience, I knew he enjoyed it as much as I did. As his mouth crushed mine, his hand hauled me closer and closer as his impatience grew to fill the aching hunger we both felt. Totally besotted, I got light-headed. At some point I pulled my face away, feeling weak like I needed an oxygen tank and a glucose drip.

"Why do you taste like candy cane?" Kyle inhaled hard, his forehead pressed against mine.

I shrugged, too obliterated to answer.

He searched my eyes and his tongue flicked out and lightly grazed my lower lip.

I lost it. With a demonic burst of strength, I freed my hands and jerked his face to mine. I kissed him with no reaction from him, and I suppose with my lack of carnal skills, I was doing something wrong. When he took charge, he kissed me tenderly as if he was afraid I would dissolve. Gentle arms tethered my waist. Fingering the thin material of my blouse, he caressed my midriff with light fingers. He was…almost reverent.

All of a sudden, we heard footsteps echoing on the marble floor of the adjacent hall nearby. I turned into marble effigy in his arms. In a second, he let me go and stood on the other side of the small room. How he looked poised and cool as ever, while I was still sagged on the wall like a heap of dirty laundry, was a mystery. He even summoned superhero speed to put on his glasses and roll down his sweater sleeves.

The footsteps were coming our way.

Clearing my throat and patting down my hair, I pointed to an alcove containing a small alabaster sculpture of a voluptuous woman with a downcast face, dressed in heavy robes. "Mr. Paxton, this is a seventeen century Flemish piece, in the style of Claus Slater, by an unknown sculptor."

The footsteps got louder.

"I see. Why does she look so ashamed?" Kyle asked with a finger and thumb on his chin.

I touched the graven wings on the statuette. "See the cut-off wings here? She was a fallen woman and this likeness was made by the church as a warning for young virgins."

The footsteps stopped and an arc of flashlight hit our faces. We both turned in calculated surprise. It was Stan, the night guard. Seeing us, he pointed the flashlight down. "Oh hello, Miss Mills. Your car is here, Mr. Paxton."

"Thanks so much, Stan," I said, as we walked out.

From now on my life will be defined as BK and AK.

Before and after Kyle.

KYLE

November 25, 7:22 p.m. 06 seconds
(Outside Paxton Museum)

K yle talked with Evan, giving him low voiced instructions. His eyes were on Juniper. Peripherally. He licked his lips and tasted the candy cane on them. Juniper was something else, alright. She. Was. Special. She stood behind Evan, face downcast, as always. Why did she hate looking up? She looked lost when he took the keys from her hand. The car meant something to her. What? *Why can't she talk about her life?*

She had problems. No matter. He knew how to fix problems. To his engineering mind, all matter in the universe could be placed in two categories.

1) Broken things that need to be fixed.
2) Fixed things that need to be updated.

Juniper was in category 2. She was not broken. But there were problems. And obstacles. Problems needed long-term fixing. Obstacles were short-term. Those were easy. He knew how to overcome obstacles with minimal tinkering and optimal fixing. For the obstacle between him and her, he had a solution.

The solution was working. It always did. His pre-fab charm. The thin coating of humanity he could put on when he wanted. Just the right words. The premeditated smile. Its heat index. The exact piercing stares. Well-timed. The precise touch. Things little-town girls like her cared about.

CHAPTER 8

A chill blast of wind met us as the museum doors shut behind us. The night was misty and the wind scattered the mist in weird shapes, as if a nightmare had fallen on Ann Arbor. Wrapping the panels of my long navy coat tighter around me, I shivered. Evan was waiting for us with a driver in front of a black limo. He tossed me a cool nod and I shot him a cooler one.

What the heck is his problem with me?

Kyle had finagled my car keys and given them to Evan. He instructed my car be left in my apartment parking lot. The idea that a stranger would be driving Tomato—my precious and my one and only splurge in life—ticked me off. But Kyle Paxton was acting like such a Mussolini-style dictator, my hesitation meant nothing to him.

The chauffeur opened the back door. As I sat down, I was hit by the luxe air of leather seating, chrome trims and gleaming wood. The car was even retrofitted with plasma TV screens and a champagne bar, and I was sure some of the fittings were real gold.

Kyle slid in across from me. "Apologies for the car. It's my father's and his taste is gaudy at best."

"The old relative excuse, eh?"

He smiled. "Usually works."

"Um, Kyle?"

"Yes?"

From under my coat, I fiddled with my pencil skirt. "I'm not exactly dressed for Chrome Fig." As Ann Arbor's swankiest restaurant with a two-star Michelin rating, it attracted high-end clientele from as far as Chicago. I had only been there once when Kyle's father had thrown a dinner for the museum staff and I recalled feeling out of place.

Kyle's startled eyebrows knitted and he gave me a quick once-over. "You look perfect." He held up his phone, which was ringing. "Double apologies. Can I just check my million emails?"

"Sure. Who's working on Thanksgiving eve?"

"Silicon Valley never stops. Never sleeps. Holidays aren't really a thing there." He bent his head and started to click away.

I watched him as the flickering light and shadow from the windows whittled his cheekbones and jaw into a Rodin bust. With his sharp coat and scarf, he looked like he belonged in this absurdly lavish car, as if he posed for a magazine and the photographer captured the evolution of an über man from day to night in one shot. And I, in my cut-rate clothes and sensible shoes, belonged here as much as a Tibetan Yak in a Tiffany store. I imagined Izzy, and countless women like her—disposable things for the Paxton men—stretched on the leather seats in sexy, languid poses. Izzy would reach for the champagne, throw off her Swarovski-studded

Louboutin shoes, snatch Kyle's phone, and kiss his neck.

I looked out the window as we sped off. Holding my arms, I felt a rush of unfamiliar emotions. *What am I doing? Where do I think this is going?*

What is more, I had not processed what just took place in the museum grotto. I had never been kissed like that. Except for a few fumbling kisses in high school and a few drunken and failed nookie attempts by guys at frat parties, I had no sexual experience. Sex was my mother's bogeyman. To her, all men were future sex beasts or future criminal rapists. For them, women were jars to spill their seed. Jars to shatter.

Mom kept me on a slow poison diet of abstinence by fear. Unlike the padlocked metal chastity belt many parents forced their daughters to wear in the past (and, incredibly, some still buy on Amazon) I wore an invisible Chastity Belt. Since I was a little girl, she forced me to watch every TV crime show about female victims.

While other six-year old's were picking out their favorite Disney princess, I was picking out the worst serial killers from the FBI's Center for the Analysis of Violent Crime. When girls went dress shopping for their junior prom, I went to Brazilian Jiu-Jitsu classes to learn combat training—though I was terrible at it.

While America was instilled with a crippling fear of terrorism, I was indoctrinated with a crippling fear of men by the best man-hater in the Western hemisphere. I always imagined a chart with color-coded levels of danger, much like the Homeland Security Terror Advisory System.

Low-Risk Green: Old men in retirement homes.

Guarded Blue: Teenagers.

Elevated Risk Yellow: College frat boys.

High-Risk Orange: Drunken men at a bar.

Severe-Risk Red: Alone in an alley behind a bar.

Kyle Paxton: Off the charts Severe-Risk Red. *For sure. But he's the only man worth smashing every rule for.*

Though I was a classic rebel as a teenager, I kept away from boys—even in my dark rebel-Goth-Satanic Hard Rock music years. And now I was virtually a sixteen-year-old entombed in an adult woman's body. I had no normal adult relationships. No teenage rites of passage. No alcohol. No weed. I was as empty as the old display cases in the museum vault. And when Kyle found out, he would spit me out like cheap liqueur, and run a thousand miles. As he sat there ignoring me, stern-faced and absorbed by his phone, I wondered if he regretted taking me out. The flinty corporate drone in front of me had no resemblance to the man who had just lost control of his mouth on mine.

Confusing. Taking out my phone, I spent my time texting soothing messages to Cypress, promising to be home soon.

When the limo stopped, Kyle looked up from his phone. "Here we go."

He led me out to a long flagstone path. The Chrome Fig was a big Edwardian mansion with ecru bricks, a glazed tile roof, lead glass windows, sloped turrets, and sweeping porches. It had been restyled as a restaurant by heiress Fleur Compton and her gourmet chef husband, Silvio Aguilera. Stepping into the plush interior, it was hard to imagine this had once been a historic home. It was all modern chic with mahogany walls, marble floors, minimal furniture, cubed sculptures, and Persian carpets so dense my heels got lost in the pile.

We shrugged off our coats and Kyle handed them to the coat check attendant. Feeling out of place, I looked around. Beautiful women in glitzy dresses, men in suits, and affluent families celebrating Thanksgiving mingled with tuxedo-clad waiters who carried silver salvers of appetizers. With an arm draped around my waist, Kyle led me swiftly through a crowded hall, his head low so as not to speak to anyone. I wondered if he was embarrassed to be publicly seen with me. That hurt.

Or maybe I'm just a drill-fracking paranoid.

Outside the last door in the hall stood a man who snapped to attention when he saw Kyle. He wore a maître-d' name pin. Rafi Numi. "Mr. Paxton. We were expecting you."

Kyle nodded. "Thanks, Rafi."

Rafi ushered us into a private room with a small round table set for two. I looked around in anxiety. Edged against one wall was a long oak paneled table and a red couch. Clearly, this was a room reserved for larger parties. Why had Kyle reserved the entire room for me? Biting my upper lip, I sank down in a chair held out for me.

Rafi smiled at me. "Miss Izzy, welcome. Sorry, I missed you last month. Fleur told me you were coming today."

Awkward. I bit my tongue. So Kyle had brought Izzy here during the museum's gala weekend.

Kyle shot him a cold look. "This is Miss Mills."

"A thousand apologies." Rafi took two steps back. "I will be back. Enjoy." The door shut with a soft click behind him.

Kyle sat down across from me, frowning. "I should've taken you elsewhere. But there is no other restaurant in Ann Arbor."

"There are actually five hundred and forty-seven restaurants in Ann Arbor."

"I meant good ones."

Says you, Mr. Stuck-up GQ Pants. Annoyed, I stared down at the delicate Waterford china with its gold-edged rims and picked up a tiny silver fork. I lowered my lids and focused on tapping the fork on the appetizer plate. Our worlds were poles apart. I'd have been happier going to Stella's Diner or the hotdog stand by the museum. And now even a frostbitten TV dinner from my fridge sounded fun. I imagined Kyle taking one look at my fridge and my small apartment, gagging, and running away. Tears pricked at my eyes. This was a mistake. A big mistake.

"So. Aside from hanging from scaffoldings, curating Celtic art and driving tomatoes, what do you do, Juniper Mills?" Unaware of the storm raging inside me, Kyle leaned back in his chair, stretched out his legs, and shot me a warm and sincere smile.

"Nothing. I'm really boring and lead a lackluster life."

"I think you're the most intriguing person I have ever met. Well—aside from Steve Jobs—but he's dead. So you win."

"I'll bet you say that to all the girls you bring here."

He put his glasses on, cleared his throat, and ignored my jab. "I think only people who get bored with life are boring. There is so much to do, to see. Only losers like me, get bored. You, Juniper, have achieved a lot in your life. And now you're writing a book. The inverse of boring. Though your book title is terrible, horrible, bad, ick."

I laughed. "Well, I'm open to suggestions."

His eyes lit up with a spark of boyish light and it was such an infectious spark, I smiled back, my doubts dissolving. It was warm in the room and he shed his sweater, revealing a crisp white shirt. Flinging his sweater and scarf on the couch, he shook his head. "I'm so used to the Bay area, I keep overdressing. Are you cold?"

"Ah, you lily-livered Californians. It's shorts weather here." My arms crossed over my breasts, as was my old habit and his gaze skimmed over my sleeveless cream blouse, the corners of his mouth lifting.

We fell into an easy camaraderie and talked about art, modern painting, the new museum wing and his love of San Francisco, until Rafi and two waiters came inside holding wine bottles.

"The red is the Cabernet Sauvignon Shiraz and the white is the Domaine Ramonet Montrachet Grand Cru," Rafi said, as he served us.

Gulp. Only two of the most expensive wines in the world, over a thousand dollars per bottle. *What is going on here?* As the two waiters set up the appetizers, I was stunned. There were at least six small plates for each of us. Prawns in ramekins of mushroom mousse. Tiny sushi rolls stacked up. Asian fusion mango scallops. Lobster bake in twisted sachets. Little meat patties. Skinny asparagus spears. I would be done after the first course.

Kyle gave me an apologetic look. "I ordered six options. Wasn't sure what you liked."

"It's too much. Just one option please," I said to Rafi.

Rafi stopped in mid step and looked at Kyle. "Sir?"

"It's fine. Bring everything I ordered," Kyle said, smoothly.

When Rafi left, I realized Kyle was trying hard to make an impression and that he was maybe as nervous as I was. Okay, so what was the story? He had been with many women. But I was different. *Right? A girl can hope.* I gave him a big smile. "Thanks for all of this."

"I screwed up, didn't I? Next time you pick the restaurant," he muttered.

I am glad there'll be a next time. It was my turn to be sheepish. "You're a good host and I'm a rotten guest. Sorry."

Intense, intimate, sexy Kyle was back. As he rubbed his chin, I was floored by the hard lines of his jawline and the just-woke-up stubble. His eyes glowed and he leaned forward. "No more sorries between us."

"Okay." I felt a slow heat rise up in me. I needed a cold shower. Eyes downcast, I chewed a morsel of the seared prawn. "Oh wow, this is heavenly."

Though he looked intrigued by my reserve, he took the conversation to a less awkward place. "Did you say you are cooking the Thanksgiving meal tomorrow?"

"Yes." *Please don't ask about my family.*

"So who're you making the dinner for?"

"The usual suspects."

"Are you always this secretive about your personal life? So KGB. CIA. So NSA," he asked with a lopsided smile.

"I guess." I blushed again and looked down. *Rat crap. Why do I blush whenever Kyle Paxton is within ten feet of me?*

"Miss Mills. You are singular. Blushing and cooking. Two arts I thought girls had forgotten." His hand reached for mine and trapped it with a deliberate motion, warm fingers kneading my cold ones.

"Not arts, social traps," I whispered, eyes on his hand. I could not look up.

"Agreed. So, what are you trapped by?"

That's harder to answer, going back to your previous question. "To be fair, I only blush in your presence. And I never want to cook for you, now that I know your stuck-up taste." *Did I just say—cook for you? Someone in power up there, please cut out my vocal cords.*

"I have no taste, trust me. So were you beamed in from the Medieval Age?"

"Iron Age." Looking up, I smiled shyly.

"Ah. There it is. That elusive smile. Do I make you nervous, Juniper?"

"I don't...know. I find you to be...daunting. Intimidating. Possibly dangerous." *And from another galaxy. And so wrong for me. And me, so wrong for you.*

The rough pad of his thumb caressed the raised veins of my hand. I wanted his thumbs and fingers to trail up my bare arm. An image of me throwing off the tablecloth, smashing the china, jumping on the table, and kissing him popped up in my thoughts and I blushed again. Freeing my hand from his finger prison, I picked up a water glass and drained it.

"Juniper, I'm really not what I seem. No big syllable words. I'm actually very chill. Very easy going."

"Bare-faced liar."

We both laughed.

"Well, I'm really glad I took you out."

"Liar."

"Why not? We are both simpatico. Can't you feel it?" he asked, raising both his hands as if the air rang with our simpatico-ness.

Simpatico. What a lovely word.

"Not yet." I shook my head and looked down again.

Kyle shoveled the entire sushi roll into his mouth with chopsticks and changed the mood by changing topics. "Turkey day, huh? You've no idea how much I wish I could crash your family's dinner tomorrow."

Nooo please, you are never allowed at my place.

My back became stiff and I took tiny bites of my sushi roll by impaling it with one chopstick. I twirled the lacquer chopstick on the tablecloth like a one-legged dancer and flipped it on its pair with a *twang*. Lost in thought, I picked up both and made them walk across the table like stick people and when I noticed he was watching my antics with a half-smile, I put them down.

"So you're not a fan of Thanksgiving with the family?"

"I meet my extended family on Thanksgiving only and even once a year is too much. Paxton family dinners are the circles of Dante's Inferno."

I leaned forward. "Really? I thought growing up a Paxton would be a cross between a Norman Rockwell painting and a Vogue magazine spread."

"More like a cross between a Malibu rehab and Alcatraz. Too much alcohol, drunk cribbing and no escape."

"Oh. You have many siblings, right?"

"Yep. Ten. The most dysfunctional family, ever. My father married six times and we call him Henry the Eighth. My mom was wife number four.

128

God, I hope you never have to meet my family." He winced and shot me a wry smile.

"You forget that I know your father."

He froze. "What?"

Stopping in mid-bite, I put down my mango scallop laden fork. "He was the museum board president before you."

His face relaxed. "Oh, for a second, I thought you knew him like half of Ann Arbor women do." My gut reacted as if he'd punched it. My eyes got bigger and I hoped he'd apologize, but he leaned in, his eyes raking my face. "God. I was right. They do change. Your beautiful eyes. This morning they were gray. In the dark they were brown. Now they are silver. At the gala, I thought you had green eyes. You have some scary pigment granules."

"Oh, yeah. My eyes are moody."

"You must reserve a color for me."

"Tell me which one you like."

"Until I met you, I liked dark eyes, now I think I like your green ones." He was watching me with a wicked grin, and his...big, dilated...aroused pupils.

Dark eyes, like Izzy's? My heart skipped a beat. I sucked my cheeks and took a sip of the Cabernet Sauvignon; I needed an entire bottle now.

I cleared my throat. "Did you know all blue-eyed humans alive today, share one ancestor? Geneticists tracked down a genomic mutation to a man who lived ten thousand years ago, near Afghanistan."

He laughed. "I didn't know I had a baby blues granddaddy."

I leaned back in my chair enjoying the genuine burst of his laugh. "Yep. So, Kyle, when did you move away from Ann Arbor?"

"I was ten. Mom got divorced and took me to San Francisco. I just—." He inhaled and took a deep swig of water. I noticed he did not drink more than one glass of wine, which was curious. "I recently reconciled with my father.

He didn't want to have anything to do with me until I became successful."

Guessing I was not the only one reluctant to talk about family, I felt he had skipped a decade or two in his history. "Tell me about your brother Royce, the congressman at the gala. Your family must be so proud of him." I had noticed a cold war between the brothers that day and it made me curious.

"The old man's proud of him, I guess. But Royce and I aren't close... probably because I've cut myself off from everyone." Kyle's eyes were far away and he clammed up again.

When I urged him to tell me about his business, he told me that seven years ago he had founded BirdsEye from his garage. The product was a lens that turned smartphones into high-resolution cameras. He struggled for four years before making it a mad success. I was impressed. With the exception of our museum founder, Kyle's grandfather, the Paxtons were not known for their meritocracy.

After we had been served the second course, he put his elbows on the table and leaned closer to me. "See, until this selfie craze, Juniper, business was slow. We got random clients from military and surveillance. All ten Paxton kids have trust funds and I dumped my entire fund to launch the business. We lost capital and suffered so much loss, I thought of shutting down. With business hanging by a thread, I lost every penny I had. I lived for years in total poverty. Ate lots of canned food, sold my apartment and moved into my grandfather's musty old house."

"Really?" I found it hard to associate total poverty and this man in one universe.

"I kid you not."

"Wow. What then?"

"Then the social media self-love paid off for us. In a big way. From Japan to Germany, all the kids who wanted clear duck-face selfies ate us up. We are now a fortune 1000 tech company."

"That's amazing, Kyle."

"Thank you. After that, my father recharged his dad-batteries. Because of the museum, I'll have to see a heck-load more of him."

"I see. So when are you returning to see him?"

"No clue."

"Not even on Christmas?" My voice was hollow as I tapped a spoon against my water glass, causing it to vibrate.

"Nah. Every Christmas break, I go rock climbing."

"Where do you go?"

"New Zealand. Nepal. Argentina. This year, I'm going back to *Piedra Parada*, a volcanic formation in Argentina. December is the best time, when the air is clean and dry."

"How exciting. I can't even climb scaffoldings. Any sports?"

"No team sports. Surfing. Parasailing. Scuba diving."

"With sharks?" I joked.

"Once in Bimini Island. In a cage. I'm an adrenaline junkie."

"Cool. Cool."

Suddenly the air cooled between us. Sad and frustrated, I threw down the spoon and slumped back in my chair. I was not thinking about his exciting outdoor activities.

He won't be back, not even on Christmas. I don't know when I'll see him again. Kyle Paxton is now the most anticipated part of my life. Pathetic.

He picked up the red wine to top off my glass and I put my hand on the rim. *No more wine.*

"Juniper, I will see you in a few weeks in San Francisco. For the museum training."

"No. I can't come." Instantly stunned, he demanded a reason. I shook my head again, realizing how I sounded—as sad as the last line of a favorite book. "Can't. I'll talk to Mr. Ipswich. I'm sure he'll understand why I can't go."

His jaw twitched. "The training is mandatory. You must come. I've pulled a lot of strings to expedite this."

"It's not possible…with my current circumstances," I said, eyes downcast.

"And what circumstances are those?"

None of your business. Nosy kahuna.

"This is the best meal I have had. Thanks for inviting me. I have to go soon."

"I know this is not normal, Juniper. Nor is it for me. It is—insanity. And all moving too fast. But I want you to trust me. Look up." From across the small table, his hand shot out and lifted my chin so I was forced to meet his eyes. I eased away. Exhaling hard, he let his hand drop on the table.

"Why? I live here. You live in San Francisco. You're an international tycoon. I'm a geeky curator stuck in one place."

"International tycoon? You watch too many old movies."

"Where is this going, Kyle?"

"I want us to go far."

"What do you want from me?"

"You. I want you."

My heart skipped a lot of beats. "What about Izzy? Was she not with you here last time? Am I just flavor of the week? Isn't she your girlfriend?"

"I don't have girlfriends, Juniper." His mouth lifted at the corners and his eyes glinted with a dangerous light.

"Excuse me?" My eyebrows rose in disbelief.

"I have fuck-buddies."

KYLE

K yle stared in interest. The girl's face changed colors faster than a chameleon on a prism. Right now, she was a white sheet of snow. He braced himself. It was possible he was wrong about her. No one ever reacted like that. No one. This was usually when they broke out in seductive smiles and poses and tried to prove they were worthy of his selection.

He needed her. Wanted her. In his bed. Every night. Till the date she needed to go. And now she was speechless. What if she said no? No, that was out of the question. No one said no to Kyle Paxton.

He just had to explain the system to Juniper. He needed to clarify the reward outweighing the risk calculation. Planned to the tee, like everything in his meticulous life, there was strategic trajectory in his system. It worked. It was infallible. It was his complex systems design.

1) It studied patterns of behavior.

2) It noted human fallacy and predicted outcomes.

3) It found the bugs and errors.

4) It debugged the errors.

5) It updated the pattern formation.

6) It carried out the bug free system.

It worked. Always.

CHAPTER 9

I have fuck-buddies.

A hot color rose up from my throat and my cheeks seared with red flags. The room became smaller, the walls closing in. My chair scraped and I got up. Taking a step back, I looked around. I wanted to rush out of the room. Now. *What in hellish of hells?*

"Sit down."

No more smiling Kyle. He was stony. Icy. A hand shot out and my wrist was ensnared. Kyle pulled me back in my chair, my wrist in a titanium grip. I struggled to free myself, and when he let go, I saw crimson marks from his fingers. Furious, I rubbed them and shot him a look of disbelief.

"I'm so sorry."

"I…I thought this was just dinner," I managed to say.

"Finish dinner. Listen to what I have to say. Then you are welcome to leave. My car will drop you off alone. If you say no, I will never bother you again. We go back to our professional relationship."

Another punch in the gut. A kick in the teeth.

He wants me as a fuck buddy?

"No."

"Juniper, you are so stubborn. Please. Just hear me out." He put two fingers on his forehead as if ironing it out.

"Don't…n…need t…to," I stuttered. I was shaking. This was a dance I did not know. A game I didn't play.

He gave me a concerned look. "Breathe in. Breathe out."

Just then the door swung open and our main course arrived. A cheery Rafi announced the dishes. Hot and tender lobster with farm butter and lime. Crisp and soft slices of Kobe steak. Plate after plate of…God knows what. I had lost my appetite. Maybe forever. The food began to swim in circles across the tablecloth, like plops of oil paints.

Teeth on edge, jaw tight, my nails stabbed my palms. Nausea rose up in my gut.

Fuck buddy? What does that mean? Friends with benefits? Why couldn't he say that? Somewhere from the recesses of my mind floated the meaning: a friend or acquaintance with whom a person has sex regularly without the expectation of a romantic relationship.

Mom's right. Men are scum.

As soon as Rafi and our waiters left, Kyle's taciturn face swam in front of me. He handed me a glass of cold water. "Juniper, are you all right?"

"Tell me what you have to, so I can leave."

Just my dumb luck. The one man in the world I want to have a relationship with wants me just for my body.

"Before I tell you anything more, you have to sign this NDA." He held his smartphone out to me.

"Oh Kyle, you're too precious. You want me to trust you. But you can't trust me?" My voice was laced in contempt. The trained man-hater living inside me took over, her emergency exit walls closing in on the real Juniper who liked Kyle way more than he deserved.

"It's standard issue, Juniper. In California, we whip them out at every meal." He grimaced and set his phone beside me. He held out the stylus. "Sign please."

"This is not California. And I'm not a girl used to being treated like an object." With trembling fingers I pushed his phone away as if it were an anti-Eucharist dagger.

"Please, sign it. I am a very private person with a very public image. This way you can ask me whatever you want and I will answer truthfully. Full disclosure."

"Please, can I go now?" My voice was small. Peevish.

"Read it."

"Do you also have a restraining order handy? I need one."

He sighed. "Just read it. Please."

Scowling, I picked up his phone and read silently as he scrutinized my face.

This Nondisclosure Agreement is entered into by and between Kyle Paxton ("Disclosing Party") and Juniper Mills ("Recipient") for the purpose of preventing the unauthorized disclosure of Confidential Information.

1) Confidentiality:The parties agree to enter into a confidential relationship with respect to the disclosure of certain exclusive and confidential information by the Disclosing Party to the Recipient.This binding agreement shall be ruled in all respects by Governing Law of the State of California.

2) Purpose: The verbal or written confidential information is only revealed by the Disclosing Party to the Recipient for a specific and timely personal, individual and privileged purpose.

3) Nondisclosure Obligations: Recipient agrees to take all steps necessary to protect the secrecy of the Confidential Information, and to prevent it from falling into the public domain or into the possession of unauthorized persons. At no point shall the Recipient disclose the information to third parties, personal and professional contacts, including and not limited to all media, press and forms of social media.

4) Survival: Recipient apprehends that Nondisclosure Obligations shall survive the termination of any other relationship between the parties. Upon termination of relationship between the parties, this provision allows the Agreement to stay in effect.

5) Breach: Any breach of the Recipient's obligations under this Agreement will result in irreparable damages to Disclosing Party for which legal scrutiny will be sought and enforcement of any of these obligations will be entitled (in addition to other resolutions) to preliminary and permanent injunctive and other equitable relief to prevent, discontinue and/or restrain the breach of this Agreement.

Receiving Party: Juniper Mills Disclosing Party: Kyle Paxton

How dare he? Seeing my name on the document, I got angry, and after reading the last clause I became angrier. My breach of this NDA could cause legal damages! But my curiosity about his secret sex life trumped my anger. Like a python's prey, I was hypnotized, afraid, repelled and compelled—in short, real stupid.

As I scribbled my name with his stylus on the screen and slid the phone across the table, I felt like I had signed my soul away. Arms crossed, I sat back and watched as he signed it as well, asked for my email and sent us both a copy.

"Clause four is the only one that matters. Termination of the relationship. Not that we have one, which is why this is all so laughable," I said, hotly.

"Juniper, you are—being harsh. I have had a life before I met you. I'm a man of thirty. I—I…am not what you think."

"Just tell me, Kyle," I spat through clenched teeth.

"All right. What do you want to know?" He pushed his plate away and when his eyes met my hostile ones, he gritted his teeth.

"Why the hell? I mean you are not exactly Cyrano de Bergerac, so why?"

"I don't do messy relationships. I can't. I don't have time. I don't do girlfriends. I have—"

"Friends with benefits?"

"No. Not quite friends. Let's say companions."

Companions? I gulped. A painful lump formed in my throat, as if I had been crying for days. "Seriously? Companions?"

"Yes."

"Why not call them girlfriends?"

"Because that implies relationships." He shrugged. "No one has relationships anymore."

"Um. You're wrong. But go on. You were saying companions."

"Yes. Set ones. Two a year."

"What. The. Actual. Fuck. Did you just say set ones?" I rarely swore, so we were both shocked at my language.

He frowned. "May I?"

"I'll shut up."

"Set ones. One for summer and one for winter. Summer from January to July. And Winter from August to December. Izzy was Winter. Each of them has a set ending date in advance. They sign contracts to enforce the ending date."

Oh my God, so that's what Izzy meant when I had overheard them. Her voice floated across the hedges. *So winter is almost over. I'm Winter. I'm almost over.*

Trying to process it all, I finally found my voice. "Wow. That is so...not okay. Why do you have set dates?"

"So there is no drama. No stress. No messy breakups. And five-and-a-half months is the perfect time to not be strangers, yet not be in a relationship. Time limits work. It's clean and efficient." His expression was aloof, as if he could not get why I made such a big fuss.

"So how does it work?"

"We attend all the events I need a date for. Parties I need a companion for. We travel together. Some are in other states, so I fly them over. Or I travel to them. Sometimes, I work in London. I have a small office there. Summer comes with me."

"Why—do you need to do this?" I held on to the edge of the table, my knuckles so taut and white, they looked like they would crack with a tap of my butter knife.

"Convenience. Time. I don't have time to go to bars or pick up girls anywhere. I don't have time for lowlifes. I also don't have time for a committed relationship. I'm too busy as BirdsEye founder. Being my companion is a physical thing, not an emotional one. But it has to be just right."

A physical thing. Why? Are you incapable of emotions, Kyle?

"It sounds like girls are things to you."

He shook his head. "It's not like that, Juniper. I am a very busy person. I have a lot of time constraints. My system is proven. It works. People know what to expect and *when* to expect it and you walk away drama-free. No romance. No jealousy. No nonsense. A girlfriend or wife would be miserable with a man like me."

"You've just messed up the entire system of dating and hooking up."

"Let's just say, I've upgraded it," he said with a cocky smile.

Ugh. Don't get carried away, chump.

"You do realize they have apps like Tinder for hooking up?"

"I have no use for hookups with strangers. Or tacky apps like Tinder."

"Okay, try Hinge. Hinge is the perfect alternative to Tinder. There's Happn. Also try Coffee meets Bagel. And there's Plenty of Fish, another great app for horny hookups. Which reminds me—why am I still here? I need to go buy a barrel of pepper spray and a small pistol."

In spite of the gravity of the situation, he smiled. "Look, Juniper. I'm not a one-night-stand kind of guy. Nor have I ever been with a professional... escort. And I need someone who can move easily in and out of my world. So I select only those who can be with me socially and intellectually. The only way I can avoid—"

"Come on. Cut it out. Stop polishing mud. It's not about your social and intellectual needs. It's about sex. Do they sleep with you on set dates, too?" I interrupted him in my best Moral Police voice.

"No. Anytime I want."

The hairs on my arms stood up. Did he really just say, anytime he wanted? *Oh Great Spirit, give me the confidence to deal with this arrogant prick.*

"So they agree to sleep with you at the snap of your finger?"

He weighed my words and flinched. "I don't get why this is a big deal. We have...a lot of fun. It's very...mutual."

"Do you have multiple fuck buddies?" I closed my eyes, shaking slightly. Why did I keep saying those hideous two words? The worst two-word combination in the English language.

"No. I'm not polyamorous. To avoid complications, both parties have to sign an exclusivity contract."

"Not much exclusivity when you move on to another girl in a few months."

He looked displeased and we both went quiet. I picked up a fork and stabbed my steak with it. He watched as I perforated it with savage stabs.

I took a deep breath. "So what do they get in return?"

"Whatever they want. Great company, great—."

Okay, I get it, Kyle. You have moves.

"All great things, without the fear of becoming a one-night stand. Being used or abused. Tossed aside without notice. Knowing I am theirs for a perfect five months. I give them what they want. It's a reciprocal exchange." He spoke as if he was describing a business transaction, a detached merger between two parties, not human emotions.

"Why…are you telling me this?"

"I want you to be my Summer."

His words sliced into me like a butcher knife in raw liver.

"What?" I knew his words were inevitable but hearing them was hard. My eyes snapped shut as if they were heavy box lids. This was the Twilight Zone, right? Or Candid Camera? This guy was an actor…this was an elaborate joke…Lila set me up…I took a shallow breath.

"Juniper, you look like you need air." He got up and came to me. His gentle hands tried to lift me up.

Let me go. No, hold me.

I rose from my seat. A warm arm went around my waist and he led me to the panoramic floor-to-ceiling window. The curtains were parted and I leaned my head on the cold glass, taking ragged breaths. Outside the swirly mist had turned into the first snowfall of the season. Fat white flakes danced in the black horizon. Even in the dark, I made out the thin white line on the tops of distant mountains. On the lawns, I saw a sprinkling of fresh snow. Like white powder. Virginal and untouched. Tiny flakes and crystals idly drifted down on the glass. Like the cold dripping inside me.

"I want you, Juniper. Badly. And I know you want me too. This is the only way." Behind me, his low voice sent shivers up my spine. One of his arms rested casually on my waist. But I sensed the evident possession in his touch, as if I was ready for livestock branding with his hot iron.

The only way?

Had this uppity twitch not heard of dating? Girlfriends? Relationship? Marriage? Norms set millenniums ago? The social institutions time-honored by society and favored by our biological function? How could a person surgically cut emotions from desire? Love from physical urges? Are we animals now? No, even animals are faithful. Animals love. Are we cyborgs now? Was Kyle an alpha who escaped from the World State of *Brave New Worlds?* Had he not—my mind ran riot.

"God, you are so cold." His arms went around my waist and he drew me close to him from behind. Cradled me.

I recalled the time he brought me down from the scaffolding. But the man who saved me was a fading illusion. Any foregone conclusions of his character were now confirmed. Even so, I wanted badly for him to hold me like this forever. His body was all rigid planes, soft flesh, hard muscles. Warmth. Strength. Security. I felt so safe. No, unsafe. Danger. Off-the-chart alert. Severe-Risk Crimson Tide Alert.

"If you say no, we go back to a professional relationship and never talk of it again. Juniper, it is your choice."

Your choice, your lifestyle.

His chin nestled in the curve of my neck and his voice was raw and tender. "I want to make you happy. Tell me what you want and I will make it yours. Anything. I feel bad I laid this all out after knowing you for such a short time. But I've never been so sure of anything in my life. Truly."

He eased me away from the window and turned my face to him. A palm cupped my chin and an errant thumb traced the curve of my lower lip. His lips parted and a shared pulse of desire ran through both of us. Like a tuning fork in the air.

"Beautiful Juniper."

I shivered. *Would he ever know, no man had called me beautiful before?*

"God, I love your name. Listen, I have never asked anyone to be with me after meeting them twice. I usually take months. You are—." He took in a sharp breath. "Different. I want to make you mine."

Mine. The word hung heavy in the air like something alive. Sentient. Threatening.

"Say something. Please," he whispered, his fingers playing havoc with my jawline.

I wanted him too. So bad. But never on his revolting, repulsive, icky terms. "The only way I can be yours is if I agree to your terms?"

A muscle began to twitch in his jaw and his hands let go of my face. "Yes. You sign a contract of rules and both parties are legally obligated to meet mutually agreed terms."

"No, *your* terms."

He carried on as if I had not interrupted him, "And the Termination Contract is the most important part of this arrangement. We set a date for starting and we set a date for ending it."

"Why do you need to terminate anyone?"

"The Termination Contract ensures none of my companions stay longer than the end date."

"Oh, yes. God forbid they should stay longer. The horror."

"I mean no disrespect. In fact, I consider it to be more respectful to women this way."

"Ha."

"No, really."

I touched my throat. "I am choking...speechless."

He released me and moved a step away. A chill cloud wrapped my body. "I did not mean to shock you. And I don't expect you to understand. But please believe me... when I say that I will never hurt you, or do anything against your will. Take a few days. Think it over and then tell me."

I folded my arms. "Nothing to think about."

"God, I'm sorry. I did not expect it to be such a shocker. I thought you were the ideal candidate. Aloof. Mature. Unemotional."

"Well, you thought wrong. Try demanding. Immature. Emotional."

"A lot of busy people do this, you know. A lot. In fact there's a whole group who started this in Manhattan and now it's common in San Francisco." As if he were in a docket making his case before a hostile jury, Kyle held up his hands in the air. "It's just a practical solution. A better solution to...all out chaos. Most men have over fifteen partners on average in a lifetime. The players have upwards of fifty. The men with my...advantages—upwards of a hundred."

Damn, did he mess with the wrong girl.

"Charming. And how many hundreds of girls have you been with?" I sneered. My arms wrapped around my waist as if I could shield myself from him and his *filth*. But I knew I was lying to myself. Though he was a pitiless heartbreaker, I still found him striking. Dangerous. Irresistible.

"Juniper, I think you misjudge me. I've had six partners in the past three years. Only six. You'd be my seventh, if you agree."

"I'd rather be girl zero."

We were quiet for a bit, each of staring off into space.

He took a long breath, eyes on the ceiling. "Listen, when you have a set date to start and a set date to finish, it works. It's a great system. The fulfillment of our natural needs without the drama. With no emotions vested, no romantic expectations, you get no heartbreak. No anger. No hatred. No chaotic ending. No bad breakups. No divorce. No children suffering. Just a clean, well-organized fresh slate to start and end."

I looped a finger in the air. "Slow clapping for you in my head. You deserve a medal for your liberating treatment of women. And unborn bastards. Simone de Beauvoir would be turning in her grave. I think—"

"Enough."

At the tacit fury on his face, I shut up. Why was I being so judgmental? We were almost total strangers. I met him a month ago, for God's sake. *Preserve your dignity, Juniper. Walk away. Move on.*

I weighed my words carefully. "I did...did not mean, I have no right to judge you."

A sliver of hope flashe d in his eyes. "No one has ever even questioned me before. But I get it. It's too sudden. Just know that I'll factor in what you want. Being mine is all about what you want. You're in control of your schedule. Your life. Come to me when you can. Leave when you need."

"How kind of you."

He sighed.

"Has anyone ever refused you?"

He shook his head.

"Has anyone ever left before the time you assigned them?"

He shook his head.

"Have you ever left before the time you assigned them?"

146

He hesitated and then nodded.

"Why do they agree?"

"The girls who enter into agreement with me get life handed to them on a platter. Some want to travel the world. Some need the connections. Some need strategic business partners. Some need capital to start a new business."

"You mean, you *pay* them? Wow. Isn't that a highfalutin way to say… prostitute. Incidentally, another word for companion." I choked back an acerbic laugh.

"It. Isn't. Like. That."

"I agreed to have dinner with you. This is so—"

Messed up.

Keyser Söze, no, Jeffrey Dahmer…serial-killer-level messed up.

Kyle reached for my hand. An electric current sprang from our touch and I jerked back as if his fingers were fangs. Frustrated, he took off his glasses and rubbed the bridge of his nose with two fingers. "I know. It's a lot to take in. But I'm clear about my intentions from the start to avoid wrong ideas. And I *want* you. I have wanted you since I first saw you."

"And you always get anything you want? The problem is, Kyle, I am not a thing."

"It was not my intention to make you feel like that. Say yes. You won't regret it. Be my Summer, from January to July. For three months, we'll be in London, at my office there. Come to Europe with me. See the world. Schedule your work around it."

"And what are the exact dates?"

"Summer starts on the last day of January and ends on the first day of July. Winter starts on the first day of August and ends on the tenth of December."

My mind struggled to do the math and I gasped. Stumbling to get away from him, I walked backwards until the table hit the back of my knees.

"So you mean…Izzy will be with you till December ten. Three more weeks. While you are with her, you are already on the prowl? And you picked me? So really, my dinner with you today…was cheating on her."

"No." Across his hard cheekbones, a dark flush vied with his tan.

I faced him squarely, struggling to keep the contempt out of my face. "I can't even imagine—I would not agree to this if we were the last two people left on earth."

For a while, he was silent, rotating his glasses in his hands over and over again. Finally, he looked up and shot me a strange smile. "I hope for a zombie apocalypse then, so we can test that."

I was not smiling and seized the edge of the chair for support. "My God. I thought I had heard it all. But you, Kyle Paxton, are a class act. *Check your privilege.* Get your deviant mind tested. The ego and narcissism of your life physically sickens me. I feel sick. The cold-blooded way you treat girls hurts me. Human girls. For your depraved needs. So I do not need time to say: Never."

Kyle said nothing, but I saw a white ring circle his mouth, as if I had physically hit him.

I continued in a polite but icy voice, "Just out of curiosity, what about me screamed that I was interested in becoming your harem girl?"

He paled under his tan. His face hardened and his eyes became ice chips. His jaw clenched hard and he looked to be seething through gritted teeth. I was reminded of a majestic, solitary, dangerous falcon.

I should have shut up but my reckless mind and tongue ran out of control. I jabbed a finger towards him. "And what's more, I know what you are doing in Ann Arbor with our two-bit museum, Mr. Bay Area. There, you are just one in a million of successful tech-biz CEOs. With your new museum wing, you'll be big news. Your intentions are hardly the same as your grandfather's. You are a poser doing it for publicity, not philanthropy."

Keeping it classy, Juniper.

"You are so far from the truth, I will not even dignify your accusations with an answer," he slurred, gritting his teeth. He looked as if I had broken him in half.

"Please, excuse me. I have to go." I walked to the table and collected my purse.

In one quick motion, Kyle sat in his chair. Avoiding my gaze, he poured a tall glass of white wine. In a clipped tone, he said, "Rob, my driver, is waiting for you. He'll take you home. Goodbye, Miss Mills."

I left without another word.

My blood sang in my head. I ran through a crowd of loud guests to the exit. The car was parked by the pebble-lined path. As soon as he saw me running towards it, Rob jumped out and opened the door. I slid inside. Only when I was almost home did I realize why I was shivering non-stop. I had walked out in such a rage, I had forgotten to get my coat.

KYLE

When the limo came back for Kyle, he had been standing outside a total of 34 minutes and 16 seconds. He came out in the cold 11 minutes after she fled. In his hands was a coat and inside him was nothing. Just a numb echo chamber. With her slicing words.

He tried to remember them, but instead of words came numbers.

It had been exactly 24 days, 5 hours, 48 minutes and 45 seconds since he met her.

Now he wished he hadn't.

CHAPTER 10

I am fuck-quality. Not girlfriend-quality. Like Mom.

I spent that restless night attacking my sheets, quilt and pillows. I was too numb to cry or throw a fit, but I was already on the train to Misery Town. Even in the morning, all I did was think about Kyle. His touch. His lips. His words. The words stuck in an infinite loop in my head. Like an earworm. *I want you, Juniper. I want you to be my Summer. I want you. Now.* The most tempting words of all: *I have wanted you since I first saw you.* And the sad finality in his last words. *Goodbye, Miss Mills.*

I wondered what my life would be like if I—frigid Juniper Mills, the oldest virgin in Ann Arbor—said yes to him.

He might be worth it, argued a crazy voice inside me.

Why can't I let go and have fun?

Because I'll fall in love and won't be able to let go. That's why.

Wait, why did I say love? It's the furthest thing from what he offered.

Love? Is that what I really wanted? I knew I wanted him. But not in the way that he wanted me. I wanted someone who could show me the good times I had missed, make me feel safe, hold me when I cried at night…someone who could take it slow and chase the cobwebs away from my body…gradually… and not use me for some sick twisted perversion of his own.

Even if I said yes to his offer, once Kyle found out I was a virgin, he'd probably stamp reject on my forehead and walk away snorting with laughter. Until Kyle, I'd never wanted to be with a man. Before I met him, I thought logically (as I had waited so long to lose my virginity) that I would just end up waiting until I got married.

Growing up with a mom who told me only unfairy tales, I wasn't sure I believed in the institution of marriage. I decided that if, one day, there was a remote chance I *did* get married, it would be with a safe guy who'd make a nontoxic husband. A safe, kind, ordinary guy from suburban Ann Arbor—the human equivalent of a tuna sandwich.

A guy whose face was fuzzy and who wore khakis, had a phone belt clip, and struggled to make his mortgage payments but had season tickets to Ford Field to see the Detroit Lions; a guy who thought Chipotle was exotic food and whose idea of the ultimate getaway was Vegas. My bland ideal— who I'd love to pieces. But in my mind, he was also a guy who laughed at all my jokes and spent every night spooning me, who was caring and would never hurt me, never cheat on me and never leave me.

The kind of guy who was the total opposite of Kyle Paxton.

After years of fighting my circumstances, my life was getting close to painless. Did I want to destroy it? In three meetings, Kyle had smashed up a lot of it. What would happen if he was with me for five months? I'd get too into him. I'd fall in love.

For him, you'd be a casual fuck buddy.

For you, he'd be everything.

He'd move on and you, Juniper Mills, are weak and pitiful, and would never forget him.

Never. He wasn't the type of man one forgot. He and I were over before we began and I just had to manage my dumb expectations. And get on with my life.

I dragged myself out of bed to cook the damned Thanksgiving meal. As I stomped into the kitchen, Cypress and my mother noticed my messy hair, the half-moon circles under my eyes, and my tight-lipped answers. Curious and worried, they kept asking me what was wrong and I explained I was tired from work. Cypress bought it, but Mom gave me a long look and tried to get me to go back to bed. I refused.

Being alone was like electroshock torture right now.

Usually, I cooked Thanksgiving dinner a day earlier, but now—thanks to Kyle—I had to rush. Only Cypress was happy, for he loved it when we tag-teamed in the kitchen. To our surprise, even Mom pitched in. When she came to help us, Cypress and I exchanged pleased looks.

I basted the turkey, Mom made mashed yams and green bean casserole, and Cypress cleaned up around us. He was over-efficient, catching every speck of flour, every crumb, every vegetable peel and fruit seed, while getting in the way. We laughed and prodded him often with our soiled hands and spatulas, just to bug him.

It had been a long time since we felt like a family. I smiled at the only two people in the world I loved. I had space in my heart for a third. Kyle.

Kyle—if only you were not a hair-raising creep, you'd be the perfect candidate.

Even memories of Kyle were as intrusive as he was in the flesh. He was here, in the tiny kitchen, leaning against the fridge, navy eyes fixed on me. If I closed my eyes, he clasped me from behind, hands around my waist. His lips moved on my neck, his words GIF images stuck in my head. I could not delete his (now) pointless images, so I did everything wrong. The vegetables were cut too thin. The gravy was over seasoned. I spilled the broth Mom made. The bread stuffing was so awful and ooey gooey, I threw it away. The turkey was not basted enough and I fretted it was dry. Checking on the turkey, I burned my wrist twice. After two hours of cooking, I wanted to cry.

This was also because holidays made me sad.

Since I could recall, no one ever joined us. Mom's family had not seen her for thirty years and they didn't even know Cypress and I existed. I had no freaking idea who my father was and, at times, I thought Mom didn't either. In my late teens, if I asked her to reach out to the men she had been with, she usually lost it. Once, in a fit of fury, she said she had been with so many men in one month, we could have been conceived with one of twelve men, like a dozen eggs in a carton.

That had shut me up. Lost in my grudge, I did not talk to Mom for almost a year. Getting into college, Lila's friendship, and my museum internship helped me get over my crippling self-pity (though not my fatal flaw of blaming others) and I did mend fences with my mother. But last night the angst and fear had come back—all because of Kyle.

Enough. Turn him off.

I redirected my anger at Mom. "So, another Thanksgiving, huh. By the way, have you thought about reaching out to your parents? They are alive, right? Thirty years and you never looked back. You just ghosted on them. Why don't you—"

"Juniper. Stop." The oven was open and she was checking the turkey. She smacked the door hard, the sound reverberating in the small kitchen like a crack of thunder.

Cypress stopped cleaning and looked at us.

"Mom, do you know I hate Thanksgiving? Hate it. Cuz it's a holiday about family and it's always just us. It's just the three of us. Year after year. It sucks. Why can't you reunite with them?"

She gazed at me, her face careful and passive, as always. "What brought this on? You know I'm not welcome in my parents' home. How many times do I have to tell you that?"

"Give 'em another chance. I'm sure they'd be happy to see us. I'm sure they've forgiven you…it was ages ago. You have kids and you did alright. At least, try."

Veiled anger and stainless steel reflected on her face as she put a big pot of boiling yams in the sink. "Why don't you get your own family, Juniper? It's about time you had a boyfriend and got married."

"What? That. Is. Hilarious. What chance do I have for a relationship? You scared the bejesus out of me. 'Juniper, be scared. Be very scared. There are monsters that walk in the shadows. Don't date. Don't drink. Stay home. All guys are wicked rapists. Boo.' That's what I heard all my life. And now— you want me to get married? Where do I get a guy? Download one from Amazon? Order wholesale from Alibaba?"

"Juniper. Calm down. I protected you from the crazy shitstorm out there."

"So you thought two wrongs would make it all right?"

"I never wanted you *not* to have adult relationships. I want happiness for you. I want you to meet a nice guy. Get settled. Raise a family. I am your mother. Not your enemy."

"Liar. The psycho dysfunctional way you raised me…how can I be with a guy when all I see are evil dickwads and Satan's tadpoles?" I was regressing into my teens, when I saw Mom as the root cause of my shitty life. When I felt Mom had imprisoned me in a tower and I was her Rapunzel project.

"I had to stop you from turning into a teenage slut like I was," she said.

"I am not you!"

"Maybe because I raised you not to be."

"You didn't raise me, you caged me."

"Junie, stop shouting," Cypress whispered.

Tears pricked in Mom's eyes. "I love you and Cypress so much, I didn't want you both to suffer like I did. And look how great you turned out."

"I turned out to be a loser unable to have normal relationships."

My mother was looking at me with wet eyes. "That's not true. You are so accomplished, exactly as I raised you to be. Independent, educated, on your own two feet, with no need for a man to fund your life. I just wanted to protect you when you were young."

"Mom, don't be sad," Cypress said. In his natural empathy, his hands went around her waist and she buried her face in his shoulder.

"You didn't protect us. You hid us in a goddamn prison from the world."

"Tell me, how can I fix this?"

I took a deep breath. "You can't fix me. I am broken. Beyond repair. Every time I meet a guy remotely into me, my first instinct is to reject him. Mistrust him. Hate him. I *hate* men who like me. And I hate who I've become. I've tried…but I can't turn my trained mind off. Why'd you do this to me? Why?"

"Okay. Fine. I was tough on you. But I did it so you didn't repeat my mistakes."

"Mom, you can't hit the reset button of *your* life on *me*. I'm not your do-over card."

"That's not what I did…"

"Yes, you did! Why didn't you change yourself instead of screwing me up?"

"I did. I left everything bad and kept you away from it."

"Well. I'd rather learn from my own mistakes than be punished for yours."

"We were having a nice, peaceful day and there you go, ruining everything." Cindy eased herself from Cypress's arms. No longer teary-eyed, her face was a cold brick wall.

"I did not ruin it, Mom. You did, by not telling us who the hell our father is."

"God, isn't one issue enough for you? Yes, I ruined your life. I stopped you from seeing your grandparents. Your not-dating is my fault. Made you get a job at a Burger Buns. Didn't get you braces. Didn't get neuro-therapy for Cypress. I'm the posterchild deadbeat mom. Everything is my fault. But I told you, I don't know who the hell your father is."

"You're hiding something," I snarled.

"I am not."

"Nooo…" Cypress covered his ears and rocked himself back and forth. Our fighting was hell for his condition.

Staring at him, I lowered my voice. "Look, sorry I yelled. Just pick up the phone. Go on social media…you'll find them. You changed your name. They didn't. Let's meet on Christmas. If you can't. I will."

"Juniper Mills, stop right there. You have no right to dig into my past." Picking up a knife, she threw it in the sink with an angry thwack. She grabbed the counter edge for support, her plump (and still Goddess) body sagging against it.

I got celery out of the fridge, slammed it shut and went to the sink. Washing the celery stalks in hot water, I scalded my skin. It hurt, but the pain forced me to think clearly. It dawned on me that at my age, she was already a mother of twin toddlers.

What led her there? The drugs? The stripping?

She told me often that stripping was all she could do with her limited skills as a pageant queen. When we were kids, she told me she had been a ballet dancer, before our birth ruined her figure. Dumb schmuck as I was, I believed her, until a jock told me in high school that my mother had stripped for his daddy and that I should strip for him. It was a tough way to find out my mother was once a stripper.

You have no right to dig into my past.

Why was her past to be buried when it affected my future? If I could find my father, maybe things would be different, especially for Cypress.

Taking a step towards her, I said, "If you won't, I'll do it. You worked at the diner and before that the strip club in Detroit. I'm gonna go and find out who your clients were. One of them was my daddy. Cindy Mills, what was your stripper name? Lemme guess. Was it Candy?"

Hands clenched, my mother put one fist under my chin. "Juniper, you're too old and smart to behave like a bitchy teenager. Stop it. Leave me be. All I am is roadkill lying by the side of the road. I'm dead. Done with life. And don't you dare look into my past. Or I'll kill myself."

Did she really say that?

I gasped, my tears coming fast and hard. I had never cried in front of Cypress. I had to be strong for him. Forcing my tears back, I reached for a cutting board and started chopping my celery. What was I doing? After all, Kyle was my mother's worst fears collected and poured in human form.

"God, no, Mom. I won't. I am sorry. I was just saying—"

Cypress began to groan, his hands still on his curly golden retriever head. "Stop it. Stop it, both of you. I can't stand it."

Both my mother and I turned to hug him.

"Okay, sorry, buddy. Look, I stopped," I said and kissed his forehead.

"Say sorry to Mommy." His wide chest heaved like a sensitive rock star belting out a sad song.

"Forgive me, Mom. Truly." She did not respond. Cursing silently, I chopped a tough stalk of celery and gasped. The knife sliced into my left hand forefinger. Spurts of red mingled with the crisp green on the cutting board

"Juniper. You are bleeding," Cypress cried out from behind me.

"I'm fine." I pinched my finger.

Just then the doorbell rang. We all froze. It rang again. It was jarring. The doorbell never rang. I swallowed and walked towards the door. "Were we expecting anyone?"

Mom shook her head. So did Cypress. We were never expecting anyone. No one ever came to visit and on the rare occasions Lila did, she knocked like a hailstorm. Peering through the peephole, I saw a man in the hall. A man pacing outside my door. At first I did not recognize him. It was Evan.

What in the world is he doing here? Oh no. I hope he didn't hear anything.

Unbolting the lock, I opened the door a crack. "Evan?"

He nodded coolly. "Miss Mills. Can you open the door, please?"

Behind me, Cypress yelled, "Juniper. Juniper. Juniper, who is it? Tell me."

"Buddy, someone from work." I opened the door a crack and slid out before Evan could catch a glimpse inside. The door shut with a firm clang. In the hall, I looked around to see if Kyle was lurking around. I was not ready to face him in my candy cane pajamas and fuzzy mint bathrobe. "How'd you know where I lived?"

An elegant eyebrow arched up. "You do remember I dropped your car off last night?"

"Oh right…thanks." I blushed as I tied the belt on my robe.

Great, so the only two men in the world I blushed in front of were Kyle and his Executive Assistant. *Shoot me now.*

I noted the casual chic of his clothes, the stylish Burberry scarf and the polished designer boots. He was dressed for travelling. "What is it? Is

159

everything alright?"

"Yes. Mr. Paxton sent me. He wanted to give you this." He pointed to a box sitting by my door. Wrapped in brown paper with a string like a vintage package, it was the size of a small suitcase and atop it was a smaller box.

"What is all of this?"

"No clue. Just the messenger here."

"I don't want it."

He gave me a frosty glance and I wondered why he was such a judgmental snowman. "Okay. Just throw it away. I'm going to the airport right now so I can't."

Heart sinking, I wondered if Kyle was leaving too. The idea of him gone sucked the light out of the hall. "Are you going back to San Francisco?"

"Going to New York for Thanksgiving. Have a family reunion there."

"What, you're flying out now?" It was past noon.

"I'll be there by dinner and leave again by dawn. Fly back here and Kyle and I fly out to San Francisco tomorrow morning."

"What a crazy schedule."

"I work for a very busy man—Christ, you're bleeding," he exclaimed.

Damn, I forgot. "It's fine." I looked down. I was clutching my finger, but the blood kept seeping through, quite a lot of it. I let go of my finger for a second and tried to wipe it but it smeared everywhere. Red. Sticky. Fishy.

Evan looked at my door as if to see if I was in the middle of a crime scene. "Are you okay? Do you want to go take care of that?"

Inching back to my door, I shook my head. "A mere nick. Don't worry about it."

"Um. No. It's a deep cut. You might need to go to the ER for this."

His sharp eyes noted the burns on my wrists from the oven and I saw him vacillate and dismiss my problems from his mind. I was persona non grata for his boss now, I supposed. My heart ached at that.

Evan slipped a hand inside his blazer pocket and handed me an envelope. "Here. Mr. Paxton said to give this to you."

Kyle mail. I got lightheaded. "Thanks. Oh, and happy Thanksgiving."

He circled on his heel to leave and tossed me another frosty look. "You too."

What was his problem with me? I had seen him smiling and chatting with everybody at the museum. I could bear it no longer and spoke to his back, "Excuse me. Evan, is there a problem?"

He stopped. "Huh? What?"

"It's just, every time we meet, you have such an attitude. Did I do anything to you, by accident?"

He walked back, his entire face looking like an eye roll. "No. You are an *employee* at the museum where my *boss* is the president of the board."

Innocent words with such weight.

I searched his face. "Mr. Evan, nothing is going on between Mr. Paxton and me." Great, I sound like Bill Clinton.

"Don't care. It's none of my business."

"I don't want any rumors flying around."

"Then you are speaking to the wrong person. My job is to protect Kyle." He gulped and looped his scarf tighter around his neck. "He is more than just a boss. He's my mentor. My brother." Furious at being emotional, he turned his back to me and then rotated again. "I don't know what you did to him yesterday, but I've never seen him so disturbed."

"Excuse me? What do you mean?" I squeaked like a mouse whose tail had been stepped on.

"Since dinner with you he was…is a mess. You sure did a number on him."

"I did not."

"I dunno. He looks like he got shot."

"I had nothing to do with it."

"You know, I know you."

"Excuse me?"

"I know what type of girl you are." His voice was soft and low. A threat. Rubbing his beautiful hipster mustache, he looked up and there was no mistaking the *j'accuse* of his velvety brown eyes.

"Explain yourself." I held up my bleeding hand now dripping on the cheap green carpet of the hallway.

Looking down, he scuffed the ragged—now bloody—carpet with his designer boots. "I've lived all over the place. East and West Coast. And I've seen many girls like you. Foolish girls who think they can change a man by latching on to him. By playing games. Men, who they learn the hard way, never change. Men, who destroy them."

"How dare you." My hand itched to slap him. With a fish.

Unfazed at my words, his pretty features were set in a blank mask. "Stay away from him, small town girl. He is not in your league. Nor can you change him. He has laser-like focus on a ten-year plan."

"Bite me."

"Look, no offense. But you're never gonna be more than what he asked you, so don't even try."

"He told you?" A flush of humiliation spread on my neck.

"No, but guess who rewrites his contracts?"

"I think you should leave."

"Stay away from him. He'll hurt you. I like you and that's why I'm warning you."

I want to sucker-punch you.

"Aren't you the little bleeding heart!" I slipped inside and slammed the

162

door shut in his face.

Immediately, Cypress and Mom were all questions. When I made sure Evan had left, Cypress dragged the giant box inside. "A present. A giant present."

With glee, he ripped the brown paper to reveal a massive catering box. Inside was a fully cooked gourmet meal, complete with a full turkey, several sides, and even dessert. It smelled aromatic and was enough to feed a dozen people.

Mother was wary. "Who sent you this?"

"Uh…Mr. Paxton, the new museum board president. He sent it to everyone at work," I lied, kissing her forehead. "I am really sorry. I was having a crapfest day and I took it out on you. It doesn't matter if it's the three of us, or thirty of us—we're family. I love you and Cypress. That's all that matters."

"Okay." She pulled away from me.

"Are we okay?"

When she gave me a ghost of a smile, I beamed and Cypress exhaled.

"Cuddle attack," he said. Charging at her, we hugged and squeezed her until she yelled and pushed us away, though her smile got bigger.

Snatching the small box with my name on it, I ran to my room. I leaned against the door, breathing hard. *What just happened?* Evan's harsh words had gutted me. Who the hell did he think he was?

Flopping on my bed, I looked inside the parcel. It was my coat. Dry cleaned. The one I had left at The Chrome Fig. How thoughtful. I opened Kyle's envelope. Inside was a small card with an upraised silver African tribal mask. In his neat bold writing was a note.

Miss Mills,

I hope you have a good holiday. First of all, I have to apologize for last night. I want you to know, I regret everything I said. My intention was not to scare you or hurt you, though it is what I did. Second of all, I never lie to anyone. In business and in my personal life, I am upfront about not leading anybody on. As soon as possible, I let them know exactly what I stand for. Exactly where they stand. I hate misleading people.

Your feelings were received loud and clear. Rest assured, I will never press you again. I hope that from now on we can be professional coworkers. I deeply value what you bring to the museum and I will see you in San Francisco for the staff training.

I know you probably did not have time to make a holiday meal for the usual suspects. So consider the contents in the box my peace offering.

Take care, Juniper.

Kyle

Conflicted and confused, I sat up in bed and put the card down on my lap. My heart ached at the finality of his words. *Take care, Juniper.* This was such a nice gesture, though. I wondered if I should send him a thank you note. Or a grateful text. No. Not after what Evan said. Nor after what Kyle revealed to me last night. Better to keep an unflappable front. I picked up the note and read, "In business and in my personal life, I am upfront about not leading anybody on."

Oh, but Kyle, you blur the lines.

Personal life should never be handled like business, but Kyle Paxton had a way of ingratiating his way into your life and not allowing you to even hate his cad moves. In spite of the sadness I felt, I smiled at his card. And gasped. Red plops fell on the expensive cardstock. Blood. My finger needed to be taken care of.

KYLE

Kyle blinked as he looked around the dining room in his father's mansion in Ann Arbor. The long polished table was set for 26 and seated around were all 10 of his half-blood brothers and sisters with their spouses or significant others. Everyone there had a plus one. Except Kyle.

His father, Davis Paxton, sat at the head of the table in a wheelchair, and right next to him was Marissa, his sixth wife. She fed him soft food from a little fork, and when the old man tried to bite her fingers she giggled and called him a parrot.

Though Kyle labeled Marissa—like most of his father's wives—as a gold digger, he did not loathe her like his brothers and sisters did. She was a sweet and basic girl, who genuinely liked the smelly, dying old man. Marissa was 3 years older than Kyle and that made him curious about the logistics of wheelchair sex. That feat was enough to earn her a medal of valor along with the millions she'd get, in his estimate. He shook his head and took one

166

more bite of the tart cranberry sauce, ready to throw up.

The room was set with his stepmother's version of what rich elegance meant and Kyle hated the kitschy nouveau riche Thanksgiving décor. Fresh fall flowers spilled down giant urns in a big centerpiece of candles and crystals and frou-frou items that Kyle could not name but would have happily doused with gasoline and lit with a match—just to clear the space.

The décor jumbled his mind's algorithms. The light hurt his eyes. The car-sized Swarovski chandelier glinted on the crystal glasses, edged off the Hermes Balcons du Guadalquivir plates, glittered on the Buccellati Torchon silver cutlery, and flashed on his glasses. He calculated there were 28,000 cut crystals and 320 lights in that stupid chandelier.

Too much.

The loud conversation was like fire ants going up his auditory canal. Except for Kyle, all 25 people at the table seemed to be talking at once, and no one was actually listening. Uniformed servers, mercifully silent, moved up and down filling glasses, serving seconds from the buffet laid along one wall. Kyle wished he could eat with the servers in the kitchen—in silence.

All of his nephews and nieces were in a separate dining room. God forbid they should be heard or seen. That was his father's philosophy. Until children grew into adults, they were best left in the corners of the goddam monstrosity he called a home. Like dust bunnies swept under rugs. Or old furniture in attics. Or moth-ridden coats in Salvation Army boxes.

Useless things.

Like Kyle, when he left this house as a kid.

Thanksgiving was the one day of the year Kyle was forced to be here. Cynical as ever, he looked around at the laughing faces. It would have been easy for him to hate everyone. But he didn't. He was just...indifferent to them all. Except Willow. Kyle loved Willow. He didn't care about the others. He didn't care if they lived or died. He didn't care if they had babies, weddings, birthdays, funerals, celebrations, in-the-news-trending milestones. Dead inside, he was indifferent to their pain and happiness.

He wondered if indifference and hate were the same things.

Today, he was quieter than usual, his mind still on Juniper Mills. The girl whose words had cut him like knives filleting fish. He was done with her. So he forced her out, taking the serrated blades out of his skin one by one. He removed her words from his mind.

I thought I'd heard it all. But you, Kyle Paxton, are a class act. Check your privilege. Get your deviant mind tested. The ego and narcissism of your life physically sickens me. The cold-blooded way you treat girls hurts me. I do not need time to say: Never.

Never. That blade was harder to take out.

Marissa clinked on a wineglass with a fork. "Children, your father would like to address you."

"Listen up, Paxtons," Davis said, coughing slightly. "We have so much to be thankful for this beautiful Thanksgiving. What joyous blessings of the season. I am so happy to see all my children gathered here today."

Yeah. All your children. Visible now that you're half-dead. Freaking awesome.

At first, Davis stuck to traditional clichés like family and love. Soon the three glasses of Madeira got to him and he went off the deep end. "This will rattle your cages, kids. Once I'm gone…oh God, I hate saying that. Once I'm gone. Now that blows. But I am thankful to be dying in peace. You won't see me groan, hiss and yell about my aches and blisters. Anyhow… what was I saying?"

"The trustee stuff," said Marissa.

"Yes. The trustee mess. Today, I want to talk without goddamn lawyers and auditors about who I've selected to be my sole trustee to handle my beneficiaries and protect their assets once I'm gone."

"Who is it? Tell us," a few voices muttered. The people who knew his choice was Kyle, tossed sly looks his way. As he had not accepted this position, Kyle ignored them.

So did their father. "Once I'm gone...oh God, I hate saying that. You should all be happy this old man is going to croak soon and leave you with truckloads of money, assets and companies I worked so hard to build. And look at all of you, now drained of your trust funds, excited to be flush again. Hey, did I mention what a beautiful room this is? Look at you, such pretty boys and pretty girls sitting here. You should be grateful I married extra beautiful women. Look at my darling here." He slapped Marissa's ass and prodded her with a fork until she stood up. "See my wifey, what a beauty."

Next to Kyle, Willow's shoulders shook and her hand cupped Kyle's knee. "I. Can't. Even."

"Holy fuck," Kyle said as they exchanged looks.

"Do you think you all look like this because of some random act of fate or blessing of God? No. No. No! I fell in love with the most beautiful, most ethnically mixed women in America, simply so that I could give my children this genetic advantage. You're welcome," Davis said.

Marissa shook her head and removed the glass of sherry in front of him. "No more drink for you."

Cringing, Willow leaned closer to Kyle. "Never a dull moment with that man, even with both legs in the grave."

"Yeah, always with two themes in his life, money and women." Irritated by his father's lack of Toastmaster's skills, Kyle began to peruse his work emails on his phone. Until...he heard a voice calling his name, a voice he never wanted to hear again.

Denise. Always Denise.

She was sitting across from him, hidden behind a tall display of flowers. She had the nerve to move the urn and address Kyle. Swallowing hard, he looked at his phone, hoping she'd shut up if he ignored her.

No such luck.

"So, Kyle, how is Min-Jun? I hear from our lawyers that you're very close to her. In fact, so close she stays with you when she comes to San Francisco. How very cozy. And intimate," Denise said, her voice as sugary as the candied pecans on the yams.

Kyle's head shot up he met her eyes coolly. "Well, somebody's got to take care of Colt and look out for Min-Jun."

Denise snickered. "Look out for? Is that a euphemism for getting frisky?"

Kyle gave her a fake smile. "Since looking out for someone other than yourself is not a concept you're familiar with, I'll let this howler slide. Now back to my cranberries."

But Denise would not let it go. "Come on, you and Min-Jun are no secret."

"Careful, now," Kyle said, his eyes cold.

Denise rolled her eyes. "We get it, she's exotic and alluring, with almond eyes. How. Original. But how can you betray your own brother this way?"

"Discretion, Denise," Willow said. "Also, racist much?"

"This is not the PG-13 table, darling. I think you should keep out of it. Kyle's a big boy." Denise's voice dripped with saccharine sweetness.

"Shut up, Denise," Kyle and Willow said in unison.

"You needn't be so mad and rude. I'm just concerned, that's all," Denise said with a peevish face.

"Concerned?" snapped Willow. "More like a radar for trouble and seeking revenge."

"Good thing, Willow. I've heard people seeking revenge die young," said Kyle.

Willow giggled and hi-fived Kyle. "Let's hope hell hath fury and cholesterol."

Denise sniveled in her cloth napkin. "You see. You see. This is the respect I get for helping your brother win his congress seat. And now that we're fighting his senate campaign, with all of America's eyes glued to us, we need support. And all we get is ridicule."

Royce slammed his wine glass down. "Kyle, why is family always second to you? How can you side with Min-Jun?"

"Talk later," said Kyle.

Denise recovered her cover girl composure and said, "There is no later with you."

"At the museum gala you didn't even deign to talk to us. Who do you think you are?" Royce asked.

"Nobody," Kyle said.

"Enough bull. I need a real answer."

Kyle shot his brother a furious look. "Don't start that again. Not today."

Willow looked worried. "Stop. Please. For me, Kylie."

"How could you betray me like that, Kyle? After all I've done for you?" Royce hissed across from him.

Kyle noticed his father had stopped talking. His raspy voice floated down the table. "What's happening down there? Now you boys behave."

All 24 heads swiveled around to the two brothers snarling like pit bulls.

"Why can't all my children have a nice peaceful Thanksgiving?" asked Marissa with a sexy little sigh.

"Don't want you and Royce fighting. Can't you see that's what she wants? Plus, we have Clive Anderson at the table," Willow hissed in Kyle's ear. Beside her, Clive cleared his throat and took a giant gulp of his wine.

"Did you hear me, Kyle? Do you not get this could ruin my life? Do you not care that my political career is on the line?" Royce persisted.

"One, it's scary that people like you are running this country. Two, who has been filling your head with ugly propaganda, Royce? Let's guess, shall we? Someone whose job is fucking propaganda?" Kyle asked.

Royce slammed down a fist on the table causing a server, behind him—about to pour wine in his glass—to jump back in fright. "You stay away from Denise. I see the way you look at her."

Kyle slammed two fists on the table. "If you mean with pitiless hate, you are correct."

"Pitiless hate, huh? I'll show you, coward. Picking on my Denise," Royce muttered.

Denise sniffed and buried her face in Royce's shoulders. "Royce. I'm sorry."

"Why are you sorry, babe?" Royce said and put a protective arm around Denise, kissing the top of her head.

"She's sorry for being an excellent little publicity bitch," said Kyle, raising his Broadbent Madeira Boal wine glass to Denise. "Good job."

Royce threw down his napkin across the table. "You stupid sad little prick. What did you say about my future wife and the love of my life?"

"Yeah, wrong use of the word love, bro." Kyle smiled calmly at Denise.

"Enough. Let it go," Willow whispered, sweeping Kyle's hands off the table. Kyle sat back in his chair, ready to let it go, but life had other plans.

"God damn you, Kyle," Royce said, getting up from his chair.

"Oh, he did. You're a little late," Kyle said.

Royce pushed back his chair and marched to Kyle. "You think we're all blind and deaf to you just because you are flashy Mr. Silicon Valley now? To the way you live your life, the scheduled depravity, the way you treat good women, the way your business runs with zero integrity. You should be ashamed, Kyle. I tried. I tried so hard to be there for you."

"Oh, I'm eternally freaking grateful. Just try being there for Colt," Kyle shouted. He shot up in his chair and threw down his napkin. "I am leaving, Father. Happy Thanksgiving to you all. See you all next year for this great American family tradition."

All the Paxton heads turning back and forth followed this new turn with interest.

"But we haven't even served dessert yet. It's raspberry sorbet and pear crumble," said Marissa, her Botoxed lips set in an unnatural line.

"Oh no, you are not leaving. Not until I'm done with you." Royce was behind Kyle's chair, his nostrils flaring.

"Royce. Not here." Kyle tried to go around his brother, but Royce blocked him.

"Oh, yes. Here. Now," shouted Royce, a few inches from Kyle's face.

"Stop at once, boys," their father roared across the room. Kyle could not help but notice an undertone of glee in his father's voice.

The man adored chaos.

Kyle faced Royce, a sick pain pooling in the pit of his abdomen. "I'm done wasting my time with you. You won't see the truth, if it came out of your own ass. Clean up your mess before you attack me. You ruined your family. You ruined Colt's life and now you don't want me to help him."

"The only reason you want to help him is because you are fucking his mother," said Royce, his hands knotted into fists an inch away from Kyle's nose.

At the back of his head, Kyle made out the clatter of dropped forks, chairs pushed back and voices telling them to stop. Fury flowed in Kyle's ready fists, but he controlled himself and shoved Royce back. In response, Royce tossed Kyle's glasses off and punched him squarely in the eye. Several people gasped. Willow screamed both of their names.

Kyle saw red and felt a black liquid ooze in his brain. In a flash, his fists connected with Royce's salt-and-pepper-stubble jaw. Hard. Far away, he heard the Paxtons shouting at him to stop. But he didn't stop.

A few hands tried to stop him, especially the superhero Clive, but he could not be contained. Kyle kept striking Royce. Some happy demon inside egged him to be even more of a jackass. The last 20 hours of anger and self-loathing and all of Juniper's cutting words came back in a single second, driving his rage. Kyle felt nothing but the rage, black and thick as hot tar, take over him.

It was only when he saw her face in the dark floating like a pale moon that he stopped. Juniper was there. And she was looking at him with round, sad eyes. She hated what she saw. Her baby owl eyes blinked and Kyle jolted back from Royce's face. He saw red. Blood. Blood on Royce's face. Kyle's knuckles were wet and cold with blood. He did not realize some of the blood was his.

As Kyle stumbled to the dining room door, away from the shocked faces, he heard Denise say, "I don't think you should trust Kyle to be your sole trustee, Mr. Paxton. I mean look at him. He's a bloody mess. Royce, my honey, are you all right?"

Kyle walked out of the room, but he took Juniper's eyes with him.

CHAPTER 11

After Thanksgiving break, I went back to work, numb on the inside, like my nerve endings were frayed. I spent a lot of time chewing pencils, crunching candy canes and staring blankly at my PC monitor while daydreaming about Kyle. Most of my fantasies alternated between gold skies where he and I explored the ruins of Petra, and cobalt ones, where I went knockout ninja on him and kicked his perfect jaw for being such a sexist prick. The latter was rarer than I cared to admit and the former was more like kissing in Petra than exploring. I was pathetic.

I also spent a lot of time confused about his weird and wonky lifestyle. I knew being an F-buddy was a casual, normal thing. But did people agree to be someone's sex slave in this day and age? Did they agree to set time limits on affairs? Termination dates and contracts for lovers? Or was that just a Kyle thing? I had signed an NDA, so I could not ask around.

I knew Stacy had a lot of boy toys and would know the right answers, but she'd also ask the invasive questions I wanted to avoid. And though Lila was a doctor (and in the ER, had her share of fishing out weird and hilarious things stupidly used for sex) my bestie knew as little about such matters as I did, for she was planning to lose her virginity to her fiancé on their wedding night.

Even my posse was pathetic.

So I went to the Internet to fill in the blanks for everything related to F-buddies. I learned there were no more rules in the revolving door of casual dating. Fueled by technology and time constraints, being an F-buddy was quite a thing. Almost an institution. A lot of people did it, and there were many common rules set up for such arrangements.

To make sure their friends with benefits followed the rules, many people signed contracts. I found dozens of versions of F-buddy contracts, Booty-call Agreements, and Friends with Benefits Legal Documents floating around cyberspace. Limiting time span on being someone's F-buddy was also a very accepted thing.

The Termination Contract was a Kyle invention, however.

As I read on, my stomach twisted into knots. Boxed in by museum crates and Celtic research, trapped in my domestic life, and a dud in the dating game, I knew so little about the real world. When I was at college, I went out on three dates with Keith Logan, a guy I liked from Archeology 202. On the second date, I allowed him to kiss me, but I refused his offer to go back to his dorm. On our third date, he took me to a party that got a bit wild and when I wanted to go back home—instead of going upstairs to hook up—he told the entire room I had a thorny twig up my ass. I laughed and left, but it hurt.

Maybe he was right.

I was a misfit in contemporary life. Not for the first time in my life was

I glad Mom had sheltered me from the brutal rituals of girlhood, with its heartless laws. Laws favoring men. I was free to live my life as a spinster, in my blind but blissful quest of Celtic history. And Kyle Paxton, living on his super-rotten cosmos of depravity where he used and terminated girls could find another candidate—a vapid, alluring sexpot like Izzy—as long as it was not me.

The thought of him with other girls made me cringe, though.

As I surfed the Internet and browsed dozens of articles, the prissy virginal miss in me was shocked by how people made a mockery of their vows and cheated on their loving spouses with their F-buddies.

One name that turned up a lot on the web was Felicia Grunde, who was some kind of F-buddy guru. She had a popular blog, Candy Call, on the topic. Her catch phrase was, *Sweet hijinks*. I began to read Candy Call and all of its archives regularly. One evening, I read in the comfort of my bed while sucking a mint tea candy cane, and a certain post caught my attention. It explained what the F-Buddy rules were. Reading them, I realized with a sinking heart, I had broken half of them already.

Ten Mandatory Rules for F-Buddies
By Felicia Grunde

As all of you Grundites know well, after my husband cheated on me, I decided to shun men. Forever. But alas. A gal has needs not always satisfied by electronic devices. Since men are filthy pigs, I decided to become one myself—albeit a sexy one. The past ten years, I've only been in F-buddy arrangements. And what a hot decade. Sweet hijinks.

As your F-buddy guru, I counsel you chin-drool crusted idiots on how to ride this wave of life. However, there are rules and regulations that are mandatory. Rules that should become laws, to be an F-buddy. So enter the no judgment zone.

Rule Number 1: Be Upfront. Be Clear

Be as clear as water with your intentions. Right away establish your lack of obligation to the relationship. Your lack of commitment. Respect the other partner by being upfront and honest, early on. This way they have NO expectations from you, even if there is physical attraction. Zilch. Nada. Zero. Let me be clear: When you meet someone you wanna bang: Do. Not. Give. Them. False. Hope. Let them know instantly what you expect from them. This way no hearts will crack like eggs, no one gets wounded, no hospitalization is needed, and no lawsuits will take place. More clarity. Less chaos. You're welcome. *Felicia bows.*

Rule Number 2: Never Fall for your F-buddy

Snip-snip emotions at all cost. Emotional connection is the opposite of a physical connection. Even casual relationships get ugly and messy. Enjoy the bedroom acrobatics and walk away, bitches. If you see any signs of emotions, any pitter-patter of heartbeats, run away like your F-buddy has the Zika virus.

Rule Number 3: No Expectations

Going in, you should both be clear there is no future with each other. No dating, no relationships, no becoming a girlfriend or boyfriend, no becoming engaged, no getting married. Not even daydreaming. No. *Nyet. Nein. Non.* You are having fun, not making a wedding scrapbook.

Rule Number 4: No Dating

No movie dates, candlelit dinners, Sunday brunches, dog parks, lazy picnics, or concerts, *capiche*? No likes on social media. No Netflix and chill—just chill. No dating—no confusion. No contact outside the bedroom. You are a booty call, not a social obligation.

Rule Number 5: Keep F-buddies Out

Never invite a buddy to meet friends, family and co-workers. No double dating—perish the thought. This can elicit risky gossip and speculation. You are not a couple, so no need to share a social life. Don't talk about your social or work life with your partner. Keep quiet, except for the puffs of pleasure.

Rule Number 6: No Green-Eyed Monster

Banish jealousy. If you are jealous, I'm not saying I hate you, but I'd unplug your life support to charge my iPhone. Find a hobby like collecting stamps, making Minecraft empires, doing calligraphy, baking macaroons, so I never bump into you. Stay out of the F-buddy biosphere. If you are jealous, then you are emotionally connected to your F-buddy. Flapping red flag.

Rule Number 7: No High Fidelity

Don't expect your F-buddy to be exclusive. You are both having casual fun without the tatty strings attached. Don't expect fidelity! If you don't get this, please proceed to the nearest bar and stand in front of the dartboard. You can see/date/be with other people, and even be in a committed relationship or be married. However, there is no need to discuss others with your bed buddy. That's just not classy. Okay?

Rule Number 8: Don't Spend the Night

Enjoy the roll in the hay, just don't sleep in the stable. Repeat after me: Being an F-Buddy. Is. A. Physical. Thing. Not a cuddle-with-someone-all-night-long thing. If you are asked to spend the night, cool. Stay. Sleep. But don't turn it into a big deal. Don't curl up in a fetal position and cry when you are sent home.

Rule Number 9: Lay the Ground Rules Early

Become Nero and lay down the law early. Decide on mutually acceptable rules. Rules are key; impose them with contracts. If you can't follow those rules, poke your eyes with a fishbone, stop reading this and go chew on your dog-eared *Pride and Prejudice*.

Rule Number 10: Respect the Protocol

If you follow the rules and get the F-buddy protocol, you will succeed. If you don't, the gutter-stench of failure will stink up this good thing. So as your F-buddy whisperer, I say keep things simple, my Grundites. Sweet hijinks.

Wow. It does not get any clearer than this.

My stomach knotted after reading the article.

Has the world gone mad? Right is wrong now.

Kyle was the norm, and I was the odd one out. Even if in some alternative reality I agreed to be his, I'd break every single one of the rules. I liked Kyle and was halfway to falling for him. Yet, I gathered this was a far cry from what Kyle was proposing. He wanted exclusivity. And dates—he had taken me to a special dinner and was very curious about my life. He wanted his Summers and Winters at events. He traveled with them. He broke the universal rules of being an F-buddy to begin with.

Upgrade, indeed.

What was his game? Maybe, it wasn't about getting laid for him. That'd be too low on the challenge notch. Maybe, Kyle was lonely. His life was insanity on crack, after all. And when he went home at night, the solitude got to him. Maybe he wanted company and slapped a label on it to avoid commitment. No strings attached, with contracts to enforce the no strings. Or maybe…not. I was an ignorant spaz about adult relationships, so maybe I was wrong. It didn't matter now. I had said no.

Like I said no to all fun things (or as I saw them, risks) in my life.

Thinking about Kyle made my head hurt. With two fingers, I eased the knots from my forehead. Sucking another candy cane, I went back to Felicia's blog post. It had been read a total of one million, twelve thousand times. I whistled. I read a few comments. There were over five thousand comments. Some disagreed but most applauded Felicia. I frowned and made a user name, Human-Minerals. And then I wrote my comment:

November 30th

Hi Felicia,

A guy asked me to be his F-Buddy. I said no to him. It hurt. A lot. I really like him. Maybe he didn't see it, but I know there was a spark. A real one.

What is happening these days? Is this the Romance Apocalypse? Am I the only one who misses the way it was? There was a time when love was prized in novels and poems, and not hushed up like a dirty secret. When a couple's worth was not sized up by their kinkiness, designer diamonds, limos, mansions and jets, but how much love they had—like in the *Gift of the Magi*.

Is love dead? Busy in survival, I missed when love became equal to stupidity and its declaration a mistake. Sex is physical and love is invisible, but both as intense. And linked. So why is one obsolete now?

Reading this, Miss Felecia, I imagine millions of people fall in love with their F-buddies, but only hear crickets chirp at night, because of your inhuman, nonsensical rules. Look, civilization began 10,000 years ago, but humans have lived on earth for 200,000 years and our ancestors have been around for six million more. In the double helix of our DNA exists the universal traits of our species—molecular codes millions of years in the making.

No matter how blasé we may get and how we may cringe at emotions, the fundamental blueprint of human behavior remains the same as our Paleolithic ancestors. We cannot simply wish away our primal instincts and indelible chemical data like jealously, bonding, love, mating, protection, and procreation by shaming them. So I wonder how many relationships finish before they start, relationships that could have led to a lifetime of happiness—all because of our (very recent) need for disposable junk and for using people like disposable things? Humans are not recyclable.

Also, I can only imagine the hurt of infidelity. Cheating on your spouse and then covering it up, smacks of a life of illusion, where the *idea* of morality is more important than morality itself. Be honest. This is a great century for fun. You no longer have to hide in caves. Or lie. If you want casual sex, drop the deluded "loved ones" in your life. Release them and you'll both be free.

So I ask: Is love dead?

Confused,
Human-Minerals

I hit the post button on my preachy comment and went to eat dinner. Two hours later, I rushed back and fired up my laptop. I was stunned. I had dozens of responses to my comment. Most of them attacked me for defying Felicia. What did I know? And who was I to judge anyone's lifestyle.

Fair enough. I've no right to judge.

Others went to spell out how they were stuck in a sexless relationship for years and being someone's F-buddy was the only way to get action. One woman said her husband had severe psychological problems and they had not had sex for years. They had a son, so she did not want a divorce. She had an F-buddy who was younger and always available when she wanted. And that I should not knock it till I try it.

Others were angry name callers. I was probably effing-ugly. A basic bitch. A backwater bitch. A fat hoarder. A cat lady. I would die a dry old virgin. *Well, that one is possible.* One funny guy said my birth certificate was an apology from the condom factory. Another said, I'd bring joy to the chatroom, if I left. As I read the ugly things, I almost deleted my comment. *Wow. So much hate cloaked by anonymity.* The Internet was troll paradise. I slammed my laptop shut. I wished it was that easy to shut Kyle out of my brain. I thought about him an unhealthy few hours every night. And several during the day.

KYLE

December 2, 9:47 p.m. 36 seconds
(Palo Alto, Silicon Valley)

T his was an epic waste of his time. He had been at Chad's party for 47 minutes and 31 seconds too long. Chad Brody was the CEO of Cirrus and wanted to partner with Kyle on his Birdseye AI prototype. No matter how many times Kyle refused, the Teflon-skinned Chad kept asking. And asking. He had become Kyle's corporate stalker. Today, Sylvia had forced Kyle to come and talk about a possible Cirrus deal. Chad had just bought a juggernaut mansion in Palo Alto and thought a party there and its price tag (14 million) would impress Kyle. He thought wrong.

Dodging the cameras, selfie takers, and a local news photojournalist, Kyle spent the agonizing minutes and crawling seconds in the corner of a less crowded room checking his email and scowling. Kyle's social skills were limited to 3 rules:

1) Avoid useless people.

2) Avoid getting invited to useless things.

3) If 2 was unavoidable, deploy In-and-Out.

Kyle twitched to run out. Chad's bachelor style party was bursting at the seams with newly minted tech millionaires, their power drunk assistants, random party animals, half-clad servers, and sleazy displays of naked sushi models lying on tables all over the house. *Not keeping it professional: Chad's rookie mistake.*

Making his way out of one of the living rooms in a series of living rooms, Kyle called Pat, his driver. "Did you pick her up?"

"Yes. She is with me," said Pat.

"How far are you?" asked Kyle.

"Ten minutes away."

"Good. I'll come out."

At the entrance of a Japanese dining room that led to the front hall, Kyle was host-blocked by Chad. "Hey, don't leave."

"Excuse me, but I have to go," Kyle said. He found it hard to believe D-bag was a data processing genius whose company was now a big cloud computing success. Chad had gone from being a lab rat to a lionized Mr. Moneybags overnight. Rumor had it, he stole data from his ex-employers, formed his own company and crushed them in a legal settlement with his new investors.

Chad's ginger brows rose and he gave him a weak smile. "We haven't talked about your company yet."

Fuck, no. "I prefer talking about my company at work." Kyle's icy eyes cut Chad's smile in half. This meeting should have been in Kyle's office. During business hours. But Kyle was a social gold trophy in human form and Chad was a slimy opportunist.

"After the party, I want to show you how our lip-reading digital signal processing software is a perfect match for the BirdsEye AI," Chad said. "It's gonna blow your mind."

Kyle clenched his jaw. One type of human that irritated Kyle was a liar. Another was a bootlicker. And Chad was both. "Thanks. I can't stay. I fly to New York in the morning."

"C'mon, stay. We'll shoot the biz breeze later. Have fun now."

"I'll have Sylvia contact you." Giving Chad false hope was Sylvia's fault. She was not a rookie and she should have known better. Kyle imagined strangling Sylvia and Chad in one spot with two hands.

Looking around as if to see what had upset Kyle, Chad said, "You know, I got the sushi models because Mr. Hoshi and co came today. They'll appreciate their national food adorned on our Frisco babes. Have some with me."

Chad pointed to a sushi model on his dining table, naked under strategic palm leaves stacked with sushi. The paper-thin ash blonde girl, who looked no more than nineteen, smiled seductively at Kyle.

Kyle winced, thinking she was probably in California escaping her small town right out of high school. Looking for her dream, living her nightmare. Plus, why would he want perishable sushi from the contamination Petri dish of a human body? "I'm good."

D-bag winked, leaned over and cupped the girl's palm-covered petite breast. "Made sure these girls were special-order-rolls for the after after after party. So stay."

100 million sperms and this was the fastest? Using sex to lure a serious business partner: Stupid. Not knowing Kyle's publicly known taste for privacy: Fatal.

"Next time," he said, marching fast to the iron-forged double doors. To freedom.

"Wait." Chad followed him and had the nerve to grab his upper arm. "So when do we talk about BirdsEye and Cirrus? How about I drop in on Monday?"

"I won't be back till Tuesday. Evan will contact you. Goodbye." Kyle flicked Chad's fingers off his bicep, pulled the front door open and shut it on his slack-jawed face.

Out in the cool breeze, Kyle sighed in relief. Chad did not follow him. Lucky break. He pulled up his phone and saw two missed calls from Izzy. Kyle stabbed his phone to yell at Sylvia. Lately, she had been getting out of hand. Then he saw an incoming call from Pat and picked it up.

"I'm here," said Pat.

As the limo slid up the driveway, Kyle hurdled in before Pat could get out. His heart leapt up. *Min-Jun.*

"Kyle. So good to see you again," Min-Jun said in the soft, breathless voice he knew so well. She smiled at him and held out her arms.

He pulled her in a tight embrace. "You all right?"

"Yes, thanks to you."

"After dinner, can you come to my house?"

"Yes."

"Spend the night there. I fly out to New York in the morning."

"Okay," she said with a sad sigh.

"Pat. Take us to Oishii," ordered Kyle. "I feel like having sushi tonight."

CHAPTER 12

A few days after Thanksgiving, Lila visited me. In my gloom and doom over Kyle, her coming was a godsend. The NDA I'd signed barred me from talking about Kyle's sicko lifestyle, but I could surely tell her about his brief fixation and my lengthy obsession. Lila and I had been best friends since the day her parents moved to Ann Arbor. When they moved to Detroit, Lila stayed back to do pre-med at the University of Michigan, just because I was there. She lived on campus while I lived with my family, but I would schlep over to her room every day. Even after she left Ann Arbor to do residency in Detroit, we stayed besties.

Cypress was my twin, but she and I were soul twinsies. Lila was one of the few who had been kind to Cypress in high school, so he was also excited about her visit. We took him out to his favorite deep-dish pizza place for lunch, and afterwards, Lila and I walked from my apartment to the Silver Tree Lake nearby.

It was a cold but clear day and the air had a special bite to it. It had snowed yesterday and the brittle snow was packed into low banks on the road edges. We took a path through the bare ash trees to get to the semi-frozen lake and began circling it—like we used to when we were younger.

Shivering, I wound my wool scarf tighter around my neck and asked, "So, Dr. Lila. Is your wedding date set?"

"Ugh. No, it's been changed three times." She rolled her eyes. Lila was engaged to Sam, a doctor she had fallen in love with during residency. In our duo, Lila was the only one with a life. She was also the talkative one. I mostly listened to her talk about her fiancé and how much she loved him and how much she hated his mother.

"Sam's mom strikes again?"

"If I wasn't a doctor, I'd consider stabbing her. But she'd turn up at my ER and I'd have to stitch her up."

I giggled. "You are the worst doctor ever."

"Oh, it gets worse. When she talks, I sit there and imagine suturing up her lips. Am I evil?"

"Very. But she's probably sticking pins in your rag doll right now." I pulled two candy canes out from my jacket pocket and offered her one. She shook her head and I ripped one open and popped it in my mouth.

"Who cares, as long as Sam is by my side? And he's just perfect. God, I love him so much." She tucked an arm in my elbow. "Anyhow, forget us. What's going on, Junie?"

"Nothing, as usual."

We trudged along the path to the pier, the frozen blades of grass snapping under our boots with a satisfying crunch. My heart jumped as I looked up. A man with dark hair stood on the pier. *Kyle.* I took the candy cane out of my mouth. I blinked. Of course, it wasn't him. It was an ice fisher, a burly guy with a beard and black hair. I recalled my dream of drowning and Kyle saving me. I shook my head; he was more likely to throw me in than save me.

"You gonna tell me your secret or do I ice-board you?" Lila shoved a sharp elbow into my waist and I was shielded from rib damage by my thick puffer jacket. "I know something's up. You're kinda out of it."

"Yeah. You remember Kyle Paxton?"

"Who? Oh, speech guy from the gala?"

"Yes."

"Hotstuff who was drilling eye holes in you?"

"Yep. I went out with him."

Brown eyes glittering, she whooped, and squeezed my arms so hard I knew it'd bruise. "Oh my God. Are you dating him? He's like a demigod. I mean hello, the Paxtons."

"Lila, we are not dating."

"I still need details, Junie."

"We just went out for dinner. Once. He was intense and kinda over the top. Out of my league, for sure. I thought he was kinda nice until he said he doesn't do girlfriends. Just casual hook-ups."

"He said that on one date? Run like a train."

"I'm not seeing him again."

"Good. He sounds creepy. Creepy Hotstuff," she said, tapping a button on her jacket sleeve with a shiny acrylic nail. It made quite a little drumming sound. It was her tell; when she was upset, she tapped things.

"Lila, there is more." Without violating the NDA and revealing Kyle's bizarre way of switching girls every five months and calling them Winters and Summers, I told her what had passed and how shocked I was to learn he wanted me as his at-call F-buddy.

When I finished, her eyes popped in outrage as she swore softly in Arabic, French, and English. "How dare he! I don't get why you are confused. He sounds like an over-privileged, entitled prick."

I put the candy cane back in my mouth and massaged my temple. "I know. I know. He thinks the models of this planet are his own petting zoo. That's the type of guy he is. But I can't stop thinking about him."

"Oh my God, Junie. You're not seriously considering it, are you?"

"I'm pretty sure it was a one-time offer, so there's nada to consider. But the real question is—what's wrong with me?"

She put her hands in a tent to her nose. "Ah. Where do I start?"

"Rhetorical, Lila, rhetorical. Maybe if I say yes to stuff, I can live a little, you know. In college, guys used to say I had a twig up my ass. Twig. I don't even get a stick."

"Screw college. You have a great life now."

"What great life? My life is artifacts and Cypress. Museum and home. In my free time, I read books written by dead people, Netflix with *no* chill, and fall for unavailable guys. Remember Reza?"

"So? You have high standards, that's all."

"Another way of saying…I'm a loser who'll die alone. And now I look around, I see most of our friends are married and some have kids. I've never been with anyone and I'm sure my eggs are expiring. Old eggs."

"Don't be mean. We are not old. Twenty-six is the new sixteen. Junie, you're amazing and have so much love to give. And since when are you defined by having a man in your life?"

"Since I met Kyle. And it's not a general need for a man. It's specific. To him."

"Why are you letting a shallow player make you feel small?"

"If he was a shallow player, I'd have forgotten him in a second."

"Remember what we used to say? Boys play the field. Real men stay. Kyle's an immature boy. You just need to find a real man."

"You know how many boys I've dated and rejected. Kyle's different... he's intelligent, deep, kind—"

"And uses girls like Kleenex. Babe, he does not sound kind at all. His behavior shows he likes to voodoo mind control women for his sick pleasure. God knows what other sick stuff he's into. You should steer clear." Her hands went to my sleeves and she idly tapped two nails on my wrist. When it began to hurt, I pulled my arm away.

"And now I have to work with him. Awkward."

I started up the timber stairs to the pier and Lila followed. From her rare silence, I knew she was worried about me. The wood planks were slick with thin ice and our boots slid like skates. She suggested we head back, but I did not heed her and stumbled along, not caring if I fell and hurt myself. Kyle had broken something inside me and I did not know how to fix it. Leaning over the edge of the dock, I stared down at the floating masses of ice in the shadowy water, my heart heavy. I threw down my leftover candy cane and watched it struggle to float and then drown.

"Look, I get his appeal and I'm not as strong as you. If Douchey Boy asked me, I'd leave Sam and run off to become Lady of Silicon Valley. And let's say he asks you again to exchange bodily fluids with him...and you say yes...ask yourself...is that a good idea? He'd be your first and kinda unforgettable and you'd just be a fling to him."

"Or he could be a great memory. I said such cruel things and he listened. What if I could be with him and he'd realize—"

"No, no, Junie." She planted firm hands on my shoulders and spun me to face her. "You know men like him don't ever change. They make promises. They lie, they cheat, they invent new ways to break a woman's heart and body. Isn't that how your mom raised you, to see men with reality glasses? You deserve a nice guy, okay? Someone stable, kind, funny, like Sam, who'll love and respect you, not make you a bus stop to Fun Town."

"You're right. It's just...I've never felt this way...about anyone. I haven't been able to work all week." Tears pricked my eyes and I looked up, breathing hard.

"Oh, Junie, I didn't know you felt this way."

"I like him. A lot."

She pulled me into her arms and gave me a choking hug. "Wow. You never get emotional. It's strange seeing you like this."

"It's my thing now. I thought we had this connection and it tears me apart he doesn't feel the same way. At all." Against her warm shoulder, my voice was muffled.

For a while she just held me and patted down my puffer jacket. When I eased out of her manic grip, she began to giggle.

"Doll, the connection you feel to Kyle is not real. Love is not real. It's science. There are three stages of love. First, lust. It's just the trigger of a pheromone, the releaser that mixes androsterone and androstenol in our bodies. Second, attraction, which is the neurotransmitters of adrenaline, dopamine and serotonin in our bodies. Third, nesting. When you're attracted to someone, your body produces oxytocin, the cuddle hormone. During sex this grows in both men and women and makes you want to go beyond lust to mate, to procreate. Love is just an irresistible cocktail of chemicals. Pure biology, not poetry."

"Oh shut your pill hole, doc."

We both laughed.

"What has this guy done to you? Tell me, did he—"

"No. We just kissed a little."

"Hope you got some tongue action."

I took a long-drawn breath. "It was amazing."

She gave me an assessing look. "Listen, Juniper. If you want him so much, go after Kyle and have fun for a few months. You're free to choose."

"I may be free to choose, Lila, but I'm not free of the consequences of my choice."

"Oh my God. You are so dramatic. Just kill emotions and move on like he will. Be fearless, babe."

Kill emotions. I groaned inwardly. This was literally what everything in the universe was telling me with big neon signs and I knew my stupid heart would lead me in the opposite direction. "No. Nothing's going to happen. Ever. I am sure he's already stringing another girl along. I have to face him and be professional. Let's go back."

We walked back, our boots clicking on the frigid pier slats. At the stairs, she turned and said, "And by the way, if this Kyle hurts you, I'll gut him and stitch his intestines to his fingers and ears."

I slapped her cheek playfully. "Ew. People should use you for teen birth control."

I wished I could keep a clone of Lila in my office to kick my butt and stop me from thinking about Kyle. The next few days, all I did in my office was chew candy canes and think about him and surf the net for news about him. The only person that distracted me was Dr. Dean Dillon. For the past few weeks, I had worked with the University of Michigan to set up his lecture at our museum. He sent me all of Dr. Scott's unpublished essays, and over time, shared his own work. I sent him my manuscript and was grateful for his feedback and editing. We connected on so many levels, I could not wait to meet him.

As far as the museum was concerned, the air crackled with excitement. The staff acted like kids on Christmas about the upcoming trip to San Francisco. The past few weeks, I'd seen a flurry of emails between our staff and the staff of the Modern Museum of San Francisco, with Evan as the intermediary. I was copied on all of them. So was Kyle, though he never responded.

Wistfully, I perused the travel itinerary every day. The plan was to arrive on Thursday for an orientation, enjoy the weekend as tourists and spend five days training at the Modern Museum of San Francisco. On Friday there was a dinner at Kyle's house, a sendoff of sorts. And on Saturday—the flight back. Ten days in San Francisco. Ten days of Kyle.

It all sounded both tempting and terrifying because he would be there. There were two reasons I did not want to go. Cypress and Kyle. One I did not want to leave and the other I could not stand to see again.

I read all the escalating number of emails flying back and forth as a spectator. Everyone responded. Except me. Soon came the day of reckoning. Evan had collected all the information and his assistants had booked everyone's flights. One Tuesday I got an email from Evan with twenty-five people carbon copied on it.

From: Evan Marquez

Sent: December 2, 3:09 PM

To: Juniper Mills

CC: All

Subject: Re: Travel Documents Request / IMP

Miss Mills,

If you could send me a copy of your license, that would be great. We have tickets for everyone and have finalized the travel. Even after repeated requests, we have not heard from you. Please scan a digital copy of your driver's license and send it ASAP so my coordinator, Lucille, can book your flights.

Thanks,

EM

EA to Kyle Castillo,

BirdsEye Universal

Tech Sech Floor

555 Mission St, San Francisco

Chewing on the malachite pen Lydia had gifted me after a visit to London, I dashed off an email:

From: Juniper Mills

Sent: December 2, 3:20 PM

To: Evan Marquez

CC: All

Subject: Re: Travel Documents Request / IMP

Mr. Evan,

Thank you. Regrettably, I am not going on the trip, so I will not need any travel arrangements.

Best,

JM

Jr. Curator,

Ann Arbor History Museum

777 Paxton Way,

Ann Arbor MI

Instantly I got a ping on my desktop. An email from Walrus. It was a private email and he had carbon copied everyone. My tummy dived to my knees. The very idea of Kyle reading that email had me hyperventilating.

From: Ipswich, Walrus
Sent: Tue Dec 2, 3:21 PM
To: Juniper Mills
CC: All
Subject: Re: Travel Documents Request / IMP

Juniper? Come to my office immediately!!!!

Executive Director,
Ann Arbor History Museum
777 Paxton Way,
Ann Arbor, MI

Oh joy. Clenching my malachite pen like a lifeline, I walked into Walrus' office. As always, he was fenced in by a thousand files in toppling towers all over his desktop. He avoided computers and still filed things the old-fashioned way. Apparently, Walrus hated trees. His anxious assistant, Annabelle, was organizing one of his bookshelves. Seeing me, she scuttled out of the room like an insect fleeing a pest controller.

Walrus was holding a half-eaten ice cream sandwich in one hand and a file in the other. He pointed to a chair, ice cream drops plopping onto the desk. "Sit, Juniper. Explanation required."

"I'm confused. Is something the matter?"

"I don't have time for histrionics. Explain why you are not going. And let me preface that. Unless someone has terminal cancer or you are medically allergic to planes, you cannot get out of this. Period. Sit down, I said."

Oh sour schnapps. With bated breath, I sat down across and clicked my pen. "Mr. Ipswich, I have extenuating circumstances at home…so I can't go this time."

I recalled the two weeks that I had spent in Egypt and what my absence did to Cypress. He had locked himself in his room and did not come out till the day I came back. Mother kept him alive by leaving a food tray outside his locked door. Only when she slept did he come out to collect the tray. I came back to find him still barricaded and screaming like an animal in his room and mother red-eyed on the couch. When he heard me, Cypress came out of hiding, hugged me and cried, "Don't ever leave without me, Juniper. I'll die. I'll die without you."

His words had gutted me.

After that, he spent two days sleeping at the foot of my bed, curled up like a pet. To my horror, he had regressed, badly. Some of the motor tics he had when we were little kids—rubbing his eyes, tearing off his eyelashes, blinking constantly, twitching his nose, scratching his jaw till it bled, grinding his teeth so hard he needed a dentist—had cruelly revisited him. The sight of his eyes with no eyelashes had broken our twin hearts. Since then, I wriggled out of all museum-related trips and opportunities.

"Juniper Mills. You are going and that is final. If not, I will have to penalize you." Mr. Ipswich's silver eyes bulged with irritation.

I snapped out of my reverie. "If not, what? Shall I speak with Kathy?" Kathy managed our HR and knew of Cypress's special needs, as in my official records I'd had to declare dependencies.

"There's strange and there's Juniper Mills. Every museum employee in America would jump at a chance like this. The San Fran team just raised half a godforsaken billion for their own museum expansion. The same Ace-team will be training you unworthy sops." The ice cream in his hand sagged and a plop of vanilla fell on a pile of papers. Flicking a finger at it, he sucked hard.

My stomach turned. I was reminded of a giant walrus on an iceberg eating a torn-apart seal. I had a lot of useless curator info in my head:

Walruses eat five percent of their total weight per day. They like to eat Junipers, no, mollusks—bivalves such as clams and benthic invertebrates and worms, gastropods, cephalopods, crustaceans, sea cucumbers, and other soft-bodied animals.

"You are my primary fundraiser and I need you to go."

"About that, sir. I've requested many times for someone else to take over the fundraising. I'd love to devote some time to my research. Can't we hire a development director now?"

"No. We're a lean operation. We all have to double up, Juniper. And you're a better fundraiser than researcher."

"But—sir." I was stumped. I hoped this was not true; Walrus could lie through his rotting teeth to an archangel for museum funds.

"Do you know how many goddamn researchers I have on my staff? All of them. Every single one. Even Stan, the guard, wants to be published. But how many are good at raising money? One. You. Raising funds is like squeezing blood from a stone. And you do it so well. I need you to work closely with Kyle Paxton."

"He seems super busy. I'm sure he won't have time for me."

"Juniper Mills. You test my patience and insult my intelligence. The man is hands down the best board president, ever. Do you recall he's donating four million of his personal funds? Do you realize his staff is an invaluable asset for us? Do you realize he shares an office building with Capture? He serves on its board. Can you imagine the worlds he can open for us? When he says come here, I expect you to swim, fly, or drill a tunnel through the earth to him."

I mulled over this. Firstly, I would promptly drill a tunnel through the earth to Kyle, if he weren't such a misogynistic bleeping Lothario pig. Secondly, I did not know he was on the board of Capture, the latest social media craze, which allowed gamers to play and connect with millions of other users. Cypress loved it and was always on it. All so inviting. Maybe

I could take Cypress with me. An image of him trapped in a city like a vampire in sunlight, popped up in my head. *Nope.*

"While I appreciate this, I simply can't go," I said slowly.

"Juniper, the problem with you is that authority is a joke to you. You're the youngest curator we've had. Ever. I had such high hopes for you. I told Kyle you can run this whole enchilada before you are old, gray and fat like me. But with this attitude, my hopes are dashed." He began licking ice cream off the edge of his palm.

My lips wobbled. Along with the staff, I was used to being yelled at and picked apart like a carcass by hyenas, but never had his words cut me so deep. "Mr. Ipswich. Please, please, don't let it affect my work."

"When I promoted you to Junior Curator, one of your job descriptions was—" He stuffed the bar in his mouth, wiped his hands on his pants and picked up a file. "Aha. I had Annabelle print your Employment Contract. It says, 'Candidate must travel to off-site meetings, conferences, archaeological sites as determined by immediate supervisor.' Lookie here. Your signature. You've opted out of every travel request in six years. Shame on me for that. Pack your bags. Is it clear?"

"But—"

"Let me give you an ultimatum. Go, or suffer a week's unpaid suspension."

My mouth fell open. "What—wait, what? You can't."

"I can and I will. So make your decision now or deep kimchi."

Thanks, Caligula. I got up, trying to keep a straight face, while silently cursing him in various ancient languages. "Fine. I'll go."

I *had* to have that dreaded talk with my mother to finally assume her maternal duties. *Hit the dirt, Mom.* I had to cut the umbilical cords. It was bound to happen. And Cypress. I gulped. That talk would be harder.

KYLE

December 4, 11:17 a.m. 47 seconds
(Modern Museum, SFO)

K yle looked around the Modern Museum of San Francisco's conference hall, his hollow heart knocking his ribcage. Hard. Local museum staff welcomed the visitors from Ann Arbor, their animated voices too loud for his comfort. In a 4-second scan, he made out Juniper wasn't there. His heart stilled.

Why? Why? Why?

Kyle hoped it wasn't solely because of him she hadn't come. He hoped she had better reasons not to come. But if those reasons hurt her, he hoped they didn't exist. She had said circumstances prevented her from coming. He could find out in a second what the circumstances were. But he wouldn't.

At this point, it didn't matter anymore. She was nothing to him.

Then why are you looking for her?

One of the girls who worked with Juniper came up to him. She was a perky young thing with bright, happy eyes and a good energy radiating from her like electric pulses. Happiness was an anathema to him and he recoiled involuntarily.

"Hello. I am Stacy Crafter-Price, antiquities intern. Thank you so much for doing this, Mr. Paxton."

"My pleasure. Uh…is your whole team here?"

"No." She shook her head, her blond bob whizzing.

"Is your funding curator coming? Miss Mills, I believe."

"Did she Juniperize you?"

"Excuse me?"

"Oh, you know. When she emasculates those in power with her rebellion and angst?"

Kyle smiled but he did not respond.

CHAPTER 13

The plane soared over San Francisco and I caught my breath. Beautiful. I had a window seat and the world below tilted in a patchwork of misty colors, the grid of steel buildings charted like little dominos below. California was known for its micro-climates and I saw fog-blurred edges of the Bay, while pristine skies and jade hills cast sunny shadows inland. Except for my trip to Egypt, I had never been out of the Midwest. And here I was in the world's Technology Empire, the land of bold badass innovation.

Kyle's city.

I didn't know how I would react to meeting him. I was a cocktail of blender emotions. Fear, cautious joy, soul sucking anxiety, and wide-eyed panic.

Turning on my cell, I took a picture of the city view and texted it to Cypress, whom I already missed. *Almost landed. Miss you, Sunshine. Check out the view.*

I had promised to text and chat with him multiple times a day, which was the only way I could pacify his fear that I'd get lost in the black hole of California. Besides, I had worn down Mr. Ipswich until he allowed me to shorten my trip. Instead of all ten days, I was going from Monday to Friday. My colleagues had been in San Francisco for three days now.

My phone pinged. It was a picture of Cypress playing Capture on his laptop. *Nice view.*

I texted: *Come with me next time, Bud.*

He texted back: *No. The Bay area: 7 million people. San Fran pop density 18,187/sq. mi-7,022/km2. Too many people. Too scary.*

Oh, Cypress. A lump formed in my throat. I wished he had friends outside his virtual world and that I could balance my life with his. We were unnaturally codependent.

The plane taxied down into San Francisco International Airport and I walked into an ugly glass and concrete terminal. Before my flight took off at the Detroit Metropolitan Airport in the morning, Evan had said he would pick me up. I had refused and said I'd take public transport, but he had insisted. I was not looking forward to meeting the rude Mr. Marquez again. I glanced at my phone and saw another text from him:

At terminal I-C. Silver Tesla. Model S.

I walked out of the terminal and spotted several silver cars. Dragging my small wheelie suitcase behind me, I ran to the pickup walkway. My earbuds blasted "Humans" by the Killers and for a few happy moments I danced across the median, eliciting surprised glances from bystanders.

Hello, world.

It had been snowing when I left Michigan and here it was lukewarm and sunny. Lifting my face up, I basked in the Pacific coast's balmy heat and its curious balance with cool air. Mercifully, I was dressed in layers—a flowy green top, a sweater and a coat over skinny jeans thrust into boots. Feeling too warm, I peeled off my coat and in my struggle to get out of my tight turtleneck, I let go of the suitcase. It began to roll away. All of San Francisco was built on hilly terrain and Ann Arbor was flat, so I was not used to things tilting. Still stuck in my sweater, I yelped and dashed after my suitcase. I clutched it only to feel someone else had seized it too.

"Hey! Mine."

"I promise not to steal it," said a familiar voice.

Kyle. A spike in my body's adrenaline. A rush of blood to my face. I yanked the earbuds away, twisted the sweater off and spun to look at him.

"Hello, Juniper."

I could not breathe. I heard a ringing in my ears. I felt like I had just dived off a cliff. Unforgettable navy eyes framed by sunglasses peered at me with a sardonic look. I was not expecting to see him till Friday. And here he was—the occupier of my dreams and thoughts—in the flesh. My heart beat so loud I was sure he could hear it colliding against my ribcage.

"Hi." Staring at him with the curtain of my hair on my face—like a horror movie girl—I was out-and-out embarrassed. How I managed to be in a jam whenever I met Kyle Paxton was beyond my grasp. My voice low and my hands shook as I pulled my hair off my face. "Why are you here? I thought Evan was going to pick me up."

"I hope it isn't too much of a surprise. Just wanted to drop you off at your hotel. Promise. Not a kidnapping." He smiled and I smiled back.

My edginess blurred like the fog on the bay. Rambling apologies—the first things I thought I would say to him—for the way we had left things off and the indelible memory of the hurtful things I said, never left my lips.

"Thank you. You didn't have to."

"Actually, let's run to my car or I'm going to get a ticket."

He took a firm hold of my small suitcase and shook his head when I tried to take it. With his other hand, he gripped my arm. Across the median was a silver hybrid car, a Tesla. Scurrying with him, I was surprised. No limousine. No driver. No grandstanding.

Why how un-fancy, Mr. Kyle Paxton. How times have changed you. Me likey.

Settling me in the passenger seat, he put my suitcase away, slammed the trunk shut, and slipped into the driver's seat. As he navigated the choked airport lane traffic, I observed him with sidelong glances, my heart racing out of control. In his flawless and casual signature style, Kyle wore dark jeans and a robin's egg blue shirt. The well-sculpted stubble lining his jaw, the sun-ignited mass of black hair, and the sunglasses made him all the more devastating. He had the kind of unearthly looks that take a moment to get used to. Skeptical he was really in front of me, I stared in blatant awe.

Seeing the corners of his mouth twitch at my appraisal, I looked out the window and said, "What a stunning city."

"First time in San Francisco?"

"First time in California."

"You'll like it then." Eyes on the rearview mirror, he took the highway exit.

The car picked up speed and I enjoyed the air blasting from the open windows. The wind pressure lifted my hair and blew it around my face. When a gust whipped my hair his way, Kyle smiled at the long strands tickling his face, but he did not angle away. Feeling self-conscious, I pulled my hair into a makeshift twist. "I'm stoked at this warm weather. So sunny for December."

Kyle rolled up all four car windows with the flick of a switch. "Yes. But it's usually foggy in downtown. You're staying at the Q Hotel there."

"Is your company in downtown?" I let go of my hair as the air stilled. My hair slithered down and I sighed, for the split-ends reminded me how badly I needed a haircut.

Watching me sideways, Kyle flicked on the air conditioning. "Yep. Financial district."

"Oh, I expected you to be in Silicon Valley."

"The past few years, tech startups have been getting a pushback from the titans in Cupertino, so we moved to the Northern Financial district in droves. Plus, it's convenient; I live close by, in Seacliff."

"Seacliff. That sounds lovely."

"It is. The house was my grandfather's and since my mother doesn't live here, she tossed it my way. I recently got to renovate it."

"I see. Where does your mother live?"

"She remarried in London when I was ten and has lived there since."

Leaving you alone here? The same year she got a divorce? Mother-of-the-Century award mentally delivered. I wondered who raised Kyle, as his father lived in Ann Arbor, but I didn't have the nerve to ask him. "Do you have any siblings in London?"

"One child was misfortune enough for my mother. But her husband had two from a previous marriage. My stepbrothers—Charles and Finley."

Misfortune enough...what does he mean? Resting my elbow on the armrest between us, I asked, "Do you see them often?"

"No. But I did spend three years in London."

"Oh yes. When you went to the London School of Economics."

"Yeah, before dropping out. How'd you know?"

"I read your bio."

He flashed me a charming smile. "Read my bio? So you've been cyberstalking me?"

"Not at all. Just doing research for the museum's new brochures." I blushed and got a lingering stare.

"There she goes again. Changing colors like a chameleon," he said in a husky voice that sent shivers up my spine.

Kyle's forearm rested on the armrest between us and slowly moved until it was a hair's breadth away from my arm. The air in the car seemed to thicken and my heart raced at the patent physical connection between us. Time stopped. For a few minutes, there was only silence. It was lovely.

Eyes lingering on his hands, I noticed that his knuckles had faint red scars, like he had been in a bloody wrestling match. *Curious.*

I decided to shift gears and spoke up, "Again, thank you for picking me up. It was not necessary, you know. I could've taken the BART."

"Juniper, you can't take your sweater off without losing your luggage. You can't climb down a ladder without getting paralyzed. You seem to lose your coat and shoes wherever you go. I just saw you dance across the median. Jaywalking with headphones. Don't think you'd survive the complex trip from the airport to the hotel and museum. So I came," he said, eyes gleaming and teasing.

He saw me dance...right now?

Transfixed by the friendly intimacy in his tone, I shot him a smile. "Are you always so protective, Pops?"

All of a sudden serious, he looked out at the endless gray highway. "Don't know why I'm protective about you, Juniper. I'm never protective about anyone. You're the exception."

"Thanks for your concern. No need. I can take care of myself."

He shot an amused glance at the small bandage on my finger. "Really? Evan told me that when he met you on Thanksgiving, you turned a green carpet red. Did you get hurt?" Then his voice dipped so low, I barely heard him. "Or did someone hurt you?"

"Oh, that. I cut myself chopping celery. No one has ever hurt me. Why would you think that?"

"What am I supposed to think when you don't tell me anything? You're the most evasive person I know. Can we discuss—"

"There's nothing to discuss."

What is this? Not again. We had been together for a microsecond and we were already speaking on intimate terms. Breathing hard, I cursed myself for not letting him finish. I was sure the man thought I was rude and whatnot, but I always got Foot-In-Mouth Disease around him.

In the long silence that followed, I stared out the window, taking in the scenic drive. The highway cut through rolling hills dotted with bright Mediterranean homes and flat buildings. It was nice to see bottle green palm trees, evergreens and tropical foliage with flowers after the snow-laden branches back home. If I craned my neck, I could see the blue waters of the bay with the outline of the famous bridges far away. There was not a cloud in sight on this fogless day and bars of sun filtered in the car.

Running a finger down the sunlit dashboard, I felt warm. With a start, I realized I was not warm but happy. Happier than I'd been for months. Maybe years. Maybe all my life. It wasn't the sun, the palm trees, or the wonder of being in a new place, but the company of Kyle Paxton that made me happy.

I looked at him and froze. Kyle looked angry. Brows puckered, jaw padlocked, temple muscles twitching kind of anger. He had looked the same when I had left him a few weeks ago with my cutting words. I was sure both of us would never forget those words as long as we lived. My hands shook and my knees felt weak at the memory of his words: *I want you to be my Summer.*

A million questions raced through my mind and one kept repeating in a loop. *Why is he here after the way I treated him?* I was lost, not sure where I stood or where we were going. Not sure I was happy or sad. Not sure what he felt now.

I broke the silence. "Um. I just wanted to thank you…for sponsoring our museum's trip. That was kind."

"After I saw your email I didn't expect you to come. I'm glad you did."

"And I'm glad you came…today."

"Juniper, I came because I wanted to clear the air between us. Before we met for work."

Is that all? "All is good. Also, I'm…sorry…for my words. Um…for the last time we met."

"No. I should apologize for misreading the situation. It was all in my head what was between us."

I held my breath. *Wait, what? He thinks I am not attracted to him? God, is he wrong. Is that why he looks so mad?*

"You didn't misread the situation. I…um…was an equal participant."

Facepalm. Am I describing a relay race? Why is this so hard?

"I'm confused."

"You didn't misread the situation. I was also interested in you…just not the way you were in me. We are…very different. We want different things."

Kyle shot a surprised look my way. On the steering wheel, his knuckles turned white as he swung around a hairpin turn. The car swerved, the wheels screeched and I realized just how quiet the hybrid car was. "But whenever we meet, it seems as though whatever we have going on is not mutually exclusive. So maybe not that different," he said.

"You're right," I said softly.

At my admission, he was taken aback. "I was clear about what I want.

211

I will not bother you with it again. The thing is, I don't know what you want, Juniper."

"I want a lot of things. I want peace. I want the Nuclear Disarmament Treaty to pass. Ketchup chips to be made in the US. Vegemite to never be made in the US. Jar Jar Binks to never have been created. An Iron Age course in colleges so my book is a raging success."

I made light of it, but he did not respond. At his silence, my mind was flooded like an Atlantic Basin hurricane. Maybe, I misread the situation. Maybe, Kyle was here just to pick me up. To extend professional courtesy and nothing else. Maybe, what I felt existed only in my pulpy jelly heart. He only wanted me as his F-buddy for five months. As a master of clinical pigeon-holing, he could remove emotions from his life—but I wasn't like him.

Maybe I should heed Evan, whose warning was stuck in my head like pins in a dissected frog. *Stay away from him, Miss Mills. He is not in your league. Nor can you change him. You are never going to be more than what he asked you.*

No.

I couldn't stay away. I felt something genuine that Evan wouldn't get, even if it hit him with Thor's hammer. All I wanted, more than anything in my life, was Kyle. At that moment, I wanted to spend time with him. To make him see what I felt. Being in his presence made me aware of how right it felt. Like we belonged to each other. This was my only chance to make it right.

I turned to him. "Is there any way we can meet this week? If you're not too busy?"

"I'd like that. I think it's time we made a fresh start, Juniper."

My heart skipped a beat. *It worked.* "When?"

"I saw your itinerary to track you. On Wednesday, you have a tour of my office. On Friday, a dinner at my house…"

212

"Track me? Stalker much?" I chuckled and bit my tongue. *Too soon, moron, too soon.*

"Meticulous planner. Not stalker. On Friday, you'll be free at 10 a.m. and I'll pick you up. Spend the day with me and I'll take you to my house for the dinner. How would you like that?"

"I would love that, Kyle." I could not keep the joy out of my voice. *Spend the day with him? Yes. Yes. Yes.*

Without warning, his posture stiffened again. His eyes narrowed to slits and he gritted his jaw. *Now what? Jar me Jesus.* I could write a language based on the muscle twitches of Kyle Paxton's jaw. What had I said to get such a stone-cold response? Was it my specious use of the word *love*?

I stared out. By now we were in the city and the traffic was gridlocked. Here the buildings were taller, the homes narrower and the crooked roads curled up and down. Tall townhomes on steep hills reminded me of the zigzagging triangles in Odili Donald's paintings. For a while I admired the complex architecture of the city, though Kyle's silence was killing me. When the car stopped in front of the hotel, I was relieved.

The driveway was jam-packed with cars and a valet with a welcoming smile hung at Kyle's window. "Checking in, sir?"

"No, dropping off." Kyle pressed a twenty-dollar bill in his palm and the valet stepped back. Kyle dashed out, went to the trunk and returned with my rolling bag.

I smiled at his obvious efforts to prove he was a gentleman. This was a different man from the corporate drone I had met in Ann Arbor who had been glued to his phone and ordered his staff to take care of me. And yet... this guy was just as moody and confusing.

Kyle held the car door open for me and I smiled. "Thank you so much for dropping me."

"Sure. You wanna grab a bite to eat?"

"No. I'm good." In truth, I was hungry, but our last date was such an unmitigated disaster, I lied. As if recalling it too, Kyle nodded. He shut the car door and leaned against it, eyes pinned on me. Flushed at his silent stare, I looked up. The Q Hotel was a sleek glass building close to the Modern Museum of San Francisco. "I guess I'll go now."

"Do you want me to stay while you put your luggage in? I'll drop you at the museum."

"Really, Kyle? I can see it from here." I twirled and pointed to the concrete structure I knew from photos.

The corners of his delicious lips tilted up. "Try not to become roadkill in the two hundred feet trip."

I laughed. "Seriously?"

"Christ. Now I'm gonna worry about you." He groaned and ran a hand through his hair, ruining his stiffly set style. "Stay safe, Juniper. There are some terrible parts in the city. And they come so swiftly jammed into the good, safe parts—promise me you'll stay with your group."

The trained man-hater inside me picked up a shield. I liked his concern for me, but this bordered on suffocating. It must be his Paxton gene pool need to control all situations and people, including the girls he liked for a few months. I had enough battles to pick with him, so I faced the hotel lobby as the glass doors swung open. "This is a beautiful place."

"Yes." He handed me a tiny envelope. "Here, I had Evan check you in. Floor and room on the key."

"Thank you." Grabbing my luggage from his hand, I pivoted away and swayed in the air, tired now.

"Whoa." His hands held my upper arms to steady me. "Get some rest after the lectures tonight."

"Aye, aye." I shot him a military-style salute.

"Ah, wait. Before I forget, give me your phone."

With a raised eyebrow at this odd request, I handed him my phone. From his jacket pocket, Kyle took out a small lens and snapped the tiny toy on my phone camera. "Now your phone is a kickass BirdsEye cam. Download our app and it'll auto-synch your photos on a cloud so you don't need a bigger SD card."

"How exciting. So this is the BirdsEye? Your original invention?"

"Yes. It's a digital SLR module camera."

"And that means?"

"Cell phone cameras are about eight megapixels. This bad boy is fifty megapixels, as high res as a professional camera—the highest res phone cam in the world. Except, it's bug-sized." Eyes bright with boyish pride, he clicked the camera on. My phone screen looked crystal clear. Out of the blue, he took a picture of me. I squinted in the sun, as he showed me the photo, zooming in on my eyes. "See? Clear. High-res. Perfect. Look it even captured the neon lipochrom in your eyes."

"Amazing."

"My new screensaver." He shot me a wicked smile and texted the photo to his number.

"Um, nice." I blushed and took a step back. "Goodbye, Kyle."

"Goodbye, Juniper," he whispered. He made no effort to leave and just stood there, staring in his intense way at me.

My heart did a sad flip. The air felt stale and dry. Though we were almost strangers, there was something aching and familiar about him. About us. As if I'd known Kyle in a life before this. As if, long ago, we had been atoms joined like bone to tissue and then separated. Some elemental beast in us longed to be joined again, fused by any means—stitches, adhesive, blood, heat, fire—anything to be one again.

Argh, what is wrong with me? Like that makes sense. That was a whimsical explanation for the science of human attraction. What Kyle and I felt was not mystical, but biological. Like Lila said, the trigger of pheromones. Simple biology…we humans are helpless to resist.

He watched the shifting reactions on my face, his hands going to my shoulders. I caught my breath as his lips brushed my cheek. "I'll see you on Wednesday, June-Bug."

June-Bug? My heart skipped two beats. Was that because of my scarab necklace I wore at our gala? I liked that—*June-Bug*. I watched him stalk to his car in a few swift steps.

I could not wait to see him again.

In the glass and marble lobby, I stared up. The hotel was all cool ambiance, ultra-modern furniture, modern art and sculptural lights. Glass installations by Dale Chihuly mingled with long metallic lights dangling from a hundred-foot ceiling. I loved it. My room turned out to be on the topmost floor. Level twenty-seven. Once inside, I was stunned to see I was in one of the most luxurious penthouses of the hotel. I guess I was given preferential treatment as Kyle's hook-up nominee and it made me…uncomfortable.

I had to make sure my colleagues did not find out.

Like the lobby, the suite was minimalist and beautiful. Larger than my apartment, it had a drawing room with roll top couches, a raised platform dining room, a huge bedroom, and a marble-and-glass sculpture of a bathroom. Rushing to the floor-to-ceiling windows, I released the automated shutters. Below me lay panoramic views of the skyline ending at the fog-drenched bay crisscrossed by long bridges. My eyes widened when I spotted the famous red Golden Gate Bridge. It was breathtaking.

I stood there for a long time, thinking of Kyle. I could still feel his breath on my neck, the roughness of his stubble as his lips grazed my cheeks. *Lordie, how I want him. Like now.*

Thump. There was a loud knock on the door. Startled, I went to open it, thinking it must be Stacy. It wasn't.

Kyle.

I caught my breath, as I always did when I saw him. Was I hallucinating? I had just been thinking about him and here he was, in the hot flesh. Materialized in the thin air by my supernatural powers. Kyle tilted his squid ink hair, lips pursed at my silence. He smiled. I tingled. His rare smile could melt chocolate…aluminum and iron.

KYLE

Kyle smiled as if he knew a secret about her and held something behind his back with one hand. Enjoying the flushed shock on her face, he leaned leisurely against the doorjamb and asked, "Forget something?"

She took a tiny step closer to him, her lips parted. She said nothing... and for a few beats they just stared at each other. The air snapped and got electric. Kyle noticed her cat eyes had changed again. In the sun, they had been jade and now they were olive with tiny triangles of gold. Color bloomed on her face, traveling from her neck to her cheeks. He crushed an instinct to drop a kiss on the hollow of her neck...and continue on to her clavicles...then dip down to her perfect breasts.

He forced himself to focus on her and not her body. "I asked, didja forget something?"

She came out of her coma with a jerk of her frail neck. "I don't know. What?"

"This." He held a black leather wallet. "Is it yours?"

Her hands flew to her mouth. "Oh my God. Thank you. Thank you. Yes."

It was an altar to hard rock with logos of Van Halen, Metallica and Motorhead on it, a petrifying pierced skull with silver tusks and quotes like, "Now scream and Rock" and "I'm a Metalhead and I can't fucking keep calm."

Kyle held the wallet out in his palm, his shoulders shaking. "I thought maybe I gave a ride to a Hells Angels guy and forgot about it."

"Yeah, I kinda love hard rock," she said with a soft laugh.

He mentally groaned...when she laughed like that...her sweet and generous lips distracted him. He wanted them all over his body. He clenched his aroused body. *Focus, asshat.*

"Kinda? Or can't-fucking-keep-calm-love hard rock?"

She smiled. "I'm crazy about it. Especially the old stuff, because Mom had a lot of records. Where did I leave it?"

For a brief second, Kyle thought about her family and why she still lived with them. It was odd for a girl of her age. Well...that was a cold shower.

"I was about to drive away, when I saw it on the passenger seat floor." He shook his head. "Juniper, how you have survived to this ripe old age without being a news headline is a mystery to me."

He took a step forward to give her the wallet, and at the exact same moment, she took a step forward to take it. Their bodies slammed together. She gasped. Kyle froze. His entire body became a livewire. Electric. Alert to her. Instant images flashed in his mind. Of the bad things he wanted to do to her. In that suite. The suite where he had spent many nights...with other girls. He pulled back slightly. No. Juniper had not said yes to him. She was off limits.

CHAPTER 14

I felt him stiffening. Pressed against his hard chest, my body caught fire. I relished the heat of his proximity, enjoying his masculine scent mixed with the cologne of sandalwood, clementine, and of…pine trees…as if he had been hiking in the mountains.

Grinning, he stared at my nose pressed against his neck, sniffing hard.

With a sheepish look, I stopped smelling him like the perfume counter at Sephora. To compose myself, I pulled a few inches away and looked up. My eyes were struck by the light reflecting and glittering off his glasses. "So what's up with your glasses?"

"Huh?"

"Is that your disguise?"

"No, just how I can see the future."

"I refuse to believe the great Kyle could be near-sighted or far-sighted. If you took them off, the world would be blinded by your dazzling glory or annihilated and turned to dust."

A smile twitched at the corners of his mouth. "Nothing in between? Glory or dust...only?"

"Yep."

With a mischievous grin, I snatched his glasses off. Swiveling around, I threw them on a chair by the door and turned back to see him blinking in shock. I stepped closer and peered into his eyes.

As his pupils dilated, I saw Kyle's irises go from the blue flame of deep fire to cobalt. His arms curled around my waist and my arms looped around his neck. To purge my pent up feelings the past few weeks, I needed to kiss this man. Like now. I could bear it no longer and pulled his face down to mine.

The man-hater in me did not even try to put up defense shields.

My lips parted over his and he gave me a tense look. Ignoring it, I kissed him, crushing my lips amateurishly against his, my hands going up his back to massage his shoulder deltoids, and drifting down to the hard muscles of his lower back. *Man, does he lavish time working out.*

At first, he held me in a loose hold, but when I pulled him in the room and slammed the door shut, Kyle lost control. His hand splayed my waist and went down in a swift motion to cup my hips, hard. He pulled me up to his body, the denim of his jeans chafing against mine. Kyle's lips hardened over mine with such force, the sharp stubble against the ring of my mouth began to hurt in delicious pain.

We kissed like that for a long time and gradually his lips became persuasive, as if asking me to submit to him. At first, he had been ruthless in his invasion of my mouth, his fingers impaling the soft skin of my back to pull me against him. He took a sharp breath and let his rigid body melt, his hands dropping to his sides. The softer kisses made me realize that this was not his usual modus operandi. I felt he was checking himself, reining it in. I suppose the girls he had been with were so skilled that restraint was never on the menu.

When I pulled away, we stared at each other.

I was lost. He was confused, his eyes asking me unsaid things.

"I'm sorry about that," I whispered, looking down at the floor.

"Don't be sorry for the best thing that's happened to me." His hand flew to my chin, the pad of his thumb stroking my jawline. He bent and brushed his lips on my cheek. "Okay, Juniper?"

I shivered. The way he said my name was sexier than a kiss. With a slow grin, he took a step back to let me know that I was free and was not going to be seduced or coerced into something. And I appreciated that. Despite his alpha male swagger and his philandering system, Mr. Kyle Paxton was turning out to be kind of an old-timey gentleman, like Cary Grant.

"Do you have to go? Or can we talk for a minute?"

"I always have time for you, Juniper."

Smiling, I walked across the room to the window wall. He followed me, stopping on the way to pick up his glasses from where I had thrown them. We stood silhouetted against the glass, the sunbeams falling on us in serrated bars. The light caught the blues in his black hair and rimmed his face in a glossy ring.

"Thank you for all of this. The suite is wow," I said, rubbing my bare arms, which were popping with goosebumps from the cooling, but mostly because Kyle Paxton could turn me into an iceberg or a fire, just by standing in the same room.

"Don't thank me for something I didn't do." He shrugged and fixed me with a searching look. "You said you wanted to talk. So shoot."

What now? I don't have a game plan, do I? I gulped and looked at the floor. The dark brown Macassar wood was streaked with thin orange veins that stretched out like winter branches. So pretty. Being named after a tree and studying tree species had given me the ability to recognize any wood grain in the world, but not the ability to converse easily with men. *Come on...just say something.*

My head shot up. "I just wanted to know are we...okay after last time? I hope...that you...dang it—I don't know what I'm saying."

"I get it. You're saying sorry. And you suck at apologies."

I nodded. "Pretty much. My ego cons me into thinking I don't need to."

"No need, Juniper. We are good." He paused and one of his hands went to his hair, mussing it up from the back. "You earlier...what does this mean? Are you having second thoughts about my offer?"

Whoa. That is direct. "So the offer still stands?"

"For you. Always."

"Oh."

"Is it a yes now?"

I chewed on my lips and slowly shook my head. "Frankly, no. Clearly...I want you. But not in the way you want me."

Kyle's face became distant and my heart raced in dread.

Is this the last time I'll see him?

"So I can't convince you?" he asked.

"About what?"

"Convince you to leap over to the dark side. My side."

"Are you no longer with Izzy?" *Oh, shut up sulky, jealous girl.*

His jaw set and his eyes tightened. "I told you, I expect and give fidelity in the time I give. But I don't want to talk about anyone else. Only you, Juniper." His hands went to my upper arms and he held me like a thick book. "I'm glad we got a chance to talk. Now, do you want to get something to eat? I'll get room service."

223

"No. I'm fine." In point of fact, my stomach was grumbling.

"Well, I'm not. I'm starving. Let's get room service." Kyle turned and picked up an elegant paper menu from the desk by the window. "Hmm. I like their burgers. Love, actually. What about you? Glazed salmon? Salad? Steak?"

"Burgers sound good."

"Thank God."

"Why?"

"Uh…a lot of the girls I know think eating is optional."

I wagged a finger in the air and clicked my tongue, like I was an auntie. "Um. Tsk. Tsk. That is so wrong."

He shrugged. "Huh?"

"Well, you *chose* them. So you can't skinny shame them."

"Okay. I'll concede to that. Though I've never picked anyone solely based on looks."

"Yeah, sure. If that helps you sleep at night."

With an amused smirk on his lips, he said, "You're beautiful, Juniper. But your smarts outshine your beauty. Chew on that."

Still smiling, Kyle walked to the phone and placed the room service order, while I just stood there, flustered and wondering what was next. Kyle hung up and led me to the sitting area. Settling on the L-shaped sleek white couch, we faced each other from across the cocktail table. An awkward air hung between us. I bit my lips and tried to think of where to start…how to broach things we flat-out disagreed on. At first, Kyle and I talked about the museum and my travel. I could tell he was biding his time to get to the meaty, tricky topics.

When he started talking about the weather in San Francisco, I burst out, "Hey, do you have any questions for me?"

Digging his big shoulders back into the couch, he nodded. "Yes."

"Shoot."

"Well, the last few weeks have not been...fun for me. I've wanted to know about my offer since Ann Arbor. It was a definite no. But now I'm confused. What's going on in your mind?"

I inched closer to him and wedged my hands under my thighs. "The way I spoke to you in Ann Arbor, Kyle...I had no right to judge you. But, I am twenty-six and unlike other girls my age, I've not had much experience... with men. You shocked me."

"Not many men in your life. Hmm, I like that."

I smiled. "Not fond of equality, are we?"

He gave me a wicked smile. "I need details." When I shook my head, he said, "Who was your last boyfriend? When was that? For how long?"

I looked down, fingering the wavy mint ribbon on my blouse hem. How humiliating for a twenty-six year old American woman to admit she's never had a boyfriend—let alone had sex—to a guy who's only been with sex goddesses. So I was silent.

"At least tell me what you expect from the men in your life."

Oh great. Talking to Kyle: worst idea ever.

"Not sure. But...I guess...I believe in relationships and seeing if I want something that leads to intimacy." I was grasping at straws. What if he knew I had no men in my life? He'd fly up-and-away like Clark Kent, tearing the roof in his flight.

"So you want a relationship from me?"

His direct question was a shot to the heart. A long pause later, I whispered, "I didn't say that."

"Juniper, I need you to tell me what you want. From me."

"I don't know, Kyle." I picked up a silver pear from the table décor and walked it across the glass table.

"At least tell me where you think we stand."

His interrogation methods would do the NSA proud. I twisted the pear like a top and scooped it up when it fell over the table edge. "Again...I don't know where we stand. It's just a beginning."

"Okay." He gave me a look of drained patience. "What about the other men in your life? Did you want flowers and diamonds and dates?"

"No. Only time and care. I could care less about diamonds." *Flowers sound nice.*

"Time and care?"

I caressed the pear like it was my Magic 8-Ball that could reach into the future and give me all the answers. "I guess...I am slow, dull. I am...old world. And you are so different from me."

He shifted closer, his arm sliding around my waist. "I knew that when we met. And I knew I was wrong for you. I tried. I tried to stay away from you, Juniper. I really did. I could not."

I can't, either.

"I don't want you to stay away, Kyle. I like being...with you. Just maybe not the way you want me to." I reached for his free hand and pressed my fingers in his.

He took the silver pear from me and put it on the table. Reaching for my other hand, he stroked my frozen digits with his warm ones. "Christ, why are you frozen? What are you afraid of, Juniper?"

Too many things. Afraid of his question, I asked my own. "Kyle...is there a way we can compromise?"

"First tell me, is there no way you'd accept my offer?"

I shook my head. I had no interest in being one of his Winters or Summers. "No. Is there a way you'd be willing to meet me halfway?"

"No. I don't comprise, Juniper. In business or my personal life. I don't negotiate."

"Oh." An alarm went off in my head and I tried to draw my hand away, but he held on tight.

Kyle Paxton, my gushy heart yelled, *is your soul blind? Can't you see there's something more than lust between us?*

"We are at an impasse then."

"Yes." I turned my face away to stare blankly out the window, willing this conversation to end.

"I told you I'd never repeat myself if you said no. I lied, Juniper." At those words I turned to him. "See here I am, repeating myself. But I don't play games. So let me be clear about my intentions. I want you. That has not changed. And the only way to be with me is to be my Summer. That has also not changed."

I was crushed. Moving my hands away from his, I scanned his poker face. "Why?"

"I want us to enjoy each other for five months and walk away. Without the mess. The drama. It's all I have to offer. I want you, but only that way."

Your way. Only that way. "If I say yes, do I have to sign the Termination Contract?"

"Yes. We have to plan. Sign contracts. Make sure you know the rules."

I exhaled like I was smoking a hookah. "Can't you be spontaneous? Why does life have to be planned? Why does it need contracts, lawyers, rules and regulations?"

Visibly stung, Kyle ran fingers in his hair until the waves fell on his forehead. "Juniper, why can't you follow my rules? They're a safeguard. I can't function any other way."

"But why are you this way?"

"You know how I work, how I live. I told you and you reacted…God, I thought I'd never see you after that day."

"That doesn't answer my question. Tell me, why are you this way?"

"Speaking of telling." He shifted to a different seat cushion to see me better. "You never tell me anything. I know nothing about you."

"What do you want to know?"

"All of it."

There was a knock on the door and Kyle went to the door. It was room service. Nate, a smiling young man, set up the trolley near the couch and opened the silver domes on the plates, revealing mouthwatering burgers. When he left, Kyle fell next to me, handed me my plate and began devouring his food. He had also ordered truffle fries, ginger ale and brownies. I loved the tiny ketchup bottles and he thought it was hilarious when I filched one for later. Though I was still thinking about our conversation, I was too famished not to eat. We ate in relative silence, talking like polite strangers about the week and the museum partnership.

Kyle's phone was lying on the food trolley and buzzed constantly with incoming calls and he ignored it until we finished eating. Snatching up the phone, Kyle got up and paced in the entry hall, talking to Evan. When he came back, I was stunned by the change in him. My friendly, polite Kyle was gone and a stony, business-like stranger had replaced him. Feeling shy all of the sudden, I picked up a steak knife, balanced it on its tip and twirled it like a top.

With a curt nod at his phone, he said, "Hate to cut our talk short, but I have to go. Work stuff."

"Of course," I said. When I looked up, he was watching me and waiting for my knife to stop dancing. The knife fell from my fingers with a clatter and I got up. "I'm sorry I delayed you."

He shot me a reserved look, his eyes distant. "Please stop apologizing,

Juniper. Big waste of time. I will see you on Wednesday."

"Sure." I orbited the glass table and walked him to the door.

With a peck on my cheek, Kyle turned to go, but not before his phone rang again. He picked it up and said, "Sylvia. Evan just told me. I'm coming. Relax."

Watching him stalk down the hall, I felt the oxygen had been sucked out of my lungs. I shut the door and leaned against it, eyes shut. *What just happened?*

I didn't have time to process it. My conflicted feelings about Kyle would have to wait—I had work to do.

I changed into professional clothes, ran down to the lobby and made my way to the Modern Museum of San Francisco. Once inside the concrete citadel, I was struck by the ascetic grandeur of it. I visited Chicago museums often (where I could make a day trip without unsettling Cypress) but this was as modern minimalist as Zaha Hadid architecture in Europe.

I walked around until Stacy came to collect me. "Junie. Where were you? Evan texted me that you landed like three hours ago."

"Just getting ready at the hotel," I lied. The ride from the airport had lasted an hour, though we were just twenty minutes away, and I was sure Kyle had taken a circuitous route to prolong the trip. The very idea warmed me from head to toe.

"Let's go, homie." Grabbing my wrist, Stacy dragged me through several corridors. Heels plinking on the marble as we ran, she told me all that I had missed. "The first day was the orientation. Ugh. Infodumps. Friday we met some dope modern artists. Saturday we saw art galleries and

229

Sunday we did cheesy touristy stuff. The peeps in charge are like forty, but everyone looks so young here."

We entered a small conference room where Jennifer Swift, the museum's Public Relations Director, was giving a talk about their standing collection. It consisted of a hundred thousand art pieces, most of them not on display, as they rotated their exhibits frequently. She explained Kyle wanted our little museum to become exhibit partners with them and use their standing collection.

After her talk, I was introduced to the young, laidback and friendly museum staff. Luckily, as I shifted into work mode, I stopped thinking about Kyle. Later on, Stacy and Trevor took me on a tour and the day passed, swift and pleasant.

Tuesday was a repeat of the same. The Ann Arbor staff fell into a routine of getting up early, eating breakfast in the Q's bistro, walking to the museum, and spending the evenings exploring the downtown area.

To dispel my guilt, I spoke with Cypress every two hours. Frequent contact seemed to comfort him, and Mom said he was doing fine. I was glad Walrus had twisted my arm to come on this trip. Based on my degree, I knew only the bare basics of postmodern art that I needed to be a curator in this day and age, and this was a fab opportunity to become semi-literate. It was all new but uplifting and my fears about the changes to our museum slowly dispersed.

On Tuesday, I got to my suite at midnight, after a nightcap at the hotel bar with Stacy and Trevor. Worn-out, I sank on the pillow-top bed and pulled the goose down covers over my head. It was a cotton womb. I shut my eyes and Kyle popped up, as if he were scored on my eyelids. Though I hadn't gotten a call or text from him, we were to tour his offices tomorrow and I wasn't sure I was ready to face him. I was totally petrified and totally elated at the same time.

"Hello there, Kyle," I said to my tall Giuko art lamp. I wished he hadn't come inside my room. Not only did I think about him all the time, I saw him everywhere. The hologram of Kyle stood by the window, sat on the couches, ate burgers with me, kissed me by the door, leaned by the arches, and followed me with his eyes.

I flipped on my belly and looked out of the glass wall. The starless night did not make Kyle vanish. Slipping out of bed, I went to the window to admire the glittering city that never seemed to sleep. Holding my midriff tight, I pressed my forehead on the cool glass.

I wondered what Kyle was doing right now at his Seacliff house. Was he alone? Or with someone...maybe Izzy. His Winter past. Wait. No. Were they done? I recalled her Winter schedule and tensed. Wasn't December tenth his last day with her...*gulp*...this upcoming Thursday? So on Monday, after he picked me up at the airport, kissed me, and had lunch with me, he would've gone back to *her*.

Oh God. Please, no.

The hair on my neck stood up and I wondered if she was in bed with him at this very moment. The very idea of Kyle's lips on hers, and his arms on her supple body made me sick. Physically sick, like being green around the gills. The green-eyed monster was strong with me. Felicia Grunde would, no doubt, happily unplug my life support system to charge her iPhone.

A few days ago, I had googled Izzy to find pictures of her with Kyle. I found none, but to my surprise, I found out she was not just a pretty face. Not only was she a model, she had a business degree from Cornell and had recently launched her own makeup company. Maybe she wanted Kyle's help with that. Super-Izzy had it all. Beauty, brains, killer confidence, and sheer sexiness. How could I measure up? And why did Kyle even want me?

Maybe he's not with Izzy. Maybe he is in bed with a new Summer.

That hurt. I felt the prick of hot tears in my eyes. I knew I had a few drinks too many, but this was insanity. I did not just want Kyle. I felt… something deeper. I had never felt like this about any man in my life. What a waste. I wished I felt like that for someone I had a future with.

I could not figure him out. No woman had ever refused him—of that I was sure. Maybe he was just excited by my restraint, my foot-dragging. I guess I was his personal challenge. I knew he liked playing games, like any garden-variety rich degenerate. I worked with a few wealthy and privileged museum board members and knew how their minds worked. Once they got the nth degree of money, power and success, they became seekers of the next challenge. The next rush.

And Kyle Paxton was an admitted adrenaline junkie, the way he dived with sharks in Bimini Island. Maybe, I was just a hunted thing to him. He was a hunter after its target, a treasure seeker diving for gold coins. I was a marathon, and the game was to get the ribbon, not cross it.

Round and round went my wonky thoughts.

Stop, Juniper. You're only gonna get hurt in all of this. Stop before you go too far.

But. I. Could. Not. Stop. Kyle Paxton with his smoky blue gaze, his lopsided smile, his hard-and-soft lips, scruffy jawline, his entire damned universe had crept into my mind, perhaps forever. I had lied to him when I told him I would never consider his offer.

I wanted him—no matter the price.

KYLE

December 8, 1:07 a.m. 07 seconds
(Seacliff, San Francisco)

The house stretched long and dark and the minutes ticked loud and clear. Kyle sat in the darkness staring out the folding doors he had opened to his patio. For the thousandth time in the past two days, he pulled up the screensaver on his phone and looked at her photograph. She was so different from anyone else he knew. The photo was as confusing as her, a puzzling mix of innocence and sensuality. Of wisdom and idiocy.

Juniper. Barefoot Girl. Bug in his system girl. Juniper Bug. June-Bug.

His phone buzzed with an incoming call. It was Izzy. He took her call.

CHAPTER 15

O n Wednesday, we left the museum early to get ready for Kyle's office.
I had just put down my purse when Stacy banged on my door, her
cheerful voice shouting, "Helloooo. Oppppen pleeeeze."

Reluctantly, I let her in. She got wide-eyed at the unexpected luxury of
my suite. Whistling, she trekked through all the rooms touching the bric-a-
brac. "Awesome! We should have a party here."

"No party," I said. I knew that as a trust fund heiress from Connecticut,
she instantly grasped this penthouse was an overindulgence for a lowly
junior curator.

She stopped at the glass wall and looked down on San Francisco, her hair
lit up like an orange torch in the sun. "Dafuq? Who'd ya bang to get this?"

"Excuse me?"

"OMG. I am just LOLing. But, look at this tricked-out palace. How
didja get this and our pimps the teeny weeny rooms below?" She grinned,

twin dimples cleaving her cheeks. Though a brilliant archiver of historical artifacts, if she could only talk in hashtags, emojis and comic book speech bubbles, she would.

"Directors, not pimps, Stacy. Who knows, maybe a registration mistake."

"Sure. Uh-huh. Is there stuff you wanna spill?"

"Shouldn't we get ready? Don't we have to leave for Kyle's office soon?"

"Spill, spill, spill." She nodded like a curvy Barbie bobblehead. I walked to my bedroom and she followed me. Kicking off her shoes, Stacy flopped down on my bed, grabbed chocolate bonbons off my pillow and popped them in her mouth. Fixing me with a shrewd stare, arms folded under her neck. "Now it all begins to make sense."

"What does?"

"All of this. The truth is IMHO, Kyle Paxton totally wants to tap your ass."

Two red flags burned my cheeks as I glared at her. "Hey. Stacy, you just crossed a line."

She shot up in the bed, her cheeks rounded by the chocolate. "Yeesh. Don't drag the rug over me. Okay, so you don't, but he hashtag totshearts wants ta nail ya."

"Just because I'm a nice supervisor doesn't mean I'll take bull like that."

I felt light years older than her. She was twenty-two and life was still a fun game. For the past two years, Stacy had given me a play-by-play of her every date and the long chain of men-boys she dangled, all interested in casual hookups like she was. No matter how many times she asked me about my love life or lack thereof—no matter how subtle or overt—I always avoided her personal questions.

She was an intruder in my isolation chamber. My mother's fears had left permanent scar tissue. In a world where social media was everything, where private lives spilled like fish guts in a market, I was a glitch. I wished

I'd been born before the age of mobile phones, satellites, computers, and the Internet. I took to social media only to market the museum's Twitter feed. On Facebook—where I posted political articles and Celtic art—I had added only ten friends and even Stacy and Trevor's requests were denied. They Tweeted and Instagrammed every beat of their life, while I could beat a hermit crab at his own game.

"Please lemme finish." Eyes filled with concern, Stacy held up her palms in protest. "I'm never mistaken about the hookup vibe. I'm like a hookup whisperer. It's not just the suite. On Thursday, Kyle came to welcome us at the Museum. He asked me if you were coming. He had such a long face, but when I said yes you are, OMFG, you should've seen him. Like fireworks. He looked so damned relieved. Honestly, I've never seen a man react like that. It was...kinda hot. Open yer eyes, woman."

"Stacy Crafter-Price, Mr. Paxton is the board president and there's work protocol I will never cross." *Killer Whale crap.* If Stacy knew, the others would too. I had to be cautious.

"Hey, don't kill me...but you get all cute 'n red when you say his name."

"Stacy."

"So what I said about Kyle. UGTI."

I sighed. "What is UGTI?"

"You Get The Idea. He likes you."

"Bull. And please stop murdering English. Speak, as your position requires. We have a coordinator job I am vying for you to get."

Scrambling out of bed, Stacy came by me and mouthed a sorry, looking like an impish kitten. I smiled. It was impossible to stay mad at her. I swung open the closet and flipped through the navy and black suits hanging there. It was a fashion cry for help. All blah-boring career clothes, nothing to shock-and-awe Kyle. I selected a pair of black pants and a matching black blazer with a navy button-down shirt.

Stacy frowned at my selection. "You going to a Men in Black convention? Or a funeral in Mordor?"

"Okay, Funny Girl, is there something you need?"

"Oh, yeah. So after Kyle's office, we're going to this epic club."

"So go." I held up a pair of brown pants. Maybe I could mix-and-match.

"Yucky, don't mix blue with brown." Stacy snatched the brown pants from my hands. "I want you to come along. To the club."

"Ha. No way." I grabbed the pants back.

"Why not? Trevor, Evan and peeps from Kyle's office are also going. On Saturday we went to a nitrogen drink bar with Evan. It was sick."

"Evan? I wouldn't have pictured him as the fun type."

"He is and so hot, isn't he? Gotta love delish Cali guys."

"Isn't Evan gay?"

"I think he's bi."

"Careful, Stace." I gave her a warning look, worried she might develop feelings for him.

"Ew. Barf. I'm not attracted to him. At all. He's just fun to look at. Come, please."

"Nope. I'll stay back with the grown-ups."

"Oh come on. You never go out in Ann Arbor. This is our one week away."

Exhaling, I collapsed on the bed and wagged a finger her way. "Stacy, what I'm going to tell you has to be our little secret."

"What is it? I love secrets and you're a secret glued in foil paper, stuck in a stinky bean burrito, buried in concrete."

"Focus, Stacy. Well…I've never gone to a club before. I've danced with friends at parties, went to prom…but I've never been to a club. I think my window of opportunity is gone. So I'll pass today, thank you."

Her eyes got round as Ping-Pong balls. "What? How? Are you kidding me? Are you a twenty-six-year-old club virgin? Now you have to come."

A virgin in more ways than one. "I said no."

Pulling my arm, she forced me to look at her. "No to your no. Say yes or I won't leave and I'll eat all your chocolate. Come on. A tiny drop of fun won't kill you. You know what Walrus calls you? Nonstop Ant."

"Pretty sure that's not a compliment."

"Look, we all know the insane hours you put in. You're young. You're gorgeous. And it's time to partay."

"Hmm. Maybe...I'll go. But I don't have anything to wear."

Stacy did a victory dance in the air. "Woo-hoo. Lemme worry about the swag. Wear your skinny jeans. I have a sexy top for you."

"No sexy top, Stace. We have to go to Kyle's office first."

"Put a blazer on it. I'll get you club ready."

When we all met downstairs, I felt really self-conscious. My hair was blown out and Stacy did darker makeup on me than I would have dared. I wore midnight blue skinny jeans, Stacy's four-inch strappy heels and her blouse half-hidden by my sensible blazer. Though too large on me, her blouse was a lovely black chiffon creation with a silk undershirt decked with geometric beads that shimmered dully with each step I took.

Our colleagues Lydia, Reza, Ruben, Aggie, Dave, and Trevor were waiting in the hotel lobby. On seeing me, they smiled and the men bumped their elbows. I knew they were surprised at my appearance. In the six years I worked at the museum, they saw no hint of the club-ready girl in front of them. Trevor, who looked sleek as always, shook his head sheepishly, but

I noticed how long his eyes lingered on Stacy, who wore a seductive black cocktail dress with a white blazer.

"You two going somewhere else?" Lydia asked.

I looked blankly at her. "I thought we had to dress for the meet-and-greet?"

Stacy and Trevor exchanged looks. "Gonna hit the town later on," Trevor said.

Ruben shook his head. "I guess us old farts are not invited."

"Our cars are here," Trevor shouted, smiling in relief.

Kyle had sent a fleet of limo sedans. Four to fit us all. The office was barely two miles away. *Kyle and his limousines.* Trevor, Stacy and I excitedly hopped into one.

When we were settled, Trevor turned to me. "Hmm. There's something different about you today. Can't quite figure it out."

"It's the makeup," I said.

Trevor gave me a teasing look. "I know! I just found out you're a girl. Bow-chick-a-wow."

I reached over Stacy and punched his arm. "Ha."

"You look good different, Juniper. I like the icing on you," he said.

Stacy put an arm around his neck. "Hala. It wasn't easy to get her dolled up."

Trevor whistled. "I can't believe she convinced you to go."

"I am a bitchin pimp. Say it," Stacy said.

"You're not a bitch, babe." Velvety brown eyes peeled on her, Trevor unhooked her arm around his neck.

I shot him a sharp glance. *Hmm. He likes her.* So for all of Stacy's perception about hooking up vibes, she was clueless about Trevor.

Oh Stacy, how oblivious to your own state of affairs.

She leaned over him to grab an Evian from the car door and he flinched.

As she pressed against him and drank, Trevor gritted his teeth. Staring out of the passenger window, he thrust his hands into his black curly hair in frustration. Light glistened on his nutmeg brown skin, throwing into relief the sharp bones of his sensitive, handsome face. A gifted young man, Trevor was diligent, quiet, shy—an introvert—the opposite of Stacy. He definitely liked Stacy, and from the looks of it, she had no idea. I wondered if he had made a move and been turned down or if he hadn't even tried for fear of being rejected.

"I wanna get wasted tonight. Can I pop a champagne bottle?" Stacy asked, giggling.

"Nope. I'm still your boss till eight. After that, we party," I chided.

"Wet cat," murmured Stacy.

"Girl, behave." I sank deeper in the luxurious leather seats, my hands glued to my knees. *Will Kyle be there today?*

Kyle's office was the tallest skyscraper in the Financial District. A modern mix of business and art, it was a green glass curtain cut with charcoal steel beams. Odd aluminum fins jutted from the top of the building as if a spaceship had landed on the rooftop. We walked into an airy garden plaza that had cube topiary walls, fountains and postmodern sculptures.

My heartbeat sped up as I looked for Kyle and relaxed when I saw Evan waiting for us in the lobby. He said a polite hello and at my cool nod, his brow wrinkled. *Meh. Let him stew.* I had not forgiven him for his nasty insinuations on Thanksgiving.

In the elevator, Evan informed us that BirdsEye owned the top floor office and that Kyle had gone into a bidding war with the founder of Capture for the vaunted space, as it came with rooftop gardens and the best views of the city. And now, he explained with pride, the two CEOs were great allies. The elevator slid open to a huge domed reception. From behind a long slate desk etched with the BirdsEye logo, a trendy young man and an elegant girl got up and greeted us. A few employees walked past, shooting us curious looks. The BirdsEye office was all glass, slate, and birch wood with sparse décor, postmodern art and flashing LED screens. The bleached colors and muted design of Scandinavian minimalism made sense for Kyle's controlled personality.

Where is he?

My belly was a charm of hummingbirds as I looked around. But he was nowhere to be seen. We followed Evan to a large atrium with ceiling-to-floor windows and a Plexiglass wall of stacked glass boxes. While Evan talked about the company, I drifted away from the group.

Drawn to the display wall, I saw the glass cubes were filled with hundreds of vintage cameras. Slim labels were marked with each item's model and date. I saw vintage cameras from Canon, Nikon, Minolta, Konica and Yashica next to lots of the Pax Rangefinder models, Kyle's grandfather's brand. From huge daguerreotype cameras dated from the mid-nineteenth century to 1980s Polaroids, this was an impressive collection.

It made sense.

Kyle Paxton collected cameras. Just the way he collected supermodels and F-buddies. I hope he didn't collect and pin butterflies as a kid. My heart sank. He was a collector. Of various items. I imagined a secret dungeon in his Seacliff house with a wall of stunning naked beauties in glass cages, trapped in liquid crystal, frozen in time. Maybe there was an empty case, its door swinging under a plaque stating: *Reserved for Miss Mills, Museum Curator, circa Iron Age.*

Shaking off my loony ideas, I ran after my group. Evan led us past modern shared workplaces, curved steel offices, glass labs, and ergonomic test centers. Before he gave us a tour of the labs, we had to sign NDA forms.

I remembered Kyle telling me at our disaster date how in California they whipped them out at every meeting. The irony of that made me laugh.

Stopping at several labs with huge windows, Evan explained the cool new gadgets BirdsEye was developing. Their cameras were hot commodities and now they were testing new products—all in the prototype phase—like smart-pens to replace phones, tiny drone cameras, facial recognition cameras, and cognitive robot cameras which led them to AI technology.

Strolling through Tomorrowland, I felt Kyle's identity in all things. Judging from the laid-back staff, I saw an innovative, dedicated, happy workforce. It was also like the UNO here—very diverse. Evan informed us the office culture had put BirdsEye in the top fifty Career-Bliss rated companies. He went on and on about Kyle's business acumen, his ingenuity, and his genius inventions. I was duly impressed and awed. But I was also edgy and impatient and was startled every time I heard Kyle's name.

Kyle, please tell me I will see you today.

At the end of the tour, Evan halted in front of a conference room of etched glass. "Mr. Paxton is super busy and will not join us today. Right now he's meeting a big client from Argentina. We partner with cell phone providers in Europe and Asia and now we're hard launching in South America."

Heart beating way too fast, I scanned the glass room and saw several people sitting around an oval glass table at the head of which sat...Kyle Paxton. I gulped. Kyle was talking and beside him stood a statuesque woman, her head inclined his way. When he paused, she turned to a screen and at the click of a remote control, a product video sprung to life. With a smug smile, she sat down, her eyes still fixed on Kyle. I wondered who this Venus was.

Dear angels, I hope she isn't one of his ex-F-buddies.

Tiny bumps prickled my skin. My eyes lingered on Kyle and I got dizzy.

It was a scary feeling of raw excitement. The kind that flows in your lungs when you do something stupid and thrilling. Like waiting at the top of a roller coaster to plummet down the biggest loop. Or diving from the edge of a waterfall.

As if he felt me, Kyle swiveled in his chair and his gaze sought me out. Instantly. Even from twenty feet away, I saw his eyes blaze. Getting up, he murmured a few words to meeting attendees. Much to the stupefaction of the woman next to him, he stood up and headed to the glass doors. Eyes fixed into mine, he stalked straight to me. I stopped breathing. I think I needed a respiratory inhaler.

Dear gods of fate, why does this man have such power over me?

KYLE

December 9, 6:18 p.m. 51 seconds
(BirdsEye Office, San Francisco)

Kyle felt her presence before he saw her. It unnerved him. She was under his skin. And when he looked at her, it scorched him from inside. Her eyes made him out like a heat-seeking thermal device hunting an animal.

Blindly, he got up and said some words he could not recall.

By his side, Sylvia tensed. "Kyle, please tell me you're coming back."

He smiled at her and the team visiting from Argentina. "I have some urgent matters to attend to. Sylvia will be helping you for the rest of the day. Thank you, gentlemen. And ladies." And with that he walked out the door.

CHAPTER 16

Our worlds collided. Again. Totally ignoring his meeting attendees and his staff, Kyle Castillo Nolan Paxton, founder and CEO of BirdsEye, came to stand beside me. Though his eyes were glued on me, I exhaled in relief when he did not verbally acknowledge my presence.

"So happy to have you all here. I'll join you in the lab now," he said to Lydia.

Our staff clustered around him like he was a rock god. As he shook their hands, his eyes remained locked with mine, the corners of his mouth up. Kyle's sharp gaze assessed my attire and I tried not to blush in front of everyone.

Rats on a stick. He thinks I dolled up for him.

Evan made his way, elbows first, through the crowd around Kyle. "But, but, but," he sputtered. "Isn't the meeting going on another thirty minutes?"

"Sylvia will handle the rest," Kyle said, tearing his eyes away from my face. Sylvia must be the über-poised woman I had seen with him. I turned to the conference room and saw her watching us coldly even as she addressed the conference room.

"But what about Mr. Ignacio's request to meet you?" asked Evan, as if this was the most atypical thing he had seen his boss do.

"Cancel it." Kyle waved to him.

Getting a grip, Evan began to text instructions.

Stacy shot me a knowing little smirk and I frowned at her.

"Follow me." Kyle walked down the hall, fast. He stopped at a curved steel wall that said: BirdsEye Advanced Engineering Lab. At the press of a button, a small hatch opened. A laser scanned his eye, and the curved wall parted. Trevor gasped in excitement. It looked like we were bound for the future.

I shivered as I entered the lab. Not only was it an icebox but it was... clinical, spotless, cold-blooded almost. Rows of shiny steel desks were clustered with laptops, computers, monitors, and plasma screens, and giant processors blinked at the far end of the room. One end of the lab had a Plexiglass wall with hundreds of tiny cubes full of tinier BirdsEye camera prototypes. So this was Kyle's bat cave. The lab's very air crackled with power, ingenuity and cutthroat competition. Kyle's brand. He looked ahead and I looked back in time.

I sighed. *We're so mismatched.*

A few Birdseye staff in white lab coats turned to smile at Kyle. Nodding at them, he marched to a long steel table and introduced the two men by his side as the company's chief hardware engineers. Evan handed him a tablet.

Folding his arms, Kyle said, "At BirdsEye we design camera modules with integrated image processing. Our slogan is Picture Clarity and we now have four models of our flagship camera, each with more clarity."

"I read your original camera was the Optic BirdsEye 009. How did you come up with the idea? I mean weren't you like in college then?" Trevor interrupted him, eyes shining in reverence.

Kyle smiled at him. "More like a college dropout. The idea came to me when I went rock climbing in Argentina. I almost lost my life taking a photograph with a huge bulky camera. My friends saved me in the nick of time. My camera fell. I saw it smash into a thousand pieces on the ravine below. That could've been me. All of us had useless phones, and I thought—*what if we had tiny cameras that take super-quality pictures?* When I came back, I holed up in my garage with a few engineer friends, like Thom here, and we created the first BirdsEye camera."

"That is freaking awesome. How long did it take?" Trevor asked.

"Took a long time and a million mistakes. They say, if at first you don't succeed, destroy all evidence that you tried. We did. We kept trying. And today we have fifteen products out in five continents. And a hundred million users. Now. Look above you."

We did. My mouth hung open. It looked as if there were a dozen bees buzzing over our heads. "Wow."

Lydia and Pam ducked their heads and Kyle smiled.

Without warning, he jumped up and snatched a tiny insect from the air. A few people cheered. Grinning, he gave it to Lydia. "Pass this around. These are our new drone cameras. The BeesEye. Feel free to wave at them and see the live feed on the screens behind you."

I held the bee camera on my palm. *Kyle Paxton probably had a few BeesEyes circling around my apartment and my office.* I looked up and swallowed when I saw Kyle was staring at me as he talked.

"The museum board wants BirdsEye to streamline your website, photography, social network and up your media game. Each of you got a BirdsEye camera. My software and marketing team will create an app using your input and photos. Before I show you my new baby Kronos, which one of you is the best photographer?" Kyle asked.

"Reza is. He photographed the pyramids for our website. Trevor is quite handy and Juniper does our catalog shooting," Lydia replied.

"Reza, I want you to use our new cam for a three-sixty panoramic view of the lab and everyone in it." Kyle handed him a small, flat camera. Reza nodded and started walking around, clicking it. Kyle's eyes rested on me and he signaled me with a finger. "Come beside me, Miss Mills."

Obviously…he would pick me.

My knees got weak as I walked to Kyle. He asked for my phone. Flicking off the camera he had put there, he picked up a tweezer, dipped it in a Petri dish on the workstation and held up the tweezer. It looked like a clear gel contact lens.

"This is Kronos, the world's tiniest but most powerful camera. Our new prototype. One of seventeen models only."

My colleagues murmured in admiration and Lydia called out, "You sure you can trust her with that?"

"Don't worry. We're good at seagull management here," Kyle deadpanned. He flicked on the lens of the BirdsEye cam and one of his engineers dabbed a liquid on it. Blowing softly on the lens, Kyle reattached it and gave me back my phone. "Miss Mills. Your phone is now worth half a million. The cost of each prototype."

"Oh no. What if I lose it?" I stared at my phone as if it were a sack of diamonds on my palm.

"No sweat. We have an in-house dungeon. And we exact punitive measures for exemplary damages to our *property*."

Everyone chuckled.

Yeah, Kyle. I bet you love punishing people who break your rules. He caught my probing look and his lips curled. I got the feeling the way he said "property" he was referring to more than the camera.

"Miss Mills, I want you to take a close-up picture. Make sure it's something smaller than a foot in size. And it must be three-dimensional. Take images of all sides."

"All right," I said, looking around. A sharp silver glint caught my eyes. Trevor's belt buckle, which I'd given him for his birthday. A Taekwondo black belt master, Trevor loved the leather belt with its silver buckle and the raised yin and yang design.

Without thinking how it would look to the others, I stood in front of Trevor and leaned down to his jean waistband. At first, he shrank back but when I aimed my phone, he caught on. Trevor hooked a finger and pulled at his jeans waistband to give me better access to the buckle and I saw his dark washboard abs. Impressive. I took a few photographs of the belt's edge as well.

Stacy giggled and a hum came from the rest of the museum staff.

"Miss Mills, when you're done assaulting the young man's belt, please bring Kronos back." Kyle's voice was strained.

Assaulting? Strutting back, I gave him my phone with a bit of attitude. "Here."

"Very good," Kyle said, in a tone that implied good was bad. He gave my phone to one of his engineers, brows knotted and jaw set. He looked crabby.

Luckily, only Evan noticed, and he looked from Kyle to me, his face nosy. Was Kyle Paxton jealous? Impossible. But he was without doubt acting like a brooding Byronic teenager. Confusing. I knew he felt something for me…and I figured it was pure, distilled lust. I also know that jealousy fell into his hated category of drama. One of the cardinal rules of the F-Buddy system was no green-eyed monsters.

"Into Trevor's crotch the archeologist digs," Stacy whispered when I went back to my group.

"Behave, lassie." I wagged a finger at her.

"Oh, I am. Not sure you got the memo," she retorted. We giggled and she leaned real close. "Um...I was right. Kylie Wiley is eating you with his eyes." When I looked at Kyle, she whispered, "One, two, three, four, I declare an eye war."

"Zip it, Stacy. This is the wrong place for...such jokes."

"But it is the right time."

Thom Lee, the VP of hardware engineering, gave us a tour of the lab and walked us through the steps of the Kronos design. While Thom talked, Kyle spent his time gazing at me. Stacy was right—he could not keep his eyes off me. Alert to Kyle's magnetic presence, I could barely focus on what Thom was saying, and prayed the others did not notice my pink cheeks.

Thom uploaded Reza's photos in a laptop wired to a flat white apparatus. The box buzzed and a rectangle hologram popped up from its lens. Around four feet in diameter, the hologram was a blueish white projection of the lab. Reza had taken pictures of us exploring the lab and all of us starred in the hologram. Thrilled and amazed, we gasped, and a few people even clapped.

"I give you HoloEye," Kyle announced. "The future of photography is holograms. So is BirdsEye's. Current cameras don't reach the gigapixels needed to create a hologram. Our engineers made a frigging cool lens— with variable aperture and a shutter of variable speed— capable of such a task. Then they made it tiny. This box is a holographic scanner and uses lasers to make a photographic light field."

It was strange to see a life-size hologramic three-D version of myself. I whistled and roamed around the table taking it in. Aside from Sci-Fi movies, I had never seen anything like it. My mind was further blown as Kyle changed the hologram to a panoramic view of the Golden Gate

Bridge. "This is an aerial view from a helicopter...of the famous bridge."

I noticed that he looked away from the bridge, his lips pursed, eyes hollow. *Hmm. Strange.*

"And here's my personal favorite, the Redwood forest," Kyle said.

The lab came alive with the sentient magic of the ancient trees and I could not help but walk through the huge hologram and not around it. The light deluged my body as I did a quick spin in the trees and I saw Kyle smile at my childish antics. After a few more spectacular holograms, he turned off the machines and the lab lights came on.

As people began to scatter, I piped up, "Hey. What about my phone?"

"Let me show you," Kyle replied.

He came over and clasped my arm, his fingers cutting through my thin blazer. I did not dare budge my lucky arm as he led me to the Plexiglass wall at the end of the lab. The walls parted and closed as we stepped into a dark room. I heard humming and clicking and made out the outline of a few cylindrical machines. He stopped in front of an oddly shaped printer and smacked it. When he smirked at me, I knew that Kyle Paxton was peacocking to impress me.

"Check this out." Something hard and oval was plonked in my hand. It was a silver belt buckle. Identical to Trevor's. Except it was pearlescent white.

"Wow. How is this possible?"

"Three-D printing. The material is glass-filled polyamide. Kronos takes an in-depth picture and this baby prints a three-D version of your boy's belt."

"Er. Trevor's not my boy." I flushed and hoped he would not notice in the dark, but he did.

"Good. I'm glad." Kyle moved so close to me, his breath fanned my cheeks. "Or I might've tossed him in our virtual wood chipper."

"Really? I thought you said your lifestyle has clean edges. No jealously.

No red-rum. Looks like you lied."

He laughed and I caught the white gleam of his teeth. Long fingers grasped my chin and stroked my jawbone as I shivered. "Lots more in store for you. Just hang with me, June-Bug."

"Looking forward to it, Kyle." Worried that someone would follow us, I eased away from him. "Let's go back."

"Wait, there's more." Kyle disappeared in the dark, came back and put something in my hand. He switched on his phone flashlight app and I gasped. I held a small lifelike sculpture of Trevor and me. It captured the moment I was leaning over Trevor's belt. Awkward. I shook my head. "But how in the world?"

"Guess."

"The bees?"

"Bingo. We've developed the world's fastest 3-D software scanning and printing."

"Mind officially blown."

"I wanted to show the museum staff how we can make scale models of sculptures using 3-D printing, but this isn't exactly a professional result." He took the sculpture back and gave me a disapproving look.

I giggled. "I have no regrets. This is a better artistic composition than if it was just me. What are you gonna do with that?"

Kyle was not amused. He cracked the sculpture in two pieces, tossed the Trevor part in the garbage and stuck my part in his blazer pocket. "Memento."

The particles shifted in the air. I took a step backwards, overcome by his actions.

Whoa. Kyle is intense.

Back in the lab, Kyle plunked the newly printed buckle in Trevor's palm and explained the technical process. "On arriving today, you all signed

NDA's protecting our proprietary info. So you must be wondering why show you all of this? Kronos will be used for 3-D printing movie sets and NASA engineers are taking Kronos to the first manned mission to Mars. Three-D printing will also renovate historical artifacts reproduction. Your museum staff will be the first testers. We'll use Kronos and three-D printing for exact replicas of museum exhibits in Europe. And now the big news. Next year, some of your staff will go to Europe to test this."

His eyes rested on me, and I shivered, wondering what was in store. I could hear his voice echoing in my head. *Be my Summer and come with me to Europe, Juniper.* I inhaled. Kyle wanted me for six months. And in six meetings, I wanted him forever.

At that moment, Sylvia entered the lab, her impatient dark eyes following Kyle. Striking, stylish and bone thin, she had boyish razor-edged blond hair and wore a gray power suit, a sheer blouse and pencil heels. When Kyle paused, Sylvia made a beeline for him. Draping an arm around his waist, she whispered something in his ear. Taken aback, Kyle wrapped up the meeting and walked out.

"All right, visitors. Please follow me. We are going to the rooftop," Evan announced.

I felt a pang of frustration. Was Kyle not going to join us? We petered out of the lab and I saw Kyle striding the opposite way with his blonde shadow. Damn that Sylvia. Why was Kyle always knee-deep in beautiful, seductive, predatory women who looked like they wanted to lock him up and toss the key into another dimension?

"Hello, Junie. Had fun in the dark room with Mr. Tall Dark and Nerdelicious?" Stacy cocked an eyebrow up. "Those glasses are so on fleek."

"Ugh. Sometimes I'm glad I don't have a sister."

We were climbing the rooftop stairs and she ran a hand up and down the steel guardrail. "Admit it. You have the hots for him. I mean, a girl could get pregnant just by looking at him."

I pulled a skein of her silky hair. "Jeez. Keep those hormones in your panties."

"He was wiping yours off his glasses."

Laughing, we entered the rooftop. It was a green oasis of potted trees overlooking the compact city, the space spectacular in the sunset. Beaded lights twinkled over the seating areas of plush couches set around fire pits and tall palm trees rustled in the breeze above. Stacy and I walked to a secluded spot behind a few red-flowered gum trees and watched people pour onto the rooftop.

"Love. This. Can't believe it's December and we're outside," Stacy marveled, arms up in the air.

"Yeah. Hey, can I ask you something?"

"Ask away."

I crossed my arms and cringed. "Um...I haven't dated in a long time. After how many dates...are we supposed to put out?"

"Put out? You mean have sex? Okay, Lucille Ball. By the third date, I guess. But if I'm super into someone, it's cool on the first date. And if they're just, you know, friends with benefits, it's about the banging. From the first second."

My mouth fell open. "I don't 'you know.' I'm lost...so far behind and... Kyle's so experienced."

"Trust me, their experience doesn't matter. We're in control. Hot bods and all."

"Oh." I blushed.

Stacy gave me an odd look. "Are you like, shy or something? He totally wants to bang you. Do it, I say."

I turned to the half-wall rooftop edge, looking down. "Stacy, I don't know."

"Come on. You both act like bloodthirsty vampires around each other."

"Fine. I'll admit...I've never been more attracted to a man. But, what's between us isn't real. Look, as cultural anthropologists, we know humans are pattern-seeking primates. Everything we do—love, hate, fight, create, destroy—is an upshot of our primitive ancestry. Me with Kyle is just my gatherer DNA reacting to his caveman hunter attributes. What we feel is as fleeting as the life span of a mayfly."

She shook her head, flaxen bob whizzing like a flag. "Wow. I can't even. Stop being a curator, Juniper. Try being a girl, sometimes. An empowered one. It's easy."

I wish. I wish it was easy. I wished I had parents who loved me in a boring way and had taught me mundane social stuff. Instead, I was raised with an unhealthy daily dose of fear and hate. I wasn't like Stacy. Her loving family let her Spring-break in Cancun, go alone to Burning Man, hook-up in their pool house, gave her a weed allowance, and cheered her on no matter how wild her shenanigans. I wished it were as easy for me.

You're all grown up, Juniper. Drop your daddy baggage and mommy pity party.

"Hey, I need a drink. You?" Stacy asked.

I shook my head and watched her walk to the seating area of the rooftop, where the BirdsEye and Ann Arbor Museum staff mingled, and waiters served them appetizers and drinks. I sighed. Unless it was an event I organized, I was always the girl behind the curtain. Content to be a social pariah, I was usually a happy outcast. Now, I was conflicted. My first day in Kyle's world and I was already on the sidelines.

My phone pinged. I groaned. Cypress had sent ten texts. I texted him a few pictures of the view and called him. "It's lovely here. I wish you were with me."

"I miss you too. Don't stay too long, Junie," he pleaded. "Don't get stuck in sticky San Francisco."

"Hey there, bud. I'll be back on Saturday."

We talked until he was pacified and when I hung up, my heart ached. We were joined at the ribs and our bond made him way too dependent. Cypress needed me...so what was I doing with Kyle? My duty was to Cypress, who would be in my life forever, not to Kyle Paxton, who'd be gone like smoke in the wind. My fixation on Kyle was my fault. From our first date, he had been clear about exactly what he wanted. But I had ignored his caveats and left my heart unarmored.

I am just a stand-in, till the next Winter comes along.

Even Sylvia, who worked with him, was more permanent. Sylvia. *Who is she?* Flicking on my phone, I searched the BirdsEye website for her. A Stanford grad, Sylvia Langston was the Vice President of Business Development and "a fearless, dynamic, go-getter." Before working for Kyle, she had pulled off one hundred million in sales at other companies.

I whistled. The women who buzzed around Kyle Paxton were not only mad-beautiful, but also mad-accomplished. I was a basic frozen meat patty found in every diner and the women he knew were caviar rolled in gold leaf.

So why the hell is he into me?

Maybe...he has bad taste.

That made me smile. Leaning over the balcony railing, I shivered in the chilly breeze, glad I was wearing a blazer. The last rays of sunset drew pink and orange chalk lines on the gray sky. The panoramic city below me was as daunting as Kyle. It was incredible, beautiful, big, sexy, scary.

"But mostly beautiful," I whispered, out loud.

"Mostly beautiful, except when she challenges me," said a deep voice behind me.

I spun around. Kyle stood there, smiling. The light pierced my eyes and I put a hand on my forehead and smiled in what I hoped was an alluring way. "Hello, again."

He took off his glasses and leaned on the balcony beside me. The breeze ruffled his hair and the falling sun ignited it. Contrasted with the black, the gold rim was a halo. It was so ironic, I almost laughed. He angled his head and studied the length of me, his eyes lit up by tiny flecks of sunset. "You're so beautiful today, I find it hard to look at you."

My cheeks heated and I got a skosh bit shy. "It's just make-up Stacy put on me."

"No. It's not that. You look better without all of that...stuff. You have a...timeless beauty and every time I see you, it grows." I froze as a bold hand lifted my chin and stroked my jaw. "Blushing again, June-Bug? You can't handle compliments, huh?"

I can't handle your touch.

My lips parted and my throat got parched. I longed to run my fingers in his hair and kiss him senseless in front of everyone. I wanted him to carry me to his lab, throw me down on a cold steel table, take off my clothes, and make love to me. Crazy monkey style. But I did not even know how to do that. Because I had never been anyone's lover and I would disappoint him. Kyle Paxton was an expert connoisseur of women, with his own damned rules and social construct of relationships...or...hookup upgrades.

Trying to figure out my silence, he scanned my face.

I inhaled and said in a polite and prim way, "Your products are amazing. Thank you for today."

"My pleasure." Noting the wicked curve of his lips, I was sure it was a double entendre.

"I can't believe how successful you are."

"Success is relative, Juniper."

"Um. You built an empire at an age when most of us are barely scraping our lives together. I feel we're playing checkers and you're winning chess."

He thrust his hands in his pockets. "We're all capable of it. Success is encoded in our DNA, but some of us are twisted enough to wrestle it out."

Twisted enough? "Encoded or not, you are phenomenal."

"So Juniper Mills is impressed...hmm. Victory is mine."

I looked down at Stacy's crystal encrusted heels on my feet. "Not impressed by money and power. Impressed you are self-made."

Looking ill at ease, he pushed against the guardrail. "I had funds to invest and a ton of help. But it means a lot coming from you. Hey, I wanted to ask you...if we are all set for Friday. I'll pick you up at ten sharp."

I smiled shyly. "If you're still up for it."

"Wouldn't miss it for the world. So where to? Pick your pleasure. The Arts District? The wharf? Touristy? Historical? Nature?"

"Oh, I'd like to see the beach." I twisted away so fast, I dislodged us from the railing and his hands shot out to steady me. Looking at our coworkers not so far away, I slipped away but Kyle pulled me back, his hands taut on my waist.

"Really, the beach? It's not exactly beach weather."

"Just the seashore. You know, I've never been to a beach."

"June-Bug, how's that possible?" He whistled and then laughed. Used to his grim Anubis face, my heartstrings tugged. The happy mood made him seem oddly young and carefree. "Where have you been hiding? Were you rescued from the Heaven's Gate cult?"

"No, from a high tower in the woods. I cut off my hair, tied it to the window hook and climbed down."

"I see. Plot twist. And, am I the hero or the villain of the story?"

"Only time will tell."

"Know what I think?" Kyle's voice was husky.

"What?"

"I have a theory about you. I think you were time transported, not born. I'll bet they found you frozen in a museum crate. So they scraped the ice off and you just ended up hanging around the museum."

I laughed quietly. "Yeah, true story. I've got a theory about you too. I think you were made in a lab. A synthetic cyborg. Half-man, half-machine."

"You got me." Kyle stroked his chin and frowned. "Hmm. You find me inhuman?"

"Just as much as you find me frozen."

My eyes gleamed and he mouthed touché. Shivering, I wrapped my blazer tighter around me. The sky was dark now and the breeze frigid. My hair whipped against my face. A few strands lashed his face, but he made no move to brush them off. He just stood there, smiling. Mortified, I tucked my unruly mane to one side. "So this is why songs complain of the cold in California? I get it now."

"You cold? Let me—"

Just then, Trevor and Stacy came up to us, holding champagne glasses. Stacy handed me one and Trevor asked Kyle if he wanted one. Kyle shook his head.

"Your work's inspiring. I think I'm in the wrong profession. I'd die to work here," Trevor added.

"If we ever need curators with giant belt buckles we'll hire you." Kyle tossed Trevor a half-amused, half-glacial look.

I wondered if Kyle was still jealous and mock-glared at him. "Hey, don't go taking away my well-trained staff."

"Juniper, we're leaving soon for The Cave," said Trevor.

A dark shadow passed across Kyle's face. "The Cave? The night club?"

"You guys ready?" Evan strolled up to us with five other people—three men and two girls, all dressed in club gear—and when they saw Kyle with us, they hung back.

"Why are you going to The Cave? The Cave gets disruptive. Why not a classy place like The Alcove?" Kyle asked with an icy look that had Evan worried.

My happy mood faded. Kyle looked like a forbidding, guilt-inciting male version of my mother. *Hypocrite.* This was the last thing I needed. I took a big swig of my sparkly champagne, lacking the audacity to defy him in public.

Evan looked at his boss square in the eye. "When were you last at The Cave, Kyle?"

"Six years ago. I'm too old and too busy for nightclubs," Kyle said.

"It's revamped now and I booked a private room. It is just a few of us hanging out," Evan said, rocking back and forth on his heels.

"Are you going?" Kyle asked me. It was an accusation and I felt I was testifying at a Senate House Hearing.

"Yes."

"I think I'll come along, then," he said, blinking.

All of us were stunned and Evan was about to drop into a coma. The five employees of BirdsEye looked revolted and melted away. No one ever wants to go dancing with their boss, especially a head honcho like Kyle. Trevor scuffed his toe on the floor and Stacy arched both her eyebrows at me.

"Are you sure?" Evan asked.

"You kids have fun with your friends. I'll have fun with mine." Kyle wrapped a self-assured arm around my back, and if there was any doubt about his intention, his possessive fingers threaded mine. With both his arms on me, I was trapped.

What's happening? Has he lost his digital marbles?

I drained my glass in one gulp. The champagne fizzed like Pop Rocks on my tongue and my heart went snap-pop, as well. If this was not a public declaration of our affection, I don't know what it was. An alarm beeped in my head. But what were we doing? What was Kyle thinking? Friends, not quite F-buddies? Was not the first rule of being an F-buddy utter secrecy?

"Should I send for Pat?" Evan asked.

Kyle held up a hand. "No. I'll drive Miss Mills."

Wow, Kyle in charge. Ordinarily, I'd have been irritated by his pitiless tyranny and his complete disregard for the feelings of others, but all I could think about was dancing with him. Burying my face in his shoulders as he led me in a slow dance. Or spinning to a fast beat, my body molded to his. I cringed. I had become a silly girl, the kind who melted like wax at a man's heat-lamp of attention.

When we were alone, I unhooked my arm from Kyle's and said, "Let's be careful. My job's important to me. I don't want anyone talking about us."

Kyle clenched his jaw. "Fine. I have to work now. Evan will call me when you leave." His expression was inscrutable, his voice cool.

I watched him stalk off. I was sure office gossip was not on his social-radar and so he did not get what I was trying to say. For an hour or so, I walked around and made a few lame attempts at networking, but my mind was not in it. Hungry and numb, I sat down by a fire pit and snatched appetizers from every tray server passing by. I could not stop thinking about Kyle's shifting moods. Perhaps he was upset I blocked his advances. All I wanted...actually...I didn't quite know what I wanted because the rules of normal relationships did not apply to us.

I just had to muster through this trip and let the chips fall where they may.

KYLE

December 9, 7:42 p.m. 01 seconds
(BirdsEye Office, San Francisco)

K yle Paxton was furious. He lost control of the tightly compressed mechanism inside him. Was she rejecting him—again? He had no idea what the hell was going on in her mind. And he hated being in the dark. About anyone.

Why is she so hard to control?

Exiting the first floor elevator, he took 56 even steps to reach the gym door. He flashed his badge on the scanner and went in. It was usually empty after 6 p.m. and this evening was no exception. Ignoring the 77 aerobic, cardio and muscle machines in the gym, he strode with determination to the wall-mounted heavy punching bag.

He began to punch. Hard. Fast.

After punching 28 times, Kyle took a deep breath—only 472 to go.

CHAPTER 17

The Cave turned out to be a lackluster building that looked like an abandoned warehouse, and in a very dubious neighborhood. A long line of revelers on a red carpet moored off with a velvet rope were the only indication that it was a nightclub. There was no signage, no lights, no music and no entrance per se. Instead of waiting in line like a normal person, Kyle knocked on the large barn doors.

A pocket aperture slid open and a voice said, "Only VIP entrance. Regular Admission, get back in line."

"Not regular," Kyle said.

"VIP Password?" asked the bouncer.

Evan, who was scrambling to catch up with us, panted, "Licorice. The password is licorice."

"You heard the man." Kyle looked annoyed at the farcical spectacle of it all.

I shivered. When we were not alone, he was so hostile, bossy, and kinda...despicable, that if I did not know him, I'd probably despise him. Kyle Paxton was not a man one dared make an enemy of.

At the entrance, two burly bouncers checked our IDs. Evan led us through a few halls into a circular room. Kyle held my hand and the small of my back and maneuvered me through the crowd. Looking around in sheer delight, I felt the blood rush to my head. This was truly my first time in a club and I hoped Kyle would not find out, as that would be totally humiliating.

The vaulted space was banded by multilevel balconies. It was painted slate and had a wall of natural stone, which gave a womb-like glow and why it was called The Cave. It was all at once primitive and modern and dirty and clean. Seductive music thumped through the club and only a few people were dancing while others stood around a stage where a band was playing.

Evan led us to a private lounge in the mezzanine level. Lined with curved white couches and small tables, it had a half-moon balcony overlooking the dance floor. We huddled at the balcony looking down, until a waitress appeared and we ordered a round of drinks.

When she left, I remarked, "It's not as packed as I thought it would be."

"It's too early for real clubbers," Trevor said.

"We're stupid early. The real fun begins at eleven. Partay till dawn," Stacy said loudly, trying to talk above the music.

"Really? We have to work early tomorrow," I said. The three younger ones stared at me and I realized I knew nothing about clubbing.

It was warm so I shrugged off my blazer and adjusted my halter top. Stacy's blouse was too big for me and revealed more of my cleavage and back than I liked. Not used to wearing revealing clothes, I felt self-conscious and nervous. When I felt Kyle's eyes burning into my back, I turned. His brazen gaze flicked over my naked shoulders and slid insolently down to my legs and strappy heels. I shivered, but not because I was cold. The man could slay me with a look.

Kyle sat down, grabbed my wrist, and pulled me next to him. "You look stunning in that flimsy excuse for a shirt. But it upsets me. Don't ever wear it in public."

"Hey, don't ever tell me what to wear. I am confused. Public affection. Possession. Isn't that against your own rules?"

"They apply to regular girls. Not defrosted Celtic girls. For them I bend the game rules."

"Inflexible much? Or maybe, confusing your quarry is part of the game," I asked, cupping my hand over his ear.

"Them? Just you, Juniper Mills. I like confusing you."

"Careful, Kyle. People will talk." Shyness flooded me as his lips grazed my ears and his hand snaked around my waist.

"I don't care. My mind's made up. I can't obey your no-public-display-of-affection order."

Already buzzed from the champagne I'd had earlier, I gave him a crooked smile. Kyle carved me to the hard ridges of his body and a thrill of elation shot through me.

Startled at this unexpected display, Trevor, Stacy and Evan exchanged uncomfortable glances. They looked nauseated and trapped, like they were being held hostage in the room at gunpoint.

Just then, the drinks arrived. The perky and pretty waitress put a tray full of shots in front of the younger ones. "Jäger Bombs for all of you." She gave me a snooty look. "Mojito for you. And Manhattan Rye for you. Great choice, sir." She handed Kyle his drink accompanied by a flirtatious glance.

I was pleased to see he ignored her.

After she left, he put a heavy arm on my shoulder blades, and I sank against him. Watching him swirl the gold amber of his glass, I said, "They say drinks say a lot about you."

"What does this say about me?"

"Manhattan Rye. Whiskey, Vermouth and a dash of orange bitters. Old, smooth, tangy. An old-school guy who thinks he is modern. Who thinks he is easy-going, but loves control. He has dragon armor that hides the dough boy inside."

He smiled at my analysis. "You're wrong. Under my rough exterior lies an even rougher interior. Now do yourself."

"Mojito. Icy, minty and lemony. A little sour, a little sweet. Sometimes nice…sometimes naughty and always confused."

"I'd like to meet the naughty side. Didn't know it existed."

"Oh, it does," I lied.

Lips parted, I moved his way as if my flesh was tied to his by invisible twines. Sparks ignited and sparkled in the space between us. Kyle's eyes glazed over and my eyes shut on their own accord.

"What did I say, Juniper? You should keep those beautiful eyes up."

My eyes flew up and closed again at his amused but heated gaze.

Then Stacy cheered about something and I realized with a rude shock that we were not alone. Kyle and I pulled away from each other.

"How do you know so much about drinks?"

"Mom was a bartender before I was born." *In truth, a stripper at a bar.* "She taught me how to blend drinks for her when I was a kid. I used to make her favorite oldies. She had a lot. With funny names."

"Like?"

I took my straw and drummed it across the rim of my glass. I was becoming aware of the fact that I always tapped things when I wanted to deflect topics. "Lemme see…Brass Monkey, Alabama Slammer, Fuzzy Navel…oh yeah…

Singapore Sling, Sex on a Beach, Blue Lagoon, Woo Woo Cocktail."

Kyle laughed. "Woo what?"

"Woo Woo Cocktail. Vodka, peach schnapps and cranberry juice, served in a highball glass. I was a drink expert before I was an alphabet expert. Sadly, before I became a teenager, she became a teetotaler. Sneaky, sneaky Mom. I'd drink a lot more if I didn't recollect her stinky intoxicated breath."

Kyle said nothing; he just listened and I wondered if he thought I was rambling.

"Bombs away." Stacy raucously downed two shots.

"Cheers, mates." Evan also drank two shots, though soberly.

"Juniper, join us for shots." Trevor tried to put a tiny shot glass in my hand.

I raised my mojito glass. "No, I had two champagne glasses and now this."

"Shots. Shots. Shots. Come on, Juniper, don't be a fun sucker. This is your first time at a club after all. Craptastic. Did I say that out loud? Not sure." Already drunk, Stacy giggled with a lime wedge between her teeth. She drained another Jäger Bomb and looked with contrition at me.

The three men swung to me in shock. Trevor's mouth hung open and Evan shook his head. Kyle's arm ripped into my shoulder. I flushed and sucked my straw. Stacy and her loud pie-hole. I wanted to stick a bunch of Tabasco-sprinkled lime wedges in there.

"First time in a club? For real? Come and dance then," Trevor said.

"Join you guys later," I said.

"So my origins theory was not far off," Kyle said in my ear, drawing my attention away from the others.

"Yeah, I get it. I belong in a museum case."

"How is it you've never been in a club before?" His voice lowered. "What else have you never done? Now I'm intrigued."

My eyes challenged him. "What about you? Doesn't look like you go clubbing either."

"I am an antisocial bear. Unless an event is related to work, I rarely go out."

"Really?" He could have fooled me. On first meeting him, I pegged Kyle as a playboy extraordinaire. It pleased me to learn that he was not a party animal. I clinked my glass to his. "To not going out then."

"To uncertain but delicious odds." Those words and his hand caressing my back even as he leaned innocuously back, sent tremors of anticipation up my spine.

Delicious odds, indeed.

Just then, the music turned up in beat and volume. The club hammered with a popular dance song and Kyle balked like a grumpy old man.

"The band is done. DJ Lord Mixer's in the house." Evan went to the balcony. Drawing the pocket doors, he closed off the area. The dance floor was visible through the glass, but the genius soundproof panels reduced the music to a faraway throb. Evan turned to Kyle. "In case you need to talk."

Kyle shot him a look that spoke volumes. *Go.*

"Woo-hoo, dance time." Stacy guzzled another shot and picked up yet another glass. Trevor prevented her from taking another shot and Evan hustled her out. The door finally shut and our club space became an intimate room.

"Thought they'd never leave," Kyle said.

"Poor toddlers. Mr. Paxton, you're terrible to my little charges."

"Listen, Mary Poppins. I'm not on limitless time. I only want to spend my time with you."

"I feel the same way." My voice was breathy and low. Our eyes met and even in semi-dark, I saw his pupils dilate. The smoke rising the whole night between us turned into a flare. The alcohol kindled in my veins and my insides lit up.

"Juniper. Juniper." I loved the way he said my name. Like it was a prayer, not a title. "I was wrong. You're not beautiful, you're lovely. And that's not even why I like you."

In concord, our bodies moved closer to each other. His hand cupped my chin and he drew me even closer to him. In lazy appreciation, he traced my lips and then my jawline. His fingers dipped to my neck, caressing the column up and down and then moved to my clavicle bones. Kyle's stubble-lined jaw teased and grazed my cheeks. His hands clasped my waist and mine went around his neck. A low sigh escaped my lips as he trailed a line of soft kisses on my jaw and neck.

Our lips met, both equally hungry and forceful. Demanding and pushing my lips against his hard mouth, I was in control for a bit. Not expecting me to be so bold, Kyle was surprised. For a second he tore away to stare at me, and it was so hot, I quivered under his gaze.

"Juniper." His voice was low. Broken. "June-Bug, what are you doing to me?"

Afraid it would end, I wanted more and arched my entire body towards him. He responded by easing me down on the settee and pulling me as close as possible while his rock-hard thighs trapped my body under his. With a growl, his lips began to devastate mine again. His kiss deepened, his tongue dipping inside, and I yielded to his lead as his lips hardened and became more insistent. The sandpaper of his stubble scraped and scratched my jaw in delicious pain. I don't know how long we kissed. I lost time and reason.

Only when Kyle's hands edged inside my shirt making their way to my breasts, I woke up. I had never been touched like that. No man had ever gone past the casual kiss-n-grope before I ended things.

His hand slid higher under my blouse. "You've no idea how hard it is for me not to rip off this flimsy thing."

My man-hater trained reflexes turned on. In the innermost recesses of my mind, an alarm began to beep. Elevated Risk Yellow. Kyle's hands spanned my back, finding the flap of my strapless bra. It was louder now. High-Risk Orange. In an expert split second, he snapped open my bra. I did not know how to proceed and froze, my eyes widening. I was conflicted. I wanted him to stop but also for him to continue. I whimpered as his hand paused over my bare breasts. *What are you waiting for, Kyle?* My breast ached to be touched by his hands. By his mouth.

The alarm was louder now, burning in my ears. *Kyle Paxton: Severe-Risk Red.* Something burst inside me like a bullet to the gut. The coldness spread and I clenched every part of me shut.

Noting my reticence, he stilled. "Are you all right?"

"Maybe not here?"

"June-Bug, yes. I want you. But not like this."

In the most distrustful corner of my mind, this triggered a sour memory. *Juniper, I want you to be my Summer.*

His eyes impaled me and then he pulled up. "I'll stop."

"Don't."

For a second he was confused, then with a frustrated groan, he clenched his hands into fists and boxed in my body. His lips traced my jaw, found my lips and locked me again in their merciless hold. We kissed long but tender this time and it was tenuous and aching. It was deeper than a kiss—as if he sought something beyond the urges of his body.

This was for my benefit, as I knew he had gauged my lack of expertise and felt the earlier violence of his kisses had freaked me. I knew from the hesitant hands that moved over my body and the restrained heat of his lips, tenderness was uncharted territory for him. I am sure he was taken aback that he even had it in him. Grateful for his restraint, I was drowning—lost

270

to another place where alarms did not exist. Nothing did, except for us.

At some point, we heard a discreet knock and Kyle pulled up and looked at the door. Cold air drifted between us, cooling my body. When no one came in, he shrugged, and his lips went back to mine...but the spell was broken. I went still as the fears crept back like a dream gone dark. *What am I doing?*

Did he think I was saying yes to becoming his...oh God, why couldn't I even say it now? It was not what I wanted. I just wanted him without contracts, without conditions, without timelines and without—what terrified me most—termination dates.

"Kyle. Stop." Gasping, I tore my lips away and wriggled until he freed me.

"What is it?" He eased himself off me, his eyes torpid.

"What if they come back?" Raising myself up, I looked around. It was a lie I told to keep him from reading what I was actually thinking.

"Fine." He leaned forward to fasten my bra in one fluid motion—and this particular talent of his made me a little jealous.

I fluffed and fixed my hair as he put back the sofa cushions that had been dislodged by the frenzy. Once he was done, he sat down next to me, his face inscrutable and his eyes distant. Confused at this, I scooted closer and pressed a few chaste kisses on his cool cheek.

He gave me a searching look and then his forehead pressed against mine. "Juniper, I lose control around you...I try, but I can't stop." He sounded almost angry.

"Oh."

"Ever since I met you, I can't stop thinking about you. Can't stop thinking about doing this to you." An errant finger traced the hollow of my throat and ran up and down its length.

I exhaled. My lips still burned with the pressure of his lips. My cheeks longed to feel the scruff of his stubble and my hands longed to explore every inch of his hard-and-soft body. We were both helpless in this damned pull between us. Like green slime in a horror flick, it could not be contained.

Then why contain it? "Then, don't stop."

"You are a very confusing lady."

"I may have cognitive dissonance," I said, in a lighter tone.

Kyle gave me a sharp look, one jet-black eyebrow raised. "You've changed your mind about my offer?"

"No," I said, but when I saw his face darken, I shrugged. "But I'm yours tonight."

Great Spirit, what am I saying? Even I did not know what I meant by that.

"Don't say things like that. I'll kidnap you and take you to my house. And keep you awake all night long. All week long."

"Then do it, Kyle," I whispered, my body heating up again.

What is happening to me? Will the frozen and frigid Juniper Mills please stand up?

I had lost my fears and inhibitions. With a shaking hand, I picked up my mojito and shook the minty dredges of my drink. As I drained my glass, I realized I rarely drank, and this bold badass stranger was a really Dutch courage creation.

"Tempting as that is, I won't. It's not you talking. Once you're no longer buzzed in the morning, I'll have to face your regret."

This is hard. Knitting my fingers, I looked away. I wanted Kyle. I wanted him enough to give up my moral dogma, my mom's twisted fears, my deep-seated neurosis, and the few things I had in my little life that weren't shitty. But he was right...if I gave into him now, I'd regret it. I guess, the man-hater in me had not fled the building.

"Let's pick up where we left off at your hotel and tell me where you think I stand. Just be honest with me." He gave me a contrite smile, picked up his untouched drink and pressed the icy glass to his cheeks.

"All right, I'll be honest." Tucking my legs under me, I snuggled closer to him on the couch and cleared my throat. "Kyle, I think you're special… intriguing…and I'd like to get to know you…more. But even if I really want to jump into bed with you, I won't, not until I am sure of us. That may be the way kids are doing things these days, but it's not how I do things. I have scary self-control. If it makes me a backwaters basic girl, so be it." I hesitated, feeling like I was in the Felicia Grunde chatroom again, trolled by judging voices, out of place and time.

He was listening intently, his eyes on my face, a slight smile on his lips. He had not even taken a sip of the drink in his hand. Perhaps he needed to be clear-headed as I was rambling and semi-drunk. "Go on."

"Well, I'm not ashamed of the way I am." Lifting my chin, I stared defiantly at him. "I accept myself. And my choices. Just because the world is going in one direction, it doesn't make it right. And I give zero fucks about the evolution of modern relationships."

"I see."

"And, yes. I'm really attracted to you. But I'm torn. You do things another way. You and I, Kyle, belong in different worlds. A different time, a different place…maybe even dimension. So I don't know…where we stand."

"I'm sorry." Kyle chuckled. "I zoned after you said you are very excessively, ridiculously, insanely attracted to me."

"Just saying what my body has already confirmed. Maybe more than my body." *More than my body, what the hell?*

At that, he squared his shoulders and turned from me, his eyes stony again. "If I was a good person, Juniper, I'd stay away from you. For I'll just hurt you."

"Hurt me? How?"

When he did not answer, I extended my numb legs and walked to the window. I squinted at the shifting laser lights, trying to spot Stacy or Trevor, but I only saw a mass of dancers in flashes of psychedelic colors. Kyle followed me and leaned against the doorpost, watching the lights turn my skin into alien shades. Laser red, orange, green, blue. I returned the favor, enjoying the red light on his face that made him look sinister and hawkish.

I should tell him now...that, so far, he is my one and only sorta-relationship.

Nope. He's scared stiff of commitment.

My confession will make him run away like Speedy Gonzales.

He spoke up, his voice low, "You know what I think? I think you should walk away from me, Juniper."

His words were an icy bucket splashed on my numb brain. I felt a pang of anxiety. So this was what it felt like to be forced to leave Kyle Paxton. A man who knew time was all we had to give, and gave this precious commodity in small doses, addictive as crack.

To control us all.

The sharp shooting pain in my ribs that I now felt...was this what Izzy felt? In an odd moment of female solidarity, I felt bad for her. He offered only his body and gave us no other choice. *He forgets the mind and heart are attached to the body.*

I inhaled sharply. "I can't do that, Kyle. I...think...I need you in my life. Even if it is for a short time."

For a few moments, he looked down at the white synthetic fur on the floor, lit up with lurid colors from the club and then he said, "You don't need me in your life. I've done things I am not proud of. You don't know what I am like."

"So clarify Mr. Kyle Paxton for me. Right now, I'm lost. Are you slamming the door in my face or inviting me in?"

"I want you. In. Always. But you're so different from others I've been with. And it would kill me if I hurt you. That's the last thing I want."

"But why do you have rules and systems then? Why do you not have girlfriends? Why are you this way?"

"Lots of reasons."

"Give me one."

"Time. There are few things I can rely on as constants. Time is one of them."

Puzzled, I frowned. "Okay…"

"What is accepted, like you said, is not always right."

"I don't follow."

"A mind is a powerful thing, Juniper. It also tricks us because we are not as advanced as our brain's potential. It tries to synchronize the sensory info it gets from our bodies in a way that will make sense to us. This is why society is set up to be—basic and stultifying to our potential."

"So you are above it all? A demi-god laughing at us measly mortals?"

His expression grew somber. "I don't understand why you're having such a difficult time with my system. The end is always inevitable, Juniper. I just set it in a calendar so that it's easier to swallow. Now, would you be alright with me dating you, going out with you, making false promises… like all men do? And then cheating on you and dropping you like a hot potato, when a new girl comes along…like men do?"

"Not all men are like that by the way. And it takes two to cheat. So you're saying you're incapable of fidelity."

"Don't put words in my mouth. That is not what I meant. Wouldn't it be better if you know what to expect and when to expect it?"

"Okay. I get it." I gave him a look that made it clear I thought he was a masochistic jerk.

Pained, he shook his head. "No, you don't. I am mostly this way… because…I have an odd mental condition."

"What is it? Tell me. Please. Help me understand."

All of a sudden, he walked away from me to the couch and stood with his back to me, arms up massaging his neck. Then he came back just as quickly as he had left. "Okay, I'll tell you. Juniper, don't freak out if you don't believe me."

"Why would I…freak out?"

"It's hard to explain…I have this damned condition. It's my mind. My clockwork mind. You can't diagnose it or heal it with therapy. I have a systematic, goal-seeking time bomb in my head. I don't need alarm clocks. I don't need schedules. Or calendars. Or calculators. It's all in my head. Picoseconds. Nanoseconds. Seconds. Minutes. Hours. Months. Dates. I need a system. So I can plan my life…years ahead. Sometimes decades."

I went slack-jawed, trying to process the shift in the conversation. "Wait. Are you serious? You can tell time in your head?"

He nodded solemnly. "My mind also calculates automatically. I can see size, space, length, distance, the freaking cubic square volume of every object around me. Millimeters, inches, feet, yards, miles. It's constant." With a faraway look in his eyes, he pointed to his forehead, his voice low and flat. "This is a calculator. A timepiece. Tick tock. That's all I hear."

"Literally or figuratively?"

"Both."

I shot out a hand and enclosed his watch. "What time is it now?"

"10:15, fifty six seconds," he said, without so much as a flicker of the eye.

Stunned, I uncovered the face of his watch. "You're right."

"In Córdoba, Argentina, it is currently 3:15 a.m. The couch we sat on was 32 cubic feet. This room is 8 by 10 by 8, a total of 640 cubic feet."

"Come on. Maybe six hundred forty-ish," I said with a raised eyebrow.

"There is no ish with me, it is all exact. Absolute."

"Oh my God, Kyle. That is amazing. But how in the world?"

He shrugged. "God knows. I found out the hard way I'm a freak. In first grade when they were teaching telling time, I raised my hand and asked why we need clocks when humans know what time it is? Let's just say, the teacher gave me a weird look and I ended up with a bloody nose in recess."

"No wonder you're a genius inventor. Your mind is a gift."

"And a curse. My clockwork mind fucking rules me, Juniper. I don't know how to be spontaneous, how to enjoy life without arranging fun, how to survive without a plan, how to live without structure, how to lose control. How *not* to fit and control other people in my clockwork code like cogs and gears."

"I've never heard of anything like that. I guess it explains a lot."

He looked at me, his navy eyes cloudy. "Funny, I've never told that to anyone before. I've spent my life pretending to fit in. Watching others to figure out what normal is."

"Normal...I don't know if there is such a thing. People are only normal from a distance," I whispered.

He smiled. "I don't want to burden you, nor do I expect you to understand, but I want you to know why I am a monster."

"You are not." A lump formed in my throat, for despite the blank way he spoke, I felt the ache in his voice, the loneliness in his words, and the vulnerability in his eyes. I had never seen him falter from his alpha-male façade at any time, and so this fragmented man in front of me was fascinating. Intriguing. Complex. Just my type.

Danger bells again.

I inched closer to him and smiled consolingly. "I understand. Most of the stuff we fight is inside us. And you...you're just coping with life."

"Juniper, you are pure. I can tell. Please don't idolize me. See me as I am. I am not coping. I have a psycho need to control others. I'm a total sociopath."

Instinctively, I took a step back. "But why?"

"I don't know why. I can't live with variables. I must know what the future holds. So I use my present to control my future. Mostly I don't get why people do what they do. I can't predict how they'll behave. But I must know what they will do. So I set legal bounds to control other people's behavior. My staff, my family, my…companions. That way I control their future as it relates to me."

"Is this why you have these rules, Kyle? For the girls in your life?"

"Yeah, I guess. You were right. I am part machine. I am calculating. Inhuman. I am not a person. I'm a system."

"You know, Kyle, I may mess up your system."

"You already have." He looked up with a sad smile that made my heart twinge.

"I like that I messed up your system."

"I like that too." Pausing, he faced the dance floor. "It kills me that I cannot be with you any other way."

I made a small move to touch his tense shoulders and he dragged me into his arms, in a vice-like embrace. Trapped in his limbs, I felt his pain drifting to me like an icy wave. I knew Kyle was not a human clock…he was just broken. I wondered who had hurt him. What traumatized him? What made him rely on planning as a coping mechanism? Grief? Neglect? Anger? Or hate. I did not know if I should ask him or shut up. So I just let him hold me for a few minutes.

When he eased his grip, I spoke up. "Did something happen? With… someone?" I knew I was pushing my luck when I saw the light go from his eyes and he sucked in his breath.

Letting me go, he shrugged. "It's a long story."

"So something did happen."

"Yes. Long ago."

"Tell me."

"It will not answer your questions."

"Tell me about her, Kyle." Palming his cheek, I turned his face towards mine.

His large hand cupped my jaw and a stray thumb stroked my cheek. My face nuzzled in the warmth of his hand. "No, June-Bug. I can't. I've never told anyone."

I let it go.

I did not know what troubled him. All I knew was that Kyle Paxton had something dark and warped clawing him from inside. He had a history more complex than the average childhood loneliness that is the product of divorced parents.

I took a deep breath. "Kyle, I get it. You can isolate your heart and mind and remove intimacy from relationships, but I can't. To me it is all…linked. I think we are at an impasse. Again."

"You're right. Maybe there is a solution. Meet me halfway."

"How?"

"I have never done this, but you, Juniper Mills, are the strangest person I've met. I want you. And I think you want me too. So let me offer a negotiation span."

"What do you mean?"

"Stay with me for two days."

"How? I'm leaving on Saturday."

"Easy. I'll change your flight from Saturday to Monday. Stay at my house."

My heart raced. The idea of staying in the very house of this handsome urbane man, who made me forget everything I knew before I met him, was heady. I flushed and asked, "Kyle, so you mean—?"

His lips parted and his eyes smoked. I felt the heat rise up again between us like a slow forest fire. After a long moment, he shook his head. "I can't think, then. So I promise you, nothing physical. Let's just get to know each other this weekend."

"You realize what it means when you say nothing physical?"

My head swam. I'd been a virgin all my boring adult life, and I was not ready to lose that part of me, just yet. I had decided—or perhaps a subconscious part of me had decided—that I would lose it to Kyle. I'd only been on a handful of pathetic dates with men and my lack of interest was a turnoff, so I was rarely asked out again—let alone asked to spend the night.

The idea of us, alone, in his beautiful Seacliff house was scary— and hot as hell. My life was getting exciting, pretty damn quickly.

"That will be torture for me, I promise. I expect nothing. But I want you to know what I am really like beyond all of these first perceptions of me. Stay with me. Please." Kyle pulled me into his arms and I felt the length of his entire body molding to mine.

"So what will we do? Exchange cards? Read poetry? Eat heart-shaped pancakes?"

His laugh rumbled over my head, his breath fanning my hair. "No, June-Bug. I'll take you around San Francisco. And you can see what being with me will be like. I will be yours completely for two days. No distractions. No work. Just you and me."

For two days. Stop putting time stamps on what we have, Kyle.

"What do you see as the outcome of this?"

"Think of it as a trail. A preview. If you like it, become my Summer. If not, we part ways."

KYLE

December 9, 9:56 p.m. 19 seconds
(The Cave Club, San Francisco)

K yle Paxton never backtracked in business. He never negotiated. There was a good reason for that. Negotiation was weakness. If you negotiated, you failed your own business. Now he was negotiating with her, and his system, which had always succeeded, would fail.

But, it's already failed with her.

The bugs were back. The errors were back. The shooting pain in his left eye was back. Kyle's system was splintered. And the numbers, the hours, the minutes, the seconds fell and fell in his mind like a black rain.

A rain of metallic numbers torn from old watches and clocks.

Glossy and sharp like a black metallic cut-out.

He tried to focus on her beautiful face, the face that haunted him every nanosecond, but all he saw were numbers of metal.

Falling. Falling. Falling.

CHAPTER 18

Part ways. *Part ways. Part ways.* I had never heard more defining words. Did Kyle know how dangerous he was? I could not bear the thought of parting from him. I did not want him for a day or two. Nor for five months. *I want forever.*

A sick feeling pulsed in my midriff. I realized there was something really wrong with me—just like there was something really wrong with my mother. I obsessed. I became too quickly attached. I wore horse blinders to avoid signs and omens. My heart raced ahead of logic, far ahead of any indication of emotion from the object of my affection. His clear-cut offer was twisted in my heart as forever. That word and others came crashing in my mind like high tide breakers.

Forever. Together. Love. Kyle.

No. No. No. Please don't go there.

Enjoy him for a brief moment. Hold that memory forever. And carry on.

Then, with my usual guilt, I thought about Cypress. I could say I had to stay back for work. He'd understand, wouldn't he? And he seemed to be doing all right. For once in my life, I had to choose me over others.

"Yes," I said. "Let's do it."

A rush of hope glittered in Kyle's eyes. "Juniper, I'll make it worth your while."

"You'd better. I am not cute when I'm disappointed." We exchanged smiles.

"Good. And after you stay with me, make your decision. Yes or no to being my Summer. If your answer is yes, I will send you the Termination Contract. Sign it. Send it back. Then—"

"Can we discuss this later?" Shooting away from him, I picked up two Jäger Bomb shots. I drained one and grimaced. What was this wicked concoction of energy drink and alcohol? It tasted like crushed charcoal and acidic black licorice.

I needed to breathe again. This back-and-forth between emotion and desire was too intense. Right now, I was in the power of his wizard influence. I was the low food-chain prey in a lion's claw. A peasant trembling at Lenin's Red Terror regime. I needed to be myself again. I needed to get out of here.

I handed him a shot glass and he shook his head. "No. This is pretty lethal stuff. Teenagers have been known to get heart attacks from it."

"Oh come on, Grandpops."

"Nope. I'm your designated driver."

"You don't have to drop me. I'll ride with the others. They're headed to the same hotel."

"No. You came with me and you're leaving with me."

It was then I noticed he had not had a drop of his drink. "At least have yours. Why don't you drink?"

"I found out the hard way, only absolute sobriety agrees with me."

"Why?"

"I like my head clear. Not jumbled."

"More for me then, Buzzkill." I picked up his Manhattan Rye.

"Enough. You've had enough, Juniper." In an instant, he took the glass from me and then poured the drink, ice and all, into a potted plant in the corner of the room.

"No. The ice. The ice. It's precious! Like crystals. I want the ice!"

"So drunk."

I laughed. I think a part of me was drunk and a part of me wanted to tell him off. "Kyle Paxton, you are such bossy guy. Such a Lenin. Paxton, the Godfather. Even your system is like the mafia." I started to talk in a deep voice. "Girls. Girls. Girls. Be my Summer. If you leave, I'll terminate you. If you don't, I'll terminate you. If you meet me after termination, don't make eye contact. Or I'll have you terminated."

Serious gaze fixed on my face, Kyle crossed his arms. "Judging how quickly you get drunk, you don't drink much, do you?"

He was right; I was barely a social drinker. "Nope. But I wanna dance, so who cares?"

"Do you really know how to dance, Miss First-Time-in-a-Club?"

"Is that a challenge? Challenge accepted." Arms akimbo, I tossed him an injured look and his lips curled in amusement. I went to the window and pulled open the panel doors. The deafening blare of music hit us. I swayed to the beat. I was happy. Animated.

Instantly Kyle was behind me, arms snaking around my waist, spooning me from behind. "I don't dance."

"Well, I do. So I'm going down there."

"No. Stay here with me." He draped my hair on one shoulder and planted a hot kiss on my nape.

I was breathless…but I twisted in his grip and freed myself. "No. I don't wanna be terminated like the ice." Stumbling to the table, I seized the last shot glass and went for the door.

"Juniper, what are you doing? You are plastered."

A thrill raced through me as I thumbed my nose at him and drank the last shot. Turning quickly, I ran out to the crowded hall and made my way down the stairs. On the main dance floor, I merged with the dancing crowd. I looked around for Stacy. All I saw was a mass of drunken bodies, jumping to loud music. The alcohol and energy drinks gave me a crazy adrenaline rush and I lifted my arms, dancing to the center of the dance floor.

On one end of the club was a DJ in front of a giant screen with a laser display. Under the screen was a stage where six young men were performing a K-pop dance. Hypnotized, I watched. They were excellent. When it ended, the dancers darted off the stage to booming applause.

"Yolo. Feel the beat. Time for the Cave's weekly dance-off. The winners get a thousand dollars. And top bragging rights. Five groups competing tonight. If there's anyone else, give your name to Yuri here. Yurrrrriiii." The DJ pointed to a young man standing next to him.

Hells yeah.

Pushing through the crowd, I went to the stage by Yuri and called him.

He jumped off the stage and yelled in my ear, "What is it?"

"So anyone can dance?"

"Those who know how. With any luck."

"Put me down," I screamed in his ear.

He looked at me in surprise. "You sure? The competition's pretty tough."

"Uh-huh." I nodded, wounded. What was wrong with people? Was it tattooed on my forehead that I could not dance?

He handed me his tablet. "Fill out this form. Do you have other people with you?"

"Uh…yes." Frantic, I looked around. Stacy, Trevor, Evan, and Kyle were nowhere to be seen.

"What's the name of your dance group?"

"Um…Museum Turtles, no…Celtic Cure. Yeah."

Yuri made me sign release forms and when he went to put them away, I grabbed his mic. "Hellooooo, clubbers, find my cute interns. Stacy and Trevor. Come to the stage, please. It's meeeee." My mouth was too close to the mic and my voice echoed even with the earsplitting music.

Yuri came running back and wrestled the mic from me. "Hell to the no." He covered the mic and said, "Look, lady, don't ever take my mic again." Then he spoke in it. "We request dance group Celtic Cure to please come to the stage. Stacy and Trevor."

I giggled and hiccupped. "Thank you, Yuri. You're the shizzle."

He frowned. "So what song you dancing to?"

I cocked my head. Cypress's favorite dance song was "A Light That Never Comes" by Linkin Park and Steve Aoki. I told Yuri and he climbed up on the stage to talk to the DJ. They both nodded at me. The broadcast worked. In a few seconds, Stacy and Trevor stood in front of me, and even in the shifting beams of light, I saw they looked concerned.

"What the hell is going on?" Trevor asked.

Yuri motioned to us. "Come on. You're up in five."

"Let's dance, my little lambchops." I swayed my arms.

"Are you okay?" Trevor asked.

I put both my arms on Stacy's shoulders and giggled. "Don't look so sad. You both look like Maastrichtian fossil eggs."

"Are you all there?" Stacy asked, peering into my eyes.

"Never been more here, goose." I guess I was a happy drunk.

"All right, Curator Gone Wild, come with us. We'll dance with you, but not on stage." Trevor grabbed my arm and started to lead me away.

"Dance on stage," I screamed, digging in my heels. A small part of me filed away that I was acting like a total loco but I was so drunk and high on life, I did not get how off-beam my behavior was.

"Nope. Not on stage. That's for professional dancers," Stacy said.

Frustrated, I shook my head. If there was one thing I knew how to do, it was synchronized dancing. Cypress and I had spent hundreds of hours in front of his dance video games, dancing to every club song known to mankind. On the restricted list of things that I could do with Cypress, it was my favorite. If Stacy and Trevor could imitate my moves then I could show Mr. Kyle Paxton I could dance.

"Look, Fruit Loops, we're gonna dance and we're gonna win."

"Is she nuts?" Trevor yelled over my head.

"No, just smashed." Stacy's pretty brow wrinkled.

I poked her forehead with one finger. "Don't do that. You'll be a wrinkly pruny. Teehee."

"No wonder she never drinks," said Trevor. "Or goes to clubs."

"Junie. Kyle is looking for you," Stacy said.

"Where's my Buzzkill?" I rasped, my voice hoarse from screaming.

"He stepped out to make a call. Let's go," she said, grabbing my wrist.

"Nope." Tearing myself away, I ran back to the stage.

On seeing me, the DJ announced, "Give it up for the Celtic Cure dancing to Linkin Park's 'Light That Never Comes.'"

"Don't let me die alone," I yelled, running up the stage stairs.

Stacy and Trevor just stood there looking stumped. I pleaded with puppy dog eyes and, shaking their heads, they bounded up the stage stairs. I led them to the center of the stage.

"It's okay, little Pampers. Just copy me. I'm in the middle, but gimme space."

Just then the beat got louder and my adored song vibrated through the club. A few feet in front of Stacy and Trevor, I swayed my body in synch with the music. They were still confused but copying me well. Our rhythmic steps escalated to a complex dance, which was a little hip-hop, a little tap dance, a little K-pop, a bit of Samba, a lot of hops and landings. From time to time, I turned to check on Stacy and Trevor. They were doing a pretty good job of keeping up.

I had danced to this tune a million times on our PlayStation, but never in front of a bigger audience than a mirror and my twin brother. At first, there was little interest from the club goers, but as I got more engrossed in the beat, we attracted some attention.

We got some hoots and even the DJ yelled, "Yeah. Check out Celtic Cure."

Before I knew it, we had the crowd whipped into a frenzy by our moves. As adrenaline spiked through my body, I got little goose bumps, like someone was watching only me. Was he here? I scanned the crowd looking for a pair of cool navy eyes. I felt his presence even before I saw him.

There he is.

Kyle stood still at the head of the staircase, leaning over the railing, his face inscrutable. Even from across the space between us, I felt his eyes pin me. Even from across the room full of people, I felt a shared jolt. My heart slammed into my rib cage. My stomach knotted with panic. And elation. In that moment, I knew I was going to belong to Kyle. I had never felt this way before. And I knew it was not possible to feel this way for any other human on earth.

Stumbling for a second, I forgot a step and missed a beat of the dance. We were four minutes into the dance and almost at the end. Tearing my gaze away from Kyle, I recovered and pirouetted smoothly. And then as the song's finale rocked the club, I threw my arms up and slid across the stage on my knees, the burn of velocity making me glad I was wearing silky jeans.

The crowd went wild and there was loud applause as the DJ shouted, "Wow. Give it up for Celtic Cure. Yolo. Feel the beat at the Cave."

Heralded as heroes, we walked down the stairs proudly.

"How in the world?" Trevor hissed in my ear.

Stacy pumped my hand. "That. Was. Freaking. Awesome. I had no idea our nerdy little curator knew how to dance."

"You have no idea what I know, Tinkerbell." I leaned on her shoulders, looking at the stairs, hoping to see Kyle smiling at me. But he was not there. Feeling needle jabs of defeat, I wondered if I had just imagined him there a few minutes ago.

As we made our way back to the dance floor, several people hi-fived us and others shook our hands. Hovering around Stacy and me was a long line of young men waiting to dance. That was a shocker. This was every weekend in Stacy's life, but this had never happened to me before. She melted into the dark with one of the Korean dancers and I stood in the middle of a group of guys, all asking me to dance with them. One blonde young man was particularly tenacious. The other men had left when I told them no, but he would not give up. Half expecting Kyle behind me, I scanned the entire hall. But he was nowhere to be seen.

Feeling let down, I finally smiled at the young man. "Okay, one dance."

"Can I get you a drink first?"

I nodded.

Pulling my wrist, he led me to the bar. "Pick your poison."

"Ginger ale. Please."

"Very mild poison."

"I've had half a dozen already." I observed him as he ordered my drink. He was short with a muscular physique, his boyish good looks enhanced by his long blond waves. He definitely looked a few years younger than me.

"Hey, I know a good joke," he said.

"Shoot."

"A bar is just a pharmacy with a limited inventory. You like?"

"Limited in humor, I'd say."

"Okay. I'll try harder. Two guys walk into a bar. They drink a lot. Guy one says, 'Hey, this drink gives you energy.' Both guys order the drink. Guy one jumps from the ten-story bar and flies away. The second guy jumps out and falls down dead. Guy one flies back in and sits at the bar. The bartender shakes his head and says, 'You're mean when you're drunk, Superman.' Huh?"

I smiled. "Still lukewarm."

"Okay, you go."

I only knew nerdy stuff. "How's this? Dyslexic man walks into a bra."

He laughed. "You win."

"So you gotta name? Or only bad jokes?"

"I'm Joshua," he yelled in my ear. "You?"

"Um. Jessica," I lied.

"You're a great dancer, Jessica. Amazing." He handed me a ginger ale glass and picked up a beer bottle.

"Thanks." I sucked at my straw.

"Tell me where you go? I'll hit the same clubs."

"I'm just visiting San Francisco from New York."

"Oh." He frowned. "I'm a lucky guy tonight.

"Not tonight. Just one dance, 'member?"

"Yes, ma'am. So Jessica, what do you do?"

"I'm a securities broker. And you?"

"I surf."

"All day?"

"Well, I'm a chef. I'm usually not off at nights. I own a restaurant on Ocean Beach. Bistro Voltaire."

"Cool name. I approve. You look too young to own your own place."

He tugged his shoulder length locks. "It's the damned hair. I have some contracts. So I gotta keep it. I'm twenty-five. You?"

"One year older."

"Damn you are hot, babe. Don't look a day over barely legal." He whistled and gave me a once over.

We flirted until we finished our drinks and then he led me to the dance floor. DJ Lord Mixer was rocking the house with a Swedish House Mafia number. I allowed Joshua to dance close to me but I did not allow him to hold me. We danced well together and when the number ended, I screamed in Joshua's ears. "You rock at dancing. And cooking. And surfing."

"I want you to come to my restaurant. And see me cooking. And surfing."

"A surfing kitchen? Wow."

"It is beachfront."

"Cool. Okay, I gotta go." With a slow smile, I blew him an air kiss.

Damn. I did not know I could flirt.

"Don't go. One more dance. Please," he begged, his warm honey eyes crinkling at the corners.

All of the sudden, I was pulled into the arms of another man dancing close by. I had noticed him watching me.

Joshua glared at him. "Hey. Get lost. I was with her."

I smiled at him. "It's all right. I'll come back to you."

In the end, I danced with four other men before Joshua reclaimed me. He led me to the edge of the dance floor and we danced close together to a hypnotic number. His arms went around my waist and he swung me around. "I've been watching you, Jessica. I can't peel my eyes away. You're so beautiful. Give me your number."

Smiling enticingly, I shook my head. "I don't have a number."

"No cells in New York?"

"No cell towers either."

"Dang. Jessica. Girl. You are killing me."

This was fun. I was going to regularly attend clubs. The life of Juniper Mills—frigid, boring museum curator who wrote about Celtic history—seemed to be another life. This was the life of my virtual reality avatar: hot broker from New York who loved dancing and drinking and was in control of all aspects of her life.

The music became low, soft and seductive. Taking cue from the couples around us, Joshua pressed me to his chest and his hands tightened around my waist. He smelled like the beach, balsamic vinegar and beer. I stiffened and though I tried to move away, he did not let go. Thinking about Kyle, I felt uneasy. I wished he was dancing with me. Even dancing with another man felt oh-so-wrong. Damn Kyle. He spoiled my fun even when he was absent. I looked around for him. I had not seen him for two whole hours. Stacy had said he had to take a few calls outside and I wondered if he had left.

Well. That's depressing.

Craning my neck, I spotted Evan at the bar deep in conversation with a handsome young man. Besides him, Trevor stared sadly at the drink in his hand. I guess he had struck out with Stacy again. *Kids these days.* And that's when I saw Stacy. She was dancing near me with a couple in a risqué way—the girl was pressed against her and the man was hugging her from behind. *Stacy is insane.* Catching her attention, I winked at her for mastering the ménage-a-trois dance.

"Have you seen Kyle?" I screamed.

She lifted her arms and pretended to be talking on an invisible phone.

"He's on the phone?"

"Outside." With a dramatic nod, she pointed to the exit.

I sighed. Kyle Paxton. Ruined my evening. This was not my plan. I wanted him to follow me and dance with me. Not take work calls outside the club.

"Who's Kyle? Your boyfriend?" Joshua asked when he saw my face fall.

Boyfriend. Ha. "No. Far from it."

"How do I get a hold of you? Come on, babe." Then he proceeded to roll up his sleeves to reveal a tanned and muscular forearm full of skull and surfing tattoos. "Tattoo your number here."

"Where? You're as inked as the Rock."

"Find a spot." With a flourish, Joshua produced a sharpie and handed it to me.

"How is it you carry a sharpie? Some kind of narcissistic disorder?" Hmm. My thoughts were clearer, looks like the alcohol was wearing off slightly.

"I appear on a few cooking TV shows and get recognized quite often," he said, with a hangdog grin.

"Dude, I did not know I was dancing with a celebrity. So truly a narcissistic disorder." I started to write my phone number by his right elbow.

"Thank you, babe." Leaning forward, he kissed my cheek.

Suddenly he was dragged away from me and I found myself starring in the furious glittering eyes of Kyle. "Time to go."

Inserting himself between us, Joshua met Kyle's glare with equal fire and said, "Excuse you. I am with her."

Kyle gave him a look that would have frozen a scorching coal. "Listen, boy. Don't want to soil my knuckles with your brain-sauce, so vanish."

"I'll smash your teeth in your diaper, old man. So you vanish."

Whoa. Whoa. How'd that escalate so fast?

"Hey both of you, chill," I said, but no one was listening to me.

"Time for a lesson, Goldilocks," muttered Kyle to Joshua.

Examining Kyle head-to-toe, Joshua's hands formed into fists. "Bring it, Pappy. Or fuck off."

"You should, if you value chewing."

"Stop it," I yelled. People around us were beginning to take notice of the testosterone soaked threats and a circle of onlookers formed around us. A few people held up their smartphones to record the scene. I groaned.

Kyle pushed me behind him and hauled Joshua up by his collar. Joshua tried to punch his taller but leaner opponent, but somehow Kyle moved faster and punched harder. Momentarily reeling, Joshua took a few steps back. Cursing and gnashing his teeth, he charged at Kyle with both fists clenched. He began battering Kyle's chest while Kyle tried to shake him off. When Joshua did not let him go, Kyle smashed two fists on his opponent's chest, shoving him away. He then turned to me and gestured for us to get out.

I had never seen a bar fight in my life and just stood there—scared stiff. With Kyle's back to him, Joshua took the chance and grabbed two beer bottles from a waiter passing by. First, he threw beer over Kyle, which spilled all over on me. Then he hit Kyle's back with a beer bottle. I gasped as the bottle smashed in amber glass shards.

Turning blindly, Kyle's rage got the better of him and he landed a chain of blows on Joshua. It happened so fast, I only saw a blur. It ended with Joshua lying on the floor with a bloody nose in a pile of broken glass.

Seeing the blood jet from Joshua's nose, I bent down by him. "Oh my God, are you all right? I'm so sorry."

He groaned and put an arm on his face. "Stay away from me, crazy lady."

"Let's go." In a jiffy, I found myself being hauled up. Kyle wrapped an arm around me and moved me through a quickly parting crowd.

I twisted in his arms. "Hey. Hey. Kyle. Stop."

"Hush, we will talk in the car."

"Don't you hush me. Lemme go."

Holding me with a firm grip, he strode out of the big barn doors of The Cave. A chilly blast hit my face as I tried to pull myself away from his manic grip.

A valet stood there with Kyle's car keys, trying to ignore our scuffling. "Here you go, sir."

Kyle handed him a note and led me to the passenger side. "Get in."

"No," I screamed. "I'm going back with the others."

Frowning, he gathered me in his arms, lifted me so very easily and seated me in car. I writhed against his chest until I realized he was not even trying to hold me down, so strong were his arms compared to my puny efforts. Bending over, he put my seat belt on, securely.

"Kyle, you've gone insane. Return me immediately."

"Miss Mills, I am taking you back to the hotel."

"Just drop me back. Do *not* talk to me."

"We *will* talk." He sealed my door shut and went around to sit down in the driver's seat. Coolly, he locked the doors and started to drive away.

"How could you do that? You freaking broke his nose!"

"Please lower your voice. I hate drama."

"Oh, well *you* created the drama."

His face was impassive and his eyes briefly flicked over me. "He was salivating all over you. I don't like to share."

"Are you kidding me? Share? I am not your plaything! And I haven't signed anything yet. I haven't agreed to *any* of your terms. You said we'd talk about it. If you don't mind, just forget the idea of me staying back."

"No. I want you to stay."

"You behaved like a crazy person in there, Kyle."

"I protect what is mine."

"Oh my God. I am not yours and you're not mine, do you understand?"

"Not yet. You will be." His voice was clipped and cold but the meaning behind it warmed my heart.

To be his...

Damn it. Get a grip, Juniper. He's a raging lunatic. Not to mention a bigoted, chauvinistic control freak bull. Run away. All two thousand miles between California and Detroit.

Crossing my arms, I sagged against the black leather and rubbed my eyes. I was bone-tired. "Why... why, Kyle?"

"Juniper. I told you, I expect and give fidelity." His hand arced in the air towards me as he drove with his left hand. My heart sank when I noticed his knuckles had blood on them, until I realized it was Joshua's blood, not Kyle's. Not caring about Joshua's spilt blood made me a terrible person, I supposed.

"You do realize the definition of fidelity is devotion to one person. One person. Not the flipping rolodex of dolls you use. Fidelity. Allegiance. Loyalty. Commitment. Things you know nothing about."

"I am not what you think." His hand came to rest on my knee and a quiver sprung from his hands and ran up my thighs.

"Oh yeah? But I know what sexist bullshit looks like." I slapped his hand away, my hands forming into fists on my knees. "So for five months you expect utter medieval loyalty slash fidelity and then you don't care a fig about who I go off with?"

"Don't ask me that."

"Answer my question, Kyle. So now I am virtually your ethics prisoner.

And after five months, you won't care who I dance with? Sleep with?"

"No." A muscle jerked in his jaw and after a long pause, he muttered, "After you are no longer with me, I won't care."

He is unhinged. Even in my furious state, I was hurt. I already cared too much and my feelings for him would not change after five months. Tears rushed to my eyelids and I gulped, forcing the tears back. "It doesn't make sense."

"Only predictable outcomes make sense."

"What the hell does that mean?"

"I told you I hate unpredictability. It causes instability. Too many variables. Total chaos. And this kind of garbage is exactly what I was talking about."

Garbage? A bitter ache swirled in my bloodstream with the alcohol. My eyes traced his profile that was already so dear to me, with the dark sweep of his lashes, the arch of his black brows, the slight aquiline contour of his nose, the etched jawline with its dark stubble, and the sensual compressed lips—lips that had mad skills. Kyle Paxton was under my skin, in my blood; he was already too much a part of me. I would hate to tear him away, like flesh from bone.

Yet...the end is inevitable.

Five months of memories would not ease the pain that would come after he left. I could not sign the Termination Contract. I could not be with him the way he wanted. And I could not turn my private life into a cheap public drama exposed to my colleagues and friends. I had worked too long to quarantine myself in my little family unit. The first relationship I was *sort of* having was turning out to be an epic fail.

I knew I had to end it. End it now, even before it began.

"Look. We tried. But I feel we're not going to work...even for five months. We're just too different."

"Don't say that. I want us to work," he said.

I want us to work too. I squeezed my eyes shut. "Then you cannot act like this. You cannot exert this Taliban-like control over my life, about who I dance with, what I drink, where I go for fun with my friends, which hotel room I stay in, who picks me up from the airport, and know every bit of my travel schedule. I want complete autonomy of my life. Is that clear?"

"Crystal." He nodded, and to my chagrin, his profile looked entertained.

Is he patronizing me? "Be serious, Kyle."

"I am. I told you it's hard for me to lose control over any part of my life. When I first met you, Juniper, I thought you were very organized, very predictable and would stick to a schedule, but I now see that you are very unpredictable."

"So is that your criteria for picking a girl? Must be predictable? Must schedule life? Fit in a gelatin mold?"

"No. It is not. But I look for stability so that they can understand the cold-blooded way my mind works. And can fit into my system."

"Kyle Paxton, you are so fucked up."

He clamped both his hands on the steering wheel and frowned in concentration as he navigated a perilous downhill road. "I know. It's why I created a system to prevent me from fucking up more. It works—my planning. So far I have not had anyone mess with my system. Except you."

"Tell me something. Do you treat all your other fuck-buddies like this? Your Summers, your Winters. Do you control who they dance with, who they talk with, who they go out with, what they drink, when they travel? Do you stalk them when they dance and act like a jealous boyfriend?"

"No."

"Please elaborate. So you've never been jealous of Izzy?"

He turned to look at me and our eyes met in the dark. "No. Never.

You're the only one I am possessive about."

The only one. I flushed and looked out into the San Francisco void. "Christ, when you say things like that, I get so confused." This sort of talk was so unlike what I had expected in his clinical arrangement. This sort of relationship-py talk was dangerous for me—like giving a drug addict a tub of the finest Colombian Highland cocaine.

"Things are never simple with me. Rules make it easy for me and whoever I am with."

"I don't want to hear about your rules for another second," I yelled.

"Calm down, Juniper."

"Alright." I lowered my voice. "Tell me about the other girls." Pins and needles of anger jabbed me...I hated the idea of Kyle Paxton and other girls. The image of him making love to—no *fucking*—the others, holding them, kissing them, made me sad and angry all at once. Even more reason to end it before he caused me irreversible harm.

"What do you want to know?" His voice was frosty. Distant.

"How do they feel about ending things? How do you pick them? Why did you pick me?"

"None of them are like you."

"Well, that's obvious. I'm no supermodel."

"No, I mean that in a good way. They've been all calculating and cold. Businesslike. It was a transaction—a reciprocal interchange. Most of them wanted something from me and gave into what I wanted."

"Which is what? Complete and utter possession of their bodies and lives?"

He groaned. "It's not like that."

"Then what is it like?"

"Enough. Rest now. On Friday, I *will* pick you up. We *will* go out. After that you *will* come to my house for dinner like a good girl. You will schmooze with all the San Francisco Museum board members I invited. And afterwards, you *will* stay with me for two days and I'll answer all your questions."

I twisted my hands in my lap in frustration. Part of me wanted to protest, to keep on fighting and resisting the Red Terror Lenin in him, but inside me was a wide-eyed girl belting out romantic ballads and telling me that we wanted nothing more than to give in to this man, listen to and obey his commands, and be with him. Deeper inside me was a seductive drunken creature, coiling in pleasure, who whispered how turned on she was and all she wanted was to be in bed with Kyle Paxton. Outnumbering man-hater Juniper, they muzzled her.

"I want us to work and I'll do anything to make it happen," he said.

"I do too—I think."

His jaw clenched and I knew he was done talking when he turned up the low music coming from the car stereo. I recognized it as epic movie music, some composition that I was too weary to identify. I gave into sheer exhaustion and dug into the leather seat, tucking my legs under me. My eyelids felt like tomb lids. Heavy as ancient stone.

I must have dozed off. The next thing I remember was standing in an elevator with Kyle. My body was curved to him and his arms were curled around my waist. I looked around, blinking. "Where are we?"

Just then, the elevator doors pinged open and I recognized the beige carpeted hallway to my suite at the Q Hotel. With an indulgent smile, Kyle pulled me out of the elevators and walked me down the hallway. Even as I tottered in my unsteady heels, I was slowly waking up.

I giggled. "Boss, is this my walk of shame?"

He laughed. "Sort of."

All of a sudden, I turned and he stopped in mid-step. I wrapped my arms around Kyle's waist, nuzzled my nose in his neck and laughed softly.

"Thank all of yous, Godfather Paxton, for dopping me."

"Dopping?"

Semi-asleep, my upper body slumped against his chest and my arms tightened around his waist, stroking his back. Feeling a rip, I gasped, pulled away and walked around him. He spun around in surprise, but I kept stumbling around until my hands touched the back of his shirt. The sight of the tear in his shirt made my heart constrict. I traced the rip and saw a tiny wound on his left shoulder blade. He stiffened as I caressed it.

"Baby. You're hurt. Beer bottle blood smash hurt."

"Don't. I'm fine." He swiveled me around like a top and dragged me in his arms.

"I'll take you to ER. Lila. Doctor. She'll suture you up."

"I don't think so."

"Uh-huh. You can snow now."

"Oh, I'll go when I want to." He snorted in amusement and bent down, one of his steel arms going under my arm sockets and the other under my knees. In a fluid motion, he picked me up and proceeded to carry me, Rhett Butler style, through the hallway, as if I was as light as a cloud.

Too tired to protest, my arms wrapped around his neck on their own accord, as if I had been used to him carrying me for years. Taking a long sniff of his airy cologne, I let out a sigh of contentment. "Kyle smells like cotton candy. Cypress and I like cotton candy."

"Who is Cypress?"

"I love Cypress."

In front of my suite, Kyle opened the door and strode in, still carrying me. "You're lucky you're cute when you're drunk-sleep. Or else you'd be in danger tonight."

"How does Cotton Candy Man have my room key?"

"He just does." Walking towards the bedroom, he hit the half-open door with his elbow and made for the bed. Easing me down on the bed, he tucked the sheets around me and pulled the comforter over my prostrate body.

Fighting against being tucked in, I threw off the sheets, kicked the comforter and lifted my arms up to him. "Make love now?"

He froze and stared at me. And then he half-smiled and half-grimaced. "No. I'd rather you were conscious for that experience." He bent down and I closed my eyes in anticipation. It was just a kiss on my forehead. "June-Bug. I'll see you Friday morning."

"Oh no. I forgot my purse." I shot up in bed, my eyes still shut.

"No, I have it here. You left it in the club with a half million dollar camera in it. I asked Evan to keep it safe. I'll charge your phone before you go and set your alarm."

"Okay, Mr. Bossypants." I giggled and slipped back under the sheets.

The last thing I heard before I slipped into a deep sleep were his quiet words, "Dear God, you will break me, Juniper Mills..."

KYLE

December 10, 2:47 a.m. 28 seconds
(The Q Hotel, San Francisco)

She would break him. Kyle knew that. Already the numbers in his head had shattered and lay on a bloody battlefield like slain soldiers. He had to bury them somewhere. Little tiny numerical graves. In a matrix graveyard.

He leaned over and stared at her as she slept. Her eyelashes fanned her cheeks like black moths. Tossing in sleep, she kicked off one corner of the sheet. He smiled. A glint of silver made him realize she was still wearing her shoes. He sighed and slid her fragile ankles towards him and slowly undid the narrow buckled straps. The shoes were at least two sizes too big and Kyle wondered who had loaned them to her.

What was that smell? He sniffed. Revolting. Like Vegemite. No, concentrated beer. She smelled of beer. Goldilocks had spilled beer on her when he'd hit Kyle.

Goldilocks. Maggot fucker.

303

Her jeans were scuffed with dirt from sliding across the dance stage on her knees. He eased the sheets off, put an arm around her waist and pulled her up. She moaned and wilted against him, her neck arched and lips going to his, instinctively. Kyle froze, every cell in his body wanting to suck her luscious lower lip and not stop. To possess her—what he'd wanted to do since he met her. She wanted it too. *Make love now?* She'd asked him, just before she slept. Teeth on edge, hands fisted against her ribcage, he paused.

Think: Resistance. Control. Strength.

Resistance, he thought, like swimming against water velocity. Control, using force to stop momentum, like slowing down in a bullet-speed dive. And Strength: Resistance and Control applied. Mobilizing great strength he did not know he had, Kyle inched back from Juniper's lips. It took every avoirdupois ounce of his control not to slip into bed with her.

The moment passed and he held her upright and pulled her shirt off. Then he undid her zipper, pulled it down and slid her jeans off. Once she lay bare in her underwear, Kyle was about to tuck her back in. But he stopped short.

He could not help but stare at the long delicate legs before him. There was something strangely pure about them, as though no one had touched them before except him. He heard his deep-rooted guilt sneering at him for leading her on. For ruining her purity.

Ha. What purity?

She was a 26-year-old woman. She was a little kooky and a little immature, which was why she acted like a teenager at times. *That's all.*

Shaking off his crazy thoughts, Kyle tucked her back in the sheets, put her shirt in a laundry bag, and folded the jeans neatly on a chair. Throwing one last, long glance at her, he crept out of the room.

CHAPTER 19

The next morning, I awoke to the beeping of my phone alarm, accompanied by the worst hangover-migraine combo I had suffered yet. Not only was last night my first nightclub experience—it was also my first time drinking as much as I did. It was a small miracle I hadn't thrown up all over Kyle. I suppose I had inherited Mom's tolerance for alcohol.

Stretching languidly in bed, I flushed as last night's sleazy memories flooded my mind. They were fuzzy at the edges but clear in content. What had I not done last night? I had made a public display of myself, drunk too much, danced on stage, gyrated with half a dozen strangers, had two men fight over me, quarreled with Kyle Paxton (the great BirdsEye CEO) and passed out in his car—after which—he had picked me up in the hallway and carried me to my bed. I wiggled my toes.

P.S. He had also taken off my shoes.

P.P.S. I had also asked him to make love to me.

And, drum roll please, had he really said, *You will break me, Juniper?* Or was I already asleep and dreaming by then?

Skull pounding and brain aching from the alcohol still detoxing in my blood, I threw off my bed sheets. Stumbling out of bed, I gulped. I was not wearing my jeans. Or my blouse. Did something happen last night that I was too knocked out to remember? Looking around wildly, I saw my jeans neatly folded on a chair nearby. Gripping the bedside table for support, I stared at my bare legs. I must have fallen asleep by the time he took off my clothes. The thought of him seeing me in my flimsy sapphire panties and bra made me hot and cold, all at once.

The migraine and hangover made my head ring like I was in a tunnel with two trains screeching on two tracks. I took three Excedrin pills and jumped into the shower. Still fighting the migraine, I put on sunglasses to hide the dark eye circles and ran like a madwoman through the hotel, somehow making it only five minutes late for the stupid farewell breakfast. Lydia, our head curator, was at the podium handing out bronze plaques to our new Bay Area friends to thank them for hosting us. Around thirty people were sitting around the room, clapping.

I made a beeline for the breakfast buffet table. Cradling my coffee cup, I sat down next to Stacy and Trevor. I was taken aback to see them looking cool, flawless, and alert. "You two are revolting meat sacks. How can you look fresh? What time did you get in from the club?" I slurred, scowling at them.

"Five," Trevor said, and they both grinned at me.

My jaw dropped. "I hate your generation."

"Junie, you're four years older than us, for God's sake," Trevor said.

"Damn you, Pampers, I am from another time."

I took off my sunglasses and tried to listen to the speeches, but I could not focus. All I could think about was my conversation with Kyle. Did I agree to a trial to be his Summer? Was I just drunk or did being drunk make me admit what I really desired all along? And what was I to make of Kyle's strange confession about him being a human calculator? A clockwork man. Could he really tell time in his head? He had called himself a psycho—no, a sociopath, and he had brutally beaten up a man. Joshua had a broken nose, for sure.

Kyle Paxton was more distracting than galaxies of Candy Crush, Angry Birds and kitten memes. Being obsessed with him meant I was no longer obsessed by my job and I had become a bungling idiot at it lately. I pinched my arm to force myself to shift into work mode.

Once the talks were over, I ate a hearty breakfast and circulated the room, making suitable small talk until Trevor came to stand beside me. He looked lost. I noticed he was watching Stacy as she talked in her customary flirtatious way with Zeke Pena, the older and handsome curator of painting at the Modern Museum of San Francisco. It hurt my heart that this wonderful young man was pining for his best friend.

Taking a deep breath, I asked, "Hey, Trev, why don't you ask her out?"

He tensed and twisted to look at me. "Who are you talking about?"

"You know who. I mean, I can tell you like her."

"Not in that way."

"Come on, dude, what's going on? After last night, we're a squad. You can tell me."

He gave me a wan smile. "Okay. I kinda like her. But I know she's not interested in a relationship...and I'm not interested in shacking up with my colleague and friend. It would be awkward afterwards. I don't want to ruin a great friendship."

"Are you dating anyone?" When he shook his head, I asked, "Did you ever ask her out?"

"Hell to the no."

"At least let her know how you feel."

"A privileged white gal from Connecticut and the dorky black boy from the wrong part of Detroit. It won't work."

"Hey, wrong century, buddy."

"Um, no. You live in a white girl privilege bubble."

I sighed. I lived in a bubble, not so much the privilege. "Trevor. You know me and that's not true. Have you approached her?"

"Let's see. I like Tupac, World of Warcraft, LARPing and going to Comic Cons, and she likes brunching at the Greenwich Country Club in her hometown, shopping on Fifth Avenue and dates Wall Street stockbrokers with Manhattan penthouses and Hampton weekend homes. So no."

"She is cool. Maybe you can—"

"Give it a rest." His dark brown eyes were taciturn now.

"Well, don't not try. I'm telling you, Trevor, don't let good stuff pass you by. Take all the chances you can and at least let her know how you feel."

Wow, I sound like a pharmacy greeting card.

Before he could answer, Stacy came up to us, dancing like she was raising the roof. "What's up, bitches?"

"Nothing." With a warning look at me, Trevor walked off abruptly.

Stacy stared at his retreating back in surprise. "Who got his goat?"

"No idea."

"So, how about last night?" She smiled and pretend head-banged.

"Hush. Delete the memories, Nosy Barbie."

"How can I? Stage dancing. Insane amount of shots. A real fight. Over you. Beer bottles broken and all. Girl, you should never go to Vegas."

"Now you know why I never drink or go out. I have a tingly twitchy side."

"Let out the animal from its cage sometimes, will ya? Hey, you left early, guess what? We won third prize for the dance."

"Really? No way." I whooped and a few people turned to stare at us.

Her eyes shone with excitement. "Hail to the riches. Certified for three free drinks at The Cave."

"Ha-ha." Arching an eyebrow, I scrutinized her. "Speaking of certified, how was the ménage-a-trois?"

"WTF? Oh, you mean the dancing couple. Nothing happened. I came back with Trevor." She paled and looked so shocked I was ashamed at my blatant question.

"My bad. Stacy, is there anyone else…I mean are you seeing someone?"

"You mean aside from three guys I hook up with from time to time? And separately."

"Um. Whoa. But, yes."

"Nah. They are fuck-buddies."

Fuck-buddies? My heart jolted and I thought how fitting it would have been if Kyle had asked Stacy instead of me…if he had brought her down from the scaffolding…there would have been no conflict. No story.

"So…F-buddies. Are they in Ann Arbor?"

"Juniper. What grownup woman says F instead of fuck? But yeah. One there, one in Connecticut, one in New York. Nothing serious. Just wandering through Funland."

"Oh. May I ask how that works?"

Taken aback, Stacy scanned my face. "What do you want to know?"

"I…I am kinda clueless about that lifestyle—"

"I see. Well, it's just to satisfy a nookie need, y'know. Minus the relationship boloney. It works well if the guy is detached. Doesn't get involved. Doesn't want to cuddle or see a movie. It works if you don't care about them as a person, just bones to jump."

"Oh." I was dispirited to hear that. Was that how Kyle saw his companions? "You have three at once?"

Stacy's brow wrinkled. "Why do you ask, Judge Judy?"

"No. No. Trust me, I'm not judgmental, just naïve. And curious, that's all. I consider you a friend. Sorry, if I crossed a line."

"Nah, it's fine. I get it. So the one at college is kind of a dick. Literally. And so it's a once in a while hook-up, y'know. And the one in New York, met him at Burning Man—damn he was super-hot—hardly ever now. And the one back home in Connecticut is my holiday gift to myself. Trust me, Junie, I'm not doing the cha cha more than once a week. Sometimes less. Kinda busy with work and studies."

"Fascinating. But, would you consider it? Real dating, I mean. Or a relationship."

"Nope. I am having fun. You know like the saying, 'Today was good. Today was fun. Tomorrow is another one.'"

"Oh, I'm not familiar with the philosopher."

"Dr. Seuss." She whooped with laughter at my mystified face. "Your parents didn't read *One Fish, Two Fish, Red Fish, Blue Fish* growing up?"

No one had ever read me anything, so I'd learned to read by staring at grocery labels. "No. And, thanks for ruining Dr. Seuss. So you are not dating…but what about trying. Like someone at work?"

"Wait, who are you talking about?"

"That's inconsequential. If, let's say…I was to set you up…would you agree?"

"Projectile vomit. No." Stacy burst out laughing.

Gulp. My stupid Cupid arrows needed sharpening. "Feel bad I asked."

"NP, all's peachy-keen. Anyhow, on Friday, Trev and I are off at ten. You coming with us or the elders?"

"Where are you going?"

"The Mission District murals. Then sushi. You wanna join us?"

"Where's everyone else going?"

Her pretty blue eyes grew round. "Haven't you checked your email? They are going to art galleries, then antique shopping. Lame."

"Stace. Please cover for me. I am going to hang out with Kyle tomorrow."

A wide smile split her face. "Last night? Did you two hook up?"

"Oh no, you don't."

"Come on. You two are so hot together. It's like watching Anime porn."

I clasped a hand over her mouth. "Dammit, Stacy, get your tongue out of the gutter. Whatever we have going on is nobody's business. And it's super inappropriate at work. So, if anyone asks, let them know I am with you and Trevor. Okay?"

Yuck. I sound uptight. Like I have a twig up my ass.

Stacy winked. "I understand. Squad rules."

That evening when I got back to my hotel room, I got dressed for another night out with Trevor and Stacy. We were going to go bar hopping, though I had informed them I was swearing off alcoholic drinks and was looking to taste every virgin drink known to humanity.

While putting makeup on in the bathroom, I dialed Mom and Cypress and switched on speaker phone. I lied about spending the weekend with Kyle and explained I had been assigned extra work forcing me to stay back in San Francisco. Cypress was traumatized because he was looking forward to seeing me back on Saturday morning—changing time and scheduling was a big problem for him, common with his specific psychological issues.

I stared at my face in the bathroom mirror, hating what I saw. I hated lying to him. Guilt weighed down my heart as I assured Cypress over and over again that I would definitely be back Monday afternoon. Though he finally seemed to understand, my voice hovered close to tears. My mother snatched the phone from Cypress and said not to worry. She assured me that he was doing quite well, unlike my trip to Egypt. I felt better and my guilt evaporated.

It was all set. From Friday onwards, I would spend precious time with Kyle Paxton.

Then I phoned Lila.

"Junie. Where the hell are you? You have not responded to my texts."

"I know, babe. I've just been so busy in San Francisco," I said.

"Hope you're not having a blast without me."

"Too late. Listen, hon, can you meet me when we get back?"

"Sure."

"I'll come to Detroit. Your hospital. Wednesday, okay?"

"Perfect. What's this about, babe?"

"Kyle. A lot happened."

"Exciting. Are you coming back without your hymen?" She shrieked and I giggled and held the phone away from my ear.

"Shut up, Colon Handler. I mean, I think we're going to be together but it's complicated. I need my bestie."

After I hung up, I caught my reflection in the bathroom mirror. A week in San Francisco and I had already changed. My eyes were lime and all lit up, like fireflies in my irises. The sun had added gold to my skin, and a glow that came from joy. From Kyle.

Joy that's to be short-lived.

I turned away from my reflection, my heart sinking. His confession to me, the way his mind worked, and the way he manipulated people made him a bit of a psycho. Kyle was going to be my undoing. My crash-and-burn disaster.

I don't care. I squared my shoulders. Time for Juniper Mills to grow up. To finally learn what it means to be a woman. To throw off the torc my mother put around my neck when I was a little girl. I needed to make my own mistakes. She was wrong. Just wrong. I was not her, nor she me, so the poison in my veins against men was wrong.

And Kyle Paxton was the antidote.

The only problem with an antidote is that it's often made from the very venom it neutralizes.

The next morning was the last seminar at the museum and it ran late. I tried to focus but in the back of my head was a beeping alarm. *Kyle. Kyle is coming to pick you up at 10.* By around 9:30, a cold-sweat panic had set in. There was little chance I would be done by then. I picked up my phone and saw a message from him sent an hour ago.

I'll see you @ 10 June-Bug

My heart raced to see his text. I texted back.

Thanks. Kyle, please come at 10:30.

Immediately I got a text back.

OK

So short. Damn it, what is going on? Moody man. I shot him another text:

Plz don't pick me up from hotel lobby.
I don't want anyone else to see.

In an instant, one more text:

northside exit, no one uses, back of hotel
pick you up there @10:30

I did not respond.

I made my way to the hotel's Northside exit, wondering how Kyle knew about this exit. Clearly he had used this hotel before, and with a twinge I guessed I was not his only companion who had stayed here.

I swung the exit door open and a sun flare on the glass blinded me. I put on my sunglasses and that's when I saw him. My heart raced at all my pulse points and dipped to my gray sneakers. *Swooning starting in 3-2-1.*

Leaning against his car, muscular arms folded over his burly chest, Kyle was my personal heartbreaker. He had on mushroom cargo pants and a fitted black t-shirt and I swore the casual attire made him even hotter. His slightly damp hair was slicked off his forehead and the two-day spiky stubble lining his jaw made me tingle, as always. Even behind sunglasses and the transparent twin reflections of the scene, his navy gaze impaled my body.

Trembling under his gaze, I was glad I had taken time to change into jean capris and a flowy turquoise t-shirt. My hair was tucked in a caramel ponytail and from my ears dangled silver wing-and-skull earrings. I had packed a khaki jacket if it got chilly. Right now it was warm and sunny with just a whiff of crispy cool.

Kyle took both my hands in his and kissed my cheek. "Juniper. No one should look so lovely so early in the day."

Recalling he had taken off my clothes that night, I cleared my dry throat. "Thank you. You are not hopeless yourself."

He laughed. "Best. Compliment. Ever."

Once we were settled in the car, I asked, "So we're going to the beach?"

"Well, San Francisco's version of it. Land's End. Okay with you?"

"Perfect."

Revving the engine, he shot me a wicked look. "Did we dodge the masses?"

"Whew. No one saw me."

"Why, Miss Mills, one would think you were ashamed of our...er...liaison."

Liaison. Great. Kyle Paxton moved from casual banter to deep topics without a hint of a segue. Nervous, I looked at the long silver-and-turquoise Turkish ring I wore on my index finger and began to tug it.

"Not at all. If anything, you should be ashamed of me. But you're the board president and I don't want this to get more complicated. Also I'm not interested in broadcasting this...um...thing we have. You did make me sign an NDA."

He gave me a long, slow look and I could have sworn that a slew of dirty thoughts chased across his mind in a few seconds. Thankfully, he chose not to share them. "The NDA was for very specific interests of mine. Interests I do not wish to broadcast either. But I would like to show you off to the world. That is, if you are ready to be with me."

"God, why would you even want to be with someone like me?" The words came out before I could stop them for they had been on the tip of my tongue since I had met Kyle.

"Hell, why wouldn't any man? Juniper, you are intelligent, kind, accomplished, beautiful, and very sexy…without even knowing it. Later, we've gotta talk about your self-esteem issues."

Ugh. He pointed out such goody two-shoes things in me. He could have said, chaste, modest, prudent, honorable, Sunday-sermon attending—though he HAD said beautiful and sexy. *Am I those things?* I'd never felt beautiful before. Guys most likely didn't give me compliments because I had a resting hostile face.

Determined to make something of myself, I had avoided boys and sex in college, and it became easy to see myself as a sexless, unsexy creature. A non-sensual being (on the fast track to spinsterhood) who devoted her life to the service of historical archiving. Who swept up the broken pieces of her shattered mother and took care of her special needs brother.

Who'd die unseen and unloved.

With Kyle, I felt like I'd been revived from death with an electro-shock defibrillator. Around him, I came alive. At a cellular level. There was a danger in such thoughts. If he knew how I felt, he'd freak out.

"For the record, Mr. Paxton, I have healthy self-esteem. Just because I don't play musical beds doesn't mean my self-esteem sucks. I am kickass and I know it."

An easy smile played on his lips. "Duly noted."

"What I'm trying to ask is…am I some kind of sport for you? Catch and release."

His smile vanished. "Juniper, I don't fish and I'm not a hunter. So, no."

He shot me an irate look and switched on music. We were quiet for a bit and then "Black Sun," a song by Death Cab for Cutie that I adored, came on.

"My favorite song," I cried out. "Well...these days."

"I like that song too."

"What's your favorite band?"

"Don't have one."

"Favorite song?"

"Don't know."

"Favorite—"

"Nope. Before you get carried away, Juniper, I don't have a personality. I have no favorite color, movie, TV show, book, city, not even people."

Chewing my lips, I let the song finish. Then I gave him a critical look. "I think you like shocking people. But really...you just have a severe introvert disorder."

"Is that so, doc?"

"Yeah-huh. And you overcompensate by pushing people away and creating your own complex paradigms for society."

"Wow. And here I thought I was just a jackass."

"Well, that too." We exchanged smiles. "You know, Kyle...we have nothing in common."

"You have ten toes and fingers, so do I. You have two hundred and six bones, so do I."

I smiled. "But I want to get to know you. More than your skull and bones."

"Well, sport, that's what today is about Getting to know each other beyond NDAs, contracts, and what the future holds."

His hand came to rest on my knee, and it was a casual gesture, but everything Kyle Paxton did to me made a gigantic impact. A knot of pleasure untied in my belly as his hands caressed my jean-clad knee.

"So no scheduling?" I asked, my voice strained.

"Nope. Today, I'm going to try it your way. Figure out the day as it goes along."

"So it's not going to drive you nuts that there's no plan. No advance booking and no control over where we end up today."

Considering how time ruled him, I was stunned he'd even consider a day without hard time limits.

"As long as I'm with you, it sounds perfect."

We turned in unison, eyes colliding. I felt the air thicken between us with pent-up need and want. My hand settled on his that was still on my knee. He clasped my hand and kissed it, his lips exploring the tender part of my palm. I caught my breath. Being with Kyle was like eating candy and blowfish in one bite. Pure sugar and pure fear.

To control my senses, I pulled my hand away from his grip and covered the dashboard clock. "What time is it, Clockwork Man?"

"10:44 and twenty six seconds."

"Wow. You weren't kidding about that."

He began kissing my hand again. "Stop distracting me."

"Kyle, please drive safely."

"What? Did you just question my driving skills?"

"Just your sanity."

"Why do I think you are daring me, Juniper?" With a bold smile, he took his hands off the steering wheel and lifted both arms up. His knees curled up to the steering wheel, navigating the car in that bizarre way.

"All right, Formula One, quit it. Focus on driving."

"Never. Question. Me."

"Even if I die today, I'd possess you and question you for all of eternity."

"I'd like to be possessed by you." Hands now freed, he began kissing my wrists. He beamed, and we were both young, carefree and happy, as he drove with his knees and kissed my hands.

Then I looked out. The car flew down a hilly road in the heart of the city and although he piloted it well with his knees, I was terrified. At the top of a particularly winding street, I genuinely feared for our lives and pulled my hands away. "Kyle Paxton. Do not kill me in San Francisco. I have a family waiting for me in Ann Arbor."

"For them." With a triumphant look, he slammed his hands back on the wheel and drove like a normal human being. "So who's Cypress?"

I whipped my head to him. "How…?"

"That night you said Cypress likes cotton candy."

"I did? Oh. Cypress is my brother."

"I see. Cypress and Juniper. Makes sense. You live with him?"

"Yes, and my mother."

It was the first time I had told Kyle about my family and he seemed cautiously optimistic that I would say more. But I clammed up and stared out at the narrow row homes clustered on hills that looked like dry green camels. It was hard for me to talk about my family without bursting into tears.

After a long pause, he asked, "How is it you have no boyfriend?"

I shrugged and yanked at my ring. "I guess I've been busy with my career. No time for relationships and romance."

"So when-slash-who was your last boyfriend?"

"Can't I have some secrets?"

"Nope."

"I thought one of the rules was no questions asked about my past or future. Nor am I allowed to ask about yours."

"You share zero personal details. That intrigues me."

"Men usually don't find me intriguing."

"Congratulations on my awesome luck. But at the club, I heroically fought a horde of men off you, so I find it very hard to believe."

I clasped my face in my hands. "Oh God. That was embarrassing. I'm sorry about that."

"Don't be. I enjoyed it very much."

"Even breaking that poor guy's nose?"

"That was my favorite part."

"Even getting beer bottle smashed?"

"Less favorite part."

"Is your back fine? Did you get stitches? God, I feel so bad."

"Juniper, my shirt ripped, not my skin." Though I was drunk, I distinctly remember seeing a red gash on his shoulder, but when I lifted my hand to argue, he quickly asked, "Hey, if that was your first rodeo, where'd you learn to dance like that?"

"You saw?" I was electrified. So, he had been standing at the staircase watching me. "When we were younger, Cypress and I danced a lot on his gaming console. Are you laughing at me, Paxton?"

"You, Mills, are singular." He laughed harder. "Now. Tell me something."

"What?"

"Every single thing about you. Birth till now."

"Okay. Let's see. I had asthma as a little girl, all cured now. I hate blue cheese. Love Lebanese food, because my best friend is from there. I hate candy, especially caramel. But I'm addicted to candy canes. Keep a stash in my office and car."

"Now I get why your lips taste like candy cane."

"And finally, if I had to pick between oxygen and music, I'd take music. Enough?"

"More."

320

"Hmm. As a teen, I wore Goth. Even dyed my hair blue. Lots of hard rock, no roll and no drugs, sadly. My life is so lame, I edit Wikipedia for history kicks. I drive fast and have a ton of unpaid speeding tickets. I like comedy and film noir and hate horror. I love saying, 'Life doesn't have any hands, but it can sure give you a punch on the nose.' Oh, yeah, I flunked high school math and physics and my SAT score sucked balls, but I did okay in college. I'm a bit Marxist. I believe in love and hate war. Did a lot of antiwar picketing in college. Got arrested for that once. Most exciting thing that happened to me. Except my archeology trip to Egypt. That's about it."

"Arrested? You're such a badass." He grinned wide. "You're adorkable. Really. I feel like I've known you for years."

"Your turn."

"Nah. I'm kinda empty inside."

"Kyle Paxton! That is cheating. Speak up, or I'll punch you in the nose."

But he smiled and said nothing.

KYLE

December 11, 11:12 a.m. 04 seconds
(Land's End, San Francisco)

K yle pulled into the parking lot of Land's End Visitor's Center, his Excel sheet mind scanning all the things that he had planned yesterday and hoping his team was able to follow through. One of his assistants, Sheila, was at his house getting everything ready. Kyle hoped she did not mess up and had executed everything on exact time. Of all the people, his team members should know how important time was for him. But not today.

Today he was on limitless time.

He turned the ignition off and glanced sideways at the girl next to him.

Juniper was looking at the view out of her passenger window, her breath catching in her throat. He saw the rise and fall of her chest as she exhaled harder and quicker in anticipation.

She turned to him, eyes shimmering. "It's beautiful. Thank you. Thank you. Thank you."

"One thanks will do."

Kyle gulped. What was this pesky tapping in the hollowness of his ribcage? *Stop*, he commanded. But it did not.

CHAPTER 20

Kyle parked the car at the Land's End Visitors center, and we got out to explore the park by the bay. At the top of the stairs that once belonged to the historical Sutro Baths, I halted to take in the view. We stood on a hilly outcrop that led to a pebble-strewn grassland beach and behind us were tall trees scattered on low hills wrapped with hiking trails.

"It's breathtaking." I twisted my head around, the rubbernecking already making me dizzy.

The Pacific Ocean. This was my first view of a real ocean. I had been to the Chicago Lakeshore several times, but never to an ocean shore. As a child, going to the beach was a fantasy, but we couldn't afford vacations—except the time we went to Wisconsin Dells.

"Thank you. It's perfect." Hands clasped in wonder, I turned to him and paused at the intensity of his navy gaze. Studying every single flicker on my face, Kyle was silent. Strange and indefinable emotions chased across his face like long shadows on cement walls. He blinked and the spell was broken.

"Come. Let's go down."

"Catch me if you can." I tore down the timber steps carved into the hill and when I saw he was following leisurely, I started to run.

"Juniper. Be careful, the stairs are often wet and slippery."

I thumbed my nose at him and ran faster, taking two steps at a time, snaking between fast athletic locals and slow tourists. He caught up with me rather quickly and I halted, disoriented by his proximity. Stumbling, I almost slipped on the last few steps until Kyle's arms seized me.

His fingers cut into the flesh of my arms. "Damn it. I am going to have a hard time keeping you alive."

"Let me go." I tried to shake off his grip, but he would not let me go. The other people on the stairs glanced at us with interest as they passed by.

"If memory serves me right, you have ladder issues."

"No, just poor peripheral vision and a big fun radar."

He shook his head and let me go. "Let me teach you how to use stairs. Step one, put one foot on stable ground. Step two, use gravity to find your balance. Step three, don't die."

Laughing, we made it down. Past the stairs, we trudged over the pebbly ground to get close to the water. Despite the masses of selfie-stick carting tourists, it was stunning. Spiky black rocks rose from the dull gray water, contrasting with the apple green grass that grew in mossy patches. Lacy mist shrouded the place in a soft glow.

The breeze was chilly so I slipped on the jacket that Kyle had insisted I bring. I stood there for a long time trying to breathe in and out with the ebb and flow of the tide, until he tugged my hand. He led me further along the beach to the ruins of the old Sutro Baths and we treaded the wet sand to go through the old flooded cave tunnel.

"Do you know the history of Land's End?" I asked.

I knew and was ready to inform him, but Kyle said, "Yeah, as a local, I do."

"Oh yeah? So tell me."

"So thousands of years ago, the whole world used to come to the healing hot springs of Land's End. But legend said it was haunted by a cray cray goddess. She was an evil creep. She fried humans into lollipops and ate them. But she was very lonely. And so very very hot. So she asked her deities to send her a warrior lover. They answered her prayers with a giant egg. She was stoked and thought her lover would be hatched soon. But then, out of the egg came a fire-breathing dragon. He *was* a fiery strong warrior, in her deities' defense."

My shoulders shook with contained laughter. "What a yarn."

He shook his head gravely. "No. True story. Then there was an epic battle. She lost and died. The dragon torched the cliffs and killed everyone in California...until the Gold Rush brought people back. Some say a cray cray lady in white haunts the baths. They even found fossilized dragon bones buried in the very sands we stand on, Juniper. And to this day people smell sulfur and say it is haunted by bad dragon breath."

Surprised he was capable of make believe, I laughed hard. "Cheesy, Kyle."

"All right, Miss Curator. Your turn."

Pointing to the waterlogged stone ruins, I explained Adolfo Sutro, a San Francisco mayor, had built a glass public bath, aquarium, hotel and pleasure grounds there in 1894. He tried to insulate the site with sea walls, but they kept collapsing into the Pacific. The project lost tons of money and was shut down.

"My history was better," he said.

Smiling at each other, we walked on further up the shoreline and I was in awe of the rough beauty of Land's End. It was a clear day and we saw a few shipwrecks lost in the water and two smashed on the cliff rocks. I gave Kyle a history of the tragic shipwrecks from various wars and it amused him that I knew so many useless facts. He teased me about being book smart and having zero street smarts. But I could tell I held his interest, like Scheherazade and Emperor Shahryar in *One Thousand and One Nights.*

Hand in hand, we walked down the beach, talking about my book and his new AI prototype at BirdsEye, the project he was most excited about. We skirted personal topics and questions; it seemed any mention of his arrangement and Termination Contract would ruin the day.

Lost to the world, Kyle and I marched on until the coastline became isolated and there was nothing but craggy rocks, the gray sky and the mist. In the greenstone basalt rocks, we saw seagulls, cormorants and the slow oystercatchers roosting. On the wet sand, we spotted crabs, washed-away starfish, and jellyfish jettisoned by broken shells.

I chased the marine life we spotted and he laughed at my juvenile behavior. I shocked him by picking up a snake we found under a rock and throwing it his way. Though it was a Western Yellow-Bellied Racer and not dangerous to humans, my unexpected audacity startled him.

As a curator, there are very few living things that frighten me.

Except the male of the human species.

At the furthest end of the track, Kyle led me to a flat rock jutting over the bay with an epic close-up view of the Golden Gate Bridge. Clutching his hand, I stood there staring at it in reverent silence. I noticed he was looking in the other direction, his expression so grim I did not dare ask why he was upset. But I knew from the distance in his eyes…it had nothing to do with me. I wanted nothing more than to find a way to loosen the nails in his skull and peek inside. His fingers had become stiff and held mine so hard, it hurt.

Freeing my fingers, I said, "This was probably the most fun I've had on a hike."

He gave me an odd look as if he had forgotten who I was. Then his face relaxed. "You know, I've hiked here the past sixteen years, three times a week, two hours each time, seven miles per time, but this is the only hike I will remember."

Why did he say such things if he only wanted me to be his for a fleeting moment in time? His time-stamped Summer. Heart pounding, I thought of a few retorts but none of them seemed right for whatever it was we had going on, so I scaled down the steep ridge so fast, he was taken aback. "Let's go, Kyle."

As we strolled back, I lifted my face to the sky. Kyle's company and the beach had me feeling something alien. I wanted to prolong this feeling—punch-drunk happy—for I had never felt this way. All the seventies records my mother listened to on her Crosley's Tech Turntable made sense now—days of uncertainty fading, feeling on top of the world, eagles soaring in the sky, hearts skimming on mountain tops. Of love being a shiny new coin of life. I had a goofy smile on my face as I sang snatches of songs in my head.

When Kyle demanded I share my thoughts, I lied and said I was imagining my travel bucket list. We were going back up the stairs and Kyle slipped an arm around my waist. "I know you want to go to Ireland, where else?"

"The Lost City of Petra," I said, without hesitation.

He looked down at me with a raised eyebrow. "In Jordan? Like from Indiana Jones?"

"Ugh, not the Hollywood version. Real Petra. It's a mystery city carved into mountains of red gold. Legend has it that it magically appeared from gold dust. The Nabataeans were a superpower civilization and built Petra to show off their architectural skills. Ever since I was a little girl I've wanted to see Petra." At my enthusiasm I saw a ghost of a smile on his face. I bit my lips. "And what about you?"

Looking unsure, he shrugged. "No place. Seen it all, done it all, can't remember most of it. I've been to so many places, I've lost count. I don't get excited anymore. My heart beats for nothing...I guess...I am dead inside."

My mood sank. I was sure Kyle was anesthetized by the constant buzz and motion of his life, while I (with relatively no life) could only meet the new and unknown in the pages of books. "I guess I have *joie de vivre*. But I'd exchange it in a heartbeat for real experiences. Trust me, Kyle. It's juvenile and rightly underrated."

"No. It's a gift. I envy you. We're all so cynical, so jaded these days. What you have is cool...and contagious."

"Maybe it's a rite of passage and if I see too much, my heart will deaden too."

I want my heart to deaden when it comes to you Kyle. So when it all ends, I feel nothing.

"I don't think so. I think I never had it."

What do I say to that?

On the way back to the parking lot, we stopped at the Land's End Visitor's Center and got water and lemonade. As we left, he handed me a shopping bag. "For you, June-Bug."

I looked inside. It was chock-full of touristy Bay Area magnets, photo frames, pins and tiny pens. Enough kitsch for an entire school class. He pulled out a Land's End magnet and put it in my palm.

"The Bay's Best Tour Guide," I read out loud.

"Me." Kyle pointed to his chest.

"Cheesy, Kyle. Part two." I laughed. However, he noticed that I palmed the magnet and caressed it until I realized what I was doing. When we reached his car, I stopped short. "Hey, guess what time it is."

He beamed across his car's silver roof at me. "2:16, thirty seven seconds."

"Are you wearing a watch?"

"Nope. Don't need to."

Wiping sand off my capris, I slipped into the luxurious Tesla and stared at the car clock. I shook my head. "I'll never get over it. How in the world?"

"I don't know. I am a freak of nature." He revved up the car engine and drove out.

"Look, kids, it's a clock, it's Super Time Man."

"What a useless superpower. I'd rather predict the future. Or fly."

"And I wish I could time-travel."

"Funny you say that. I used to collect clocks and watches when I was a kid. I tore them apart to look at the spring driven movements. I rebuilt them into weird monstrosities. I wanted to figure out time. So I used telescopes to see if I could find the timeline and its spatial location of particles at every instant in time. I wanted to figure out the space time continuum with my powers so I could turn back time and take my mother and me back to Ann Arbor before the divorce." As if embarrassed at oversharing, he muttered, "Dumb kid stuff."

Kyle, your childhood breaks my heart. I didn't know what to say.

"Do you collect anything?" he asked, at last.

"I can't afford ancient torcs, so I buy books. Old Irish books. Celtic ones are rare but I have one from 1892 that is my pride and joy. You see there was a nationalist Celtic language revival in nineteenth century England and so many writers—" I halted. The last thing I wanted was for him to get bored or start buying me rare Celtic books.

"Go on."

"Nah. I blah blah too much about the Celts."

"I love every word that comes out of your mouth." His voice was silky, smooth and ever so racy. He turned to see the effect of his words on my face. It was the first time I consciously heard him say the word love and this was getting a bit too somber.

"Oh yeah, wait five months when every word turns sour." *Way to go, blunt girl.* His face was impassive as he drove, his eyes hidden by aviator sunglasses and I spent some time cursing my reflection in the passenger window. "Do you still collect watches?"

"No. I guess I like vintage cameras. Every time I visited Ann Arbor, I stole one of my grandfather's old cameras."

"Oh yeah, the camera collection in your office is awesome. Do you take photos?"

"Not anymore. I used to." And then he pursed his lips.

I found it strange that the CEO of the hottest new camera company did not take pictures. Staring at the bay whizzing by, I thought the day was beautiful but odd. Relaxed Kyle was fun and I was at ease, as if I had known him for years. It unnerved me how natural we felt, like we were a…couple.

If Felicia Grunde, F-buddy specialist could see me now, she would say, *Miss Mills, my Barmy Blighter, since you don't get the concept of a casual arrangement, please go to the nearest rocky cliff and jump into the Pacific Ocean. Then drown. Your carcass deserves to be eaten by a mob of blood-thirsty piranhas. Then your spit up bones should be cremated in a flame spitting bonfire.*

I was basically screwed.

Kyle drove on and I tried to ignore my stomach twisting with hunger. Was he going to drop me back?

As if reading my thoughts, he said, "June-Bug, I'm going to take you to the best place to eat."

"Kyle, I'm not dressed for a fancy place."

"Who said it's fancy?"

It turned out to be a taco truck a few miles up the coastal road. There was a long line of hungry people stretching past the truck. Holding my hand, Kyle led me to the end of the line and put his lips on my ear. "My favorite place to eat."

Kyle Paxton was as unpredictable as a bag full of puppies and fireworks.

As a Midwesterner used to freezing weather and drive-through eateries, my eyes sparkled and my hands knotted in delight at the food truck on the beach. The glossy black truck had SEÑOR SABOR painted in loud orange and lime strokes. "Mister Flavor?"

"*Si*," Kyle responded.

At the truck window, an old man sporting an incredible lush black mustache set in a pudgy face leaned forward. "Ah. *Senor Kyle. Me dio gusto verte.*"

"*Qué tal? Senor Javier?*" Kyle said, his voice warm.

"*Primer vez que te he visto con otro ser humano.*" Javier seemed excited to see Kyle and stared curiously at me. Shuffling back, he called out, "Catalina."

Instantly, a woman who must be Javier's wife, appeared in the frame. Both of them were fascinated by me and I was lost as a rapid-fire conversation took place, with Kyle joining them in fluent Spanish.

"This is first time we see Kyle with one extra human," Señor Javier remarked.

"Yes. He come here when he teenager. No girls. No boys. *Extraño.* Very strange." Catalina nodded solemnly.

Kyle put an arm around my waist and said, almost timidly, "*Juniper, mi amiga especial.*"

332

His special friend. Guessing what he said from the bare bones Spanish I knew, I beamed shyly and the couple beamed back.

Grinning wide, Kyle ordered the food. *"Cuatro tacos de pescado, cuatro de pollo, cuatro de carne asada y mi favorito, el civeche de camarones.* And any other special."

Once our order was prepared, we bid the sweet couple a fond farewell and sauntered to the beach behind the truck. We found an isolated spot on a massive flat rock by the shore. Kyle had ordered a ridiculous variety of tacos and two Frescas and we sat amicably eating the most delicious tacos I had ever tasted.

He poured green salsa on his fish taco. "Isn't this the best food in town?"

"By far." Mouth full of shrimp ceviche, I sighed in pleasure. "You speak Spanish, eh?"

"Kinda normal in California. But my grandfather was from Mexico."

"I didn't know that."

"Hence the name I use—Castillo. Proud of my grandfather. I got his black hair and dark skin and grandma's blue eyes. She was Irish."

"I see. You're lucky. That's like God's Photoshop."

He smiled. "Yeah, I'm a mutt. My father's parents were Italian. What about your parents?"

I took a bite of my taco and pretended not to hear his question. "So your grandparents taught you Spanish?"

"No. They died before I was born. My nanny was from Mexico. Nina. Her husband Samuel was my driver. They raised me."

"Raised?"

"After my parents' divorce, we moved from dad's McMansion to my grandpa's tiny old house here. Naturally, Mother fell apart."

"Who wanted the divorce?"

Kyle stared vacantly at the foggy horizon and I noted he was grinding his teeth. "My cheating father. When we got here, Mom cried at her new life. Every freaking second. She was bored, hurt, lonely. After three months of tears and tantrums from both of us, she felt too broken to handle a ten-year-old. She hired Nina and Samuel Marquez to take care of me and went off on a long tropical islands trip. I was almost glad when she left. She had become…hard to live with. In Las Palmas, she met another rich old man to screw. He's British and she moved to London."

Slack-jawed, I looked at him. "How come she didn't take you?"

"Brit hubby had two kids. She's wife number three. Think about it. She couldn't handle me. Three kids from three families would have frigging killed her."

I looked away to hide the outrage in my eyes. My heart broke for Kyle. I imagined his childhood. I saw a lonely boy with round glasses on his little nose staring out of a house by the sea. An orphan with parents who were alive. How could a mother be such a Medusa? In comparison, my mother was Betty Crocker. And what about his douchey father?

"But, is it even legal? Why didn't you go back to your father?"

"Dad thinks the way to raise a kid is to sign a check. He has six wives, ten kids. A lucky day was when he recalled our names."

"What about holidays?"

He shrugged and did not answer. My mood dropped. The day got foggy and sky got dark.

"How were you able to fend for yourself, Kyle?"

"I told you. The Marquez family raised me." His voice was distant and snippy. Kyle was done sharing.

"Marquez, same surname as Evan…"

"Well, he is their son."

"Oh. It's kind of you to hire him." I smiled, realizing why Evan felt Kyle was more than a boss. They must have been raised together, like brothers.

"Not kindness. Business sense. Evan is an accounting genius. He went to Berkley and is the best, so I hired him."

"Oh."

My heart went back to ten-year-old Kyle. What level of self reliance had he been forced into? And what kind of coping skills did he construct? Oh...that clarified his clockwork mind. As I stared at him with glistening eyes, I saw two of me reflected in his glasses and the empathy in my eyes looking back at me. As if—the void was staring back.

He frowned. "Don't, Juniper. Don't look at me that way. Shit happens. There are billions worse off...millions suffering great hardship. I have no right to complain. My problems are cloud nine compared to the damned souls of this messed up world."

"Just because other people are suffering, doesn't mean you lose the right to mourn your loss."

"It doesn't bother me. I had every amenity. Every fucking financial advantage. I did fine."

But no family. No loved ones.

Lost in thought, I picked up a plastic fork and poked it in the crevices where I saw patches of grass. I knew this was an unusual day for him— actually going out with a girl, instead of just hooking up. He was terrified of relationships and I was beginning to see why. I had a million questions for him, but with the little information I myself offered, I'd lost my privilege to know the answers.

"I never knew my father, you know," I said faintly. "Perhaps it's for the better. I have this image of him being this perfect man. Loving, intelligent, kind. Funny too. Generous to a fault. If I knew him, I'd just end up disappointed. It's good I don't know him."

Disbelief flickered on his face because it was the first time I had shared family stuff. "How's that possible?"

I kept rapping the plastic fork until it hit stone and cracked in two pieces. Kyle picked up the pieces and put them in a brown paper bag. Shifting my legs up the rock, I put my arms on my knees. "Mom doesn't know who my father is either. It could be any of the men she was sleeping with at the time."

"Didn't she find out? Or contact him? Let him know he has kids?"

"No. She was with some royal jerks and was afraid it was one of them. Sometimes, I think she's protecting us from an ogre and sometimes I think she really doesn't know."

"Did you try to search for him?"

"I did. But the only clue was my birth certificate and it only states my mother's name. We don't have any relatives. It's just the three of us."

His face was awash in anger and empathy. "God, Juniper, you deserve better."

My hands crept over the stone slab looking for something to twiddle with. Finding nothing, I pulled at the spiny Paspalum Grass growing in the gullies of the rocks. My body went rigid, but my hands kept ripping the grass savagely. "At least I have a mother. Well. Half of a mother."

"Half?"

"Yeah. Growing up, she wasn't maternal or loving, just protective. Whatever hellish hell she lived in, she didn't want us to see. But instead of training us to fight the world, she hid us, kept us away from it all. She overprotected us. Suffocated me. At times, I feel I've only lived half a life."

"Hey." His arm went around my shoulder and I was relieved he just listened instead of probing.

My eyes rested on the ridges of broken rocks in the water. *How strange that our childhood never leaves us. It's like a kid throwing a tantrum from far far away. You can't see him but you hear him all the time.*

"That's why I never want to have children. I don't want to screw them up." When Kyle turned to me, I couldn't believe I had said that out loud.

"Me too."

Another thing in common. And not a good thing.

We sat in peace for a few moments. Then Kyle bit another taco and insisted I eat as well. After we ate every bite of the magic tacos, he dug into his leather jacket for gum and mints to cleanse the spicy salsa. When he also produced a miniature candy cane, I was stunned. *He remembers.* Though elated, I teased him for planning this trip ahead of time. He denied it and I said he must have an internal planning mechanism on autopilot inside him. This made us both chuckle.

Chewing breath mints, I stood up on the rock and stared at the roaring ocean. This was an isolated beach and the sea was more accessible here than at Land's End. I heard the call of the waves and despite Kyle trying to stop me, I jumped off. Rolling my capris thigh-high, I flung off my shoes and sashayed into the cold lashes of water. I shrieked as the Pacific winter water numbed my legs. Black seaweed laced my feet and I discovered tiny green crabs scuttling around. I ran in and out of the sea like a child, not caring I had a spectator who didn't know what fun meant.

Arms folded, face stern, Kyle stood on the rock, watching me. "Juniper, tell me you can swim. I'm wearing my favorite jacket. So please don't have a near-death experience."

"Hey, Buzzkill, lemme frolic."

"There's a Do Not Frolic sign at the beach entry."

"Kyle, don't voodoo my fun."

"I can't help it—you're so ham-fisted."

337

Arms akimbo I spun to him. "Really? Ham-fisted? You take that back. How about inelegant. Cutesy? Perky?"

"Nope. Clumsy. Inept. Ham-fisted. Ham-legged."

"Prepare to be sorry." Looking around for a pebble to thwack him with, I spotted a small crab running in and out of the water. Scooping it up with a handful of wet sand, I ran to him.

Instantly, he soared off the rock, took two steps towards me and said, "Don't you dare, Mills."

"Watch me, Paxton." With a spurt of maniacal energy, I ran to him, flung the wet sand on his jacket and placed the crab on his shoulder.

"Oh no, you didn't."

"Betcha didn't expect that, didja?"

He flicked the crab off his shoulder and gave me a look that made me shiver. "Juniper, watch out, you're going down."

"Where's your honor, sir?" With a grin, I ran towards the dry sands.

"No honor in war." Catching up with me in a second, Kyle seized my wrists and pulled me to him. Rammed against his chest, I saw the dangerous glitter in his eyes, even under his sunglasses.

Struggling was futile for his muscles were heavy-duty. So I played dirty. "Kyle. Ouchie. Let go. You're hurting my wrists."

"Sorry." Instantly, he eased his steely grip.

"Sucker." I freed one hand, wrenched his sunglasses off, and threw them down.

His frown deepened, and with a growl, he tackled me. He slammed into me and knocked the wind out of my lungs. I gasped hard. Somehow, we ended up rolling together on the sand, until I was under him. The chilly bed of sand caved under our weight. Trying to get him off me, I flung sand on his face. My attempt to grab a second fistful of sand failed for Kyle promptly pinned my wrist to the ground.

When I struggled to push him, he deliberately eased the entire length of his body onto mine, eyes in relentless contact. With a free hand, I poked his neck to put some space between us but he handcuffed it with his fingers. Powerful thighs imprisoned my legs. I twisted and turned but his smile meant he was enjoying my struggle, so I stilled.

"Kyle, lemme go at once."

"Uh-huh. Revenge time."

With one hand, he picked up a fistful of sand and began to trickle the cold grains on the hollow of my neck, slowly moving down. He looped a finger on my t-shirt's scooped neckline until my cleavage was totally exposed. Completely stirred and yet completely comatose under his spell, I did not even flinch. When he got to my bra underwire, Kyle pulled it up to drip a generous amount of sand there. Staring boldly at my generous chest, he was suddenly immobile.

"God. Your body is beautiful," he murmured.

At some point, the playful teasing had stopped. The electric tension that had been growing all day, ignited. His inflexible eye contact drove me wild and I wanted to hold him in my arms, but my arms were trapped under his fingers over my head.

"Let my hands go."

"Never." His lips hovered over mine and when I closed my eyes, he began to kiss me. At first his lips crushed mine in a valiant effort to exact revenge, but as soon as I trembled, his lips relaxed.

I met his mouth with eager heat, my tongue flicking into his mouth. My hips undulated and seemed to drive him crazy as he pinned me closer to him in the shifting sand. At some point, he released my hands and they slipped under his leather jacket. His hands went under my shirt, chafing my bare waist. One of his hands caught my breast in his hand and I gasped against his lips. The pressure of his lips deepened, and he pressed me closer—if that was even possible.

"Hey, you two heard of indecent exposure?"

Instantly, Kyle pulled my shirt down and pushed himself off me. Bemused, we stared up. Two teenage boys in wetsuits stood a few feet away, holding surfboards and snickering.

One said, "Yeah, you can get arrested for public indecency."

"LOL. Arrested for being too sexy," the other said.

"Get lost." Kyle jumped up, extended a hand to me and I groggily stood up.

Uneasy now, the boys took a step back. The first one said, "Legit helping, bro. A Florida couple got jail time for—"

"What you hot lips were doing," the second one added, chuckling.

"Listen, Beavis and Butt-Head, vamoose." Scowling, Kyle moved a tiny step towards them. They howled and ran off.

We stared at each other with self-conscious grins. He brushed the sand off me. "I didn't want to stop, but I promised you this weekend was going to be about something else."

"Thank you for the perfect day," I said.

All of a sudden, his hands snaked around my waist. My heart skated to my knees and I cried out as he elevated me and slid me down the entire length of his body. He kissed my forehead.

"June-Bug, this was the most fun I've ever had."

"Me too. All without a plan."

He pulled away. As we walked to the car, Kyle was moody, quiet and pensive again. Maybe it needled him that we had no plan today. Jaw locked, he spaced out like an android adjusting himself for human contact. I heard the whirring of his clockwork mind, the cogs turning and the wheels gyrating. When his smile thawed, I felt like I had won a silent battle. Like the sun had come out even in the dim and misty air.

"For the first time in years and years, I have not thought about time, clocks, schedules, work."

"Don't you go on vacation and chill?"

"Never. Even when rock climbing, I take a satellite phone."

"Oh."

Images flashed through my mind. Kyle and I exploring Ireland. Greece. Petra. All the historical ruins I loved. Endless vacations. Feeling shy, I looked away, painfully aware of the fact that he was almost a stranger to me. And yet he had become so familiar I couldn't imagine my life without him. Conflicting thoughts. Terrifying beyond belief.

"I should get back to the hotel."

"Like that?" Kyle gave me a once over. "Nice mud bath."

"Yeah, yeah. I'm a dirt magnet." I looked down. My capris were mud-coated and my shirt was filled with wet sand. Save a few glistening specks of sand on his chic jacket, he was as impeccable as ever, as if it had been his stunt double rolling in the sand with me.

"Don't go back, Juniper. Just come over. You have to be at my house for dinner at any rate."

"No way."

"My house is five minutes from here. I can hose you off in my yard." He chuckled at my incensed face. "Okay. Shower. Change there and get ready for tonight."

"But I didn't bring clothes."

Kyle insisted I go with him as he had to oversee the catering staff for tonight's party. The secretive smile on his face made me think he was bluffing. It pleased me that the idea of parting after this flawless day hurt him too.

I called Stacy and instructed her to bring my clothes tonight. Before I hung up, I said, "Get to Kyle's house early. I'll join you so they think I came with you."

He leaned against the car, watching me with a smug smile. "Why do you care what people think?"

"Are you laughing at me? You know when people laugh at me, I throw crabs at them."

"When people throw crabs at me, they get punished. Want more?" His lips parted and he reached for me.

"No." I blushed, stopping a few inches from him. The air ruffled his crisp black hair and I admired the study of contrast his face was. The depth of his navy irises, the long lashes and the full lips, the sharp angles of his face, the patrician tilt of his nose, the harsh cut of his jaw and the abrasive stubble lining it. His striking looks were even more overpowering so close up. And for some unknown reason…this man…wanted to be with me.

"Juniper, stop with the dirty thoughts about me. Or I'll take you against the car and we'll get arrested."

"I *do not* have dirty thoughts about you." My blush deepened and I looked down.

"Liar. Every time you turn pink, I know your mind is getting hot and dirty."

"No, it's not." He was right, but I shook my head. In front of the passenger seat, I brushed off as much dirt as I could. I was humiliated when a residue of sand sprinkled on the luxurious mats of his car as I slid inside. I was glad he didn't seem to care.

We had agreed to leave our phones behind, but Kyle turned the car on with one hand and his phone with the other. The Bluetooth screen began to buzz with his missed calls, texts and emails. For a few minutes, he drove while staring at his phone, then with an impatient flick of his wrist, he threw it down.

Concerned about the number of incoming calls, I asked, "Aren't you going to check your messages?"

"Nope."

"Why?"

"It's the first time in six years I've gone minus phone for more than five minutes."

"How's that possible?"

"Believe me," he said, with a sidelong glance at me. "It's how I run my company."

"So you're a micromanager?" I said teasingly.

"No—" he broke off with a little laugh. "Maybe. Some would say that. I guess, I'm on top of everything. But today, I want to let everything go. Except you."

KYLE

S omething was wrong. Something was very very wrong. He felt it spread out from deep inside like black liquid bitumen. To stop it from taking over his mind, he picked up his phone. So many missed calls. He scrolled down. Emails from work. Texts from Evan, Sylvia, Sheila, Izzy and Willow. And most important of all…Min-Jun. He longed to call her. She was important to him.

No.

He dropped the phone down. Today, it was all about Juniper. Only her.

But then why did he feel something was very very wrong?

Inside him?

CHAPTER 21

The road to Seacliff was not like the rest of San Francisco. There was no human traffic, the streets were wide, and the houses big with sweeping lawns and tall, mature trees. As Kyle drove uphill, I admired the fog-drenched palm trees against the limestone walls. I didn't know why, but palm trees made me happy.

Seacliff mansions were an eclectic mix of Spanish villas, French chateaus and Georgian mansions, and not a single cookie cutter design could be found among them. It was peaceful and Zen, yet awfully elitist. These homes must be valued above ten million and I felt a jab of unease. It was a sore reminder of the unbridgeable gaps between us.

Silent the whole way, Kyle drove with one hand, the other resting on the open window, his face guarded and flinty, as if he needed to recharge his Distant-Kyle-Batteries. As if he regretted saying, *I want to let everything go. Except you.*

"So, your grandpa built the house?" I asked, not able to endure the crickets between us.

He shot me a stunned glance, as if he had forgotten I was in the car with him. After a long pause he said, "Yes."

"When."

"In 1953."

"Tell me about him."

"What about him?"

"Anything. I never knew any of my grandparents."

"What about your mom's parents?"

"Never met them.

"Why?"

"Mom left home when she was in college. She never went back."

"Oh. So—"

"Tell me stuff," I said, interrupting him.

"Okay. Grandpa…Arturo Castillo was a travelling salesman. His parents came from Mexico to Los Angeles in the nineteen twenties."

"So how'd he move here?"

"He used to sell vacuum cleaners to homes here. He was dirt poor and had the crazy dream to move into this neighborhood. During the war, he was stationed in France, and fell in love with an army nurse, Amy Maxwell. She got stationed in the Pacific, but he never forgot her. Once the war was over, he wrote to her—a letter every day until she agreed to meet him."

"How romantic." I clasped my hands.

He carried on as if I had said nothing. "She moved from New York to San Francisco to be with him. He swore not to marry her till he built her a house. For seven long years, he saved every dime and lived with friends in mind-blowing poverty. At times, he slept in his car. Grandma thought he was mad, but she loved him and waited out the seven-year-engagement. Finally he got enough money, bought the land, and built the house. They got married in its garden. They loved each other every single moment they were alive."

"What a lovely story," I exclaimed, the hopeless romantic and history lover in me tearing up.

Kyle pursed his lips and ignored my comment. Perhaps he wanted to make sure I did not get carried away with the hope he and I had a future. Perhaps, I read too much in his aloof mood. Nevertheless, I was crushed.

Seeing my mood change, he said lightly, "Believe it or not, he got the land for four thousand bucks and built a home on it for fifteen thousand. Crazy, huh?"

It was probably worth fifteen million now. "Cool. They left the house to you?" I made sure my voice was more neutral this time.

"Mother has little use for it and gave it to me."

I nodded and looked out of the window. It seemed his mother had little use for him as well. What kind of mother would leave a ten-year-old boy to fend for himself? No wonder Kyle was petrified of relationships and commitment.

Oh...

The road wound up to the top edge of the cliff. The trees got bigger and taller and there was nothing but shrubbery on the knolls by the road. No homes. Just dense woods. The road narrowed and curved dangerously until it widened into a private lane. The street sign read, Vacuum Lane. Odd. *Vacuum Salesman, ah.*

Kyle's grandfather did not want to forget his roots.

A laminated glass and steel gate slid open and the car pulled into a long asphalt driveway. The house came upon you so suddenly you could do nothing but gape. Set on a plateau cliff facing the bay basin, it was organically built in the wooded rocky site. Kyle parked in a car porch in front of garage and I jumped out to examine the house, head cocked, like I was inspecting a new artifact in the museum.

It was not mansion-sized as I had expected, but it was adequate. Three interlocking rectangles made up the minimalist structure of gray concrete, white marble, and shimmering glass. The glass walls made it look transparent and from one end of the house I saw clear to the other side. There were wall-to-wall windows with metal cladding, cubic terraces, intersected gardens, and decks dotted with succulent and tropical plants in neat rows, giving the impression of an ecological indoor-outdoor space. It was breathtaking. Modern. Futuristic. Unique. Chic. Stony. Distant. Just like Kyle Paxton...

He came and stood beside me, his hands in his pockets. "What do you think?"

"It's so you."

My answer seemed to confuse him, and he searched my face. "Two years ago, it was a rotting wreck and I was ready to level it and sell. But I realized I could not buy better land in the city. My grandpa was smart. So I renovated it."

"You did well. Your architect did a great job of blending history with the future but I like that it still has the Mid-Century bones."

"Yes."

"Did you live here during the renovation?"

"No, I moved in a year ago."

"Where'd you live in between?"

"I have an apartment in a high-rise near my office."

Have. Not had?

"I see." But I did not see.

I wondered if the apartment was now his…fuck-pad. My belly knotted. In the course of my trip to San Francisco, I had come to know another side of Kyle Paxton. The real guy he kept hidden behind the lady-killer facade. Instead of growing on me, the idea of him with different girls every few months was now more intolerable.

"Um. Are your caterers here?"

"Nope. They arrive later." He grinned. "I just wanted you to come with me."

With deep breath, I said, "I see. Well, I need a shower. Like now."

"More like radiation decontamination."

"Ha-ha. Cute."

Kyle went to a panel by the door and a laser scanned his eyes. The door opened and I rolled my eyes. *Super-dork.* He stepped inside and beckoned me to follow. I froze at the door frame. I did not want to go in.

"Juniper?" He glanced at me and I took a cautious step inside the foyer.

They say that there are some houses with bad auras.

Kyle Paxton's house was one of them. As I followed him through room after room, the bad vibes of the house hit me and I wanted to bolt. Looking around, I saw everything was flawless, airy, sunny—nothing eerie for miles. But a solid aura of solitude, anger, loss, and relentless grief hung in the air. It was like walking in smoke clouds.

Maybe I was being ridiculous, but I could not shake the feeling. At times, I felt that negative energy when I was unpacking a disturbing and historically cursed artifact. I wondered if something bad or violent had happened and left its mark in the house. Kyle was walking with his shoulders slumped and his face was kind of lost, as if, the bad juju was his old friend.

The house was a blank white vacuum with cold marble, quartz,

Birchwood floors, and plasma screens and monitors all over—a beautiful blend of technology and art. There were some incredible art pieces too and I made a mental note to explore them later.

Kyle stopped in a sunken great room out of which the entire house flowed. It was sparse with white couches, white carpets on icy marble floors, and white sculptures on white displays. The window wall revealed an infinity pool, deck and staggered gardens outside. I could not resist walking to it and staring out. The showstopper was the view of the rocky cliffs, the Golden Gate Bridge and a small beach down below.

I whistled. "Sweet. What a view."

"You can trek to the beach from there."

"Before I trek mud on your pristine house, shower please." I turned to him.

He stood near a floating staircase, watching me in that disquieting way of his. "Come here, Juniper."

When I reached him, he extended a hand. I took it and felt the voltage charge I always did when we touched. Our eyes met and I thought of the way he had kissed me on the beach and my cheeks seared. As we walked up, the silence was heavy between us—fraught with expectation and a need to fulfill the longing.

Upstairs, he led me to a landing and ushered me into a bedroom. It had unexpected feminine touches I had not seen anywhere else in the house. There was a gray satin chaise by a window framed in long silk curtains, a white tufted bed set on a geometric wall and silver moon-and-star shaped mirrors hanging above mirrored chests. It was decorated in shades of gray and silver—very old Hollywood glamour décor. I felt Veronica Lake or Ava Gardner would appear from thin air and yell at me for disturbing their boudoir.

"Whose room is this?"

"Yours," he said, tersely.

350

Like that explains anything.

"Bathroom through here." Kyle slid open a frosted glass door, revealing a huge rectangle bathtub and a glassed-off shower.

"Thanks. Can I borrow a t-shirt?" It was an awkward moment and I felt unwelcome, as if I were imposing on a stranger.

"No need."

He stalked to another door by the bathroom. Eyes shining, he threw it open and stepped inside a massive walk-in closet. I gasped at the sight of the rows of evening gowns, skirts, jeans, t-shirts, and brand new shoes I saw. An entire designer wardrobe. New clothes with labels that looked suspiciously like my size. I shrank from the closet as if it were filled with poison ivy.

"Whose clothes are these?"

"My mother's."

"I'm fine. Don't wanna wear her clothes."

"They're from last season and she'll never wear them. So all yours."

I folded my arms over my chest. "No. Thank. You."

Frustrated, he frowned and ran a hand through his hair. "Don't be an idiot, Juniper. Mother never visits. Please. All yours."

What fresh insanity was this? Had he decided I was now to be his companion...his pay-as-you-go-along-mistress? "I'm not an idiot, Kyle. These are my size."

"Fine. They are yours."

Why did you lie?

"O-kaaay. No. Not okay. When did you buy this stuff?"

"I didn't. One of my assistants did."

"When, Kyle?"

"Yesterday."

"You mean after we talked in the club? Why the hell?"

He raised a cool eyebrow. A muscle worked furiously in his jaw. Clearly he was not used to being grilled. By anyone. "Don't turn this into a big deal. My fuck-buddies always keep a set of clothing at my place."

Yuck. In this room! This was a room reserved for his—harem girls? I flushed. I knew he was angry and said those words to put me down. "At this house?"

"No. At my apartment."

Whew. Relief. Only temporary relief. So he did have a separate fuck-pad. It made me anxious and I wondered if Izzy was still there. "So…why'd you bring me here?"

"I don't know. You're the only one I've taken to this house."

"Kyle, I haven't agreed to anything yet."

"Yet, here you are." His voice was caustic, his eyes icy.

It hurt. The coldness directed at me was a punch in the gut. I turned away from him, hands clawing at the room door. The particles of sadness drifting in the air hit me again. Tears welled up in my eyes and I wanted to run away. "I should go."

"Dear God." His arm shot out and grasped my wrist. In a second, I was pulled into his arms and I sank against him. For a few seconds he just held me, his hands stroking my shoulder blades and soothing me. "Juniper. Juniper. Don't go. Please. If you say no after this weekend—fine. Please stay."

All I managed was to say his name and bury my face in his shoulder. I felt our combined heartbeats rising together. My head swam. This was all so new for me. My first relationship—was it even one?—and it was so damned warped.

"These clothes are not to sway you. They are for convenience. Just that. Get it? I'm a planner. I like things preset. Planned. Not chaotic. Not last minute."

"How'd you know my size? Can you tell girls' sizes with your laser vision?"

"The way I can tell the cubic feet of a couch." I felt the smile in his voice. "No. I had Evan check when he got your coat cleaned."

He had my size checked in Ann Arbor? After I had stormed out on him? So he had been planning all of this since then.

He kissed the top of my head. "If it bothers you, feel free to leave them here after you're done. Or take them with you. I don't care. All yours, Juniper. Everything I do in the next six months will be all yours."

Curses. The heavyweight topics again. "Okay, I'll wear the clothes while I'm here. Thank you. But I'll leave everything here."

"Whatever. Your stuff, not mine." As if he was tired of the topic, he stepped away from me and I felt stone-cold once our bodies were separated. "Please pick a dress for tonight. I have curators and donors coming from several museums. Good networking for you. I'll see you later, then." He stepped out of the room with a polite smile.

"Why are you doing this, Kyle?" I called after him.

He stopped dead in his tracks. "What do you mean?"

"Why're you so nice to the museum? We've never had any board member go so far."

"They should." His brow furrowed in irritation and his voice was clipped, as if I was holding him against his will.

"How does it benefit you?"

Anger darkened his expression. "What. The. Fuck. How does it benefit me? You've accused me of this before. I don't like being wrongly accused. To the damned contrary, Juniper. It's all for you...I mean...for the museum."

My mouth hung open. "What do you mean, it's all for me?"

Exasperated, he massaged the back of his neck. "Juniper, why do you push me so? If you must know, I made my decision to join the board after

353

I met you."

"What are you saying, Kyle? I don't get it." My knees weakened and I was in danger of melting like clay in a kiln.

Kyle marched towards me and I found myself backtracking until I hit the wall. He placed his hands on both sides of me, caging me in tight. His face dipped down and he planted a soft kiss on my lips.

"It's all for you, Juniper. Everything the past month has all been for you."

"I don't understand."

"When I first saw you on that scaffolding, I had not made the decision to become the board president. I was way too busy. After I met you, I was intrigued. I decided to do it. It's all been for you, Juniper. My decision to be on the board...coming for Thanksgiving with my family...this trip for the museum staff to San Francisco. The event tonight. This room. Just for you."

What?

He'd done all of it for me? I did not know whether to cry or laugh. Hysteria grew in me and I did not know if I should be overjoyed or mega-depressed. No one had ever done anything like this for me before. Even if it was kinda creepy, it was sweet and poignant. One thing was clear—he cared for me. Kyle Paxton cared for me...more than he cared to admit. Did that mean he wanted more from me? From us?

Like an ivy that takes over your house, new leaves of hope popped up in my naive heart. "So all of this...I don't get it. Please elaborate."

"No. I've already said too much." His expression grew distant again. "Don't read too much into it, Juniper. I make my decisions on human capital quickly. When I meet people, I know at once if I want to work with them and if I want to be with them."

Human capital. Ouch. It was like another sock in the gut. Looking up, I put my palms on his chest to try to push him away, but I was trapped in a cage of his arms. His face tensed but he did not let me go. Instead, he moved so close our breaths mingled.

"This is a lot to take in, Kyle."

"Juniper, stop. Again, don't overthink. Stop overanalyzing me. I am not as deep as you think I am. I just want you."

His lips came down on mine. He kissed me savagely. It was a vicious kiss. Hard. One-sided. Demanding. Angry. As if he was staking his claim. As if he was in a losing battle to establish dominion over me. As if he was trying to convince himself that we were only fuck-buddies. Nothing more. But, in that moment I knew. I knew he cared more for me than he admitted even to himself, but that he would never act on it. He had a system. He had bent it for me, but he'd never break that system. Never change. For Kyle Paxton did not negotiate.

Oh, and you do, Juniper?

It was hard to think with his assault on my senses. The entire length of his body pressed into me even as his lips continued their battering. At some point he rammed me against the wall, his hands seized my hips and lifted me, parting my legs for better access. He kissed me that way until my mouth was raw, my ribs ached, and I could no longer form coherent syllables. Though I did not want him to stop (and let him know this by kissing him back) the dark force of his desire frightened me.

I managed to tear my mouth away. "Kyle. Please."

Instantly, he slid me down the wall. His lips went to my forehead and his eyes searched mine in regret. His hand cupped my jaw and a thumb gently rubbed my lips. "I'm sorry. You are red here. Did I hurt you?"

"I'm fine. But you said...no physical expectations this weekend."

He pulled away with a jerk, leaving me sagging on the wall for support. "Yes. I'll remember. The ball's in your court."

When he left, I stood rooted in the shaggy white carpet. I had never been kissed like that before. I touched my swollen lips. I still felt his punishing kiss. It was so different from the tender kisses at the club or the playful ones at the beach. Like he was seeking something more than physical contact. But physical contact was the only way he knew how to communicate.

The ball's in your court. What in the world did his words mean? Do I have to make the first move now, physically?

I locked the room, peeled off my clothes and slid into the glass-enclosed shower. Luxury jets flooded me with vertical and horizontal streams. Leaning against the textured tiles of the shower wall, I stared out the window in the bathroom. It was a bizarre luxury to see the bay views while taking a shower. I tried to process what had just happened and what he'd dropped on me. Why had he done all of this for me? It did not make sense, if I was supposed to end it all in six months.

I can't end it.

I should end it, now.

It will be harder, later.

This was all too much. Kyle was a bullet train going through my life at such speed that if either one of us applied the brakes, I'd go flying out. I admitted Kyle was trying hard with me; this level of care and attention to my needs was unheard of. But there was a darker part of him—the icy, indifferent part he kept hidden—and I had just seen it.

The part he knew would frighten me.

The part seeking total dominance and control.

A control he applied by engineering and limiting other people's emotional, social and economic choices. By his own admission, he was a sociopath. Machiavelli had said, "He who wishes to be obeyed must know how to command." And Kyle knew how to command and lure dupes like

Izzy and me with things they wanted.

The only thing I wanted was Kyle.

Yet, argued an illogical voice in my head, I wanted Kyle because he was also thoughtful.

Kind. Into me.

Tears rolled down my cheeks and got lost in the flood of the shower. I pressed against the raw-cut limestone shower wall, trying to stop the tears that just kept coming. Why the hell was I crying? I barely ever cried. With an easily hurt special needs brother who took things too literally, I had the notable distinction of going through adult life with very few tears. For the past two days, I had almost cried a frightening four times, like I was missing key chemicals in my brain. I did not know who this weepy girl was. I did not know how to stop the tears.

How to stop the pain.

I just knew that I was falling for Kyle Paxton. Already, I could not imagine my life without him. And he was making it very hard for me to leave him or to say no to his ridiculous proposition. How could I be with him in such a consuming physical and emotional way to be tossed aside for another girl—the way he had tossed Izzy aside. He'd said that there had been only six. But I wondered if he had conferred verbal terminations on many, many, many others before he set up his system.

Did all his F-buddies get special treatment? Or was I special? Was I a dice in his game? A shiny object in a bored life? Was generous n' restrained Kyle just a con to convince me to say yes? Did he *become* exactly the type of guy he thought his companions wanted?

That made me numb and my tears finally stopped.

I stayed in the shower until I was a human prune. Once out, I opened the bathroom drawers looking for a hair dryer and was shocked to see them lined with all kinds of brand new and boxed hair products, styling tools, creams, gels, lavish makeup—everything a girl could possibly need for primping. For a decade.

I washed my face and tried to de-puff my swollen eyes. I applied makeup and amped up my eyes with mascara and eyeliner. I used my own makeup from my purse as I was way too stubborn to use Kyle's purchases. I blow-dried my hair in waves while repeating a mantra silently. *Juniper, be still. Emotion is weakness.*

I walked into the closet and discovered how complete it was with purses, shoes, dresses, jeans, shirts, casual and formal wear. It even included swimwear, underwear, and...lingerie. *Jeez Louise.* Fingering the lacy edge of a diaphanous white teddy, I sighed. It was a sore reminder I had never owned lingerie. I took out the exquisite dresses and held them against me. Size four. My size. The prices had been ripped off but I saw high-end designer labels. It was all lavish haute couture. Kyle's assistant had good taste. I knew Kyle was flush, but this was too much.

The girly part in me skipped and hopped for joy in the luxury I had never experienced. The feminist part of me cringed in a corner of the room at being dressed up like a doll to please a man. It made me want to walk out of this room naked and burn the bras in the fire pit on the deck. However, the logical part of me won. I put on black underwear, dark wash jeans and a gray t-shirt. I had asked Stacy to bring my clothes tonight and there was no way I was wearing Kyle's purchases beyond convenience. It was too creepy.

But when I saw myself in the full-length closet mirror, I caught my breath. The designer jeans and low heels elongated my legs, and the deceptively simple t-shirt was loose and trendy in a clingy and sexy way. Picking up my dirty clothes, I walked downstairs. The house looked deserted. Then I heard voices coming from the kitchen where I saw a few caterers loading trays with savory delicacies. They stopped working when they saw me.

"Hello. You guys know where the laundry room is?" I held up my dirty clothes.

Some of the caterers hid their faces knowingly.

"Hello, Miss Juniper." An older woman, not in a catering uniform, came forward. "This way, please."

"Thank you."

She led me to a tiled laundry room and took my clothes. "I'll take care of this."

"I got it."

"No. No. I will do it. I am Marlene, by the way." She smiled genially. "Mr. Paxton's housekeeper."

"Nice to meet you."

Marlene was short and stocky with curly brown hair and twinkling black eyes. She was around fifty years old but her wrinkle-free, smiling face made her look younger.

"Once dry, I will put these in your room."

So even the housekeeper knew I was sleeping here. I looked at the floor, my face red. "Thank you."

"Mr. Paxton said to let him know as soon as you came down. He's in the office working. Shall I get him?"

"No. Please don't disturb him."

She gave me a surprised look and I wondered how many of Kyle's exes she had met and served. *Duh, all of them.*

"Miss, can I get you something to eat or drink?"

I followed her to the kitchen and took the iced mint tea she was offering. Sipping the delicious drink, I walked out to the garden. Skirting the pool edges, I looked at the view below. The sinking sun cast a gloomy net of light over the hills and city. The sunset and fog drifting over the silhouetted eucalyptus trees was a melancholy but breathtaking sight. I just stood there, not feeling the view for my heart had dropped when I found out Kyle was working. I felt unwelcome and out of place. Perhaps my decision to stay here was rushed and reckless.

"Juniper." I heard a low voice behind me.

KYLE

December 11, 6:17 p.m. 33 seconds
(Kyle's House, Seacliff)

A t the sound of Kyle's voice, Juniper tilted her neck sideways, her posture hesitant like she was on the brink of running away. Finally she turned, rocking on her heels. For the first time since he had met her, she was wearing clothes worthy of her beauty. They suited her. A lot. Sheila, one of Kyle's stylish assistants, had done well. He smiled. But his Rebel Warrior had not worn a dress and he was sure she had picked the plainest pieces in the closet.

Gliding in her low heels, she came to him and every cell in his body caught on fire. He wanted her. Right now. He imagined peeling off those useless clothes to make love to her on the pool edge.

Make love? What the fuck?

He had not used those words since high school.

Since Chloe.

Then he heard Sylvia's grating voice on the phone and every cell in his body numbed to ice. As Kyle shifted his phone to speaker, he noted Juniper's eyes. They were lined with half-moon mauve shadows. As if she had been crying. Kyle swallowed.

Did I make you cry?

He felt piss awful. Like someone had punched his nose so hard, his eyes watered. His brow furrowed. What did this remind him of?

It was like Chloe all over again.

No. No. No. Not Chloe. It can't be. Never again.

CHAPTER 22

Kyle stood by a glass door holding a phone, watching me. I put my drink down and walked to him slowly. When I got closer, I noticed a female voice coming from his phone. "So I met Chad's Cirrus CEO today. Got an office tour of his cloud computing biz. Impressive. He says IBM is trying to buy them out. Did you know they raised more than three billion in a major final quarter funding reload?"

Kyle grasped my wrist and pulled me close to him, his eyes drifting over me. I returned the favor. His hair was slicked back and he wore blackout evening clothes. All black slacks, blazer and a shirt with a few buttons open. The bit of bronze chest peeking through the v of his shirt looked so delectable, I wanted to unbutton the whole thing.

"I know Chad is not your favorite person, but I think a potential strategic alliance with them on our CK-290 AI prototype is—" the voice was saying.

Kyle's eyebrows shot up and he pressed the unmute button. "Sylvia, why do I have to repeat we are not ever partnering with the pricks at Cirrus. Meeting Chad the D-bag was enough for a lifetime of no and no."

The voice was Sylvia's, the striking, incredibly successful woman who worked with Kyle. Her voice was cooler now. "So your only objection to Cirrus is Chad is a D-bag and that you didn't like his sushi models? Is that how we run things now?"

"You really wanna know? Yes, nasty sushi is the first thing. The second is this Chad. Both lead to cons of liability and merged reputation. That's two cons. The third is lack of control."

"Let me handle him, you just—"

"Sylvia. I told you I was busy today."

"Kyle. You have been MIA—"

"Talk on Monday."

"Fine. See you later at your house."

Kyle hung up on her and turned to me. "I feel bad now."

"About what?

"About work."

I smiled slightly. "If you didn't work, my museum would suffer."

He grinned and pulled me into his arms and I tucked my chin on his shoulder. What was happening to us? We could not physically keep away even for a minute.

"Juniper, I'm also sorry, about earlier."

"No need. Thank you for...everything. I'm sorry I was such a pain. It's just that I am used to taking care of myself." My voice was muffled against his jacket lapel. Nuzzling his collar, I inhaled the fragrant but distinctly masculine scent I had become so used to. *Itching to rip that shirt off.*

"I can see that. You refused to wear a party dress."

"Stacy is bringing my clothes."

"Huh. I see I lost the battle."

I pulled away from him. "But you won the war."

"Have I?" he murmured. "But I did not. I can't even explain myself. My buying you clothes was not to exert control over you—"

"Aha. Just a few days ago, you said you control everyone and everything around you."

"Fine. But I could care less about clothes. I believe in the science of simplicity and practically wear the same thing every day. And baby, you'd be gorgeous in a paper bag. But I know that if you agree to be with me, you'll attend many events. Formal occasions where you're expected to dress a certain way. I want you to be comfortable and fit in." He closed his eyes. "Ah, fuck it. I messed up again. I have very little experience saying the right things to women."

"So your er…companions never speak with you?"

"Rarely."

My cheeks got hot as I considered his words. So basically, Kyle and his six former buddies did not talk. They probably just made love—no, no, no—copulated like animals in all the rooms of his apartment. In the back of limos. In hotel suites. Perhaps the very hotel suite I was put up in. This messed with my head. "So you've not had even a semblance of a relationship with them?"

"No. We attended events so I could have a plus one. They traveled with me but always lived in separate rooms, so I could work. It was simple convenience. Before my system, I took a few girls to different events and the media typecast me as a player. That's *not* who I am."

"Like when people say, I'm not racist but…"

"All right. I know you made a snap judgment about me and it hasn't changed. Listen, if I'm seen with the same girl for months on end, it works. Helps my business image. Keeps the traditional BirdsEye board from ramming down my throat. The girls with me know what I need without infringing on my privacy. Also if I'm seen as single, I get slammed everywhere I go with time-wasting offers from women."

"You poor Stud Muffin," I said, shaking my head. "Such personal sacrifice and struggle for the progress of technology and humanity."

He smiled. "But with you everything is different. You are special, you are—"

I interrupted him with a dry laugh. "Oh, am I the One? Like Neo or Frodo. Keep calm because I am the chosen one."

"Juniper, stop trolling me. Or I'll find a way to punish you. I'm serious. Until you, I saw my system as a protocol, the end to need. Not desire. With you it is different."

"How?"

Instead of answering, he took hold of my hand and led me into his office. It was all hard lines and bare bones and a plush white carpet that looked like a lifeless polar bear was the only soft accent. There was a long bookshelf, a white desk with several monitors, an Eames swivel chair, and a low bureau above which hung a vibrant painting. Like the rest of the house, it was white, bleak, minimalist, and scary organized. With a smile, I imagined the room splattered with thousands of pinpricks of paint globs by Yayoi Kusama who painted polka dots on entire rooms. It'd drive Kyle nuts.

Leaning against the desk, he pulled me close to him. With two fingers, he tilted my face up. "June-Bug, you are so different from any girl I've ever known. And when you are with me, I feel like an idiot. I feel like a moronic teenager doing the whole shebang wrong."

"Kyle, you're trying and I like that. You respect my wish not to jump into things and I can't even start to process what you've done for me. The museum, the seminar, the events, the clothes. I'm grateful, but I'm also..."

overwhelmed by it all."

"My logic was not to overwhelm you but let you know how much you mean to me. I should not have told you. I swore I'd never let you know." He took off his glasses and pressed two fingers on the bridge of his nose. Then he looked up and I caught my breath at the raw emotion in his eyes. "But the truth is, since I first met you, I wanted you. No matter what. I don't think I've been thinking straight from day one. After your trip here, I know what I feel is not simple want or need but something...more."

More? Kyle Paxton wanted more from me?

My heart stilled. It was all very flattering but I forced myself to picture Izzy standing there with him—and it made me sick. So if I agreed to be with him, a few months later he'd be hunting for a shiny new object while I waited for him in Ann Arbor? I was nauseous enough to vomit my green tea in his turquoise pool.

"What are you thinking?"

I was glad his superpower was reading time and not minds. "Kyle, you have certain rules and limits for your, er, buddies. Have we already broken some of those?"

"I guess...you're right. We've broken those rules. I never bring anyone to this house. Never take them to my office, or introduce them to my coworkers. I've never gone on what can only be called a date like today. And for God's sake, I don't talk about my childhood. Or talk. At all. Rule broken."

"So do you want to set up some ground rules for us?"

"No, doll, I get the feeling that ground rules will not work for us. I like rules. You like smashing them." He grinned wide and I smiled back.

"Should we take it day by day...and see where it goes?"

"I agree. All my rules and bylaws can go down the drain. Nothing in my life is off limits to you, Juniper. The only thing I'm not willing to compromise on is the Termination Contract." His voice was measured and careful and he watched me warily.

The Termination Contract.

His words were like a punch to my gut. Kyle could be a professional wrestler if he wanted. He wanted to end it. I wanted it to never end. Could I do this? My heart pounded and I pulled away from his arms. I went to look at the only artwork on the wall, the painting of bright concentric circles.

Eyes squinting, I said, "You have some incredible artwork in your collection. Whose piece is this?"

"Bruce Gray. He's not well known. It's called Raindrops number 4. I like it. It's loopy but complex. I picked this one in L.A. by myself. The first art piece I got that was not in a catalogue."

"Who buys your art?"

"Evan. From Sotheby's auctions."

"Hmm. I was wrong. You don't just have Hirst or Koons. Your taste is eclectic."

"No." He came to stand by me. "You were right. My house was full of Hirsts. After I came back from Ann Arbor, I took a look around and laughed hard at what you had said. And I went on a little art spree."

"Nicely done, Mr. Paxton."

"So that's how you deflect tough issues, Miss Mills. By talking about art."

"Excuse me?" I arched an eyebrow and locked eyes with him.

"I asked you about the Termination Contract and you distracted me. Smoke and mirrors."

Coloring, I walked to the desk with my back to him. His words kindled rage in my head. *The only thing I'm not willing to compromise on is the Termination Contract.*

Then how was I any different from the others?

"Fine. I will sign the Termination Contract if that's what you want. Why don't you show it to me right now?"

He followed me. "Juniper, don't be like that. Take your time. I'll email it to you—"

"Then tell me what's in it."

He frowned. "It's a notice of the termination date. It creates a record that I notified the party about the cancellation of the relationship and the end date. Kind of a courtesy reminder that the time stamped contractual obligation is done and both parties agree to part on its mutual terms."

"Why don't you email it to me right now? Or print it? Right now."

"I'll email it to you. Later. Take a look at it, read it and if you have a lawyer, ask him or her to look it over. If there are clauses you want to modify, let me know."

"I want to read it right now. Print it out." I put my hands on his desk, leaning forward in grim determination.

Shaking his head, he clicked away on his desktop while watching me. In a few seconds, the slim printer on a bureau by his desk hummed to life. Papers emerged from the printer like an egg-eating snake spitting up the shells. Moving like quicksilver, I went to the printer and grabbed the papers. I arranged them in a sheaf and saw that there were around ten sheets. I grabbed a pen, flipped to the last sheet and signed the dotted line at the end of the document.

"Juniper. Stop."

"It's too late. I signed it."

"Well, I don't accept it. For God's sake, read the freaking thing, then sign it."

With a resolute pout, I signed a few more places that required my signature. "There, all done."

"I don't want you to do this."

"Yes, you do."

"Don't be like this." Kyle snatched the papers so fast from my hands, I got a paper cut.

I gasped when I saw a drop of blood on my index finger. With a smirk, I squeezed as much blood out as I could and smeared a red line on the document he had slammed on his desk. Now I knew what Dr. Faustus must have felt like when he signed away his soul in service to Mephistopheles.

"See, signed in blood." I sucked my finger.

"What the hell, Juniper?" Kyle glared at the line of blood under my signature. With a growl, he dug in the drawers of his desk and pulled out a small tube of Neosporin. Clasping my finger, he examined where I got hurt and applied a drop of antiseptic there. "God, what are you made of? Kleenex? I feel like an ass for hurting you." He massaged my finger gently and the pain went away.

Then he picked up the papers, and when I saw he was about to rip them, I snatched them away and held them behind my back. "Nope, already signed and delivered."

"What's wrong with you? You're a total bolshie. Impulsive, crazy, self-destructive. I do not accept this." He took the papers back from me, tossed them in a drawer and shut it firmly. "I'll keep it as a token of your rash behavior. However, I'll ask you tomorrow night, as originally planned, if you want to be with me or not. Then go home, read—"

"Kyle, I trust you. I've signed the damned contract. Now let's get on with our lives. I am yours for six months. Till the termination day." Suddenly, the pain of leaving him forever hit me like a dozen paper cuts. My shoulders shook and I rotated my back to him.

"Juniper, listen—" His voice was raw and soft behind me. Whatever he was going to say I would never know. Just then the bell rang. Again and again. It was an odd digital chime that echoed all over the house. "Who the hell. Evan invited the guests at eight. Right now it's 6:36. I'll throw this person out." He stalked to the living room and I followed him.

Marlene, the housekeeper, entered, panting. "Mr. Kyle, it's Miss Willow. Were you expecting her?"

There was a loud clicking of heels and a girl burst into the room and I caught the impression of a ball of energy. Marlene stepped around her and left. As soon as she saw Kyle, Willow shrieked his name and flung herself in his arms. At first, he flinched and stood rigid. At her repeated hugs, he held her waist with one hand as she proceeded to kiss both his cheeks, French style.

"Kyle," she screamed. "Where the hell have you been? You've ignored all my calls. My assistant sent you sixty texts. Sixty. I don't pay her enough for this crap. And Evan said you were out. Out where? Seriously, dude, what is wrong with you?"

Lips pursed, he pulled away from her. "Willow, what are you doing here?"

My heart dropped. Willow lived up to her name. She was utterly beautiful and exotic with a petite and thin figure, deep tanned skin, wavy long brown hair, brown eyes, and absurdly long black lashes like an anime cartoon. She exuded an air of Bohemian chic and zany abandon evident in her ankle-length lacy mushroom skirt, white peasant blouse, piles of turquoise bracelets, the bag of vintage textiles, and the oddity of a Spanish fan in her hand as a fashion accessory. The crisp designer jacket and long heels were her only concession to mainstream fashion. Though heavily applied, her makeup was girlish and deceptively bare. She was oddly familiar and I wracked my brain trying to remember where I had seen her.

At Kyle's question, she threw her arms around his neck again and said, "You are a cold-hearted jerk, you know?"

371

"One of my better qualities."

"Always the cocky bastard."

"And I love you too." He grinned and drew her closer.

What fresh hell is this?

Did he just say he *loved* her? My heart was slowly tearing apart. Who was this diva? And why the hell was she so intimate with Kyle? Was she one of his old companions? An ex-wife? A current girlfriend? They seemed so cozy and familiar, I wanted to melt into the walls.

I took small backward steps to his office door. I barely knew anything about him.

Merde, don't I even have him for six months, exclusively?

Kyle spun around as if he recalled I existed. "Juniper, don't go."

"It's fine. You have company so I'll just…go…umgh…brevis…nach." It sounded like a cross between a satanic chant and a Latin prayer.

Kyle glared at Willow. "You have no manners." He walked to me and tugged me back, holding my wrist. "Willow, this is Juniper Mills. She and I are dating. And Juniper, I'd like you to meet my sister, Willow Paxton. Otherwise known as Willow Silver. Or Will to me."

His sister. Half-sister. *Whew.*

Willow's eyes widened in shock. She inspected me from head to toe and lifted her arms like she was at a concert. "Juniper. Woohoo. So this is why you have not answered my calls."

"Will lives in L.A. and likes to turn up out of the blue. I keep telling her we live in two cities, not neighborhoods, but she still pops up like an unwelcome gopher."

Willow threw her purse and fan on the floor and squeezed me tight. A fragrant potpourri of earthy greens, beets, neroli, myrrh, and jasmine flowers hit my nose. "My brother has never introduced me to anyone he's ever dated, so you must be really special."

"Willow, behave." Kyle's voice was a soft warning.

"Oh no, this is too delish. How did you guys meet? How long has this been going on? When did you move in? Tell me the whole thing. I need deets, deets, deets." She laughed like pretty bells ringing and clapped her hands. Dragging me to a couch, she sat us both down. She scooted her legs on the couch, heels digging into the expensive white leather.

"God damn it. Willow, I told you we were just dating. She has not moved in. Has your mind gone fruity from all the juicing?" Kyle's angry voice cracked across the room.

I had been excited he introduced me as someone he was dating. Clearly, it was only because he had been put on the spot. I closed my eyes. I was deflated by his words. *Just dating. Is he embarrassed by me?* I would be, if I were him. *Sigh.* I swiftly changed the subject before it got more awkward. "Willow, you look so familiar? Have we met?"

"Oh, you don't know my show?"

I shook my head.

"I star in the reality show The Odd Life of Willow Silver. Have you seen it?"

"How nice. I have not. I will see it now."

Kyle grimaced. "Please don't, if you value brain cells."

"Do stop growling, bear," she snapped.

I was peripherally aware of her show and it being a big hit, but I had never seen it. It was a show starring Willow and her eccentric travels around the world. Now that I placed her in my head, I recalled seeing her in various magazines, admired for her Bohemian Chic and earthy beauty—which was breathtaking from a few inches away. She was also ethnically ambiguous— she could be half Arab, Persian, Armenian, Latino, Bulgarian—I couldn't tell. It seemed like Kyle's family was favored by the gods of mixed genealogy.

"And what do you do, Juniper?" she asked.

"I work at the Ann Arbor History Museum."

"Ann Arbor. Our hometown. Aha. My spidey senses tell me you two met there. So what are you doing here?"

"I'm just here for a work thing," I said.

"Really? And what misfortune led you to date our bitter kale?"

"Seriously, Willow, I am going to throw you out on your bony ass."

"Like kale, Kyle is yucky but vital. So Juniper, you seem too nice for my brother…what are you doing with him? Was it his unfeeling heart or his callous soul that attracted you to him?"

"No. I just like big dorks," I said and was awarded with sunny grins from the siblings. Despite Kyle's starchy attitude, I liked her. She was a charmer.

"The real question is, what are *you* doing here?" Kyle sat down stiffly next to me, a possessive arm drawing me away from Willow.

"Kyle. Kyle. Kyle. Why do you make my life so difficult? Dad wants you to join everybody for the Christmas reunion thingy. He's been driving me nuts."

"I'm not going on Christmas. Especially not this one."

Willow sighed dramatically. "Why can't you just love your family? It's like breathing."

"Let's see. Daddy Dearest who was gone all my life now wants me in his. Coincidently when my business skyrockets?" The unleashed fury in Kyle's tone was unnerving.

"Listen, fish-face, don't you care that Dad is dying?"

"We are all dying, Willow, some faster than others."

"So you refuse to help your family?" she asked.

"The family who ignores me till something breaks. So what's the plan? Let's all just stick Kyle under everyone's shoes until his back breaks."

"Um...do you guys want some privacy?" I asked, surprised at the unhappy path the conversation had taken.

"No," both of them roared in unison.

Kyle's head whipped to Willow. "Don't tell my girlfriend what to do."

Wait, what? So we went from dating to girlfriend? Without my consent. What the hell had I signed? Struggling to release myself from Kyle's tightening grip, I made an effort to get off the couch, but he pulled me closer, molding me against the tensed muscles of his body.

"I am not your girlfriend," I hissed in his ear.

"Well you should be," he hissed back.

"Don't say things you don't mean."

Plus, boyfriends don't make their girlfriends sign Termination Contracts.

Willow got up and was still talking—with such histrionic flair—she missed the exchange between us. "Don't you give a damn about anyone else but yourself? We're your freaking family. And I need you there this Christmas. Everyone's coming. All six wives, all ten children. All new spouses."

"Awesome. He's not even dead and the vultures have descended. You know what they all want. And they can shove it up their platinum asses. I don't want a cent."

Barely listening to Kyle, Willow was on her own rant. "And don't even get me started on Royce and Denise. Why'd you hafta go and screw that up now? Why are you siding with Min-Jun?"

My ears perked up when I heard Royce's name, Kyle's brother, the congressman, and Denise, his fiancée. *Who is Min-Jun?*

"I'm doing what's best for Colt," Kyle said.

Who's Colt now? I was stumped.

"Well, Colt has two loving parents," said Willow.

"Two parents who put him in a war zone."

"Kyle. Talk to Royce. Please talk to him without lawyers."

"Nope."

"Argh." She fisted her hands and threw them in the air. "I want to put you two Neanderthal knuckleheads in a room and smack your heads together."

"Willow, you know the effing truth. Don't side with Royce."

"I'm not. But at least he tries. He said he even came to the museum gala to talk to you. But you ignored him. Childish much? And Thanksgiving was insane. Wish I had my cameramen and producers when you broke his jaw."

I gasped. A cold chill went up my spine. "Kyle, you broke your brother's jaw?"

He frowned and said nothing.

Willow nodded. "Yeah, well…almost. He punched Royce's lights out for saying that Kyle and Min-Jun were having an affair. Wowza." Noticing the daggers from Kyle, she looked with guilt at me.

Min-Jun…affair…what the hell? Again, who is Min-Jun?

"Shut up, Willow. I don't have time for this right now." Kyle got up, ripping his large body away from the couch, dislodging me. He went to a cleverly hidden bar, which I had assumed was a limestone décor tallboy, and poured himself a scotch.

Unmoved by the Kyle's anger, Willow rambled on. "You never have time. Listen, Dad wants you to be the sole trustee because he doesn't trust any of us with money. For obvious reasons. So you hafta come on Christmas."

"I don't *hafta* do anything."

"Kyle! None of us can handle money, except you. The lawyers and accountants can only do so much. We *all* need to make sure Royce and Denise don't get their hands on it. It is a billion bloody dollars to be chopped up into itty bitty parts."

"Willow, for the love of God, it's half a billion, not a billion. Half the money is slated for charity. The Paxton Foundation, remember? It runs eleven charities and supports hundreds of thousands of people in need. I guess the old man wants to atone for his sins before he goes to Lalaland."

"But we have to convince him charity begins at home."

"You're such an airhead." He slammed his fist into the tallboy.

"And you're not. Dad sees the way you handle your company. Handle the money, Kyle, or it'll vanish like our trust funds and I'll be forced to buy a food truck in L.A. and make my living frying burgers. Oh God, and I am vegan. We're all gonna die carnivores and paupers." Willow's voice rose a decibel with every word.

"Lower your voice, please. You know I hate drama. And I have caterers in my house…never mind why…you are not invited."

"Ooh. You're hosting a party? That never happens. I wanna come."

Cradling his drink, Kyle marched back and towered above his sister. "Look, Green Smoothie, I've a right to reject my trusteeship even when it is thrust on me. I took on the damned museum board position that nobody wanted. What else does the old bloodsucker want from me? I've had my full quota of family for one whole year."

The damned museum board position that nobody wanted. What now?

Willow jumped up, grabbed the drink from his hand and drained it in a giant gulp. Kyle snatched the empty glass back, flung the ice cubes in his mouth and crunched noisily. I stared at him in surprise…who was this man and where was cool and calm Kyle Paxton? I shifted in my seat and realized he did not drink alcohol at all—he just liked to hold a glass for comfort. Was he a recovering alcoholic? What else did I not know about him?

"Listen, Kyle," Willow began.

"No, you listen. I've said no a thousand times. Every time I'm in that house I want to kill someone. I almost did this Thanksgiving. If you want to see blood on my hands again, then freaking awesome, I'll become a trustee from behind bars. You know they're toxic cretins and I need to stay the fuck away."

"You know what? The least you can do is see Dad. Before he's six feet under," Willow screamed.

Trapped in the bizarre family drama unfolding too close to me, I shot up. "I'm just going to go. And change."

"Sure. Go ahead, darling," Kyle said, putting his arms around me.

Darling? My heart constricted. He'd never used terms of endearment before and I wondered if he wanted his sister to think we were closer than we actually were. I wished I could trust him. A voice in the back of my head was saying I had trust issues. Major trust issues. Clearing my throat, I said, "It was nice meeting you, Willow. I hope I'll see you later."

"I feel bad. I elbowed in here and ruined your romance," Willow said.

"No. No. Nothing like that...I'm gonna go," I said. Avoiding Kyle's gaze, I smiled at her and ran upstairs without looking back.

Once in the sanctuary of my room—wow, one day and I was already calling this my room—I stared at the geometric accent wall, thinking about Willow. The Paxtons were eccentric and outlandish, and I was sure Kyle and Willow were the best of the lot. I began to understand why he avoided them. Rich people were so strange. One billion dollars and they were going to die paupers. *Ludicrous.*

I checked my texts. Stacy said she was running late. That meant I had to wear something for the party from the bone-of-contention closet. I selected a dark olive silk dress and black heels, refreshed my makeup, got dressed and had fun posing in the mirror. Though I felt like a Stepford wife, I had to admit the 1960s redux dress was simple but stunning with its fitted waist, flared knee-length skirt and the v-neckline that hinted at the curve of my breasts without being tasteless. The shimmer of olive silk turned my eyes bottle green and I wondered what Kyle would think.

I perched on the edge of the bed, trying to decompress. So much had happened today. Everything that used to be normal and routine was now distant and irrelevant. Kyle had changed my life by just being in it. I recalled some of the things he had said to me before Willow arrived. *Since I first met you, I wanted you. No matter what. I don't think I've been thinking straight from day one. After your trip here, I know what I feel is not simple want or need but something...more.*

But if I was more, why did we need an end date? It had not even sunk in that I had signed the goddamn Termination Contract. I just wanted to lock that memory in a buried part of my mind and throw the key in the Bermuda Triangle. Head slung low like Eeyore, I sat there thinking until I heard a soft knock on the door.

"Come in."

The door flung open and Kyle took a deep breath when he saw me. He strode in, slammed the door with a kick, and dragged me in his arms. "God, you are beautiful in that dress."

"You don't look so bad yourself, Blue Steel." I smiled, meeting his scrutiny head on.

"Now I regret getting nice clothes for you. You are so damn hot, other men will stare and I'll want to solder their eyeballs, flay them and bury them on my cliff."

"If someone else said that, I'd file a restraining order, Kyle..."

My voice trailed off as he kissed the hollow of my neck. My breath hitched. Pulling away, he gazed tenderly at me. I went very still. This was the only time I had seen Kyle look at me in such an achy-breaky way—

devoted, almost.

"I am glad you're still here, Juniper. I thought you might've jumped out the window to an Uber."

"I was about to."

"Hey, about what just went down—"

I put two fingers on his lips. "Hush. It's fine. I know how things get with family."

He plucked my hand and kissed my fingers. "You're amazing, you know that?"

"Darn right, I know."

"I've created a fiend."

"No, Henry Higgins, I was born this way."

His thumb grazed the edge of my jaw. I gasped and closed my eyes, expecting him to kiss me. Instead he tugged on my hand. "Come. Let's go downstairs."

KYLE

December 11, 8:46 p.m. 59 seconds
(Kyle's House, Seacliff)

T he party had been in session for 46 minutes and Kyle already regretted hosting it. A week ago, it seemed like a good idea, but now it was going be a future waste of 4 hours 24 minutes he could have spent with her. He stood with Sylvia and Evan, barely listening to their debriefing on what he had missed at work, his eyes and mind on Juniper.

Through the retracting glass walls, he had a clear visual on her. She stood by the pool talking to Trevor and Zeke. She was perfection in that khaki dress, shining in the dark like a firefly. A sexy one. How she looked pure and seductive in one stroke, he'd never get. Laughing at something Trevor said, she punched his upper arm and when his arm went lightly around her waist, she hugged him.

Take your hands off her, Buckle Boy. She's mine.

At that moment, the patio string lights went on. Juniper looked up in shock. She excused herself from the two men and proceeded to walk

381

around in fascination, craning her neck up and down, checking out every single twinkling light. Like a child gaping at Fourth of July fireworks.

"Kyle, Kyle." Sylvia snapped her fingers in front of his face. "Earth to BirdsEye CEO. Damn it, we're going to lose the Argentinians the way you're acting these days. Snap out of it, okay? I have to crunch the year-end numbers for our board meeting, the most important board meeting ever. We have too much invested in—Kyle, you listening?"

Kyle walked away from Evan and Sylvia, their eyes burning holes in his shirt. He had lost his fixed visual on Juniper. As if in a trance, he hiked out to the patio to see if he could find her. He needed to feel that static charge again. His heart jolted with a million electric amps when he spotted her.

CHAPTER 23

All in all, some hundred people turned up at Kyle's house and the food and free flowing wine got the party into full swing. Unlike the rooftop event at Kyle's office, this was a livelier and louder affair, with guests holding drinks, laughing and almost yelling around the staggered food stations by the pool. Kyle's staff seemed thrilled to be there, as it was the first time they had been to his house.

He circulated with his guests as graciously as an anti-social person could and introduced our museum staff to many useful contacts and donors. Despite his insistence to the contrary, Willow stayed for the party and I was happy to see her friendly face.

When it got dark, twinkling string lights came on like a cloud of fireflies descending on the patio. I had not noticed the lights before and walked around admiring them. I covertly used the moment to peek at Kyle as he circulated with his guests. Throughout the party, we kept professional distance, as I informed him I was not ready to tell anybody about us. Though frustrated, he told me he would respect my wishes.

After dinner and dessert was served, I reached the coffee station at the same time as he did. All of a sudden breathless, I froze with an empty coffee cup dangling in the air. Amused, Kyle pressed the coffee dispenser and filled my cup. I looked around. Thankfully, no one was paying any attention to us.

"Well, if it isn't my classified file," he whispered.

"Hey, let's talk later."

"Dunno where all of this Catholic guilt is coming from. A first for me."

"Unlike some people, I don't run my own empire and don't want my coworkers to find out I'm dating the board president."

"Again, do not compute."

Just then, Zeke came to get coffee, smiling at both of us.

"Great event, Mr. Paxton. You have a great group of friends," I said in a professional voice.

"Nope, only acquaintances," Kyle said.

"You didn't invite your friends?"

"To be honest, I don't have friends."

"Kyle," a frosty voice said.

We both swiveled around, holding our coffee cups.

Sylvia stood there with a suspicious look on her Botoxed forehead. "Kyle, I was looking for you. I simply must introduce you to Vinos Pascal." Tapping her heels, she surveyed me head to foot. Rather critically. I took a step back.

Kyle frowned. "Who?"

"The new Velocity CEO. He's a big client I wrangled and he says you refused to meet him. Several times. Shocking but predictable."

"You know I hate meetings more than liver paté." Kyle smiled at me and shrugged.

"I invited him here. Come along." Sylvia linked her arm in Kyle's and carted him away from me.

I sighed and watched them go. Almost the same height, they made a stunning couple straight from a classic fifties film. His handsome face, muscular body, rebellious stubble and the blackest black hair offset her platinum hair, thin figure, classic beauty and elegance. No matter what I wore, I could never look like the lifetime-of-polishing women in Kyle's life. But he had picked me for some bizarre reason.

Me. I fingered the silk of my dress. My clothes had given Stacy a great start. She had shrieked in excitement at how beautiful I looked. I, too, felt I shone like a Tiki torch. Even though it was the day I had signed the Termination Contract, it was still a special day: the day I had found out that everything Kyle had done the past month had been for me. *Me.*

I was not going to let Sylvia spoil the day.

Evan came to the coffee station, talking to a young man with black horn-rimmed glasses and jeans so skinny he looked superglued to the denim. Evan blocked my way and muttered in the man's ear. Glasses Guy smiled and melted away. Evan and I regarded each other with our usual tacit tension.

"Marquez."

"Mills."

"What?"

"Do you mind if we talk?"

Slurping my coffee, I observed him coolly over the rim. "Sure. Is it more unsolicited advice?"

Scuffing his toes on the grass, Evan looked uncomfortable. He stroked his thin mustache with a forefinger and thumb. "For what it's worth, I'm really sorry about what I said on Thanksgiving. I crossed a line."

I shrugged elegantly. "Unless I care about someone, it doesn't bother me what random people think about me."

"Okay, I deserve that. You know, I was wrong about you. You're actually very good for Kyle. He has stopped working...like totally." He started laughing. "Which is bad for business, but good for his soul. About time he discovers he has one. And I think you might be the girl for that job."

For a second, I just stared with my mouth hanging open. "Okay... thanks, Evan."

"I trust Kyle and his decisions. I haven't always, about some of the women he's been with. But I'm like a brother to him and care about his personal life, unlike others. That is why I overdid it...with you. I've given you a bad impression of me. But I wanted to let you know, I have your back, Juniper. Even if you don't care about the fact that I do." Smiling smoothly, he walked away.

Feel free to knock me down with a feather.

I walked away smiling, as well.

The night was surreal. One part of me mingled and networked. One part of me was detached, as though I were a fly on the wall, flying and chasing Kyle. At times, I caught him staring at me over the heads of the guests... and his gaze was such a tangible force, I felt it from across the room. I would lift my drink and smile at him. And he would give me a terse look, as if angry at having been caught staring at me. It was obvious there was more between us than he dared to admit.

It was almost midnight when the guests started to leave. The museum staff left, and Stacy and Trevor stayed back to pretend I was leaving with them. The three of us stood by the pool eating desserts from Trevor's plate. I picked up a bite-size hummingbird cake from his plate and ate it. "Ah, nibbles made in heaven."

Trevor held his plate away from me. "Get your own dessert. Stay back, Stace."

Stacy massaged her rounded tummy. "Bitch, please. I've had like five hundred. So, Juniper? Are you and Mr. President a thing now?"

"Maybe. We'll see." I snatched a mini lemon tart from Trevor's plate. He scowled.

"Oh, I think you guys are a thing. He bashed in Surfer Dude's face for dancing with you," Stacy said with a smirk.

"And I was sure he'd hang me with my belt," Trevor added. When I reached for another mini dessert, he capsized the contents of his plate in his mouth. "All mine."

"Yeah, he marked you the way animals wizz on their mate," Stacy said.

"Okay, yes, he's a bit caveman, but ew, ew," I said.

"You should see the way he stares at you. The way Van Gogh stared at his love, the lady-of-the-night Hoornik."

I playfully punched her but felt a stab of disquiet. Like Van Gogh, was Kyle attracted to women in trouble? Is that the vibe I gave?

"Evan said the prince hosted this ball only for you. Seems like he wants the world to know about you guys," Stacy said.

Trevor nodded, his mouth full of three mini desserts.

"He does, but it's complicated."

"What isn't complicated, Juniper? Every relationship is," Trevor said.

Stacy's eyes narrowed shrewdly. "But you haven't had many relationships, have you?"

"Is it obvious?" I said.

"Well, you've never mentioned a man before, then pow! Kaboom! Your whole life is defined by Mr. Kyle Paxton," she said.

"So wrong. My life is not defined by him. Or by any man," I said, arms folded.

"Okay, Susan B. Anthony. See you back home. Enjoy your yummy man. Eat him bit by bit," Stacy said, giving me a hug.

"Barf. Thanks, Stacy. My lemon tarts are going up my throat." Trevor rolled his eyes and pecked me on the cheek. "Bye, Junie."

I walked back to the house and saw Kyle and Sylvia by the window wall. Absorbed by Sylvia's phone, heads almost touching, they did not notice me a few feet away and I could not help but feel a twinge of jealousy. Her short hair was set in blond spikes and she wore a short black dress, the neckline plunging to her waist leaving nothing of her fashionably flat cleavage to the imagination. Heels stroking her ankles, Sylvia had one hand on her waifish waist and one propped on Kyle's arm.

I wanted to tear those red claws away from him. Then I noticed a multi-carat ring on her hand. Sylvia was married. It was apparent from the way she leaned into him, how little marriage meant to her—she was, without a doubt, interested in Kyle. That made me hopping mad. There was something about her I did not trust, as during the party I had noted her eerie light eyes scrutinizing me.

Willow appeared by my side and hugged me hard in her overly-familiar way. "Juniper, I'm off. Fab meeting you."

"You too, Willow."

"BTW, you're special to Kyle. Don't worry about Resting Bitch Face there."

Dazed by her bluntness, I asked, "What do you mean?"

"I think that Man-eater has had the hots for Kyle, like forever. But he gives zero fucks. And it pisses her to no end."

"Isn't she married? She wears a ring."

"Blech, Sylvia moves in the elitist San Fran circles. To them, vows don't mean much. Nasty burps, the lot of them. Their tech success gives them a God complex. And people say Hollywood's bad. We got nothing on 'em."

I was taken aback. From what I had seen, San Francisco was bursting at the seams with savvy businessmen and laid-back geeks, but then Willow had a penchant to embellish reality. "Doesn't Kyle move in the same circles?"

"He's not in the habit of sleeping with his staff. Plus, she's married and he's not the cheating kind."

"I wouldn't know. It's all so new for us."

"Listen, hon, I know my bro well. You'd be surprised at his public face versus private face. He hates going out. The only thing he cares about is work. And…now, you."

"Thanks, Willow. You're a kind soul."

"Wrong. I'm tots evil. But I like you. And he likes you—a lot. I can tell. He can't take his eyes off you. The whole night I noticed him noticing you. If I ever see him with a girl, he'll never ever introduce her, jerkface. Actually, come to think of it, he hasn't since Chloe."

"Who?"

"I thought he must have told you about her." She stiffened and looked away. "Damn it. Forget I said anything."

"Who is Chloe?" My heart sank. *Lord, give me strength to deal with this.* How many women were in Kyle's past?

She pulled at the leather and silver bracelets on her wrists and I flinched as she snapped them hard on her wrist like rubber bands. "Sorry, old rehab habit. I shouldn't say, but Chloe was his girl X, I suppose. She was the first one he loved, and I think…the last. You should ask him about her. Everything he does…well he really changed after she…well, he'll tell you… I'm sure. It's not my story to tell."

"Oh."

At my crestfallen face, she said, "Let's just say, what happened to Chloe was his most shit-awful time. It was like seven years ago. The brother I knew and loved died then. If he acts like a jerk, remember it's because of Chloe. God damn, I've already said too much."

"It's all right. Thanks for telling me what you did." This information messed up my head even more. Kyle had a girl X? Was that why he had Winters and Summers? The mystery deepened. In a rotten way.

"Hey, I asked Kyle for a double date Sunday with me and my boyfriend. That okay with you?"

"I'd love that. So who's your boyfriend? Tom Cruise or one of the Duck Dynasty dudes?"

"Ick. No one that old. Or hairy. Do you know the actor who plays Professor Shadow?"

"Shut up! Clive Anderson is your boyfriend?"

"Yep. But we're keeping it quiet and not confirming the paparazzi rumors."

"You know, I met him at our event last month."

"Oh yeah. Kyle asked me to make sure he came."

I wallowed in shame, recalling how I had goaded Kyle about Clive. And gloated. Double facepalm. "We raised a million dollars that night. Thanks to Clive."

"My BEA's the best. At first, Kyle was hateful to Clive. My bro's an overprotective ass-hat at times. Now, they're friends. Well, Clive thinks he's Kyle's friend. Friendship isn't Kyle's thing." Her phone rang. She looked at it and said loudly, "That's Clive. Hey, I gotta go. Kyle, you going to see me off or not?"

With a start, Kyle disengaged from Sylvia and walked over. "Of course. My favorite part of seeing you is saying bye." He nodded at me. "Sorry to make you wait, Juniper."

"It's fine," I said.

As they left, I swiveled around and almost bumped into Sylvia who had crept up to me. With one emaciated arm, she steadied me and gave me an icy look. My stomach knotted and I felt the cold build up inside.

"Sorry," I said.

Truffle butter. Why do I always apologize for things I did not do?

"What's your name again?" Her voice was as chilly as her gaze.

"We've not been introduced. Juniper Mills. You?"

"Sylvia Langston, BirdsEye Vice President. And you?"

"I'm a junior curator at a museum in Ann Arbor."

She smirked at my title, smiled in a superior manner and folded her arms. "Then why are you still here?"

None of your business, Lady-Ask-a-Lot. I noticed she wore no jewelry save her wedding ring and diamond studded stilettos. One thing my museum job trained me to do was to recognize real jewels. Good grief, where does one even go around finding real diamond shoes?

"Nice shoes."

"Nice dress," she said, as if she knew I could not afford a designer dress. "So you're the reason Kyle's so distracted these days?"

"Excuse me?"

"I've worked closely with Kyle for seven years. He never misses meetings, ignores my calls, fails to give a damn about major deals, throws parties with no business purpose, or throws a party, at all."

Hailing from the polite and reserved Midwest, the bluntness of Californians never failed to shock me, but Sylvia was plain rude. I gave her the most nonchalant look I could muster. "I don't know what you're talking about."

"It's my job to do what's best for my CEO. And I see Kyle is distracted. Mind-blowingly because of *you*."

"Is worrying about him part of your job description?"

"As his oldest and closest friend, it's my job to prevent him from harm."

"What a good friend you are, coming in the way of his happiness."

"Oh no, darling. His happiness is my goal. And what stands against it is my call to duty. I just can't figure out what's so special about you."

"I'd like to think it's my big brain and perky body." I smiled wide.

My unexpected words made her survey me with reluctant admiration. She smiled and it was as cold as salt on snow. "What surprises me is you're not his type—at all."

How dare she? Longing for a Celtic warrior torc to chain her neck, I asked, "And *you* know his type?"

"Yes. I've only seen him with interchangeable gorgeous, successful, supermodel types, which you're not. Unless you're a hand model? Or a foot model?" She laughed and it was the sound of ice cubes falling on marble.

This is war. Afraid my rage would turn physical, I took a step back. "Aren't you going above your pay grade? You deserve a raise."

At my words, her eyes became hard chips and her composure shattered. "Listen, little Midwest girl from podunk town. Word of advice. You're out of your league here. Even the type of women he likes would eat you for breakfast. I've known Kyle since he was a boy. He is a monster and you can't change him. He *will* dump you, hard and soon. The sooner you get him out of your system, the better."

I was gutted. The knots I had released with my sass came back, hard. I struggled to find my voice and gritted my teeth. "It's obvious you being irrelevant to Kyle makes you mad. Don't you have a hen-pecked husband waiting for you?"

I wished I hadn't said that. The moment those words came out of my mouth, I realized I had made an enemy. I could have walked away but instead

I chose to be as immature and offensive as she was. Juniper Mills: Ancient Curator. Expertise: Making Enemies. Ninja moves: Knee-jerk reactions.

Just then, Kyle strolled back and looked surprised at the palpable frost in the room. He slipped an arm around my waist and hauled me close. I sank against him and her eyes widened at his open affection. It didn't matter what Sylvia said. It was obvious Kyle cared about me.

"Sylvia, I want one weekend with no work. I don't want to hear from you until Monday, okay? No emails. Calls. Texts. Nothing," he said.

Her eyes widened and she nodded. She looked small all of a sudden. "Fine."

"Now be a dear and see yourself out." Kyle's arm grew tighter around my waist and I nuzzled in his neck, smiling at her.

"See you Monday, Kyle." She stalked away.

"This was a bad idea," Kyle said in my ear.

"What was?"

"I should've spent this night with you instead of hosting this ridiculous party."

"No. It was perfect. Thank you for doing this. You are too kind." I threw myself at him and kissed his cheek.

He shot me a look of surprise and kissed me back on my lips. One of his hands moved to my nape to pull me closer and his kiss become more forceful. Just as I was melting at the salty taste of his lips, he broke away to caress my cheek. "You taste lemony. Out of candy canes?"

"Don't stop." My voice was a hoarse whisper.

I slipped my arms around his waist and drew him close again. I reached up and dug my fingers in his hair, my body tingling from want. His eyes met mine, intense, darkened and full of need, and I thought he would kiss me again, but he shot away from me as if I had hit him.

"Juniper, I promised you no physical pressure this weekend. And if I don't stop kissing you, I will not be able to stop at all."

I blushed at his words. *That's hot.*

Enjoying my discomfort, he grinned. "I am curious, do you blush with all your past relationships, or only me?"

"Only you."

"Lucky me. June-Bug, are you sleepy or can you stay up and chat?"

"Are you tired?" I asked, putting more distance between us. Why did it bother me that he kept physically thwarting me? Isn't that what I wanted?

"Never tired with you around, kiddo. You're adrenaline in human form." He made a Wile E. Coyote gesture.

I beamed. Till now, I never thought I had even a pulse of energy, let alone adrenaline. "All right, then."

"Why don't you get comfy? By that, I mean, freaking take off that dress and put on something less tempting, because I just want to rip it off your body and see where the night goes."

Jesus. Was it me or did the windows just fog up in the huge room? I looked down at the fluffy polar white carpet under my heels. "Okay. I'll put on my pajamas."

"Please tell me they're not sexy."

"Not unless you have a lollipop fetish."

"No. Only for sexy museum curators."

KYLE

Being around Juniper was like being trapped in an electric field. He sensed the static buzz in the particles of the air as he changed his clothes. He felt the electric current pulse in him from nerve to nerve, as he washed his face.

Electrons, protons and ions gone wild.

When he walked past Juniper's room, he halted. The door was shut. *So close, yet so far.* He stepped 14 inches away from the door. He fantasized about going in, kissing her senseless, throwing her over his shoulders Stone Age style, and dragging her back to his bedroom. He knew if he insisted, she would say yes. She wanted him…he had seen the reaction in her eyes. But he had made a goddamn promise and he was not a man to back down from a promise.

Think: Resistance. Control. Strength. He gritted his teeth and deliberately moved 36 inches away from her door. As he went down the stairs, his phone buzzed. With an angry sigh, Kyle picked it up.

It was Min-Jun. And in her voice was the buildup of tears. "Kyle, can we please talk?"

"Min-Jun. You okay?"

"I've been better. When are you coming back?"

Depends on Juniper, now. Everything depends on her answer. Even if she signed the contract, I need her answer. She's all I know, now.

"Min-Jun, I'm not sure. What happened?" He wondered if she was sleeping these days. She had lately developed insomnia.

"I'm back in DC. You won't believe what they've done this time," she said with a delicate sniffle.

"What? Tell me everything."

CHAPTER 24

found Kyle on the patio, wearing track pants and a long-sleeved Henley. As I came closer, I saw he was talking on the phone. It was way past midnight—who could he be talking to so late? As soon as he saw me, he hung up. Grinning at my lollipop pajama pants and mint fleece top, he motioned me to the crystal-lit firepit, which was circled by a wicker sofa.

I sat down and held my hands over the glossy hot crystals, grateful for the heat lamps above, for it was cold over the bay now. Kyle plopped down next to me and picked up a glass of scotch on the rocks. I noticed, as always, he had not downed a drop of it. I wondered if his strange holding-but-not-drinking alcohol had something to do with Chloe, the mystery girl Willow mentioned.

"Cocoa? Coffee? Dessert? Marlene can fix a snack for you," he said.

"No, I'm stuffed. Your housekeeper is a live-in?"

"Yep. There's a guesthouse behind the house. Before her, the Marquez family lived there."

"Oh. So when you were a kid, you lived alone in the house and they lived in the guesthouse?"

He nodded slowly. "Yes. They allowed their kids to sleep in the house, sometimes."

"I see. Where are they now?"

"Their daughter is in San Diego and they moved to be with their grandkids. Evan stayed with me and when I started my business, I got lucky—he agreed to be my Man Friday."

"I see. And how'd you hire Sylvia? You two seem very close." I could not keep the cold edge out of my voice.

"We go way back. Went to the same high school academy. She's a tough but effective cookie. She worked in New York before joining me. Silicon Valley's laid back and Sylvia's too New York, but she nabs the investors, so I put up with her. Why do you ask?" He looked a bit uneasy at my curiosity.

"She went all Spanish Inquisition on me."

"Damn her. I hope she wasn't too inquisitive."

"Were you two ever an item?"

"God, no." He shot me a bemused glance. "She's a friend and coworker, that's all. Where'd you get such an idea?"

"She seems very possessive of you."

"I'll talk to her. She knows I keep my personal and business life separate."

I leaned forward in my sofa. "Please don't say anything."

"Okay, but you should know Sylvia hates everyone. She's an equal opportunity offender. But if she bothers you again, let me know. I'll chew her out."

"I can fight my own battles, thank you very much," I said, sniffing.

His eyes shone in admiration. "I know you can. What did she say?"

"Forget it."

"Juniper. Spill."

"Um. She said...that I wasn't your type...I guess she's right." I felt a twinge of guilt, for as much as I disliked Sylvia, I wasn't a tattletale.

"She had no right. But she is right."

I stared at him, eyes wide in hurt. Kyle shifted over and hauled me in his arms. When I stiffened and tried to pull away, he held me tighter, his lips breathing over mine...so close that I shivered.

"Juniper. Yeah, you aren't my type. Which is why I am crazy into you. You know that, don't you?"

"That's news to me."

"Really, after I told you all I did the past month?"

"I care about you too, Kyle. Even though I don't always get you."

"I want you to get me. I wish I could take you away from all of this, June-Bug. Find a place where no one exists but you and me. No family, no job, no time zones."

"Great idea. Why don't you buy an island, burn the boats, and you and I can live fishing and drinking from coconuts."

"Are you trolling me again?"

"No, just trying to catch you, hook, line and sinker." I gave him a coy smile.

"You can hook me anytime."

Kyle pulled away from me and scanned my face with that forceful smoky look of his. Leaning back, he put one arm under his head and one around me, towing me close. Blissfully warm and secure, I closed my eyes and nuzzled in his shoulders; already, this was my favorite place in the world.

"Screw other people. I think it's time I got to know more about you," Kyle said, after a long pause.

"What do you wanna know?"

"Why do you live with your family? Not that there's anything wrong with it, I'm just curious. And tell me about Cypress."

"There's not much to tell. Cypress is my twin brother."

He whistled. "Lucky you. There are two of you?"

"Yeah, um. Cypress is on the autism spectrum," I said, with a long sigh.

"Did not know that. I'm sorry."

"Yes. It's sad but common in twins. I guess I sucked most of the nutrients in our amniotic sac and deprived him of a chance at a real life."

"Hey, it's not your fault."

"I know. But at times, I look at him and wonder what if I was not his twin..."

"Jesus, Juniper. It's not your freaking fault. It is tragic, but these things happen with no one to blame." With a swift motion, he held me tighter and I wilted against him.

"But I think he could have been so great, so successful."

"Maybe he's happy. And that's success."

I smiled. "Yes, he's at peace."

"Is he severely autistic?"

"No. Cypress is on the high-end of the spectrum. He's mentally and academically functional, but not socially."

"Was he in a special school?"

"No. Regular. He even got a college degree online in video game design."

"Wow. Does he work?"

"No. He tried, but no one hires him. See, he has severe agoraphobia. Hates social settings, gets skittish in public places. He can only work from home."

"Maybe, I can help—"

"No, thank you. We're good." When he shot me a cagey look, I said, "Look, I didn't mean to be rude. He relies on me for everything, Kyle. When I went to Egypt, he missed me so much he almost starved to death.

He has an unhealthy attachment to me. That's why I did not want to come to San Francisco."

"Is he all right? Do you need to go back earlier?" He flinched as he said those words.

"He's fine this time. He wasn't always like this…" I stopped. Moving away from him, I held my frozen hands over the crystal fire leaping in the breeze.

"You cold?" Kyle picked up a woolly throw and draped it on my knees.

I felt the prick of tears and gulped to force them back. "I'm fine. It breaks me that he has to go through life like this. He's always been badly bullied and Rivercreek High School was purgatory."

"Kids are piss awful."

"Kids don't know any better, I guess. He wasn't autistic enough to be pitied, nor savvy enough to fit in."

"What did they do?"

"What didn't they?"

"Tell me. Details."

"It was insane. The gang bullies stuffed him in lockers. The jocks taped his mouth…and forced him to wear the dirty mascot costume. They'd strip him and duct-tape him to the pool diving board. He joined band and they punched out a drum and stuck him in it. Pretty girls he crushed on played nasty tricks on him…paint on his face with nail polish…pin cruel notes on his back…lure him to the girls' bathroom and report him as a pervert. Once they Cling-wrapped him to a girl. Him and Ashley Larson, in their underwear, on the flagpole. It would be funny…if he wasn't special needs." I went quiet, watching the flames rise up in the crystal pit and dance in the breeze.

"God damn it, teenagers are hell hounds. Didn't your mother do anything?" Kyle looked at me and I saw how visibly shaken he looked, hands knotted into fists.

"Mom had adult sized troubles. She was busy making ends meet. At one time, we were on food stamps."

"What about the school? The teachers?"

"Some tried. Cypress is simple and can't defend himself. I picked fights on his behalf with everyone. We were the two most hated kids in Rivercreek High. It got so bad, I was worried he'd commit suicide."

"Jesus. Was he in therapy?"

"Years and years. It helps. But it doesn't make it go away. People like us… we get a bit messed up by bullies, but we snap back. Kids like Cypress…it stays with them forever. He's a shut-in and no therapy can cure that. Mom and I are his only human contact."

"He's got no friends?"

"Only virtual ones on Capture."

There was a long stretch of silence, until Kyle said, "I did not know you were taking care of an autistic brother. That's a lot of responsibility."

"I don't really go around broadcasting it." I eased away from him and moved closer to the fire.

"I wish I could do something."

"No need. That was the past. Cypress is in a controlled environment now."

"Do you support both of them—your family—financially?"

I put a hand on my throat as though it was hurting. "Yes, I do, but we're a lean machine, so we're fine."

Lost in thought, Kyle stared at the fire. "I should not have probed."

"It's alright. I don't mind telling you anything, Kyle."

That night, we stayed up till dawn and I told Kyle things I had never told anybody: my frustration at my mother's apathy, my missing father, and my teenage curiosity to find out who he was. In turn, Kyle told me how he resented his parents for leaving him alone in the house and how much the Marquez family cared for him and if it weren't for them, he would have committed suicide.

That chilled me to the bone.

He said he had grown mega-depressed in his teens and saw a lot of therapists and was prescribed several drugs, but he lied to the doctors and always flushed the pills down the toilet. Kyle did not want to get addicted. On the rare occasions he had met with them, his father seemed to be an alcoholic and his mother seemed to be addicted to all kinds of pills; this made him believe he was genetically predisposed to addictive behavior. Very early on, he decided to live his life as different from his parents as humanly possible.

Snug against each other, heads close and arms laced, we talked for hours.

Talking about our dysfunctional childhoods was the best way to counter the rising attraction we both felt. That night was a turning point in our kind-of relationship. And so far—the best night of my life.

I had never felt less alone, more desired, comforted, cherished.

I felt like we belonged, and in a preview of our future, I imagined us like this, night after night—after work—sitting here, just belonging to each other...at peace and loved.

Loved. Loved?

What was wrong with me? There was no love. No future. Just a short ride into the Strange Life of Kyle. If he could see what was going on in my mind, he would probably send me packing on a red-eye flight to Michigan. Or throw me off the cliff, if my life was a film noir.

I think I was going crazy—crazy with the weight of my feelings for him.

We talked until dawn lit up the sky and birds chirped in the garden. Only then did Kyle halfheartedly tell me to sleep. We slept in separate bedrooms.

It wasn't until noon that I woke up. When I went downstairs, I found Marlene in the kitchen and Kyle nowhere to be seen.

"Good morning, Miss Juniper. Hope you had pleasant dreams." She smiled, her cheeks curved into bright pink apples.

"I did."

"I wasn't sure what you liked." She pointed to the white marble countertop, where every kind of brunch fare and fruit known to mankind was laid out.

"That's a lot of food."

"Whatever we save here, I take to a homeless shelter on Sundays."

"How kind of you."

"Mr. Paxton's idea. I think he's very kind." She put a square plate in front of me. "Please, help yourself."

"You're spoiling me, Marlene."

"I make a so-so breakfast, but Mr. Enzo Marcel, Kyle's weekend chef will make a special dinner for you tonight."

"How nice."

I slipped onto a barstool and looked around the gleaming, cubic kitchen. Cold and soulless like the rest of the house, it had lustrous flat cabinets, stainless steel appliances, marble floors, and handmade glass sheet back splashes. After talking to Kyle last night, I understood why his house resonated with sadness—it had been boarded up and shut down for years after his grandparents died Since then, only Kyle's mother had lived here—briefly, before leaving him alone.

I asked Marlene where he was and she said, "Kyle said to tell him when you awoke. He's swimming. He does laps every morning. Shall I get him for you?"

"No, it's fine." I peered at a tray full of exotic fruits. I made out soursop, jackfruit, star fruit, pink guava, kiwi, mango and kumquat—but there were some I could not identify. "How fun. I love guavas. I once had them in Egypt."

"Go ahead. Please eat."

"I'll wait for Kyle."

"I think you make him happy, you know," Marlene said, out of the blue.

"Excuse me?"

"I've been with Mr. Paxton for a very long time and seen many girls come and go, but I think I've never seen him like this."

"Like what?"

"Not to be so personal—" She paused and looked at me.

Get personal. Meddle away. It seems to be a universal problem in California. I gave her an encouraging smile.

"Well, I think Kyle's different with you around. He's happy. Fresher, if that is a word. He's usually quiet and cranky—no, not cranky...brooding. And you're different from all the uptight...snooty girls he brings to his apartment." She looked up from the stove and tossed me an anxious look.

"Thank you, Marlene. For your kind words." Two things. One, I was sickened by the thought of Kyle's apartment—his fuck-pad. Two, I didn't need everyone's constant reminders on how different I was from the supermodels Kyle dated, but I knew Marlene had good intentions, so I smiled. "I'm just trying to figure him...it...all out."

"I'm glad. Take your time with him. Kyle is often misunderstood...I think. He's not good with people," she said softly.

I gave her a surprised look. "Really? He's so successful."

"Not with people. I've known him since he was yea high." She held up her hand, level with the counter. "He used to come home from school with cuts and bruises. Got beaten up a lot for being too weird...too quiet. Until high school, when he started fighting back. Then he was in trouble all the time for beating other boys up. I think he had such a terrible childhood... you know...alone in this house. When his mother first left...he was scared and would scream all night. After that, he got sad and would just stand by the door and wait. Every day after school. For months. Then he stopped being sad. Just got numb, you know. And he used to just sit there and stare out at the bay."

"Oh," I whispered, my heart torn at the image of Kyle standing by the door, just waiting.

She pointed to the glass wall. "Right here he'd sit. Wasn't fancy, like now. It was a round window then. Oh, you should have seen it then... before the renovation. It was old, moldy and ugly and dark and mean. It wasn't white...it had that brown and orange wallpaper. Pears or flowers, I think. He just sat at the window, kept waiting and waiting...for that day when one of his parents would come...and take him. But no one ever did."

I gulped, forcing back the lump in my throat. "That's awful."

"Yes. I think some people should not have children. One day, I remember, he just stopped looking out of the windows. I think he was twelve. He realized no one was coming. He just hadda figure life out by himself, you know?"

"He became an adult way too soon."

"Yes. He was angry a lot after that."

"So then...maybe love isn't a taught thing. It's a given thing. When you don't give someone love, they never learn it," I mumbled.

With a crinkle-eyed smile, she gave me a long look. "Yes, that's why he's bad with people, I think. The only good thing about Kyle being alone most of his life was that he pushed himself harder, you know. To succeed. To show 'em all he was something, all right."

I gave her a look of empathy, waiting to hear more, but she looked so pensive, I asked her about her family and that brightened her mood. We chatted amicably until I grew anxious to see Kyle and went to look for him.

I walked to the back patio where I saw Kyle swimming. Leaning against the doorjamb, I watched him. A bit down, I was thinking about what Marlene had told me.

Noticing the way he swam, my heart hammered fast. I could watch him swim all day long. Doing powerful butterfly strokes, his golden brown body sliced the turquoise waters like an Olympic swimmer. His swimming skill was scary exact and advanced—Kyle Paxton did most things with revolting, mind-blowing precision. As if he felt my presence, Kyle froze in mid-stroke. He swam to the edge of the pool, and in one swift motion, pivoted up like a robot in an action movie.

My mouth fell open. *How can a human move like that?*

He walked towards me, the sunlight glinting off his biceps and the washboard abs of his lean but muscular body, which was—in my defense—clad only in wet swim suit trunks. I held my breath; I was not prepared for how ripped he was. My skin crawled with desire. Kyle Paxton was a bronze Spartan warrior, ready to crouch in a phalanx with other hoplites and all that was missing was a helmet, an iron shield, a spear and a horde of rival warriors.

Dripping with golden drops, Kyle stopped beside me. At my wide-eyed appraisal, he beamed, grabbed a towel and wrapped it around his waist. Feeling let down, I wanted to rip the towel to shreds.

"Good morning. Or afternoon. I trust you slept well?"

It took a few seconds to find my poor constricted voice. "Considering someone kept me up till dawn, yes."

"I wish I had kept you up doing this." He bent down and kissed me, drops of water raining on my face. When he saw how flustered I was, he said in a less seductive way, "Would you like to swim, June-Bug?"

"No. I hate anything to do with moving my muscles."

He smiled. "Did you eat breakfast?"

Blinking like a spaz, I shook my head again. I found it hard to make my vocal cords function with this gilded Bernini sculpture in front of me.

"Lemme just take a quick shower," he said, eyebrow cocked as if he knew what I was thinking.

Scanning his toned abs, I saw a tattoo in small neat black letters on his lower left midriff. *Elafris.* Latin? No…Greek, in English transcript. It was a word I did not know. Without thinking about what I was doing, my finger made contact with his wet skin and grazed the tattoo lightly.

"*Elafris?* What is this?"

"Nothing." He recoiled as if I had cut him with a penknife, his hands covering the tattoo.

"I'm sorry. I was just curious…"

"It means light in Greek. It's nothing. I've been meaning to get rid of it."

"Okay," I squeaked, wondering if the tattoo was for Chloe. Was she his light? Willow's voice echoed in my head. *Chloe was his girl X, I suppose. She was the first one he loved…*

"I'll meet you for breakfast in five."

I stopped thinking about the tattoo because Kyle walked away, took off the towel, flicked it hard on his thigh, and then blew me a kiss. *Oh sweet Lord of Temptation.* I think I might have passed out after that, because all I remember next is being seated at the breakfast bar in the kitchen with him. I really have no recollection of when I got there.

Marlene wisely left us alone to eat and Kyle poured me some coffee and filled my plate. Perched on the barstools, we ate and talked about the day's plan. He said we should hit all the tourist hotspots and if there was any time left, we could tour Alcatraz Island. To pleasure-deprived me, it was so exciting, I clasped my fingers like a toddler.

"It sounds perfect."

"Anything I might have missed?" Kyle's lips turned up at my infantile display.

"I'd love to see The Painted Ladies."

"There's no way we miss the Painted Ladies."

Half an hour later, we went to his car porch and I saw a kindly older man in uniform, standing in front of a black, iridescent BMW. Kyle introduced him as Patrick, his chauffeur, who would ferry us around on our day's excursion. My heart dropped. I would have preferred to be alone with Kyle and had imagined a day like before, with him driving me around.

Kyle tossed me a concerned glance. "I thought we'd maximize time if Pat takes us."

"Sure."

It turned out to be a perfect day. It was hard to imagine a day that could top our beach day, but I was learning every day with Kyle was better than the next. We started off with a walk at the dome of the Palace of Fine Arts and I admitted having Patrick ferry us around was a convenient luxury. Then we drove through the city and I loved strolling down Lombard Street, the crookedest street in the world. But the highlight of my day was seeing the pastel Painted Ladies—the Victorian homes in Alamo Square's famous postcard row.

When we stopped at the Golden Gate Bridge, I was disappointed Kyle got a work call and had to wait it out in the car. I ended up walking with

Patrick halfway across the bridge to its towers. Moved by the hulking beauty of the bridge that had endured the ravages of time, wind, fog and choppy bay waters, I could not help but wish I were with Kyle and not his driver.

For lunch, Kyle took me to the filthy, stinky, crowded, but delightful Fisherman's Wharf where we got food from street vendors. In the madness, we found a seagull poop-splashed bench on the pier to eat our scrumptious sourdough bread bowls and crab legs. He said the natives avoided the wharf like the plague and he had not been there in a decade. I rolled my eyes at him.

After lunch, we took a long ride on San Francisco's iconic cable cars. I insisted on standing on the outer ledge and he held on to me as I leaned out to take photos. Every time I swung out on the straps, he pulled me back and I would wrestle with him to let me swing out farther. This led us to laughing fits and we behaved like silly teenagers without a care in the world, much to the irritation of several of our fellow passengers.

Armed with relaxed humor, Kyle was such a charming tour guide I almost forgot things like clockwork minds, termination contracts, supermodel exes, pitiless coworkers, and the other headaches of being with a man like Kyle.

An electric energy pulsed between us all day long. Despite the heated looks we shared, I felt more comfortable around him than I ever had. Our conversation last night had smashed some kind of boundary between us.

When the pale lilac sunset fired up the sky, Patrick picked us up at the end of the cable car line. Sliding into the car, Kyle asked, "I've arranged a dinner at home with my chef. But if you prefer dining out, June-Bug, I can take you to some incredible restaurants."

"No. I'd rather eat with you. At home. Alone."

My answer seemed to please him, and he gave me a long, lingering look. "Pat, home."

KYLE

December 12, 6:16 p.m. 59 seconds
(Seacliff, San Francisco)

K yle stood in his bathroom, staring at his unshaved face. A rapid-fire series of images imprinted on the mirror cataloged the day's touristy trip with Juniper. He stored the images in a desktop file of his mind; doubtless he would be using that file a lot.

He tried to sort out the day he just had.

Kyle had never planned a romantic day, date or dinner for a girl. As a bleak, stiff-necked, nerdy teenager, no girl except Chloe had ever wanted him. All his adult life, too many women wanted him—many throwing themselves at him in hot fits—and in his entitled douch-baggery, he had always taken the easy, time-effective and lazy way to them.

He had never planned anything remotely starry-eyed for Chloe even though she had hounded him about it for years. She'd always been the one who felt the need to go out, forcing him to take long beach walks, eat dinner under the stars at farm bistros, spend weekends in Sonoma wine castles,

411

take Caribbean Island vacations, and make way too many impromptu Las Vegas getaways. She'd sought out unique pubs and cool nightclubs in London when they lived there, and he'd simply shrugged and went along with her plans.

That thought was a stab in the heart. It made him curse his image as he stood in the bathroom. *Loser. Hateful. Bastard.*

Pushing down the teeming garbage of his Chloe guilt, he focused on Juniper.

Today, he wanted everything to be perfect for her.

Perfect day. Perfect dinner. Maybe…perfect night.

He had thought the day would be a drag in her wish to go to all the touristy things he hated. But he had loved every single second of it. Only because of her company. She made everything come alive. She made everything dark brim with light.

His mind was a mess of circuits and it needed a voltage divider switch to control the input and output across the two resistors. Juniper was his personal voltage divider.

CHAPTER 25

I went to my room and took a quick shower to wash off the day. Kyle had asked me to wear a dress from my supernatural closet and I complied without a protest. I picked a chiffon cocktail dress of ecru-pink, a color I would never have worn back home. As a rule, I wore dark navy or black and when I saw how luminous my skin looked in the beigey pink, I made a mental note to dress in Technicolor from now on. I arranged my hair into long caramel waves and slipped on my new Valentino heels, feeling girlish, uninhibited and ready for anything the night promised.

In anticipation of a night alone with Kyle, there were a few knots in my belly. I knew from the way he stared during the day, he would have kissed me senseless if we were not in public. One part of me was ready to give up the part of me that I had never given to anyone. Tonight, I decided, I would be his.

Have mercy, angels.

Though I was determined to lose my V-card to him, he had me worried.

He was a wild card. And he left me in the awkward position of taking wild stabs in the air about what he was thinking and planning. I wasn't the kind of person who likes challenges, and Kyle Paxton was a twisty pretzel of a human challenge. Lines from a Robert W. Service poem came floating in my head. "He's a rolling stone, and it's bred in the bone; He's a man who won't fit in."

I sighed. Looks like that rolling stone was going to roll right over me and pulverize me to bloody mush. I was just about to go downstairs when I heard a knock on my door.

A hunk stood in the hall, dressed in dark jeans, a white shirt and a gray blazer. He had shaved and I kind of missed his stubble. "Hey, you ready?"

"Yes."

His eyes widened in appreciation. "Come, then."

As his eyes raked my body—taking in my dress, my shoes, my hair, the light makeup—my heart skipped a few beats. He angled his head as if he was inspecting a new company product. The detached look terrified me and I had an unsettling thought.

Kyle Paxton was a collector, Like Frederick Clegg, the butterfly collector who imprisoned his obsession Miranda, Kyle liked to fix the broken things he collected—by opening them and pulling out their guts. Just like he pulled clocks apart when he was young. Just like he invented and reimagined gizmos now. Just like he gave his F-buddies all they desired, and fixed the things in their life that needed fixing.

"June-Bug?"

He interrupted my crazy thoughts and I sashayed to him, wrapping my arms around his neck. "Well, am I up to par, Mr. Castillo?"

"You are beyond par, Miss Mills."

His breath fanned my ear and his fingers twisted the soft silkiness of the dress at the small of my back. I tried to still my heart, afraid it was beating so loud he heard it.

"Come, I have something to show you."

I held his hand as he led me to a room with double doors down the hall. This was probably his bedroom. It was white and minimalist and, like the rest of the house, had an unlived look. He led me to a stainless steel sculpture of what was a block of tortured, melting pixels with hard metallic edges. I shivered. It was like looking into a metal void. How could he stare at this every night? It'd give me nightmares—and I saw my share of scary artifacts at my job. To my surprise, he pulled the sculpture panels open, under which was a safety deposit box built into the wall.

"You want to show me one of your new acquisitions."

"Something like that." He punched a few numbers in a digital panel. To give him privacy, I turned my face away. Kyle put a finger under my chin and forced me to meet his teasing face. "Juniper, you handle ancient artifacts worth millions. I think I can trust you with my safety deposit."

"What is it? I'm excited now."

"Wait for it." He bent down to the panel and a green laser scanned his eyes. "I installed iris recognition technology all over my house and office."

"You're such a geek. It's probably a 1939 Batman comic. Or Stars Wars memorabilia?"

"Ha. Nope. Close your eyes." I did and heard the soft snap of a latch. Then he spun me around. He flipped my hair to one side and when I felt his hands on my nape, I tensed. "Keep your eyes closed," he commanded.

Something cold slid around my neck. A cord-like object. For a split-second my blood froze and I thought he was trying to strangle me with a metal twine. Then I recalled the chef and Marlene were downstairs and Patrick was outside. *Again, I've got serious trust issues.*

I twisted my face towards him. "Can I open my eyes?"

"Nope." One of his hands clamped over my eyes. He propelled me forward a few steps. "Now."

We stood in front of a mirror and I blinked to adjust to the light. I gasped. On my neck was a long platinum necklace, inset with round iced diamonds, their light strobing my face and making my eyes sparkle Judging from the quality of the diamonds—and even with my limited knowledge of contemporary jewelry, I knew it was stratospheric—and probably worth more than my entire annual salary. I was speechless.

"Do you like it?" Kyle linked eyes with my reflection.

"It's beautiful…and too much. I can't." I couldn't even bring myself to smile as I turned to face him.

"Yes, you can. Why not?"

"No…please."

His smile faded. "What's the big deal?"

"Take it off." My hands trembled at my neck and I tugged at the necklace.

"Juniper, what's wrong?" He looked shocked and hurt.

"Please…take it off." I yanked the chain as if it was a noose.

His eyes glittered with anger as he swiveled me around and took the offensive necklace off. "I thought you could use it for some of the events I expect you to attend. That's all."

"Kyle…please."

"I'm sorry. I'm so used to giving gifts to my companions."

I whipped to face him. "Kyle. I am *not* one of them. The toy girls you play with. I don't give a damn about pretty things. Why can't you get that? I like you for you—not for what you can give me or what you own. Or what you put on me. Life is not about *things*. It's about people. You are a great guy…and…I'm sorry. I'm just not sure I can do this."

With a sharp intake of breath, I ran from the room, fumbled in the hall, found my room and slammed the door shut. As my tears began to fall, I thought, *Great, the Paxton penchant for drama is rubbing off on me.*

Soon I heard him outside my door. "Juniper, can I come in?"

I opened the door. Wiping off my tears, I stared at my toes. "Hey, sorry…for freaking out."

"No, I am the sorry one."

"Don't be." I laughed through my tears. "What's wrong with us? We seem to be in a perpetual state of regret."

"Well, your sorries are contagious."

"Kyle, about what I said…I guess I'm stupid idealistic."

"No, you know your mind. And I like that about you. I just feel bad that I made you cry."

"Every time you try, I ruin it."

"You don't."

I took a small step to him and crossed my arms tight to stop myself from falling on his inviting chest. "I do and…it's not that I don't care about your gestures…it's because no one's ever given me much. Growing up, I wasn't raised to fill the void inside by going to malls…like most people. We weren't better than others, just poorer. We never had extra cash to anesthetize our issues by buying stuff."

"I completely understand," he said, gathering me in his arms.

"You do?"

"Yes. These things have no meaning for you and I keep tossing them at you. I've been so used to buying my friends and girls with things… because it's the only thing I think I have to give them. Unlike you, all I had was useless stuff. I have money and people want things. So the logical conclusion is…I can get people if I can give them things."

I wiped a runaway tear on my cheek, wondering if his AWOL parents had ever told him they loved him. I supposed Willow was the only one who genuinely loved him. My arms wrapped around his waist tenderly and I buried my face in his shoulders, breathing hard. "Kyle, you have so much more to offer, you have no idea. I only want you. Didn't you ever have anyone love you for you?"

Oh my God, did I just say the L word? Just shoot me now.

Taut and silent, he became a granite tablet, with my arms still awkwardly around him. I closed my eyes and cursed myself for saying the L-word. What was wrong with me? And then, it came to me with the crashing weight of an Easter Island Head—I loved Kyle Paxton.

I love him!

Oh, no, no, no. No!

I bit my tongue to prevent myself from screaming, *I love you, Kyle.*

I, Juniper Mills, was in love with a man who wanted nothing more than a casual fling for a few months. A strange, dead-inside man who liked to control and dress up girls like paper dolls and make them sign termination contracts. A man who forced legal rules in all his relationships.

Already, Kyle and I had broken every one of the Felicia Grunde F-buddy rules. And the worst one (Rule number 11), the final nail in the coffin, the one she had not even articulated—because she was sure no one could be so doornail dumb—was Never Fall in Love with your F-Buddy. These days, it's cool to have casual F-buddies but love—that was taboo. There was no bigger fool on Planet Earth than me, at this point. Being a fool hurt. My brain mocked my heart with a heap of I-Told-You-So's.

Kyle was still shell-shocked, so I took control of the situation. "Hey, let's see about the meal your chef has prepared for us."

He nodded and we walked down the stairs in utter silence. It was only when we got to the patio that he said, "Through here."

We went past the pool and courtyard to a sunken garden hidden by hedges. Set on the cliff plateau, it overlooked the ocean and a sea-worn timber fence was the only boundary between us and a sheer drop to the shore. Compared to the well-manicured lawns of the house, this was an unexpected wild and unruly garden. In the center was a seating area of white concrete blocks bordered with grass, where a round table was set for dinner. Above the table were two ash trees strung with tiny lanterns that threw soft arcs of light over the space. The light flickered as the lanterns swayed in the breeze.

"What do you think?" Kyle asked.

"Oh my God. It's unbelievable." Twirling around with awe, I bit my lips. Kyle had planned this perfect weekend down to every detail for me and I had screwed it up at every turn with my gauche overreactions.

"Enzo, this is Miss Mills."

I turned to see a man in a black chef's uniform standing by the table with a polite smile and an attentive expression. Enzo was short and thin and had a stylish, pointy beard. "Miss Mills. A pleasure to serve you," he said, in a marked French accent.

I shook his hand. "Pleased to meet you."

"Juniper, Enzo is a Michelin rated chef and I am grateful he sometimes agrees to cook for a barbarian like me."

"Unlike many of ze American fellows, cooking for you, Mr. Paxton, I enjoy. Now I prepare a leeelte rustic French dinner."

"Sit, please." Kyle held out a chair for me and sat down, watching me with a penetrating gaze. Hit with shyness, I inhaled and looked at the table.

Enzo leaned over and lifted a silver dome on my plate. "Mademoiselle, the first course is ze red snapper salad, then will come la petit quiche, ze third one is le Marseille shrimp stew, followed by Toulouse beef cassoulet and enfin, le soufflé de chocolate."

I beamed at him. "How wonderful."

With Enzo coming in and out of the house to serve us, dinner was a quiet affair and our conversation desultory. I relished the food and turned often to take in the eye-popping beach views below us. Kyle was polite but detached and I missed the friendly, lively guy who had taken me around the city earlier.

As always, he had a glass of wine in his hand but had not drunk a drop of it. I recalled what he said to me at the club. *I found out the hard way, only absolute sobriety agrees with me.* To give his sobriety company, I had a glass of red wine with the main course, but declined more alcohol. I needed to stay clearheaded tonight.

After Enzo served the chocolate soufflés, he bid us farewell and we were finally alone. Eating my first soufflé bite, I watched Kyle as he looked out to the seaside below us. It was completely dark now and the only light source in the garden came from the iridescent lanterns in the trees and a candle in a jar on the table. Chasing shadows across his face, the light blew hot and cold on his chiseled profile.

As the slight breeze ruffled his hair, I caught my breath. There was something undefinable about Kyle Paxton that attracted me, which had nothing to do with his handsome looks or the Midas touch of his success. It was a magnetic pull beyond pure physical attraction. As this week unfolded, it had become painfully clear I had strong and dangerous feelings for him. Feelings...I wrongly believed could be love.

He turned and caught me staring at him. Clearing his throat, he said, "So is the soufflé good?"

"It's silky and custardy with crisp edges. Delicious."

He took a bite from his soufflé, then shook his head. "Meh. It's all right." With a devilish smile, he leaned over, dug his spoon into my soufflé and ate a big bite of it. "Now—yours is delicious. Mine, not so much."

I giggled. "Game on. If you eat mine, I'll eat yours."

"Nope. I eat both."

He lifted his soufflé out of my reach and took another bite from mine. Then he dug into his own dessert and put the spoon on my lips. My body ignited. My lips parted and my eyes closed of their own accord as he fed me. For awhile, Kyle teased me as he alternated between eating from my dish and feeding me from his, until every sweet morsel was gone. Though I was thoroughly provoked and semi-aroused by his antics, I laughed to lighten the mood. What I really wanted to do was to jump out of my chair, sit on his lap and taste the chocolate on his lips.

"Kyle, thank you for this weekend. You did so much for me."

"Illogical to thank me. I really enjoy hanging out with you, June-Bug."

"Hey, can I ask you something?"

"Shoot."

"This weekend, we avoided the elephant on the cliff. I think we should talk about us."

"Well, is there even an...us? Have you come to a decision yet? Even though you rashly signed the contract, have I turned you off or compelled you to stay?"

Chewing over my tangled thoughts and failing to organize them, I did not answer and asked instead, "First of all, how is this even going to work? I live in Ann Arbor and you live in San Francisco."

"Easy. One weekend you fly here and one weekend I fly there. Next objection."

"It's not that easy for me to take off. I told you about Cypress."

"How did you date other men?"

"They were…local."

And most of them, imaginary.

"So you have never lived with anyone?"

I shook my head.

"Maybe, this will actually help Cypress. At some point, don't you think he has to learn to be independent? And you've cared for him all your life. Don't you deserve a chance at happiness?"

"Is that what you are offering? Happiness? It sounds more like a preview that ends soon."

He put two fingers on the bridge of his nose and pinched it, coolly staring ahead as if he did not care to answer. His indifference made me gulp and air slid down my throat like dry ice. Then he said something I'd never forget as long as I lived.

"Don't you think, Juniper, everything comes to its natural end? Friendship ends, lovers fall out of love, marriages break, people die, cities fall, stars implode and turn into supernovas, and even this planet will crumble one day. Nothing lasts forever."

Speechless, I just stared at him. *Some things are forever. Like love.*

"All that I've seen makes me believe all things come to an end. Relationships are no different. If we can avoid the pain, anger, hatred, and enmity that ends most intimate relationships, isn't it great? I'm offering you freedom. A chance to enjoy the best relationship of your life and walk away without heartbreak."

Maybe I'm not cut out to be with a postmodern man. Maybe I can wait till they invent a time machine and beam me to Celtic times.

I sighed and took a big sip of my wine. Screw my clear head. I needed

Dutch courage. "So what makes you think there will be no heartbreak?"

"If there is an expiration date on a product, you only use it before it goes bad. And you are prepared for its end. If you think something is going to be around forever, false hope destroys its very existence."

Expiration date? Product? Did he have digital wires for synapses?

"Don't get me wrong, RoboCop. At no point am I suggesting that I want to be with you long-term. All I'm saying is I don't know if I can casually be with you and then casually leave you."

Without being hurt. Without breaking apart.

He sucked in his cheeks and tossed me a fiendish grin. "We haven't been together yet, but I can tell you, doll, it's not going to be casual. It's going to be intense. You and I are good together, really good, but like everything else, it'll end."

I picked up my cutlery and stacked it on my wineglass rim. Then I twirled a silver spoon in the empty soufflé dish like it was a lonely dancer. "All right then, unrelated to me, but I'm curious. Before your system…did you ever have a relationship?"

"Once."

Was that Chloe? "And?"

"It did not end…well."

"Did you love her?"

"No."

"How long were you with her?"

"Four years."

What, so long?

"How could you not love her in four years?" I asked, dropping the spoon with a *clang.*

"Juniper, stop."

I couldn't stop now. "What about love? Don't you believe it exists?" At my question he regarded me with such derision, my heart thumped painfully.

He picked up a butter knife and tapped his plate, knuckles white from gripping hard. "Love is a social construct. Not a reality. It is a lie created by songs, books, movies, De Beers, Hallmark. A lucrative lie. A lie people tell to force others to be bound. All I have seen is lots of holy lies, six carat rocks, pre-nuptials, greed, kids torn apart, divorce lawyers. If love existed, they wouldn't."

So cold. He is right—he is dead inside.

I sighed and waved my hand across the flame of the candle on the table. At that moment, I would have rather played with fire than wrangle with Kyle. We were an immovable object meeting a dynamic force.

"And...did you never want to get married?"

"God, never." He raised his eyebrows and moved his chair a foot away from the table. "How many marriages do you know that are happy?"

I waved my palm closer to the blazing candle in the jar. "I don't know. I guess some of my friends are happily married. Some of my colleagues are divorced. People make mistakes. And they move on. That's life."

"People live together for a while like lovers and then rip each other apart like mortal enemies. It starts off great, but the end is always ugly. Why wait till it becomes intolerable, Juniper? Why not end on a high note and keep the good memories?"

"So what are you, some kind of memory collector?" I jeered.

When he did not answer, I kept my hand on the candle flame for a second longer and it hurt. I rubbed my palm and moved it back over the flame, but his hand lashed out and grabbed my wrist. Then he blew out the candle. I snatched my hand away from his grip.

Kyle pushed back his hair from his forehead, staring at me as if I were a stranger. I shivered. His moods could alter the microclimates of a city. All of a sudden, he shot up in his chair. Pushing it out of the way, he got up and walked towards the bench by the hedges of the garden.

"Come here," he demanded.

Heart beating too fast, I got up and followed him. He towered over me with one of his knees bent on the bench. It was dark here and I saw darker shadows passing across his face.

"Juniper, what is really bothering you?"

"Nothing."

"What. Is. It."

"I am confused."

"About?"

I took a deep breath and plunged on. "Do you get bored? Or do the girls get attached to you and you're afraid they won't leave? You made the rules and contracts so you can end it?"

"You think I've created these rules so I get to push away the girls I'm with?"

"You tell me. I am lost in your system. I feel trapped and powerless and I don't like it."

"Listen, this isn't about you or somebody else. It is about me. So I don't breach the contracts and rules. I don't ever want to fall for anyone. I can't. Not again."

"I don't understand."

He was quiet for a bit and I saw his jaw working angrily as if he were trying to force the words out. "I can't be with someone because I can never care about them. I've never loved anyone and no one should love me."

"Kyle. That isn't true. Of course, you can love someone. You are—"

"No." His voice was a sharp vibration in the air. "I can't go through this hell again. Once was enough for me and it tore me apart and tore the other person apart, literally."

The other person. Was it Chloe, Girl X? "Who?"

"No more questions."

My body went limp and I sank down on the bench, rubbing my naked arms. But something inside me would not quit and I asked, "Is this because of…Chloe?"

"Who the hell told you about her?"

"I should not have—"

"It was Willow, wasn't it? Son of a bitch. One day with you and she's wag the dog. What exactly did she say?"

"Not much. Is Chloe the reason—"

"No. You do not get to ask me about her."

Kyle sounded so angry I spent a few moments looking at my taupe slingback shoes, the signature Valentino metal studs glinting in the low light and so out of place. My hands went under my thighs for support and I looked up as he was looming over me.

My tongue is a menace. "I am…sorry."

I was not expecting his next words. "Chloe is dead. And I never want to talk about her."

KYLE

December 12, 8:37 p.m. 18 seconds
(Seacliff, San Francisco)

Chloe had died 7 years 3 months 4 days 16 hours and 42 minutes ago. After 4 years of purgatory and absolution, Kyle had kept her memories at bay for the past 3 years. Ever since he had met Juniper, bit by bit, Chloe had slipped back into his mind.

No matter what he did, how he planned his life and orchestrated the people around him, Chloe always returned to him.

An image of Chloe's broken corpse was ever-present in his mind.

Kyle gritted his teeth, willing the broken body in his head to vanish.

But it was still there—lying prostrate on a steel gurney, under a white plastic sheet.

I am Chloe's monster.

He walked away from Juniper, to yank the bloody chain of Chloe out of his mind.

CHAPTER 26

O *h my God*. I stared at the sea, my face as miserable as I felt inside. "I
did not know. And I didn't mean to upset you."

He took a few steps away from me and paced around the small
garden, the gravel pounding under his forceful steps. *Good plan*. I longed to
run away, too. I stood up. My gut reaction to all conflict was to run. In an
instant, I planned my getaway: get to the airport, take a red-eye to Detroit
where my Tomato was parked, drive home to Ann Arbor, and crawl into
my snug twin bed.

I took a few steps backwards, trying to locate where we had entered,
the absurdity of it all making me wince. I did not even know how to get
back into the house.

Seeing I was looking for a way out, Kyle walked to me, grabbed my wrists and jerked me to a halt. "Damn it, Juniper. Stop running away. Just try to understand. I have not been in a relationship for seven years. Until... you. Seven years. That is a hellish long time to prove I am dead inside. But I have gone further with you than with anyone else. So say yes to us."

Until...you? Really, are we in a relationship?

"Kyle, did I not sign the contract?"

"I told you I do not accept that. It was signed in rash haste."

"I want badly to say yes. That is why I signed it. How I feel about you is absolute. I really do...but...there are doubts that scare me."

"What are you afraid of? Look, if you think I am making excuses for myself, think again. I am a pitiless jerk, but since I've met you, I have not pretended to be otherwise. I am a monster who uses people. What prevents me from being a complete demon is I give my victims a choice. And I was clear to you from the beginning about what I was offering. Juniper, either you're in, or you're out. Just tell me now."

Déjà vu. I flinched at his use of the word monster and Sylvia's cruel words came floating out of nowhere: *Even the type of women he likes would eat you for breakfast. He is a monster and you can't change him.*

Afraid my words would be as muddled as my thoughts, I was quiet. Easing my shoulders from his hands, I stumbled to the edge of the garden by the run-down fence. He followed me and put a tentative hand out. I took it and we stood there watching the moonlit sea. The waves were frothy at the edges, like a mass of white snakes twisting in laundry detergent. Beyond the shore, the ocean waves slid back and forth, uncaring of the humans and their endless spectacle of love and hate and war.

I trembled.

"Here." Kyle took off his coat and draped it on my shoulders. I nestled in the warmth still clinging to it. His hand rested on a thick wood post and he cleared his throat. "You know, my grandpa built this fence. He was kinda an amateur carpenter. All over my house, I found things he made that I did not tear down in the renovation."

"Like what?"

"A bunch. I'll show you."

"Well, this really stood the test of time and sea."

The breeze became harsher and lifted my hair in a mass around my face. Pushing my hair off my forehead, he gave me a sad smile, the kind you paste on your face when you're a kid and you have to give away your favorite toy. "I'm making you miserable, aren't I?"

I shook my head.

He sighed. "Don't lie. Feel free to walk out tomorrow and never come back. We'll go back to our professional relationship and I will not bother you ever again."

My heart broke into twenty pieces, some of which jumped over the fence and fell down to the frothy snakes below. "Is that what you want?"

"God, no. It's the last thing I want. I want you, Juniper. And since I have met you, it is all I can think about."

Warm arms went around my waist and I relaxed when I saw the concern on his face. I rested my head on his chest and his lips brushed the top of my head.

"Kyle, don't ask me to leave, please. Can't you tell I really like you?"

"I'm glad. I know I have forced you into my life because I really want you. And my anger earlier...about Chloe...was not at all directed at you, but at myself. Just don't ask questions about my past. And please know that my system has nothing to do with you. It is to protect you from me, not the other way around."

"Protect me from what? Are you a werewolf or something?"

430

"I destroy lives. I drive people mad. Maybe because I am insane myself. It's why I devised the system so that I can have minimal human contact."

"But you and me this week?"

"All a first for me. And I can tell this is all very new for you. Tell me, have you ever had a boyfriend before?"

"No. Never."

A ghost of a smile played on his lips. "I thought so. Have you ever had a one night stand?"

I slipped out of his embrace to look at him. "No."

"But you have dated? Please tell me you have had dates and been with men."

This would have been a good segue to disappoint him further by letting him know I was a virgin. Instead I said. "Um. I've dated...quite a few men." This was technically true but in reality I had not gone on more than three dates with any of them. I had a habit of dropping them before things got too serious.

"Can you handle this for the next six months? I told you I don't do girlfriends. Before you, they've all been...friends with benefits. I knew that would not work with you. So I tried to make it easier for you. I tried. I think I failed. But Juniper, I will try harder. Be in a relationship with me till the termination date."

"Relationship?"

"Yes. I know that's what you want. And this weekend has made me see I want that too...with you. I've never had a relationship with any of my... uh...let's just talk about us. We'll meet every weekend. Like this. Go out. Have fun. But when the time comes for us to part, we say a civil goodbye. And move on. Now, decision time. Yes or no?"

Say no. Say no, before he breaks you.

But I was the sleepwalker on the road. I was an animal running off a cliff. I was the broken train speeding to the end of the line. And despite the certainty of the cutting pain of loss, I knew that I would not stop, even if I had the chance. There was something about us that made me want to take it all the way—from now to the train wreck at the end.

"Yes."

"Good." Even in the dark, I saw relief flood his face. "Say it again."

"Yes." I trembled.

"You're cold. Let's go inside."

As we walked back in silence, I knew something had changed between us. Something had grown darker and I could not shake this sad lump in my throat. I heard a ticking sound, like a broken clock in my head. Was his condition contagious? I tried to process our exchange. Until Wednesday at the club, I had assumed Kyle's termination system had to do with his player lifestyle. After learning about his clockwork mind, I began to think it was because of the complex human timetable that he was.

Now it was quite clear it all had to do with Chloe. *Girl X*. The girl he loved. The girl who had died. The girl who was his light—tattooed on his waist. She was the reason he did not want to fall in love. Or be with anyone long enough to have a real relationship. He'd said their relationship had torn them he had said, so there was a story about Chloe that preceded her death.

What had he done to her?

Something that filled him with guilt and self-loathing and convinced him he was a monster. I needed answers badly but I liked Kyle—no, not liked—loved. I would never tell him, but I loved him—so I would wait patiently for those answers.

Wait, what?

I swallowed. So I was doing this, now. Admitting, thinking, stating

432

casually, (and not double-checking) I was in love. Funny thing about love, there's no blurred line in between—either you love someone or you don't. And I loved Kyle. There was no going back.

Back in the house, Kyle wanted to show me the things his grandfather had built. He started in the den with a bookshelf his grandfather had carved for his wife. In the mudroom, he opened the hidden doors of an ingenious coat closet, and in the foyer, we admired a vintage teak dresser that used to hold his grandma's clothes. In the living room, there was a low cocktail table his grandfather had built from the reclaimed wood of a boat that had washed ashore. "My favorite piece of his."

"It's beautiful," I said, trailing a finger down the rustic table. The reclaimed planks showed the age of the table with stains, dents and dings, and its history as a boat showed in its nail holes, steel bolts, and chipped pain. "What a remarkable man."

"He was."

"You have two incredible grandfathers." *And two awful parents.*

"I do. So you said you'd never met your mother's parents. Why?"

"Mom left home when she was nineteen. She never went back."

"I see."

Last night, I'd shared a lot about my family but I had not told him about what my mother once did for a living. I pictured his family finding out he was dating the daughter of a stripper, whose dad could be any of the men she had canoodled with—and my ears burned.

"Anything else?" I asked before he could ask me more.

"A stool." He held out a hand and led me to the kitchen.

We stopped short. Marlene stood by the sink. She was stacking all the dishes from our dinner in the sink. Seeing us, she smiled wide. "I'll have these ready for you in a jiffy."

"You've done a lot this weekend, Marlene. Do them in the morning. Go to bed. Thanks. See you tomorrow," Kyle said.

"All right, I suppose." Marlene looked at the dirty dishes that were so out of place in the stark, clinical kitchen. With a smile, she left.

"Hey, I'll wash the dishes." Taking off Kyle's jacket, I walked over to the sink.

"Don't be silly."

"I want to," I said loudly.

He shot me a surprised look. "Easy there, soldier."

I turned on the faucet over the stack of plates in the sink. "Cypress has germophobia and he's always cleaning up. He never lets me clean anything. He's done the dishes since we were eleven."

"Okay, you wash. I'll dry," Kyle said with a lop-sided grin. He grabbed towels from a drawer and strode up to me.

As I built up the suds, I asked. "Do you even know how to dry dishes, Lord Kyle of Bayland?"

"How dare you? Lord Kyle always punishes insubordinate subjects, wench." He smacked my bottom with a punitive thwack of a towel.

I giggled and twisted away from him. "Wench? Try female warrior."

"Don't know any."

"Really, Joan of Arc? Lady Trieu of Vietnam? Queen Zenobia of Syria? Sura, the Persian warrior princess? The Apache warrior, Lozen? Artemesia? Grace O'Malle, Irish firebrand who fought Queen Elizabeth? They were fierce badasses. I could go on. Oh, then there's my personal favorite, Celtic Queen Boudicca who pushed the Romans out of London in 60 AD. She's in my book."

"All right, I'll call you Badass Boudicca from now on. I think some of her atoms must have traveled around the world and time and ended up in your blood."

"Ha, perfect." We exchanged an amicable smile. "So you remember I said that?"

"Yes. I try to remember every word you say, Juniper," he said, with a smolder in his eyes.

I looked away with a sharp audible hiss. *Changing topic in three, two, one*: "You know, Kyle, you're the first person who's going to die in a zombie apocalypse."

"Oh yeah, why?"

"I mean, think about it. You have like six assistants, and I am sure you've never done dishes in your life, and you have drivers, security guards and people who cook Michelin star-rated food for you. So when the rest of us are eating beans out of a can in the sewers with rats gnawing on our toes, you'll be the first person to croak and kick the bucket."

Kyle threw down the towel and wrapped me from behind, his sandpaper jaw on my neck. "You know who the first person to die in a zombie apocalypse will be? A ham-fisted girl who can't climb scaffoldings. You do know I rock climb—for fun. I'll probably be your Commander-in-Chief and best warrior against the zombies."

Kyle's proximity left me breathless, but I managed to say, "If you are the Commander-in-Chief, I'll defy you and be the rebel leader."

"No doubt." He kissed my nape and I froze, my hands stuck in suds. His arms wrapped around my waist and his entire body pressed hard into mine and I was trapped between him and the kitchen sink. Every nerve in my body tingled with desire. All of a sudden, he inhaled audibly and moved away fast.

I never felt colder in my life.

As we washed the dishes, he kept the conversation light and witty, but I noticed a change had come over him. It became clear to me Kyle wanted nothing more than to kiss me comatose. Every time his hand brushed mine, my breath hitched and though he pretended not to notice, I knew he did. The mundane task of cleaning dishes together had become some kind of infantile foreplay for the two of us—so long deprived from each other physically.

When we were done, he washed his hands and I started to wash mine. Spaced out, I washed my hands six times in searing hot water before Kyle turned the faucet off. I turned the tap back on and washed my hands again, the water scalding my skin.

He pulled a face and turned the faucet off. "Juniper, your skin's gonna peel off."

"Let me just finish." I hit it on again.

"That's enough. You'll melt your bones if you keep scrubbing your hands like that," he said, turning it off again.

Hands hovering over the faucet handle, I pursed my lips. "Yeah, I guess. Um…I kind of have this OCD. Sometimes, I have to wash my hands over and over again. I know…it's irrational. Compulsive."

"That is so not cool."

"I know," I whispered.

Clutching my shoulders, he swiveled me around to face him. He examined my hands, which were patched with red splotches and his nostrils flared. I was led to the fridge, where he poured ice in a towel and gently put my hand inside. Brow knitted, he massaged my hands in the ice. "Geez, you had me worried. I thought I smelled finger kebab."

"Surely you lay it on thick."

"That's what she said." Kyle laughed at his own joke. "Okay, this is not funny. How long have you been grilling your hands?"

"Since I was a teenager. Like fifteen."

"So over ten years?"

I nodded. "It's not really bad. I use a lot of hand soap, take extra showers, use a lot of hand sanitizer but for the most part I have it under control."

"It's sad you don't think this is a big issue." Once he thought my hands looked less red he threw away the ice and dried my fingers. "You never saw a therapist for this?"

Seeing the pity in his eyes, I shrugged. "Didn't I tell you about my family last night? See a therapist for an OCD…that's funny…we've got bigger fish. Cypress has a lot of OCD's tics and issues he can't control. Like real ones. They come when he is upset, edgy…or nervous."

Kyle made the most devastating eye contact of all, navy eyes dilated to black, lips parted and so close to mine. "So, which is it? Are you edgy or nervous today?"

I caught my breath and threw myself at him, lifting my lips to his. Quicker than lightening, his arms went around me and he bent his neck. Maintaining the intense eye contact, Kyle locked his lips with mine and strong arms went around my waist as I arched my body against his. Kissing me fanatically, Kyle walked me back until my backbone hit the marble countertop. Then he trapped me there, his arms and legs making me an utter convict. I don't know how long we kissed—all I know was, this time it was different. I knew that we could not stop this time for there was a longing so desperate and frantic…it sought only the end.

My blood raged, raising my systolic pressure and contracting my heart muscles. In the distance, I heard his ragged breaths as his lips inflicted chaos on my mouth and his hands caressed my waist, my arms, my breasts, my legs—nonstop. Talented hands so shaped by experience and instinct. I could barely keep up his pace. Trying to imitate him, I stroked his back but with my lack of experience and the force of his passion, I realized I was an amateur at best.

Learning curve. Learning curve.

His hands went under my skirt to cradle my hips and he lifted me up to the counter. As he pushed himself closer, I gasped but my legs clenched and snapped shut, denying his legs entry. He stared down in surprise and with firm hands on my knees, he managed to gently ease them apart.

Our lips locked again as he pulled my legs apart further and wrapped them around his torso. Slowly, as his kisses deepened, I was pushed down, until my body was almost prostrate on the icy Carrera marble. When his lips tore away from my mouth and traveled down my throat to my breasts, I put up a hand to his chest. At that moment, I was lost and did not know what to do, my muscles taut with doubt.

He grabbed my hand and trapped it over my head. "Juniper. I can't stop."

"Can we please…go upstairs?" It was a bid to buy time.

"Sure."

I panted as he gripped my hips, hoisted me up with my legs still around him and started to walk, all the while still kissing me. In the living room, he stumbled a bit when he bumped into the cocktail table, but he recovered and smoothly moved to the stairs. I was struck by how effortless this was for him—as if he were used to carrying girls up and down the stairs while making love to them, every night.

When he got to his room, he kicked the door shut and hurried to his bed. He threw me down and stood at the foot of the bed watching me with gleaming eyes. Every inch of my body ignited and I felt every vein fill with smoke. With relentless eye contact, Kyle leisurely scaled my body. Concerned his weight would be too much for me, he rested on his elbows and knees as he began kissing me. Wanting more, I twisted my fingers in his hair and drew him down. He lost control. His hands dipped to my waist, spanned my back and drove me wild. I felt him pressing harder and harder into me, the pressure making my ribs ache. I flushed, knowing that my inexperience meant this would not be a joyful experience for him.

I have to tell him.

At that thought, I became too stressed to enjoy myself, but he did not notice the change. Kyle pushed himself up and ripped his shirt off revealing his bronze muscled chest. I smiled and touched his ripped abs, my hand trailing down to his tattoo. His eyes followed my fingers and then he lifted me to take my dress off. I put my arms up like a wooden doll.

He gave me a worried look. "You all right?"

I nodded. My dress was tossed to the heap on the floor and I sank back on the bed, a mass of congealed nerves. I had never done this before and though I badly wanted to do it right, I was petrified by my lack of experience.

Seeing me in my fancy new black bra and panty set edged with turquoise piping, Kyle gasped for air. "Juniper, you're beautiful, way more than I could imagine."

His hands trekked on my bare body which was now a slab of ice. And as he came over me once more, the roughness of his jeans chafing my skin, my legs clamped shut and my knees joined like bridge gates closing. My Chastity Belt in action led by the alert man-hater in me.

Kyle nudged my legs open with his knees but on meeting my rigid strength, he stilled. Puckering his brow, he heaved himself up on his elbows and gave me a searching look. "What's wrong?"

"I don't know what to do…"

"Been a while for you?"

I nodded. *You have no idea.*

"Don't worry, babe, it's always awkward the first time with someone new. We'll find our rhythm." With those words, he pushed his stone-hard knees into me and in a second forced my legs apart. Then he pulled me closer to his body and tried to put my legs around him, his upper body pressing so hard into me, I could barely breathe. "Relax, Juniper, put your legs around me."

"Why?"

At that, he froze and looked at me in shock. "What?"

"Well...I...uh...I've never done this before."

"God dammit—is this your first...no, it can't be."

"Yes, Kyle. I am a virgin."

"What the hell." He pushed himself off me so fast and hard, the stiff denim of his jeans scraped and burned my thighs. On his haunches at the edge of the bed he glared at me. "Are you kidding me? Tell me this is a bad joke."

I shook my head, wretchedly. "I wanted to tell you...but I didn't know how."

"Why? Juniper, how old are you?"

"Twenty-six." I covered my face with my shaking hands.

"Then how? Are you a complete virgin?"

"Is there any other kind?"

"No experience either?"

I stared at him through a cage of fingers. "Very little. You are kind of my...first."

"Holy fuck."

"Jeez. I'm inexperienced. Not Charles Manson. Why is this such a bad thing?"

"Why the hell did you not tell me before?"

"I just...I didn't know how to tell you." Ill at ease, I took one of his white pillows and placed it on my torso as if to shield myself from assault.

"Why? Is it for religious reasons? Did you take a purity pledge? Are you

440

a born again Christian? Or are you like in a pagan cult…waiting for virgin sacrifice? Christ, are you saving yourself for marriage?"

"No. No. No. And, no."

"So you were going to trick me? Not tell me and then surprise! Blood on my bed and a crying shame…then I am forced to marry you? What kind of games are you playing?" He grimaced and a muscle worked like a furious tick on his tightened jaw. His chest heaved from breathing hard and a flush of anger raced across his cheeks.

I pushed myself up and leaned on the headboard, anger rising in me as well. "How can you say that, Kyle? This is not the medieval ages. And I don't want more from you than what you can give me. I would never— what kind of person do you think I am? I'm a virgin, not a conniving bitch!"

"Why didn't you just tell me?"

"Should it be on my museum biography? Tattooed on my forehead? Why does it matter?"

"It does. I wanted a fuck-buddy not a…Catholic School girl. God damn it, this is so wrong."

"Why? Why?"

Mean. Mean. Mean. I couldn't wait to run away from this awful man.

"If you have been saving yourself for so long…then I can't. You need to be with someone who will be with you long term. Someone for whom this means something. Not me."

"Can you please hand me my dress?" My voice was a parched cackle.

Kyle jumped off the bed as if I was radioactive waste and he was escaping contamination. Looking around, he picked up my dress from the floor and tossed it my way. I gulped and put it on, realizing that this was the most embarrassing moment of my life—yet. He watched in pitiless silence as I sat on my knees and quickly pulled the salmon pink creation on.

Sliding off the bed, I realized I was still wearing my heels and tried to find my balance, but my legs shook with seismic waves and I tottered.

Instantly, he steadied me with an arm on my shoulders. "You okay?"

Tears welled in my eyes as I turned to him. "It's not a crime you know. The CDC says fourteen percent of the American population consists of virgins. Um. Look, I barely know you...and then everything on this trip was so unexpected. I just...I just didn't know how to tell you." I stopped, realizing my words meant nothing to him.

Kyle sat down on the edge of his bed near me and reached for me. "Come here."

Warily, I studied his face and then moved towards him.

He held my hands in his. "Don't feel bad. I'm sorry. I'm a jerk. I should not have reacted like that. I am just shocked. I imagined you had a low number of men in your life. I just never imagined it was zero."

"I should have told you, but on this trip I enjoyed my time with you so much...I thought it would be okay. You'd understand." I wiped my moistened eyes, worried I'd break out in an ugly, unstoppable crying fit. Great Spirit, I had set some kind of crying record this weekend.

"Help me understand. Why?" He got up and held me gently at arms distance, like I was made out of thin ice and spun sugar.

"Mom was strict when I was a teenager. I was not allowed to date. And when I got older, I did not want to be with anyone. I dated and...kissed my share of frogs...but never liked anyone enough to...well...until I met you."

His eyebrows soared on his forehead. "Not allowed to date? Why?"

I shrugged helplessly. "She was very protective of me...and Cypress. She worked so much to support us when we were kids, she thought if she could scare the hell out me about boys...it'd keep me out of trouble when we were home alone. The problem is...my fears became permanent...until

I met you."

His face guarded, Kyle dropped his hands and put some distance between us. He picked up his shirt from the floor and slipped it on. It fell around his chiseled brown abs in a way that made my mouth water, so I averted my eyes.

He cleared his throat. "Anyhow, no matter now. Look, I'm flattered you wanted me to be your first. But I've never been with a virgin and it'd be so wrong...for you."

My heart sank so low I think it hit the floorboards. "Okay...I didn't mean to lead you on."

"Don't say that, Juniper. I am the one who pursued you. It's just that... you deserve someone better. More human."

The worst type of "It's not you it's me," possible.

I gulped and took a step back. "Kyle, I get it. I'll leave in the morning. Or if you want, I can leave now."

He raked fingers in his hair with angry motions. "Jesus, Juniper. I don't want you to leave."

"I do."

"Please don't. Please. Don't. Look it's been a crazy few days, so why don't you get some rest tonight? Tomorrow we'll go out and then talk. Let's see if we can still do this." He leaned forward and kissed the top of my head, as if I was his little cousin. "Don't worry, things will be better in the morning."

Teeth clenched, face averted, I nodded and ran from his room without another word. I finally learned what the Walk of Shame felt like. In my room, I pulled the door shut and slumped against it.

KYLE

December 12, 10:14 p.m. 47 seconds
(Seacliff, San Francisco)

K yle stood staring at his bathroom mirror, something inside him splitting in half. W-H-Y was the only question in his mind right now. Why had Juniper not told him? Why was she a freaking virgin at the age of 26?

Why did I not guess?

All the signs were there, in big florescent letters. The way she had reacted to his douchey proposal in Ann Arbor—as if he had slapped her from the inside. The way she always hesitated beyond a kiss—her eyes searching his for clues, hints, pointers for what lay beyond. The way she evaded questions about boyfriends. This explained why his security team had been unable to dig up any information about her past relationships.

He had figured she was shy and maybe had been with a few boys, got busy with work and now was a bit rusty, but never in his wildest delusions did he imagine that the girl who reduced him to a hormonal teenage slush

444

pile every time she merely glanced his way was an untouched virgin.

Ugh. No. Just no.

His system was not set up for this kind of a glitch. He could not ask her to be his fuck-buddy for a limited time. Her first time needed to be with someone worthy of her purity. Someone who wanted a long-term relationship. An image of Juniper in another man's arms popped up and Kyle was dazed by the force of his jealousy. He took a step back. The idea of someone else with Juniper was hateful. Intolerable. But it was the most merciful option.

He had to let her go.

This was all wrong.

I am all wrong.

The image in his bathroom mirror mocked him, as Kyle was forced to meet his darker double's face. He glared at his image like he always did, as if it was his enemy, eyes full of lies, accusations, and the aftertaste of black bitumen on his tongue.

What are you doing messing around with this innocent girl? Kyle asked the mirror.

Why? She came willingly, said his reflection, nonchalant and cool as always.

No, she's a captive bird.

Wrong, she led us here.

No, you lying prick, you put her in your steel bear trap. Kyle lips twisted in an ugly sneer.

Calm down. Not a big deal. She'll walk away happy—in July. Like all of them.

No. There will be no time with her. I can't ruin her. I have to release her.

The image began to laugh. *You have to admit this is the ultimate irony. You wanted to chain her and keep her like a pet for a few months. But instead, she chained you.*

CHAPTER 27

That night, I slipped into bed numb as a corpse until sleep claimed me. The next morning when I woke up, I stayed in bed for an hour, still as a chameleon waiting for a katydid. Half-lidded, I studied the geometric pattern on the focal wall for so long my neck ached. When the room filled with razor-sharp light that glinted off the mirrored chests and the Venetian mirrors, I forced myself to crawl out of bed.

I paced the room until my phone rang. It was Cypress. As we chatted, I massaged my stiff neck. He was hyper-excited about a video software editing gig he had just been offered. Even though he could work from home, the interview was in their Detroit office and he was worried he'd have an anxiety attack there. I allayed his fears and volunteered to go with him. Happy at this solution and the fact I was flying back today, Cypress hung up.

I walked to the window that overlooked the pool, basking in the sun warming the room. I pressed my forehead on the glass and watched the mist pleating over the bay until a flicker below caught my attention.

I gasped when I saw Kyle stalk to the swimming pool. At the edge of the diving board, he turned with his back to the water. With a little tap on the board, he took off backwards. My heart skipped a beat as he arced in the air and then dove down. I expected him to start swimming in the pool. But he quickly emerged out of the water and scrambled up the diving board. This time he did a pike dive and his body impaled the water like a blade in flesh. In an instant, he bobbed back up and I wondered why he was not doing laps.

Up the board and down he flew, into a chiffonade of a million drops. The sheer athleticism of the man, the power of his body, was a marvel to witness and I clenched my hands in longing. With bated breath, I watched him dive over and over again, each time performing different dives. It looked like he was on an insane seconds-reliant schedule. While California was still asleep on a lazy Sunday, Kyle Paxton was diving in frigid waters like the Olympian great Greg Louganis.

I was mesmerized for several minutes before I realized this was an unusually long time for someone to be diving continually. The terminal velocity with which he rammed his body into the water was terrifying—almost, as if he were punishing himself. Over and over again. What the hell was going on in his mind? He looked like a man driven to the edge of wild impulse.

After countless dives, he stood poised to jump again, but he sank down on his knees and collapsed on the diving board. He looked up, face furious as if he were subduing some inner demons. He clenched his midriff, by his tattoo, as if in pain. And even from far away, I could tell it was not a physical pain. I stepped back from the window, worried he'd catch me staring.

What was all that about? Did it have something to do with last night?

No.

As bad as last night had been, Kyle was fighting something inside I knew nothing about. Last night, I had been too stunned to cry. Kyle's irascible reaction to my virginity—as though it was a crime against humanity—was hard to process. I knew that he would have been uneasy, and maybe briefly stunned to learn I was a virgin—I just did not know he would be so let down, so cold. So…unkind.

I did not know my being a virgin was a deal breaker. But what else did I expect, when the cornerstone of his liaisons with women was only sex. I meant nothing to him. It was just good old lust and sex for him, even after all we had gone through. It was unexpected. Painful.

I have to leave.

Lifting my head, I forced back the tears that I had been holding back since I ran out of Kyle's room last night. I was not going to cry. I was going to leave with whatever little shred and crumb and dash of dignity I had left.

I took a shower and dressed in my own clothes. I neatly put all of Kyle's gifts back in Pandora's closet and packed up only my things. I went down the stairs holding my packed wheelies suitcase. When I heard low voices coming from the kitchen, I stood at the foot of the stairs to compose myself. Heart pounding like a percussion drum, I walked over.

Kyle stood there talking to Marlene as she cooked. There was a breakfast spread on the counter and he held a coffee cup.

When he heard me, Kyle turned and smiled. "Hello, Juniper."

"Hello, Miss Juniper," said Marlene.

"Hi, Marlene. Kyle." I noted Kyle was dressed for work, wearing a suit. On a Sunday? My mind tried to process this Kyle with the semi-naked man I had seen killing himself on the diving board an hour ago.

Seeing my little suitcase rolling behind me, his eyes popped open and he put his cup down with a loud porcelain clatter. He walked over to me

448

and stood a mere foot away, his irate eyes searching mine. "My office. Now. Minus the suitcase."

Skulking, I followed him to the office. There, he shut the door and sat down on the chair by his desk. I hesitated by the door and he signaled me with his fingers, as if I were his very own dancing marionette. "Come here."

Jaw locked, I walked over. Still sitting, he hauled me to him and trapped me between his legs and his futuristic slab of a desk. Conscious of his hot gaze on my poker face, I grew breathless and writhed against the hard thighs holding me in prison.

"What are you doing, Kyle? I'd like to leave."

"You can't."

"Am I your prisoner?"

"At the moment, yes. For the future, don't tempt me." He grinned wickedly. "Come on. Stay on your own accord. Can't you see I don't want you to leave?"

"You made it clear last night, I was no use to you. That my…state…was a deal breaker."

"Whoa. Whoa. I didn't say that. You just did. Nice try there." His hands went to the back of his head and he rubbed the column of his neck. "God, I am so sorry about last night, I really am. I was not planning…what happened. It was a shocker. Maybe we need to take this slower. Look, I thought about it last night and nothing has changed between us, as far as I am concerned. I want to be with you. Now and later. If you'll…still have me."

Say no, Juniper. Be strong. Walk away, now.

My mind tried to resist him, but my turncoat heart began to thaw at the raw emotion in his voice. Feigning nonchalance, I checked out the psychedelic green shoelaces on my Supra high top sneakers for a bit.

"Say something, Juniper. If you leave like this, it will be the worst day

I've had since God knows when—." His pleading irises locked with mine.

"Kyle…" My heart melted like hot butter but I did not know what to say.

His arms snaked around my waist and he buried his face in my chest. As his large head nuzzled the valley of my breasts, my breath hitched. I threaded my fingers in his crisp hair, utterly ruining his hairstyle. His hair felt silky and rough, mink and barbed wire, at the same time.

"Juniper. My Juniper, I know I don't deserve you. Someone as dark and twisted as me should not be with someone as pure and innocent as you. But after just four days with you, I can't…I can't imagine being without you anymore. I feel…I know, I truly don't deserve you but if you stay and will be mine for the next few months, nothing will make me happier." He released me and gave me a wry smile. "If you still want to."

I can't imagine being without you…wait, what now?

"Kyle, you know I want nothing more."

"Then don't leave, June-Bug."

"Fine. I won't."

"Good."

Relief flooded his eyes and he dragged me down to him and crushed my mouth with a hard kiss. Though bowled over, I did not yield to his lips. As if recalling my revelation last night, his lips softened and his kiss became feather gentle. Too gentle for my liking. I placed my hands on both sides of his face and returned his kiss, hard, my lips forcing his open as I dipped my tongue inside, to remind him I was inexperienced, not made of glass. He responded by ejecting my tongue out of his mouth and easing away. I wanted to slap him. I liked his fanatical kisses not his wussy ones.

Nostrils flaring, I linked angry eyes with him and he tossed me a wicked look.

"Listen, I am so sorry to do this to you, but Evan called this morning and the damned Argentinians I have been dodging are leaving today. I have to go in for a short meeting with them. Okay with you?"

I gulped and checked my disappointment. In spite of what he had just told me, I could not help but think his going to work today was his way of running away from me. But then, running away was my thing—not his. Kyle was successful because he met his troubles head on and fought them, instead of running away from them.

"Sure, it's fine."

"Alright, I'll be back at noon sharp. I'd like to take you to the Muir Redwood forest, but we'll do whatever you want. It's up to you."

"I'd love that, Kyle. But Willow said we have a double date with her and Clive. Are we doing that?"

He shrugged casually but I noticed his eyes narrowed. "If you like. I love my sis and Clive is cool, but I'd rather hang out with you."

"Me too."

"I'm glad." He kissed the tip of my nose and released me. "Deal then. Hafta run now, but make yourself at home. Look around. I have paintings and books all over."

"Kyle, you don't have any fiction books. Only snoozefest biz and tech ones. Really sad."

"Okay, I'll buy books for my Hot Librarian. Just say the word and I'll buy a library. A candy cane store. Whatever she likes."

My eyes widened. "Do not. Do. Not. Please don't get me anything. Zilch. Nada. I explicitly do not want you to get me anything. Repeat after me: I, Kyle Paxton, tyrannical rolling-in-it CEO of BirdsEye, do solemnly swear I shall hereby not ever shower lavish unwanted gifts on one simple blissfully non-mercenary Juniper Mills."

Kyle chuckled. "Wow. I heard that, but it doesn't mean I will obey you.

Hey, listen. If you are interested in the history of this house, check out those boxes with photos of the house and my grandfather." He pointed to an acrylic shelf full of fat tech books with a few black boxes in between.

"Will do."

"And in case you need to go somewhere, I'm leaving my driver, Pat. Do not go out by yourself. Do. Not."

"Oh really? I'll stay put, but not because you said so, Bossy Boy." I raised an annoyed eyebrow.

"There's the sassy mouth I admire." Grinning like a kid, he swept me in his arms and kissed me again.

He left and I went to the kitchen and ate a big breakfast with Marlene. She would not let me help her clean up and we chatted while she washed the dishes. After she was finished, she said that she had to go to church and then get groceries. "Are you okay with being home alone?"

I chuckled. "Did Kyle put you up to be my nanny?"

Before Marlene left, she showed me a pimped-out control panel in the kitchen for outdoor surveillance and walked me through the alarm system if I needed to leave. Once alone, I walked around the house listlessly and then went back to Kyle's study to look at his grandfather's photos.

I love vintage photos. These photos did not disappoint. I pulled out the boxes and sat down cross-legged on the rug, flipping through crinkle-edged photos, yellowed by time. There were some of the house in the fifties in various stages of its construction and some were the milestones of Kyle's grandparents.

Their wedding, vacations in Europe, his mother's birth, her childhood, her wedding to Kyle's father, and a few of Kyle as a baby. There were also some photos of his grandmother when she was an Army nurse in the Bataan Peninsula and his grandfather had been in stationed in Normandy.

An ache settled in my throat as I flipped through them again.

The life of these long-gone lovers was reduced to a few photos.

I started looking for pictures of Kyle. I saw his grandfather had the same set jaw and thick black hair as Kyle, who owed his looks more to his grandfather than father, although he did have his grandmother's eyes. With her dark lipstick, slick chignons, pea coats, and sprigged dresses Kyle's grandmother had a timeless elegance. I noticed her husband looked dotingly at her in every photo, instead of the camera. Letting the photos drop from my hand, I felt a pang of nostalgia at the pale memories trapped in the images.

Only faded memories remain after people are long gone.

Like ashes after a fire.

That made me tear up. I sat on my haunches and stared at the transparent bookshelf. Nothing lasts forever, Kyle had said last night. What legacy did he want to leave the world? Just one of individual success, not one with his own family. No one who could be an extension of him. He was a partial life. A torn fragment of a book unwritten.

Longing to figure out Kyle and frustrated there were no photos of him as a child and a young man, I got up and rummaged through all the boxes.

Nothing.

I was about to give up, when I spotted a wooden box wedged behind several thick books on the topmost shelf. It was bound by painters tape. On my tiptoes, I managed to reach the box. Tearing off the tape, I jimmied open the box and examined the contents. I found his childhood photos, wads of envelopes, and a few letters.

I also found a stack of landscape photos taken by Kyle. They were striking views of sunsets and sunrises around the world, many taken from the death-defying razor's edge of mountains. Kyle had an earth porn fetish and he captured broken cliffs, wide-rimmed sunsets over beaches, bowing apple green valleys, and snow-hooded peaks in film. Turning the photos over, I saw notations in his handwriting. Argentina, 2014. Machu Picchu, 2013. Katmandu, 2012. Angkor, 2011. It came as a pleasant shock that he was such a skilled photographer. I wondered why he had not framed a single one in his house.

When I saw the childhood photos of Kyle, my heart went out to his mini version. He was a tiny thing with unruly black hair and sullen cobalt eyes. There were a few of him with a younger Evan and his family on holidays. They were telling. Kyle looked sad. Silent. Lost. Angry. My heart skipped a few beats.

From time to time, I scolded myself for skimming through his private photographs. But I did not stop. I could not stop. I continued intruding and discovered a large envelope trussed with painters' tape. I ripped it open.

Several photos spilled out.

They were of Kyle, looking younger…and happier. In most of them, college-aged Kyle was arm-in-arm with a mystery girl. They hiked. They surfed. They swam. And dove down waterfalls. They sky-dived. Bungee-jumped. They ate at farm-to-table bistros. I found a lot of photos of them in London. Kyle and the girl traveled Europe together. They held tankards of beer at pubs in London. Wine glasses at wineries. Cocktails at clubs. It looked like Kyle drank—a heck of a lot—when he was younger.

In several of her close-ups, Mystery Girl wore flowers tucked behind her ears, trendy hats on shimmering headbands, lots of beads down floral maxis, shorts with boots, and bras and jeans under long coats. She rocked the sexy-hippie, Coachella look. She was petite, with cropped ash-blonde hair, pixie green eyes and a sensitive expression on her face.

My heart stilled. Was this Chloe—girl X?

If I needed proof that this was Chloe, I found it. There was a fragment of a handwritten letter signed by her in the envelope. The letter had been ripped-up and taped together. Several pieces were missing but half the letter was legible. I gasped and put it away.

I should not read it.

But my curiosity got the better of me and I picked it up, heart banging with guilty knocks.

And Kyle, even when you are thousands of miles away all I think of is the bond between us stretched like a rubber band ready to snap. My love, you're more than my boyfriend, you are more than my lover, you're more than my friend, you are my anchor. My soul. I cannot call you my boyfriend anymore because it does not do you justice. You are my life.

You and I—we are more than the faults we make.

Please, please listen to me. I am truly sorry about yesterday. I promise, I'll try harder. To change. To be who you want me to be. The lovely Shel Silverstein said, "There are no happy endings. Endings are the saddest parts, so just give me a happy middle, and a very happy start." That is all I want for us. But I am scared. Scared of the end. Please don't let it fray. Don't burn us down.

Love you so much,
Your Elafris—Chloe

His Elafris. Like Kyle's tattoo.

The letter was sickly sweet, but it touched a raw nerve in me and some of her words got stuck in my head. *I promise, I'll try harder. To change. To be who you want me to be.*

What did that mean? Did Kyle try to control her? Did he break her?

It was then that the doorbell rang. Startled, I tucked the letter back and taped up the box exactly as I found it. The doorbell kept ringing, the digital notes scraping in my ear like a knife against a glass bottle. I went to the security panel in the kitchen and clicked on the outdoor camera frame. I saw a vaguely familiar tall girl by the white gate leaning on a limousine and a uniformed man pressing the doorbell.

I clicked the intercom on. "Who is it?"

The girl in the video heard my voice and ran to the gate's intercom. "It's me. Izzy."

KYLE

December 13, 10:53 a.m. 27 seconds
(BirdsEye Office, San Francisco)

yle escorted the Argentinian executives from the conference room
to the lab. The doors opened and he almost bumped into a man
exiting the lab. It was a thin, red-haired, short man who was thrilled
to see him. Kyle stopped dead in his tracks and the visitors clustered up
behind him. Exiting the lab was no other than Chad, the D-bag Brody.

Rage choked his throat and he took a few steps back.

What the hell was this pest doing here? In his classified lab?

Sylvia came out of the lab and was stunned to see Kyle. Chad made
a beeline for Kyle and she followed with less enthusiasm. A smiling Chad
shook Kyle's hand and they exchanged hellos, but when the ginger D-bag
began to blabber, Kyle ignored him.

Turning to Mr. Ignacio, the head of the Argentinian delegation, he said,
"Will you gentlemen please excuse me for a few minutes? I have an urgent
matter to attend." Then he motioned to Evan. "Please take our guests to

Thom in the lab. After that, Evan, come to my office. Bye, Chad. Good to see you."

Not.

Meanwhile Sylvia signaled her assistant to see the deflated Chad off.

"To my office. Now," Kyle said to Sylvia, walking down the hall fast.

Once they got to his office, he sat down on his chair and faced her from across his desk.

When she warily seated herself, his silent ice cracked. "What the hell is Chad doing here?"

"And what are you doing here? You said you weren't going to work this weekend."

"Ignacio wanted to meet me."

"I was handling him," she said. "Me."

"Not enough, evidently."

"Kyle, what the hell? We work as a team."

"You know very well that rat Chad stole data to form his company. What the hell was he doing looking at Kronos? In a lab needing top security clearance."

Sylvia shrugged. "Looking."

"Let me ask you something," Kyle said, realization dawning on him. "Straight up, no lies, no politics, no schemes. Are you going above my head to the Board of Directors because you want to push Cirrus and Chad down my throat?"

"What's wrong with you? Why the finger-pointing neurotic doubt?" Sylvia stared in disbelief at him, but the flush of angry red on her neck gave her away. Red on her neck was her tell.

And she has so freaking few.

He leaned back in his chair. "But it's not really about Cirrus, is it? This

458

is part of your bigger game plan, isn't it? Your shameless plan to rat out your lousy CEO to the board. That's what it's about for you. A cheap power play—a pathetic power play at that, because the board knows who the lousy one is."

Sylvia gritted her teeth. "You have officially lost it, Kyle Paxton. You never have a single minute to talk or give priorities to budget—"

"To what? Your manufactured doomsday prophecies and 'concerns' to control BirdsEye?" Kyle asked with air quotes.

At that moment Evan came in, shut the door and sat down in a chair by Kyle's desk. The two men fixed Sylvia with identical hostile expressions that were terrifying in concord.

Sylvia's composure faded and the flush on her neck deepened. "All right. Let's talk. Now that you finally have time."

"This is a clusterfuck that I do not have time to address today but I will be addressing tomorrow." Kyle looked down at his phone. Izzy was calling. He ended her call.

"What do you mean?" Sylvia asked with an arch smile. "Are you going back to your little museum distraction? Isn't she a little peach? I wonder though—"

Kyle's face erupted with fury. "Sylvia, do not finish that thought. My personal life is mine only. I've never butted into yours, so stay out of mine. Don't you dare even enter the same room as her. Now, full disclosure: I will seek to dismantle your seat on our board and will have a vote about it during the next board meeting."

"What the hell. Are you firing me?"

"No. But I am calling an internal company investigation into your actions. Legal and HR. After their review, we'll see."

Sylvia shot up, her cool shattering. "How dare you? After what I've done for you, Kyle? *I* was the one who helped set up BirdsEye. It was all me in a zoo with a bunch of fucktards." She shook her head and her eyes turned into murderous slits. "This is totally unjust."

"You should have thought of justice when you went against BirdsEye. And no, you did not help set it up. You joined once we became a corporation with an IPO and hundreds of employees."

"You arrogant asshole," she hissed.

"Keeping it classy, I see. Leave your office today for a week's suspension. Files and PC handed to Evan."

Sylvia put her hands in air. "Kyle, you can't do that. Let me explain—"

Kyle hit the desk with two fists. "For years you have. Explained. Explained. Explained. While I shut up and was all ears. I did *everything* you asked. Made every irrational change you demanded. How long have we worked together, Sylvia? I trusted you. No matter what you did, I dismissed my suspicions as my own stupidity. I can't stand two-faced people and now I get why you're always schmoozing with the board. What did you think? That they would fire me and replace you with me?"

"You are delusional if you got all of that from Chad's visit."

"No, Sylvia, this was a long time coming." Kyle swiveled to Evan. "Do you have it?"

Evan rummaged on Kyle's desk and slammed a file in front of Sylvia. "Here you go."

"What is this?"

"Some excellent reconnaissance work on your dear pal Chad from our security team," said Evan.

"I think you'll be quite unhappy with what you see here. It going to be shocker, even for you," Kyle added.

"Treating your loyal partners like traitors." Shooting daggers at the two men, Sylvia picked up the file. "You'll regret this."

"Is that a threat?" asked Evan with a yawn.

"You'll be hearing from *my* lawyers," she said.

"You do recall *our* lawyers are the most rabid attack dogs in the city?" Evan said in a bored tone looking at his manicured nails.

"Take the file. Get out of my office," said Kyle.

Sylvia lifted her neck high and stalked out.

Kyle felt sick to his gut. It hurt that his doubts had solid possibilities. Now they just needed proof. He turned to Evan. "What the hell is going on here? I spent two days with Juniper and the world flipped upside down."

Evan shook his head. "It's nothing to do with your time. Sylvia has been planning shit-hits-the-ceiling mutiny for years. Kyle, I'm worried. It wasn't a good idea to let her know your intentions. You didn't handle the situation well. You should have been objective."

Both of Kyle's hands went to his head. "I couldn't. I thought she was a friend…our best asset. God, I can't believe it."

"She will die fighting. Better to destroy her subversively. Behind her back to the board."

"Sorry, but subterfuge is not my game. Destruction, yes. Damn it. Back to Ignacio and our meeting for now. I have to get to Juniper in 67 minutes exactly."

Evan smiled as they walked out. "So how is round two with Juniper?"

Kyle clenched his jaw. "I don't wanna talk about it."

CHAPTER 28

zzy? What is she doing here? My lungs went empty. "I'll open up."

The gate slid open and Izzy came inside. I ran to the front door and stood still for a long moment staring through the glass panels at Izzy, catwalking to the front steps. I opened the door and stood in the frame. "Hello?"

She gave me a cool nod. "Is Kyle home?"

I just stared blankly at her. A ton of emotions ran through me all at once: anger, umbrage, jealousy, confusion. I took a deep breath and said, "No, he's not."

"When will he be back?"

"By noon."

Almost oblivious to my presence, Izzy breezed past me to the foyer. With slow and measured grace, she began walking through the house with me scampering behind her. She looked around curiously, as if this was her first time in the house, and I was gratified. At any rate, Kyle hadn't lied. I was the first one of his companions to come to his house.

How is that a good thing, Juniper?

Izzy stopped short in the living room and strutted to the wall of windows. Seeing her standing there, looking dressed and posed for a *Vanity Fair* cover, was surreal. She wore a sleeveless swinging white top—an arresting contrast with her dark skin—skinny jeans, heeled leather boots and metal studded bangles on her emaciated arms. Staring at the view below, she muttered, "Nice pad. Can't believe the bastard never brought me here."

I coughed softly.

As if recalling I existed, she swiveled to me and smiled faintly. "Are you one of his assistants?"

"No, I am his…friend."

"His what?" Her neutral face crumbled, and she shot me a real look for the first time, as if now I was worthy of a second glance. "What is your name?"

Gawking at the six-foot tall goddess in front of me, I gathered she did not recall meeting me at the gala and I was sure that for lionized immortals like her, mundane folks like me were instantly sent to the recycle bin. "Juniper. May I help you?"

"I just came to drop off Kyle's keys." She rifled through her Hermes ostrich purse and took out a few keys strung on an Eiffel Tower chain.

"Kyle's key to what?" I whispered.

"The apartment, of course."

My head spun like a top. "Wait. You were living in his apartment?"

"Um, yeah. I'm vacating it today. I have a flight back to New York in a bit. I tried calling him, but he's not picking up. Will you please give him the keys?" She detached the Eiffel Tower chain from the keys, threw them on the old table and turned to leave.

"How long have you been living in his apartment?" I asked her retreating back.

She spun around like she twirled a dress at the end of a runway. "Why do you want to know?"

"I just do. Exactly what dates?"

Izzy gave me a stunned look that turned to dawning realization and then to inspection as her dazzling eyes probed me from head to toe. "Are you...are you Summer...but you can't be, can you?" I was silent but my fallen face gave her the answer. "Oh my God, you're so different from all the others."

I know, I know just tell me already I'm not a supermodel like you.

"Jesus freaking Christ, I need a smoke. Can I go out?"

I nodded, drew open the patio door and led her to the rockery. I sank against a pillar and she stood ramrod straight like an elegant utility pole in front of me. With shaking hands, she fished a lighter and an emerald tin of Pall Mall Menthols from her purse.

She took out a cigarette and handed me the tin. "You want one?"

I shook my head.

"Can you hold this?" She lit a cigarette, the dark pools of her eyes on me.

"Yes." I held the green tin in my hand and looked down at the white warning label, which read: Caution. Cigarette Smoking May be Hazardous to Your Health and Can Cause Cancer. But all I read was: Caution. Kyle Paxton May be Hazardous to Your Health and Can Cause Heartbreak.

After a few puffs, she said, "I'm just surprised to see you. Aren't you supposed to start in January? I mean don't Kyle's Winters and Summers have specific dates? Set in a Fort Knox schedule."

"I guess. I am not really sure." Wrapping my arms around my waist, I shrugged, not volunteering more information. This was not a conversation I wished to have. Cringing, I looked at the silver-lined clouds at the bay's foggy edge. As always, the sky was partly cloudy, partly sun-drenched.

"How remarkable. Kyle isn't usually out-of-the-box. He seems to do very fixed things." Izzy blew an elegant puff of smoke from her wide luscious lips.

Look, Juniper, look again at those edible lips, said my jealous heart. *Lips Kyle used to kiss. Don't even peek at her endless legs. Legs that know what men want.*

I took a long breath. "Yeah. He does."

"I mean you're cute, Jennifer, but so not his type...at all."

"So I've been told," I said. "And it is Juniper." I was clutching her tin cigarette case so hard that my hands felt like I'd been repeatedly hit by a ruler. I looked down at the red lines on my palms and handed the tin back to her.

"I meant that in a good way. He usually likes posh tramps. Like me."

Recalling Izzy was an Ivy League grad with her own company, I wondered where her self-effacement stemmed from. "Thanks, I think. You're not a tramp, at all. So how long have you been living in Kyle's apartment?"

"For the past five months."

"I see." My heart sank to the grass under my feet. The clouds dimmed and the fog felt thicker and closer. So Kyle was playing a double game with both of us.

There was no flicker of emotion on her face but I could tell it upset her too. "Yes. Wait. Have you been living here all the while? Wow. And he made me sign an exclusivity contract. Fucking Kyle. Clever bastard."

"Wrong. I just got here a few days ago."

"Oh. You are a glitch then. You living here, the dates...I mean...this is so weird because the girl who was with him before me, you know, Linda the lawyer...she started at a set date and ended at a set date. I started on a set date and ended...oh my God...I guess it must be because of you." She coughed at the smoke and then spat out a dry laugh.

Linda the lawyer? Great.

"I don't think Kyle does anything because of anyone else. There is only Kyle in his universe," I said, bitterly. "Who is Linda the lawyer?"

"The Summer before me. She's a lawyer, vicious as shark teeth. She works in the company in his office building. Rapture...or something."

"Capture?"

"Yeah. After he was done with her, he never spoke to her again. Linda's cool, though. She saw me at an event with him and knew I was the shiny new item. Kyle was as white as a sheet and told me not to talk to her, as per the rules. I did, though. Asshole. What is it with his fucking rules? We should have a Kyle-exes support group, right? Or a union." She gave me a strained smile. "But that's against the rules too. The goddamn one hundred rulebook. Did you sign it?"

What one hundred rulebook?

Oh God, I had only signed the Termination Contract. That's what Kyle wanted me to sign. Not a rule book. I hoped I'd never have to see that blasted document. Plus, hadn't we broken all of his rules already? Pressing my belly, I felt sick. Enough to upchuck my breakfast on the bottle green grass.

"Um. What about the others? Did you meet them?"

"I only met Linda once and she told me about, what was her name, oh yes, Nunu...nope...Anu, the Indian British model. Then there was the actress, Mona Atkins. Now that I think of it, he has a girl type: arrogant bitch trolls. And a body type: tall, skinny Amazonians. all of us very eclectic racially." She was talking almost to herself, as if airing it in front of me gave her closure.

All of us. Izzy. Mona. Linda. Anu. Even poor Chloe.

And now—Juniper. Kyle's harem.

"Why did you agree…to this? Why did they?"

She blew out a fresh cloud of smoke and shrugged. "Personally, I like the rush. I usually like casual hookups. This was the longest I've been with someone since college. I don't know about the others. I guess he gives us something we desperately want. For me, it was h

5i41s business contacts. For Linda, the job at Rapture. For the Brit gal, it was an ad campaign. For Mona, it was a movie deal with his producer friend. What did you sell your soul for?"

My soul? Is he Mephistopheles? Am I Dr. Faustus?

Why was I so impulsive and why had I signed that contract without reading it? Oh wait…the museum. The four million dollars…no…I was wrong there—the museum was a Paxton legacy.

"Um, nothing yet."

Izzy looked calm and indifferent as she flicked ash on the grass.

"It doesn't bother you that I am with him now?" I asked her.

Her small nose wrinkled, and she gave me a snide smile as if to say, *Bitch, please. You're cute.* "Not in the least. For me it was just a work deal. No buyer's remorse. I mean he gave me what I wanted. Endless shopping. Lots of diamonds." She lifted her wrist that was draped with the Hermes bag. "Twenty thousand-dollar toys like this. Contacts and investors for my company. I have a makeup start-up, Orchid. Gotta pay my bills. Being a model is a limited liability, after all."

"I see."

"And I gave him what he wanted. I attended mind-numbing events, traveled with him and put out…what he needed at night. But, that was not just for him. He's hot in bed. But aside from that, he was kinda cold, dead at the eyes. Like he was missing a soul. He didn't want to talk—at all. Or go out. Same thing with Linda. What's he like with you?"

"Um…a bit different, but then I haven't officially started yet."

"Oh. Where did you two meet?"

"In Ann Arbor."

Interest flickered in her eyes and then it was gone as she dismissed me from her mind.

"Where did he meet you?"

"In New York. The Met Gala. He kept staring at me even though he was with another girl. And then a month later, he took me out and threw it all on me. I was flattered and said yes."

I gulped and said nothing. That sounded so…familiar. My heart hardened with anger and revulsion. All the fireflies, rainbows, unicorns and fairy dust I felt for Kyle mashed into a thick smoke cloud in me. I coughed, ejecting it from my throat like a demon from my body. I felt empty and raw, like I'd just had surgery. I could not wait for Izzy to get out of here so I could leave too.

Izzy threw the cigarette down and twisted it in the sod with a pencil-heeled boot. "My Kyle Survival advice is don't get too involved, sweetie. He's a coldblooded snake. He'll turn on you in a second after fucking you like an animal. Nothing about him is human, but then most of the girls he picks are just cultured skanks from *Maxim* covers looking for an easy handout. They're never nice like you."

"Oh."

I felt a physical pain bloom in my belly like dark watercolors on a wet page. Such harsh words. Words about him that hurt…me. A lot.

Do I matter? Am I a thing now?

What am I doing here?

Yes, what the hell was I doing here in this cancerous place, in this awkward situation with soulless people I did not, nor ever could, understand?

"Gotta go. Good meeting you, Jemima."

Juniper! My name is Juniper.

I followed her back into the house and at the front door, I asked, "Tell me, when did you see Kyle last?"

"Thursday."

"So to be clear, this Thursday?"

"Uh-huh. Bye bye now." Walking away, Izzy gave me a snooty smile, as though she thought it was droll anything she said could have had such an effect on a perfect stranger.

"Goodbye. Have a safe flight." I gave her a weak smile.

I tried to regain my composure, but I just stood glued to the doorframe, staring at the girl sashaying down the asphalt driveway. A girl Kyle had fucked on Thursday. A day after the club, a day he carried me to my penthouse and put me into bed...

Repulsive.

Slamming the door shut, I strode through the house, seeing red. Izzy was a warning from the gods of fate. A cautionary tale. Her words echoed in my mind like a shrill siren. *He is a coldblooded snake. He'll turn on you in a second after fucking you like an animal. Nothing about him is human.*

Kyle was a lying, serial philanderer, Charlie Sheen level...no, Hugh Hefner level. Mix that with the soothing whispers and lies he had fed me the last few days and my head began to throb with a bad migraine.

I needed to get out of there. But I didn't even know what time my new flight was. I dismissed the thought of calling Evan; he'd definitely alert Kyle. Maybe I could buy another ticket, but a quick phone search revealed the thousands of dollars I'd need to spend for a last minute booking— thousands of dollars I did not have.

I still had to leave, so I went to look for my suitcase. It was nowhere in sight. Thinking Kyle must have asked Marlene to put it away, I ran upstairs.

To my dismay, it was not in my room. I went to the bathroom. The closet. I searched all the bedrooms upstairs. I even checked Kyle's room. No suitcase. What was going on? Had he hidden my suitcase so I wouldn't leave?

I was done. Back downstairs, I paced and fumed for a bit. Shoulders shaking, I collected my purse and phone. I used the Uber app and waited at the door for the cab to arrive. As soon as the driver texted me, I ran out to the white gate—the gate of Hades that I never wanted to see again.

Seeing me outside, the driver Pat came running after me. "Miss, where are you going? Mr. Paxton's orders were for me to take you."

"Sorry, I have to go." I began to sprint. Before he got to the gate, I was already in the Prius on the road.

"Downtown, right?" the Uber driver asked, smiling at me in the rearview mirror.

"Yes. No. Yes. Um. No. Can you…just drive me around?"

"Sure thing," he said, surprised at my request.

For half an hour, he drove me around and pointed out some landmarks when he found out I was an out-of-towner. Breathing in and out like I was in labor, I tried to stop my manic thoughts of Kyle.

Keep calm, Juniper. Kyle is a roadblock. Life goes on.

Gradually, my wheels stopped spinning and it occurred to me that I could not spend the rest of my life in this Uber cab, drifting around the Bay area without direction. I pulled up places on my phone map I wanted to see and decided to tour the historic murals of San Francisco, something I was fond of doing in Chicago and Detroit.

I instructed the driver to drop me off at Harrison Street in the Mission District. From online guides, I learned the on-foot tour went through Balmy Alley along 24th Street, past St. Peter's Church and down to the murals at Galeria de la Raza. Once I was dropped off, I followed the online map and went from mural to mural. The painted images of racism, class struggle and xenophobia gave me quiet strength as I walked on and on.

Slowly, my mind cooled and I felt a numbness creep over me.

My favorite mural turned out to be the old Maestrapeace mural on an entire building, with female icons of history like Audre Lorde, Georgia O'Keefe, Frida Kahlo, and Kuan Yin, the Goddess of Mercy, and Coyolxauhqui, the Moon Goddess. These timeless women were once my spiritual guides, and now, bereft of their wisdom, I was lost. On one of the murals I found these words by the sage, Kuan Yin:

> *We create realities based on our own personal beliefs. These beliefs are*
> *so powerful that they can create entrapping realities over and over.*

Is that what I had done? Created my own reality on the fantasy of what Kyle promised?

Precisely at noon, as expected, I got a call from Kyle. My belly twisted and I ignored his call. Then the text messages started to come in and my phone buzzed like a swarm of wasps. I ignored it, but soon my curiosity made me check my messages.

juniper, where are you
i am waiting for you
i told u to take pat i left him for you
are you ok? call me babe
ok now i'm officially worried
is this about last night? i said i'm sorry
please, tell me where you are & i'll come n get you
what's up with the radio silence?

Radio silence was all he was getting from me until I figured out how to get my suitcase back and go home. When I saw Kyle was calling nonstop, I checked my online mural guide that led me to the Tenderloin District, where the civil rights murals were located. I made mental notes and turned off my phone so Kyle would stop calling me.

Following the murals, I walked on. After some time, I noticed the area was getting shady—the murals improved but the neighborhood got worse. But I did not feel unsafe, as there was a lot of traffic and the streets were full of people—granted, some were homeless. It reminded me of the inner neighborhoods of Chicago and Detroit with colorful murals, dilapidated buildings, dirty pavements, iron-grill storefronts, and the unemployed citizens who lived there, forgotten by progress and capitalism.

Deeper through Tenderloin, I saw people talking loudly to the air, hollow-eyed beggars, dejected streetwalkers, lost addicts in a drug-induced haze, and even homeless families who'd never recovered from the recession. A few of them asked me for money and initially I responded in kind and handed out what I had, but I soon ran out of cash and got a few angry looks.

Something Kyle had said came to me. *There are some terrible parts in the city. And they come so swiftly jammed into the good, safe, parts—promise me, you'll stay with your group.*

Dammit and damn him. Maybe I was the one who should be damned. Since I entered Kyle's world, I had become myopic and shallow and he had done nothing to rile it up. The trash rising to my waterline was all inside me. And now, navigating the flotsam and jetsam of people washed up on the streets of San Francisco, I felt a great sadness grow within me; it was something bigger than me and it connected to the world through shared misery. There was so much gloom in the dust of broken dreams here, my troubles seemed stale and selfish.

I wandered into an area that looked as bad as Skid Row and I tried to backtrack my path but ended up more lost than ever. Seeing an empty police car, I lurched around it to ask for directions. When I saw the two cops, I hurried to them, but they were busy arresting a couple, who were screaming bloody murder.

I had to leave. Turning on my phone, I groaned. It was now almost three o'clock. How on earth had I been aimlessly wandering for over three hours? I clicked on the GPS to see if I could take a cab or Uber, but the only option was public transport.

I found a route to a Bart Station and headed to it through a dirty and dicey street. This was where a group of young men loitering on the road and zigzagging through traffic taunted me with lewd gestures. Alarmed, I walked faster to get away from them and they all laughed behind me. Looking back as I ran, I bumped into legs attached to a man lying on a few cardboard boxes with syringes surrounding him.

"Hey, Missy, need a hit? I got it all. Very cheap," he rasped.

I gulped and shook my head. A girl wearing seedy clothes shoved past me, her elbows digging hard into my arm and yelling, "Eyes on the road, bitch."

Past her, I saw an emaciated and shriveled red-haired woman with soul-searching eyes. She held up a hand. "You got a buck, pretty baby?"

"I'm so sorry. No." She spat at my feet and I ran again.

I looked around with wild eyes and realized my fear was inviting undesirable attention. I had to stop looking so freaked out. I forced myself to be calm, but soon lost it when my phone map led me through more of an alley than a street and I passed by several homeless men in makeshift shelters, cardboard boxes and even garbage containers. Most looked kindly at me but some gave me varying degrees of lecherous and vicious looks.

Blindly, I ran out of the alley and made a swift right turn.

That's when I heard a loud male voice.

"Juniper. Stop."

I went dead in my tracks. And that is when I saw him.

The world stopped rotating on its axis.

Time slowed down.

Kyle was shouting at me from a car that Pat was driving. They were on the other side of the road from me.

"Juniper, stop and turn around," Kyle yelled.

KYLE

I n all of the 30 years, 5 months, 22 days, 16 hours and 27 seconds of his life on Earth, Kyle Paxton had never felt as relieved as in the moment when his eyes fell on Juniper. Relief. It was an alien emotion. Most of the time, he was indifferent to the pain and troubles of others. And now the relief was so strong, so absolute and so gut-wrenching, he sank back in his leather seat, eyes closed and knees weak.

For the past three hours, the coiled tension in him had threatened to snap into a physical shutdown. human body can go into shock when there is not enough blood circulating through it, and he felt the symptoms of this even now: his skin clammy, his breathing shallow and rapid. He felt lightheaded, a rapid pulse beating in his forehead.

In the nanosecond as his hand went to the door, the relief turned to rage.

He gritted his teeth and told Pat to stop the car.

"I will. Just a few feet now. Can't stop in the middle of the road."

"Now," Kyle roared.

"But I have to p—"

Without letting Pat finish, Kyle opened the car door and flung himself out into the moving traffic. Weaving in and out of the cars like a man gone postal, he headed towards the only thing he could see.

Juniper, standing there safe and sound, her mouth formed into a little O.

Horns blasted, car tires squealed, people rolled down their windows and cursed obscenities at Kyle, but he did not flinch or deviate from his single-minded drive to get to her.

CHAPTER 29

I saw Kyle jump out of the car. Horns blared at him as he jaywalked through the traffic to follow me. Not thinking straight, I ran in the other direction. Dodging food carts and pedestrians, I was fast, but it was no use as he quickly caught up with me. His hands shot out and he stopped me in the middle of the pavement.

When he twisted me around to him, our anger collided.

For a few moments, we just glared at each other like a Wild West showdown.

There was no denying he won the Rage Wars, for I could not match the rage oozing from him. "What the hell are you doing?" he spat through compressed teeth.

"How did you find me?"

"That should be the least of your worries." Never taking his eyes off me, he seized both my hands and led me to the black BMW that was now parked on our side of the road. Several bystanders watched us with interest as I was all but dragged through the pedestrian traffic.

"Let me go." I struggled in his arms, trying to loosen his iron grip.

It was then I noticed a black sedan screech to a halt behind Kyle's car. Two burly men wearing sunglasses and dressed in black suits jumped out and strode our way, looking armed and ominous. When they came closer, one of them asked, "Do you need help?"

"Yes. This man's trying to force me in his car," I said.

The men were looking at Kyle and ignored me. With a sinking heart, I realized they belonged to him.

What is happening? Are they FBI agents? Ex-military?

"Sir?" one asked, as they took a step in unison toward him.

Kyle put up a hand and they froze in mid-step. "All good. You can go back now." As if they were androids, the men rotated and went back to their car and drove off.

I blinked. "Who are those guys?"

"My security," Kyle said, tersely.

Who are you—Mission Impossible?

Before Pat could come out, Kyle jerked the car door open and pushed me in with primal force. Furious, as I all but fell on the seat, I flipped my hair off my face and glared at him.

Kyle slid in and barked an order to Patrick. "Home. Now."

"Right away, sir," Pat said, smiling at me in the rearview mirror. It was so odd under the circumstances that I was startled—I guess he wasn't afraid of Kyle. "How are you, Miss?"

"Fine," I managed to choke out. As the car started I turned to Kyle with an open mouth. "How dare you."

He put a finger to my lips and shook his head. "Talk when we get home."

With equal fire, I turned to stare at the window. *What is he so mad about?*

478

It was ridiculous. I needed to get away from Kyle as soon as I got my luggage back. Obviously, he was an unhinged madman and I had fallen into his crackers trap. He had warned me, though, by calling himself a psychopath—and so had just about everyone who knew him. Evan, Sylvia, Izzy. Even Willow and Marlene, in their gentler styles. I had been too blinded by my meretricious feelings and dazzled by Kyle to see the truth.

A tacit anger hung in the air between us and the ride back was the most unpleasant ride of my life. Kyle sat like a dead android and did not look my way once. A mere foot away, I kept my face hidden in my sleeves as I stared out the window.

Once we came back to his house and the gate slid open, Kyle jumped out of the car when it was still gliding in. I gaped in shock. Pat's warm brown eyes met mine in the mirror and he gave me a comforting smile. "Don't worry."

Oh, I wasn't worried. Kyle did not scare me.

When the car stopped, Kyle opened my door and grabbed my wrist— without an iota of concern for my wellbeing or dignity. He walked to the front door with me scuttling behind him. Inside, he slammed the front door shut with a kick and led me to the kitchen. I noticed Marlene was not there and I guessed she had been told to stay away. By the marble counter, he finally let my wrist loose. Recalling this was the exact spot where we had been kissing a day ago, I gulped and massaged my wrist.

He took off his black suit coat and threw it on the counter. I watched it slide on the glossy surface and halt an inch from the sink as if he'd planned the trajectory. "Talk," he barked.

"I don't know why you're doing this. I just need to go back to Ann Arbor. Where's my luggage?"

"I'm sorry, but I need an explanation. Now. What. Was. That?" Kyle rolled up the sleeves of his pure white shirt, all the while watching me. Assessing his hard-as-nails face, I began to understand how this man could make multimillion-dollar deals and annihilate his competitors to molecules.

"Nope. I don't owe you anything."

The look I got could have eviscerated a hawk in the sky. Realizing my hands were covered with dirt, I brushed past him and went to the kitchen sink to wash my hands. To my surprise, he hovered over the tap to make sure the water was not scalding hot. After he adjusted the temperature, I moved away from his body instantly. This made him scowl at me for awhile.

Can he be any more childish?

He took a glass from a cabinet, filled it with cold water and slammed the glass in front of me. "Drink. You look thirsty."

I shook my head. "I'm fine."

"If you don't drink, I'll make you." Picking up the glass, he put the rim to my parted lips.

My eyes widened and I took a step back. "Christ, what's wrong with you?"

"First, drink. You are dehydrated. Can't you tell? Your lips are parched."

I ran my tongue over my dry lips; he was right—I was very thirsty. Caving in, I swigged the entire glass in a few seconds as he watched me with arctic eyes.

"Are you hungry?"

I shook my head.

"Did you eat lunch?"

I shook my head again.

"Then, eat."

"I'm not hungry."

"Well, I am."

I watched in disbelief as he went to the fridge and emerged carrying a lasagna Marlene had made. He jammed it in the microwave and set two plates on the counter. Head stuck back in the fridge, he produced a pitcher and poured us both tall glasses of iced tea. When the microwave pinged, he put the lasagna dish on the counter and doled big chunks of cheesy pasta on both plates.

"Eat."

The basil-tomato aroma made my stomach churn with hunger, but I mulishly shook my head. "No."

"Fine, if you don't eat we talk. Now." His face was scary calm, like a Guy Fawkes mask.

"Okay, I'll eat."

I quickly sat down on the barstool and Kyle sat next to me. I dug into the lasagna that to my starved body tasted like manna from heaven. Confusion and exhaustion rendered me speechless and I was relieved we ate in silence. I barely glanced at him but was aware that he studied me unrelentingly as he ate. When we were done, I pushed my plate back and twisted to face him.

"How did you find me?"

"Your phone. The BirdsEye lens has a latent GPS and we can triangulate your position from our database. But you totally turned off your phone. When you turned it on, I found you in five minutes."

"Isn't that a penal code violation?"

"I'd find you even if it meant unlawful manslaughter."

"You're acting like a possessive loony psychopath. Seriously, I feel like I need a restraining order after the way you behaved, Kyle."

"Do you know what I went through today? Those three hours you turned your phone off were some ugly long seconds in my head. While I combed the streets, my security team searched the area where your GPS was last turned on."

"How?"

"They are ex-special forces and tuned into local police reports. A few days ago, a girl's tortured body was found by the pier and I went insane thinking of the craziest possible explanation for where you were."

"What's the big deal? I'm an adult. I go out all the time."

"I've not been so stressed since Chloe died." He shook his head and closed his eyes, as if ashamed at having emotions. Looping a finger in his collar, he gave his neck some breathing space and unbuttoned the top two buttons. "I don't get it, Juniper. I thought we had a great talk this morning and then you ran off like a kid. I nearly went out of my mind."

My heart flapped like paper in the wind. He was going out of his mind? "I did not run off. I just went to see murals."

"Bull. Spit out the truth."

"Fine. I felt like you and I weren't going to work. I needed to clear my mind."

"What is it with you and running away? After what we've been through the past few days…the things I told you. You must know how I feel, Juniper. You didn't even have the basic courtesy to give me a call or let me know that you were just going to disappear? Is this about last night? I don't deserve to be treated this way."

"Let's talk about the way you treat your Summers and your Winters."

His eyes flashed. He shoved at the counter, got up, and started pacing the kitchen. "Where's that coming from? I don't get it. I'm so done with you right now. You're always barking up the wrong tree with me. Why, Juniper? Why the hell? Yeah…well, I know why. The problem with you is, your moral compass is very different from the world. And you want the rest of us to get in line with whatever is in your stuffy repressed head."

"That's rich coming from you. With your *own* depraved compass. You don't even allow normal human behavior in your relationships." I was so loud he stopped pacing.

"What the hell does that mean?"

"Kyle, you cannot treat people the way you do and get away with it."

"What. Are. You. Saying."

I thought about Izzy and my conversation with her and the pain of it came back. My belly twisted like angry moths were trapped there. "You can't treat people like things and control them…because they've spilled ink at the end of a paper. At the end of the day, that's all a contract is. You can't control emotions with a piece of paper. It binds you, yes, but it doesn't mean a human is gonna stop behaving like a human."

I went quiet when I saw he was looking away. Kyle went to the fridge and filled his glass with ice. He put a few pieces of ice in his mouth and crushed them.

"I don't know why you can't accept such a basic thing. You keep on imposing your goddamn moral crap on everyone else. And then you sit on a frigging high horse and judge me. With your impossible holier-than-thou-morality. You can keep it. Just stop shoving it down my throat."

I guess…he's kind of right. But that doesn't excuse him.

"Kyle, what I'm trying to say is your entire system is a load of messed up bull. It doesn't work. You only think it does."

"It works. Yes, it's messed up, but it works," he said, like a robot stuck on a repeat command. "Until you."

I jumped out of my chair and went to stand by him. "Does it? Does it? It doesn't work. Kyle, don't you get it? We are hardwired to behave with big emotion. So when you try to take that away and impose your own robotic effing antiseptic rules on charged things like sex and relationships…you're messing with stuff no human can change."

483

"Juniper, not interested in your rants. Can we discuss why the hell you ran away?"

I hesitated. He had taken some of the wind out of my sails, but I was still outraged. "Kyle, please let me finish. You think if you push people away, it'll work? You think by limiting time, you limit people? You think if you pick girls hardened by lives, they won't get hurt? They won't cry inside, even if they don't in front of you. You don't think Izzy got hurt? And the ones before her?"

"No, I don't." He shook his head, his face finally drained of anger. "One, because they knew what they were getting into. Two, they go through men like socks. Three, they have a choice."

"No. They don't get a choice to be in a relationship with you."

"I am confused."

"Well. You are an ultimate mind-screw!"

"Is this about them or you? Why do you keep talking about this? Am I in absolution hell for my past?"

"I get that you have some unresolved I-hate-myself-issues you torment yourself with. I get that you think it's okay to impose them on others. It's not. Your self-loathing is not self-evident. It is subterfuge. They don't hate you. I don't hate you. I just can't exist in that rule world you created."

Kyle took the glass of full of ice and massaged the back of his neck with it. "What the hell, Juniper? You're not making sense."

I was barely listening to him and still stuck in my rant. "Kyle, you *can't* make up rules about the human heart out of thin air. You can't change a person's emotions. Not the inbuilt ones, stuck in our DNA. As a curator, I know we've got the same building blocks as our primitive ancestors. And no matter how evolved we get…we're all just flesh and bones led by the instincts of cavemen, hunters, gatherers. That's it."

And then he said, almost to himself, "Sometimes, I get the feeling my exes hired you for payback..."

"Human hearts, mine and yours, are at the mercy of our mutations. So when you mess with nature, because you are a commitment-phobe... because you hate the inconvenience of messy things that go with fun in bed, like *dumb* feelings...and love...and emotions...you fail. Real life has tears and stupid emotions and mess and dirt and filth and drama that go with every beautiful thing we do. There is beauty in everything that falls. Like this."

With a swift motion, I picked up the leftover lasagna and slammed it down, spilling it on the counter. His eyebrows shot up and we watched as the glutinous pasta strips slowly settled down on the pristine white marble, the melted mozzarella, tomato paste, chicken and basil clotting in a red, green and white glorious sticky mess.

I saw his jaw clench as he controlled the instinct to clean up the mess.

He just stood there staring in disbelief.

Fortified by my insanity, I marshaled on. "You only think you have control. But control is an illusion. Your system is an illusion. Kyle...you and I...we're not powerful enough to crack and fight evolution, millions of years in the making." I took a deep breath, my cheeks coloring as I realized how long I had been ranting. "And I am sorry...but what we have is not real. I was so wrong to stay back. I need to...go."

His eyes tired and face ashen, Kyle took a step closer to me. "Fine, whatever. My system is a lie, an illusion. If you say so. But what we have is not. And you know that. It is real. It is worth fighting for. At least...for the time allocated to us. I know this—you running away today—has nothing to do with cavemen and DNA. What is this really about, Juniper?"

Worth fighting for. Great, Kyle. I think so, too.

But not for five months. And not if you're not mine.

I went back to my stool and sat down. Picking up my glass, I took a big sip of iced tea and closed my eyes. "Izzy was here. She…she left your apartment keys."

A flicker on his face was the only indication that he was stunned by this. But he just shrugged. "So?"

The nerve of that man. Cheating rat!

"You forgot to tell me while you were trying to fuck me last night that your shag buddy was living in your apartment. And you also conveniently forgot to tell me that she had been shagging up in your apartment for five months. Everything you told me was a lie."

Right away, he strode to me and twisted my barstool to face him. "What are you talking about? I never lied to you."

"Withholding information is the same as lying."

He shook his head. "Juniper, it never came up that she was using my apartment. Izzy just needed a place to stay while she was launching her company."

"Kyle. Let me stop you right there. I know you were with her on Thursday," I said, swiveling the stool away from him.

He spun the stool so I was forced to face him again. "Are you high or something? I sent Evan during lunch but she was out. After work, I went to pick up the keys from her and she said she needed to stay a few more days. Said she'd drop the keys off at my office. That is all. Did she tell you that she and I hooked up on Thursday? That would be such a big, rotten lie. But she isn't like that. Izzy is a big girl."

I reviewed Izzy's exact parting words and realized she said she had met him on Thursday, not that she had been with him…*oh*…but her words were conveyed with a sly glint in her eyes as if she was implying it. Was she playing me in bad faith? Feeling relieved, I began to breathe easy. "So you weren't...with her this week? Even though last Thursday, December tenth, was her last day as your Winter?"

"God damn life I have," he muttered. "I have not been with Izzy. At all."

"Oh."

He shook his head, the corners of his lips lifting. "So you ran away in a jealous fit?"

I opened my mouth to deny it, but I couldn't. It was humiliating, but true. Instead I said, "I'm not usually like this. The drama way...I was this week. Look, I want you, that's all. It's hard for me with all your rules and time limits. I just can't wrap my head around that. So I make it a big deal..."

"Come." He grabbed my wrist and walked me to the living room, where he released me. He went to the tallboy and poured a drink—scotch on the rocks. He asked me if I needed a drink and I refused. Sinking down in one of the white leather couches, he patted the spot next to him. "Sit down."

I watched him with my arms folded, realizing I still had no idea about my booking information or my luggage. Also, I was filthy and clammy from walking around like a drifter. "Kyle, where is my stuff?"

"In your room. I had Pat stow it in his car in case you decided to abscond."

"So not cool to hide it. I'm gonna freshen up. Let's talk later." I looked down at my soiled white shirt and dusty jeans.

"Okay. As long as you don't want to run away again."

I gave him a watery smile. "Not anymore."

KYLE

December 13, 4:26 p.m. 17 seconds
(Seacliff, San Francisco)

F irst the clusterfuck with Sylvia. Then Juniper vanished. This was turning out to be one the most stressful days Kyle had experienced in his life. And he was a veteran of stress.

Hand on his stiff neck, Kyle went to the kitchen. His eyes went to the mess of tomato sauce, pasta and the little heroic bits of basil bravely pushing through the mozzarella. *There is beauty in everything that falls.* With a growl, he picked up the lasagna dish, intending to put it in the sink. Instead, his rage—at himself—got the better of him and he lifted it up and smashed it in the steel garbage can. The dish split and broke into exactly 17 ceramic pieces.

Control. Your. Black. Smoke. Rage.

Control is all you have.

All he had wanted to do when Juniper stood there yelling was to grab her, toss her on the marble slab, and have very angry sex with her. Had Juniper not been a bleeping virgin, he'd definitely have had very angry, rough sex with her right there in the kitchen.

Kyle had never had angry sex with anyone…except Chloe.

Since she had died, every time he was with a woman it was because of need, the animal need he wanted slaked. He had learned this weekend that his need for Juniper was not the same animal. It was based on her existence. No matter how immature and impossible she was—how much drama—his longing for her went way beyond his animal urges.

What the hell is wrong with you? Get a grip.

Reaching for a paper roll, he leaned over the counter. He forced himself to look at the lasagna mess on the counter, expecting his anger to resurface. But it evaporated and all he saw was the humor in the absurd situation. His shoulders shook with laughter.

CHAPTER 30

I changed and went to find Kyle. He was on the patio. Cradling his untouched scotch on the rocks, he faced the land and sea, his silhouette etched on the glass doors. He had changed out of his suit into relaxed clothes, wearing a black t-shirt and faded low-slung jeans and holding a khaki jacket that dragged on the ground.

He heard me and turned. "Come, I'm going to show you a secret place."

"Is that where I get thrown over the cliff as your defective F-buddy?" I asked, admiring the way his jeans hugged his lower abs and taut hips.

"Too soon, Juniper, too soon." He was terse, but I saw a ghost of a smile. He put down his drink, shrugged on the jacket he was holding, and held out his hand. I put my hand in his long fingers and let him crush them.

He led me down to the private garden where we had had our dinner yesterday. Crossing it, we went through a gap in the tall hedges on a narrow flagstone path. It went up the cliff, enclosed only by a run-down fence that looked like it should have a CAUTION: DEADLY DROP sign on it. When I stumbled on a tree root growing out of the ground, Kyle pulled me away from the cliff side and held on to my shoulders.

In spite of the tension between us, this made me smile. The path ended in a narrow clearing jutting out on a sharp outcrop. Fenced in by wild growth, it was a charming nook with a rustic bench and an old metal firepit.

I gasped and went to the fence to take in the bay views. "It's stunning. Kyle, your house takes my breath away."

"No one but Evan knows about this place. We found it when he was nine and I was twelve. We used to come here all the time as kids. Jeez, we did such dumb stuff here."

"Like what?"

"Knees-scraped-noses-broken-stitched-up-cheeks kinda stuff." He pointed to his nose. "See this bump. I wasn't born with it. When I was twelve, I was on the wrong side of the fence trying to jump from a tree. I missed and my face smashed on the fence."

"Ouch." Leaning over I kissed his nose. "I like it. Gives you distinction."

"I'm glad my pain brings you joy." We exchanged looks that spelled out things were good between us. "It's a miracle we're alive. We used to swing on ropes. Walk the fence edge. Jump from trees. Fell all the time. Never learned. And if we ever saw people on the beach below, we'd throw flour in bags and water balloons and hide."

I laughed, feeling grateful for Evan—at least because of him and the Marquez family, Kyle had a semblance of a childhood.

He walked over to the old bench and traced the wood grooves covered with scratched designs and hearts. "I carved the initials of every girl I had a crush on in high school here. My mother did too. And Grandpa carved his wife's initials in a heart, right here."

I bent down to see better. "I wish I'd known your grandfather. I saw the old photos today. Did he build this bench and fence?"

"Yeah, it was his special spot. I heard my grandparents would sit here and look over the bay. I think it was his way of saying that he had conquered the cliff."

"He did," I whispered. "And he would have been so proud of you."

When I saw the intense way his eyes were fixed on me, my belly clenched with desire and I leaned against the fence, my back to him. What an insane week. Kyle had gone from being a stranger to becoming the most important person in my life. I watched the waves glide on the silver sand and the seagulls float in the gray sky in a synchronized dance until he reached for me. Arms went around my waist and he kissed my neck. Instinctively, I arched my head back and his lips went down the column of my neck and when he got to my collarbone, he lifted his head.

"June-Bug, I need to know what happened today."

"Honestly when Izzy told me she'd seen you last on Thursday, I lost it. I thought you were playing both of us."

"I would never do that. It's why I set up my rules...to avoid all of this."

"I know it was wrong of me, now, but I just don't know how to do this...because I've never done this before."

"I am a lot of things, Juniper, but I am none of the things you accused me of today. And before. I told you I am not a cheater, nor am I polyamorous. Yes, I set time limits on relationships. But I've been upfront with you since our first dinner."

"I know but...it's hard for me to trust...men."

"Why do you have such trust issues?"

"Because people have such cheating issues."

"Did something happen to you? Tell me, so I can gain your trust."

"I don't know." *Yeah, I do.*

I was raised to hate and mistrust men. To question their motives. Dig out skeletons. Seek out intentions. Find out what lies in their twisted hearts. I was a diffused missile of mass male destruction. Kyle had broken down my metal walls, the decades of defenses around my heart, and no matter how juvenile I acted, he would not give up on me. But he should.

I looked up at him, eyes shining with unshed tears. "Kyle, have you heard of Occam's Razor?"

He shook his head.

"In Latin, it's *lex parsimoniae*, which means law of parsimony. It's the principle of truth, which states the simplest explanation is the right one. A person in doubt should pick the idea with the least assumptions. Or, as I tell myself, 'Keep it simple.' The problem is I complicate things. Especially about you. I'm sorry."

"It's fine, Juniper. Stop saying sorry. It means nothing. Just stop running away from me."

"You told me your system has nothing to do with feelings. But I feel. That's just one of the many things about me that sucks. I am petty, super-emotional, green, inexperienced and I can't stop what's inside me from spilling on people involved with me. I don't know how to please a man and I know...I don't belong with you."

He gave me a searching look. "You do. So much so that you can't see me with anyone else. I get it. If you had old flames lurking around, I'd probably punch their lights out—like Goldilocks from the club."

"There's no one but you in my life. But you have such a colorful past... and future...I'm having a hard time as your temporary present."

Eyes distant and an inscrutable expression on his face, he mumbled, "I know I can't change my past, but I will try to fix the future. For us."

I wondered what he meant, but he offered no explanation and went to the battered metal firepit by the bench. From his jacket pocket, Kyle pulled out a box of matches and small bottle of lighter fluid and began scavenging the area for tinder. Catching his drift, I joined him and we threw twigs, dry pine needles and dead grass over the few logs in the metal circle. He bent over the pit and arranged the tinder in a teepee fashion. Dousing the logs with the lighter fluid, Kyle lit a match and threw it in. Tiny flames rose from the tinder and slowly the kindling collapsed over the logs. The flames extended like smoky fingers and small embers appeared like dark magic in the pit.

"Thanks, Tarzan." I put my hands over the fire.

"Come sit." He led me to the bench and I slumped down next to him. Kyle put both my hands in his. "I know I screw up things. With you and with others. You have no idea how many people I have let down. And... I'll never forgive myself for what I did to Chloe, as long as I live." At my inquiring look, he shook his head. "I'll tell you one day about her, not today. No matter my past, you're the one person, I know, if I let down I'll never forgive myself."

"I know you are trying, Kyle. I swear, I am not asking you to change. I'm just trying to figure out where I fit in."

"There are very few things in my life that I'm sure about—and you are one of them. I want you to know I have never lied to you and I will never lie to you. Nothing I told you this week was a lie."

"I know that. Now."

"Listen. Three hard rules for us, from now on. One, don't run away. If you have an issue with me, instead of running away like a stunt kamikaze, ask me. Two, come to me. If you hear something about me that scares you, upsets you, just ask me. Three: Us first. Others later. Never talk about me to somebody else because I expect your loyalty to be with me first. Promise me that."

"I promise," I whispered, making a mental note of his rules.

Don't run away. Come to me. Us first. Others later.

"I don't know what you are doing to me. But everything else in my life has faded since I met you." He sighed and drew me into his arms. I let his words sink in, as we sat collapsed against each other, watching the flames crackle.

"Kyle, I—you must know how I feel about you. Only you."

"I know. I know, baby." After a pause, he said, "Juniper, for what it's worth, I have not been with Izzy since the day I met you."

My heart skipped a beat and my mouth hung open. "What? How? The day we met? You mean, since the gala? That was like two months ago. How is that possible?"

"Let me explain. The day before your gala, Izzy was in New York. We both flew in to Ann Arbor on the day of the event. Things were tense between us, as I hadn't had time to see her more than twice a month. I'd been very busy at work and she spent her time flying back and forth between New York and San Francisco. Here, she lived in my apartment and I was at the house. The day I came to your gala, we had lunch at The Chrome Fig and we just talked about our own companies. Believe it or not, it was only the second time I had ever taken her out."

"How is that possible?"

"It is, Juniper. I haven't dated any of the…others. I just gave them…stuff they wanted. Anyhow, I met you a few hours later. When I got you down from the scaffolding, I did not want to let you go. I felt like my life paused and that everything I had been doing until that moment was a mistake."

My eyes shone. "Really?"

He smiled, the corners of his eyes crinkling. "I resolved to find out more about you. I watched you running around the whole night, and I was taken. Totally taken. Later that night, I told Izzy on the red-eye back that we were done. I could not think about you…till I ended things with her. It was the first time in my system I was done earlier than the exact termination date. At first, Izzy was stymied and said she'd find a legal loophole to make me stay with her. I told her I'd still help her business and that she could live in the apartment. She calmed down and we parted ways politely. The way I like. No emotion. No drama. No messy lasagna. But Juniper, know this— since I met you, I have not thought about any other woman or looked at any other woman. I want you. Only. You."

"I had no idea you felt that way about me. I feel the same way," I whispered.

He kissed the palms of my hands and his lips went to each of my fingers. "After the gala, all I could think about was being with you. But I was kinda trapped in my system. I couldn't think of any other way to get you. So instead of talking with you, charming you, dating you, and gradually coming into your life like a Joe Schmo, I ruined it all by spelling out my intentions on our first date. That was a disaster."

"Hindenburg and Titanic collective."

"And this weekend, I suffocated you."

"No, Kyle. You made up for it a million times over. It was the best week of my life."

He grinned and brushed off a strand of hair that fluttered across my face in the slight breeze. "I'm glad. But when you said no to me that awful day, I was heartbroken. I knew it was my fault and I had to live in the misery of my own freaking failure. I was sure I misread your feelings for me. My last chance was this trip and if you were not still into me, I told myself I'd never try again with you. I realized you are not like other girls. I needed to go slow. I would let you be…but here we are. Finally, where I wanted you."

Letting the scale of his confession sink over me like spun sugar, I looked at the pigeon gray sky lit up by the drifting bronze clouds. It was as perfect as I felt at the moment. Twisting my hands in my lap, I tried to express what I felt.

"Ever since I've met you, Kyle, I haven't been able to work. I haven't been able to function. All I do is think about you. I can't even remember my life before I met you. It's all fuzzy, like it never happened. And it scares me." I turned to him and pressed a passionate kiss on his lips. In response, he put his arms around my waist as his lips created havoc on my mouth and then trailed down to my jaw.

We were both breathing hard when he pulled away. "Wait. Why are you scared?"

"I've never actually wanted to be with a man before so this is all very new for me."

"So how is that you've never had a boyfriend? Never been with somebody at this age. You're so intelligent, beautiful, hot, men must be battering down your door."

"Um. You'd be surprised. Not many guys look for intelligence in picking a mate. Plus you're the only one who thinks I'm hot. Most guys think I'm a cold fish."

"I think you're the total package, babe." Kyle traced my jawbone with an idle finger. "You must have had something unusually bad happen to you for this kind of isolation."

I looked away and put some distance between us. "It's a long story."

"I have time."

"There are a lot of reasons…I'm messed up. But I guess…it starts with my mom and the way she raised me. She didn't have an easy life. After you hear about it, if you don't wanna be with me, I'll totally understand."

"Your mom could be Bloody Mary for all I care." He laughed. "Nothing can make me stop wanting you, idiot."

"I don't come from an illustrious family like you do."

"They may be illustrious, but they ain't a lot of things."

I put my arms around his waist and nuzzled my head in his chest, relishing in his warmth. "In the eighties, my mother was Miss Detroit. She was a popular, beautiful girl who became famous at twenty. But then she started dating older guys…was a total badass…partied out of control. On top of that, she met a rich d-bag, who hooked her on drugs. It got bad… first coke, then cheap heroin.

"Soon she was stealing from her parents and even used her tuition for her fixes. They kicked her out. She failed…also got expelled from college. Then the Detroit Sentinel printed bad party photos of her…and her Miss Detroit title was revoked. At first, her sugar daddies paid for her addiction. When she was drained of money and guys, she became homeless. Then s-she…started stripping."

At this point Kyle's body became rigid.

I continued in a dead voice. "She worked at the stripper joint for four years. Dunno what happened…that made her hate all men with a passion. She told me that we had the same genes and raised me in the opposite way her mom did. All her life, all she heard was, 'You're beautiful.' Nobody said she was smart. She really is, you know. She could've been something. She never called me beautiful once…just said I was smart, empowered, kickass and I didn't need a man."

"And that is a good thing."

"Yes. It is a good thing. But Mom doesn't have balance. It's all or nothing. She overdid it. Told me such R-rated things, made me watch true crime and murdery TV shows…in which men hurt women. Started when I was like six. Terrified the bejesus out of me. God knows who did what to her. She's never told me, but I guess it was horrible…horrible."

After a few moments of silence, Kyle said, "God. That is awful. I am so sorry. Not very responsible of her to do that to a little girl."

"Yeah. I know she was trying to protect me, but fear is a permanent thing—once it's inside you."

"That's…enough to scare anyone off the opposite sex, forever."

"Yeah."

"Did you never rebel?"

"To enforce her rules, she'd punish me by…taking things away from Cypress. That hurt more than if she took something away from me. And she'd threaten to put us in foster care. I was too young to call her bluff…and I didn't want to be separated from Cypress. I wasn't allowed to date, go to clubs, drink, or even hang out in groups.

"She taught me how to behave coldly around guys, Turn 'em off, before they got ideas. In high school every time I was alone with a boy in a class, in a gym, I'd freak out. I ran. I wore Goth, even dyed my hair blue, and kept away from boys. Ha, despite all my mom's fears, little good it did me. There was a guy…but I guess he's not important…" My voice trailed off.

Kyle twisted against me and said, authoritatively, "I want to know everything,"

"Okay, not a big deal. His name was Drake and I kinda had a crush on him. All the girls did. He was an all-star football guy…dated cheerleaders and was the prom king. He was a blond pretty boy with big shoulders and a smile like a thousand puppies. I was sixteen and he was two years older… never noticed me. One day, he grabbed me by the collar and pushed me in the janitor's closet. Said I was sexy even with blue hair…and he kissed me. I was kinda delighted. It was my first kiss. But then he…" I shook my head.

"Go on."

"Forget it, Kyle, it was so long ago."

"Tell me, Juniper."

"Fine. Ugh...he undid his zipper and told me to eat. I was so stupid innocent I didn't even know what he meant. I just stared in horror. And then he said my mother was a stripper who used to strip for his dad...and since I was in the family business, I should be his little bitch. And that is how I came to know that Mommy Dearest was not just a pageant queen. Anyhow, he really scared me off men, forever. That's it."

"You have not finished the story."

I was startled at the naked fury on his face. "That was ages ago...so no biggie."

"Juniper Mills, assault is never no biggie. What's the prick's last name?"

"Don't be nuts. Whenever I see him, we ignore each other. Anyhow, moving on."

"Not moving on. I want you to finish. The hellhound pulled his zipper down and then?"

"Kyle, it doesn't matter now." When he insisted I carry on, I rolled my eyes. "O-kay...you want the graphic stuff. So he kind of pushed me in his smelly parts. I tried to leave but he...he tied my hands with the janitor's rags. Stuffed some in my mouth so I couldn't scream. I didn't know what to do...I started crying. So he shoved me on the ground...the mops and brooms all over me...he laid on top of me until I think he...got somewhere."

"Did he—" Kyle looked away, a muscle in his jaw twitching. "Makes me so mad, I can't even say it."

"No. I clenched my knees so hard he couldn't penetrate me, let alone move my legs apart. At all."

His brow furrowed. "But wasn't he an athletic type?"

"Yeah. Don't ask me how, but in my moment of super-panic, I got super-strength. My legs locked up. I remember thinking about medieval chastity belts and why many girls were forced to wear them."

"How did you get away?"

"When it was over... he said that I was a dirty skank and a liar and that the other boys had said I'd fucked half of them. Then he left...that is all. After that, I was scared of all guys. To this day, if a man gets close to me, my legs lock up." I covered my face with my hands. "Like...last night. God, I don't know why I even told you."

Kyle pulled me into his arms and stroked my back. "I did not know. Please, don't worry, baby. I'm so sorry. There were times I was rough with you...If I'd known...I'd never have been that way."

I smiled against his shoulder and told him I knew he'd never hurt me.

"Please tell me the fucker got juvie."

"Um. No, I never reported it."

Kyle swore softly under his breath and said, "What is wrong with the girls of this world? Do you not get when you're being violated? Don't they teach you that? Especially the way your mom raised you, Juniper? You should've pressed charges...did you not see that was a violent crime against you?"

"Horrible as it was...I didn't at that time...I just thought that was sex. When I got older, I got it—but by then, it was too late."

"Permit me to kill him, will you? Where does the bastard live? I need details."

I began to laugh. "You know you're crazy, right? I was not hurt."

"He treated you the way dogs treat alley cats. He used force and coercion. That is rape."

"Since there was no actual act...I didn't think it would hold up."

"That is insane. You were hurt at that time. It did permanent damage.

PTSD is a real thing, Juniper."

"I know." I blinked. I had so many other issues to deal with growing up, maybe I had filed this in the Do Not Examine folder of my Life in Denial.

"Did your mother tell the school?"

"No, I didn't tell her. Just...my best friend, Lila."

"What the hell! By now the statutes of limitations are way past the crime."

Kyle asked for Drake's full name again. When I did not give it to him, he did not take it well and swore under his breath at Drake for a bit. Not interested in getting Drake murdered, I sat stiffly by his side, cursing myself for spilling the beans. I had to distract him. *Smoke and mirrors.*

"God, Kyle...what are you even doing with me? My mother's rules made it hard for me to become an adult. I am like trapped in a time zone, an insect in amber, an adult in high school. You deserve to be with a sophisticated and gorgeous girl like Izzy, not a juvenile girl like me."

"June-Bug, you drive me insane with your defiance, sass and drama. And you have ruined other girls for me."

"How is it—" I whispered. "Never mind."

"No. Shoot."

"I mean, how is it you haven't been with Izzy since the gala?"

He gave me a wicked smile. "You are not the only one with crazy control, Juniper. Controlling desires has two outcomes: either you break down, or you grow stronger. I've always enjoyed calculated patience. Trust me, when you wait, good things happen. Anything worth having is worth the wait."

"Oh." Pleased, I picked up a thin branch and began to tap it against the rim of the fire pit. "So you meet me at a gala, hop on a red-eye with Izzy, tell her it's over...but how did you know I would be yours?"

He smiled mysteriously, leaned back on the bench and put his hands under his neck. "That's for me to know, baby-cakes."

"Kyle, tell me." I punched his shoulder and accidently hit his hair with the branch I was holding. I threw it down. "Sorry. Tell me."

"I gauged your body language and your reactions to me during the event. Though I knew you were not as taken with me as I was with you— you noticed me all night long. It was not much to go on. I saw you didn't wear a ring and I thought...don't care if she has a boyfriend. I decided, no matter what, I will get that girl. And lucky guy that I am, I did." He smiled like a cocky bastard.

Wow. No, I'm the lucky one.

"And when this wicked world starts bringing me down. I tell myself that I'm one lucky guy."

His eyebrows went up. "What?"

"Oh sorry. Bon Jovi, his song, you know, 'I got the Girl.'"

"Sorry. Don't know poetry, don't know song lyrics. Head's full of circuits and wires. So let's do this, June-Bug. Meet me every weekend. Fly over here. When I have time, I will come to Ann Arbor. To Chicago. We'll paint the Midwest red."

"That's a tall order. But. Yes. Yes. Yes. Can't wait."

Hauling me into his arms, he kissed my neck and asked, "So, next weekend, do you want to come back to San Francisco?"

I shook my head, my eyes gleaming. "No. Why don't you come to Michigan?"

"Alright. I'll make plans and text you."

"Perfect." I stretched my arms and yawned. "Hey. What time is my flight today?"

"Anytime you want." I looked at him in confusion and he frowned. "Now don't get hot and mad. I booked you a private jet, so you can come and go whenever."

I shot up from the bench. "Kyle."

"If you are offended, I won't next time."

"Dude, I don't want you to spend crazy money on me. Just let me be me. I will wear what I have and at the events you take me to, I'll dress up in your paper-doll gifts. And the jet is prohibitively expensive, environmentally irresponsible and so—"

He got up and put a finger on my lips. "Hush, Juniper. For once, let me take care of you. The jet was convenient. That's all. You can go tonight or tomorrow. Your choice."

I sighed, my heart suddenly tearing apart. "As much as I hate to leave you, I do have to work tomorrow. And Cypress misses me."

Kyle poked the firepit with a stick and the embers sizzled. Once satisfied with the flames, he slumped down on the bench. Scooping me up, he dragged me into his lap and wrapped his arms around my waist. "Watch the sun go down with me. Then go."

"I'd rather do this." I threw my arms around his neck and my lips went to his jaw. I left a trail of kisses along his jaw and the corners of his mouth and whispered, "Are you all right with my wishy-washy inexperience?"

"Don't worry, June-Bug, we'll take it slow."

"I want you to know that next weekend...I don't want us to take it slow."

Firm fingers clasped my chin so our eyes met. "I can guarantee that next weekend you don't get a pass." Then his lips went to my ear. "Because I will do bad bad things to you that I have wanted to do since the day I met you."

"Oh." I buried my face in his shoulder, and when he chuckled softly and tried to look at my face, I pushed myself harder against him.

"I don't care about your lack of experience, at all. Not anymore. I think it's kind of hot. All your pleasure is mine." His hands caressed my waist as he pulled me closer and closer and locked my lips with a searing hot kiss. When we parted and stared dazedly at each other, I was almost tempted to screw leaving that evening, so we could finish what he started.

The sun decided that this was the perfect time to set in a flashy display of plum and gold pinwheels over the bay.

I took a deep breath. "It's stunning."

By twilight, the fire had turned to cinders. With a heavy heart, I stared at the smoke rising from the gutted fire. My head buzzed with a thousand things we had said and another thousand we had left unsaid. I was happy about where Kyle and I were, but there was an odd melancholy between us now—vague and misty as the smoke. When I urged him to let me get ready for my flight, Kyle halfheartedly got up and smothered the embers with the wettest dirt he could find.

With considerable foot-dragging, I went to my room and got my luggage. Kyle drove me in silence to a private airport nearby. He drove right up to a gated entrance and pulled directly onto a shining tarmac. A small white jet, with a blue plume of smoke painted across its chassis, was parked there, with two crew members standing by the stairs. Oblivious to them, Kyle opened the passenger door, dragged me into his arms and kissed me again and again. Between kisses, I told him I could not wait to see him again.

My last words to him were: "I'm a pretty basic girl. I want nothing from you. Only you, Kyle."

Once in the jet, I was delighted to see the cabin featured taupe leather seats, an in-flight video entertainment center, and a mini galley. As soon as I settled in the luxurious seats with a happy sigh, I peered out the window to see Kyle leaning against his car, quietly staring at me. He was still there! I blew him a kiss and he half-smiled. He looked so solemn and unhappy, my heartstrings tugged. I was reminded of a little boy sitting by the round window waiting for his parents to come and get him.

"Good bye, Kyle," I whispered.

END OF BOOK I

Turn the page for a sneak peak of
Kyle and Juniper's next adventure in...

PART II

CHAPTER 2

Kyle shoved both hands in his jacket pockets. "Not to worry. I'd rather look at things in their natural environment."

"Naturally. This way, please." Mr. Ipswich began to walk to the offices.

As soon as Ipswich's back was turned, Kyle grabbed my hand and crushed it. My eyes widened. Horrified that Kyle Paxton was at my workplace massacring my fingers in public, I tried to yank my hand away, but he didn't let go. I flushed.

At that moment, a group of first graders on a field trip came skipping through the hall, led by our tour guides. Kyle put our hands to his heart and moped like a dejected Eeyore. At his pantomime antics, a few little girls giggled as they passed by. I bobbed like a cartoon character and managed to pull away. Delighted, the kids whispered and pointed at us. Kyle and I beamed at each other.

When we reached the offices, Walrus asked, "How long will we be blessed with your company? I'd love to talk about our new year's agenda."

"After I convene with Miss Mills, I'll be happy to meet with you."

Convene? Gulp.

"Can I invite local board members?" asked Walrus.

Like Mathilda Marston, no doubt.

"Fine. But I leave precisely at four forty five to meet a VIP."

I beamed at Kyle.

Ipswich glared at me, as if to warn me to behave. "Mr. Paxton, I am ever present. If there's anything I can do, please do not shillyshally. My doors are forever open to you. And I—"

Nodding, Kyle opened my door, led me inside and slammed the door in Walrus's face.

I whirled around. "What are you doing, Mister? At my job."

"Looking for my girl."

"Seriously, you can't walk into my office and turn my life upside down."

"Actually, I can."

"Kyle—"

"Quiet."

He put a finger to my lips, put an ear to my door and twisted my door lock. In a swift motion, Kyle swept me in his arms and his lips claimed mine. My arms wrapped around his neck and slowly he walked me back until I slammed against my bookshelf with a soft thud. Uncaring, Kyle pressed me harder and his hands wound around me, lifting me slightly off the ground. We kissed for a long time, but it did not feel long enough. When he released me, my eyes were shut, my lips parted, and my brain a melted orange slushy.

Best brain freeze ever.

I finally opened one eye and Kyle's ruthless eye contact made me close it again. I inhaled the delicious brew of his aromatic cologne, minty aftershave and his own body's odor. Was it possible to fall in love with someone's scent?

Yep. Stupid pheromones.

"Hi, there." His fingers cupping my chin and caressed it.

"If Mr. Ipswich was not talking to you, I'd think you were a GIF in my mind," I whispered, my breath against his lips.

"I'm as real as it gets, June-Bug." His lips locked on mine again.

It was what my body wanted, but my brain—used to this space as my place of work—protested the merciless assault of his mouth and the pressure of his hands on my waist that got more intense by the second. Imprisoned between him and the bookshelf, I could barely breathe.

I tore my mouth away. "Kyle, what are you doing here?"

"I wanted to surprise you. I did." His attention turned to the bookshelf behind me. Trapping me with his legs, he leaned over and read the spines of my books. "Hmm. *Saxons, Vikings and Celts: The Wars. The Bloody Beginnings of Britain. Celtic Revival: The Magic of Druids. The Search for the Myth and Mystic Celt.* And thousands more. Miss Mills, your Celtic fetish goes scary deep."

"Well, fetishes change. My latest one is wrestling with the museum board president."

"Hmm. He sounds powerful. Major league."

"He's got a lot in common with Caligula."

"Then, I'm sure you'll lose."

"Nah. Even water wears down stone over time, Lord Kyle."

"Water also evaporates."

"Okay, it's a tie." I smiled. "By the way, Kyle, I was supposed to pick you up. We decided."

"You decided, not me." He gave me a tiny bit of wriggle room to better stare at me. "Isn't this better?"

"Now you've changed plans on me?"

"Who said the plans changed?" Kyle released me and I began to breathe again.

I sagged against the bookshelf like a deflated balloon. "So we're still on?"

"Yes. For everything you've planned. Now that I've seen the shock and awe on your face, I am good. I'll behave." Reeling away from me, Kyle started walking around the room like a curious toddler. His great and tall presence made my office look old and untidy with its toppling bookshelves and oversized Art Deco waterfall desk.

"I wish you had told me."

Tour done, he sat in my chair, put his legs up on my desk and crossed his feet, face fierce and exacting like a truant officer. A really hot truant officer. "You're not happy to see me."

"This is my happy face." I smiled and posed like a store mannequin.

"Try harder."

"Good enough?" I gave him a Cheshire Cat smile.

"Come closer." He pulled out his glasses from his jacket and put them on. "You know I'm a bit blind and you'll have to come very very close so I can see that happy face better." He patted his lap. "Come closer…"

"…said Big Bad Wolf to Red Riding Hood. I'm sure your ears are fine. See how happy I sound?" I said, laughing.

"Miss Mills, are you defying the President's command?" His feet thudded on the floor and my heart skipped a beat.

"You walk in here like you're Pepe le Pew. So, no."

"As a matter of fact, I'm a whiz at cartoon improv. Moi leetle bundle of dandelions, where are vous lover? Do not come wiz me to ze casbah, we shall make beautiful musicks togezzer right here."

It was a near perfect imitation of Pepe le Pew. Hands laced on my waist, I laughed hard. "BirdsEye CEO. Skunk of many talents. Pepe, I work here. If Walrus found out about us there'd be big penalties. Major drama. For me. Not for you."

"Come here, Juniper."

"Nope."

"Such civil disobedience. Tsk, tsk. For defying me, I'm calling your boss." He picked up my phone.

"Let him know I'm filing a workplace harassment charge."

He frowned and his navy eyes seemed to shoot sparks, like bottle rockets exploding in an indigo sky. Desire pooled in my belly. Even fake angry Kyle was so delicious to look at, I gave up my pretend resistance. I shook my head and raced to him. Scooting between him and the desk, I sank down on my knees, my hands on his legs. His eyes darkened with desire and he scooped me up with brute force and kissed me again. I don't know how long we kissed, but soon my office walls melted and my brain casing was in danger of melting as well.

At long last he hauled me onto his lap and whispered, "How's this for a promo?"

"Are you just going to stay here and kiss me?" I asked softly.

"Only if you promise to misbehave." He leaned in again...

ACKNOWLEDGEMENTS

I wish to personally thank the following people for their contributions to my inspiration and knowledge in writing this book. Thank you to my wonderful Editor Beth Bruno, President of CT Authors and Publishers Association, for your countless rounds of editing and your priceless feedback. Thanks to Lena Gibson for your ninja proofreading skills! Humbled by my wonderful BETA Testers and ARC Bloggers, especially Nikki Brackett, who prized the book so much after reading it, that she advocated it far and wide voluntarily. Thank you to my mom, whose love of dense Victorian novels, made me love reading as a kid. Dearest Rahat Ali, thank you for your loving and encouraging sanction of my work. Appreciate my sisters, Ayesha and Maryam, for their daily dose of love and quirky support. In awe of the patience of my kiddos, Emad and Elsa, in waiting for their mom to finish the book. Miriam Peregrina thank you for your support and patience with this project.

Love you all.

Tauheed, my husband and best friend, none of this would be possible without you.

You are my anchor.

AUTHOR'S NOTE

Dear readers, thank you so much for your support and love of *Juniper Smoke*! You guys bought 75,000 copies of a little e-book that no one had heard of! Blessed to have inspired hearts and nerdy minds like y'all in my life. To hear about my upcoming projects and giveaways, follow my author page on Facebook. Find me and my readers talking about all things Kyle and Juniper in Sadia's Sassy Readers.

P.S. I am an indie author and rely on word of mouth recommendations, so if you like this book, pwetty pwease tell your friends to get it too. Thank you!

ABOUT THE AUTHOR

Sadia Ash works in TV story development and moonlights as a sushi monster and novelist in her not-so-free time. Currently, she's working on the development of three TV shows, including *The Memory of Water* and *A Girl in Istanbul*, which is also her next novel. She holds a MA English degree from Loyola University, Chicago and a Screenwriting Certificate from UCLA.

www.sadiaash.com

Made in the USA
Middletown, DE
28 May 2019